Greetings From Sunny Aluna

by Eric Lahti

Greetings From Sunny Aluna
© 2017 Eric Lahti

Cover Art Elements: © Pathique | Vectorstock.com
Cover Design © 2017 Eric Lahti

Dedicated to my wife and son.
And everyone who ever wanted to be a badass.

Contents

1 | Information Extraction Techniques

Felix Crow was a badass.

He wasn't a good man, or even a stable man, but his heart was in the right place and there was no doubt he was a badass.

Seen from behind he cut a mysterious figure as he stalked down an unnamed alley in the *Fànzuì Hútòng* district of Croatoa. He always felt it was loony to call an entire district crime alley, but he didn't make the rules. Felix Crow exploited rules, or ignored them entirely.

His keen eyes scanned the alley, seeking out a hidden sign that he was assured wasn't a joke. In a place like this, calling something *Xīwàng* had to be a sick joke. Hope, in a crumbling alley filled with the lowest echelons of murderers and drug dealers was, at best, a fresh box to sleep in. But supposedly there was a place called Hope that held a secret he would very much like to know.

Felix walked right down the middle of the alley. The brim of his hat hid his eyes and his long coat flapped out behind him. The hat was lifted from a body he had left in an alley a few months ago and the coat was a gift from his sometimes friend, sometimes enemy Chan. The coat supposedly offered magical protection, but Crow had yet to try it out. The hat just made the ensemble look good.

Ahead of him, a shadow stepped into the alley and laughed. It sounded like the giggle of a schoolgirl who just realized she'd traded her life for an endless supply of Johns and synthetic heroin. Madness and anger echoed down the narrow lane. The pale light from Xi□o M□qīn reflected off a long and wicked looking knife that had to have been made of discarded bits of metal fused together in one of the cheap magic shops nearby.

Little Mother's light was pale compared to Dà Māmā's light, but it was one of those rare days where Little Mother was up and Big Mother was down. The pale light did little to illuminate the alley, but at least it was daylight; travelling the alleys at night was risky even for people like Felix Crow.

Crow kept walking. He had more important things to deal with than petty thugs with cheap knives. He reached out with his mind and found the knife. His fingers snapped and the blade exploded. The would-be thug, a gaunt thing with more bones than skin stared at the handle in his fingers. Some remaining neuron knocked another neuron around and eventually the message got to the man's voice.

"Crow," he gasped.

Felix Crow paused. He knew his antics had spread his name around the city. It was impossible to kill the Clock Man and go unnoticed; even if he had gone out of his way to keep the dirty deed quiet, brother *baiju* loosened his tongue. The thing in front of him was hardly worth the time, but it was important to keep up his reputation. "*Xīwàng*," he said quietly. "Where is it?"

"There's no hope here, man," the thug replied. His wide eyes darted around the alley. Shadows moved quietly, hiding in corners and behind trash cans. Maybe, just maybe, enough of them could take down the legendary Felix Crow.

"Not for you, anyway," Crow said. "But that's not the kind of hope I'm looking for. A place called Hope. There will be a door. Where is it?"

A trash can tipped over, spilling ramen and rotting vegetables. Crow spared a glance at a kid holding a stick before looking back at the thug with the broken knife. "Not the brightest idea you've ever had."

The thug chuckled. His knife may be broken, but Felix Crow was supposed to have an arsenal on him. If he could get hold of the arsenal, he'd be a king. With that jacket and that hat, he could move out of the alley. Anyone who killed Felix Crow could write his own ticket in the underworld. Hell, it was rumored that the Beast himself offered up a fortune for Crow's head.

All around Crow the alley came to life. The people, things really, had been here so long they'd started to look like the alley itself. Dark eyes, tattered clothes, and grimy skin rose out of invisible hiding places. Some had sticks, others had knives taken from the dead hands of souls who had lost their way and wound up in the alley.

Crow sighed. It would figure a simple in and out job would turn to *lā sh□* on him. The whole alley reeked of *lā sh□*, why shouldn't the job follow suit? Maybe job was too strong a word. Job implied an exchange of services for money. Quest would be a better term. Mad quest, probably. Still, it would figure a simple in and out quest would turn to *lā sh□* on him.

He spun in the alley and took in the motley rabble. None of them had eaten in days. Their eyes were full of the madness of *Tiāntáng De Fěn*. Heaven's Powder was a new drug on the scene, something for people who couldn't afford anything more. It was gaining a toehold in the city, and even on Croatoa's streets it wasn't uncommon to see burnouts trying to visit heaven. They described it as a religious experience, but like all religion it was an addictive lie.

"Fuck off," Crow said. "I'm busy."

"Nice jacket," a voice said behind him. "Nice hat."

Crow didn't bother to turn around. He could see the shadow of the of the speaker waving something around. "I know," he said. "Now fuck off."

"I want the hat," another voice said.

That was the problem with *Tiāntáng De Fěn*; it convinced people they were already in Heaven. First time users experienced a euphoric high and usually slept it off. But, like all drugs, the effects waned and soon people were constantly chasing the religious high they got from the drug until the heaven became real all the time. A person who thinks he's already in Heaven will fight over anything. These guys had spent a lot of time believing they were already in Heaven and

Nüwa's tits were in their faces.

"It wouldn't fit you," Crow said. "Now fuck off before I turn it loose on your skinny ass."

Out of the corner of his eye, Crow saw the shadow move closer. Whatever the weapon was, it had pulled back into position. Crow shook his head. He hated dealing with amateurs. Turns of hard training with legendary Chan had made him cynical when it came to fighting. Crow would readily admit he was no Chan, but he was hardly something to be trifled with.

The shadow shifted slightly and Crow knew the attack was coming. Some young punk, looking to make a name for himself was trying to brain him with a stick. Crow spun and dodged the incoming attack. The punk hit nothing but air.

Crow didn't hesitate. He was busy and these idiots were wasting his time. He twisted his body, flexing his legs and twisting his hips. Force worked its way up from the ground, through his legs, up his torso, and through his shoulder. A fist flew, fast as an arrow and strong as stone. Knuckles hit the punk's face, twisting his head to the side. Teeth flew out of his broken jaw.

The junkies watched as their temporary friend staggered. His face went ashen and the punk toppled to the side. Crow didn't care if the punk was dead or out of it. He kept moving. The punks became targets in his mind. It was one of Chan's little tricks – it's easier to punch the life out of a target than a person.

Crow moved with random precision, drawing on the harsh tutelage of the man who had become one of Croatoa's most feared and respected fighters. Never be predictable and hit exactly what you want to hit. Chan had taught Crow to move and keep moving; a static target was easy to hit. While Crow moved, he watched for openings and struck at the places most likely to hurt. Another junkie stepped up to swing a piece of pipe at Crow's head and almost immediately found himself kneeling on a broken knee. He started to scream out in pain, but a vicious chop to the throat silenced him permanently.

Like all drugged up hop-heads, the punks didn't realize the danger they were in. They thought they were strong, but starvation and drugs had made them weak and Crow was a predator in their midst. For the time being, they worked together, but the alley was a place of constantly shifting alliances as each denizen tried to jockey for a better position. When a threat was great enough, like the time the police had shown up looking for a rapist, the alley had temporarily banded together. Felix Crow qualified as a threat and the added bonus of killing the guy who had killed the Clock Man made Crow a delicious target. The hat and coat were nice, but the street cred from killing Crow would be overwhelming.

They attacked en masse, an uncoordinated mess of junkies wielding weapons culled together from trash or stolen from other junkies. Even with the mass attacking, Crow still had the advantage. He might not be able to work the same kind of magic that shattered the knife – that required focus and a small amount of time – but he had the ability to sense when an opponent was about to strike.

It wasn't much of a sense, maybe a half second, but a half second in a fight can be a lifetime.

The next junkie slashed at Crow with a piece of rusty metal that had probably belonged to a bed frame. Crow deflected the knife and snaked around the man's arms. He drew the punk closer and head butted him. The punk's nose exploded, his eyes started to water, and he suddenly found he was having trouble breathing. He staggered back as Crow pressed his attack.

What the junkie didn't realize was Crow could move forward far faster than the junkie could backpedal. Before he could take two steps, Crow had smashed the man's ribs.

Crow assessed the fallen guy briefly before turning to find the next target. He found a burly man that had gone to seed when the drugs took hold. The big guy held a long piece of rebar over his head. A fist hit the side of the man's jaw and unhinged it with a sickening crack. A large boot slammed into the side of the guy's knee, cracking bone and tearing tendon.

A lifetime of training, a hint of magic passed to him from a dragon, and a propensity for violence turned the junkies into a simpering mess in short order. Crow took a deep breath and exhaled slowly. He looked around for the first guy and almost missed the terrified eyes looking out from behind a trash can overflowing with rancid meat and old noodles.

"Get your ass over here," Crow snapped.

The eyes shook from side to side and disappeared behind the trash can. Crow muttered a string of Chinese curses and kicked a nearby crying mass in the ribs. "Now!" he yelled.

The junkie's eyes were wide and his body shook as he slunk from his hiding place. Gone were all the thoughts of getting the jacket or the hat. He'd be lucky if he left with his life. "Please don't kill me," he mumbled. His remaining sandal slapped the pavement and squished through gelatinous puddles as he slowly made his way to Crow.

Crow's arm lashed out and his fingers wrapped around the guy's throat. With a slight grunt, he lifted the junkie into the air. "I promise I won't kill you if you tell me where I can find Hope. I have a meeting there, and I don't like to be late."

Skeletal fingers grabbed at Crow's hands. Fingernails that were trimmed like claws dug gouges in his arms, but Crow didn't flinch. "I don't have much time and if I have to kill you I'll waste even more time looking for someone to beat on. So, do yourself and someone else a favor and tell me where I can find *Xīwàng*."

The junkie croaked something that could have been anything from "it's over there" to "go fuck yourself." Crow squeezed. The man's face turned blue and the light faded from his eyes. Crow pushed his face closer to the junkie, close enough to smell rotting teeth and a shallow diet of trash and whatever insects or lizards got too close.

"What was that?" Crow asked. "I couldn't quite make that

out."

A feeble arm, more bone than anything else and shaking from lack of oxygen and food, pointed across the alley. Crow turned his head and peered, but all he could make out was decaying brick and the faintest hint of where a *paifang* used to stand. The outline of the archway was etched in shadow on the wall.

"Through that *paifang*?" Crow asked. "Is that there I'll find Hope?"

The man nodded weakly. His skin was ashen and clammy. Crow knew the junkie didn't have much time left, but also knew the man was barely alive as it was. When he'd been on the local constabulary, Crow had seen the same man in different skin time after time. It was only a matter of time before the *Tiāntáng De Fěn* caught up with him and sent him spiraling into a pain-wracked death.

"You're not joking around, are you?" Crow asked.

The man barely managed to shake his head. Crow knew exactly how long it took to the kill the average person by shutting off the blood to the brain. He'd been counting to himself ever since he lifted the man off the ground. At one hundred and fifteen seconds, Crow dropped the man.

The junkie hit the ground like a bag of meat and collapsed in on himself. With a bit of luck there wouldn't be any brain damage that couldn't be made worse by living in this place and using Heaven's Powder night and day. The drug was odious. Even Crow, hardly the paragon of virtue, eschewed the stuff. Had he still been a cop, he probably would have been stuck tracking down whoever was making and distributing the stuff. But, he was no longer a cop and would never get assigned to the Heaven's Powder case.

No matter. People could do whatever they wanted with their bodies. Crow had higher aspirations.

Felix Crow wanted the city. He wanted it in the same way that a man wants a woman he doesn't respect. He wanted to slap it around and control it, keep it on his arm during the day and scream at it at night. The key to the city was controlling the underworld. No matter what people believed, the root of all power in any capitol was germinated by graft and tended by people with knives.

In the dim light Crow could barely make out the faded, dingy remains of letters: *Xīwàng*. The legends were true, then. Croatoa was an old city, not ancient, but old. Like all cities, it was alive. It breathed and bled and heaved in orgasmic revelation. Croatoa changed and grew after the Dragon Wars. This part of town was old and decayed, quite possibly the first part built.

Crow ran his fingers along the old stone and closed his eyes. The cold mind of the rock told him stories of dreaming gods and magic and dragons bigger than houses. He thought back to his little dragons and made a mental note to pick up some meat for them on the way home. Through his fingers, he felt the weight of centuries, through wars and strife and junkies puking and killing each other for hats or jackets. The stone lived on, quietly watching the world go by, unperturbed by the goings on of Croatoa's transplanted children.

"*Xīwàng*," Crow whispered.

His fingers felt along the smooth stone. There had to be a switch or a lever somewhere. The legends of Hope had largely been forgotten, but a musty tome in a ramshackle pawn shop spoke eloquently of the place. Hope, it is said, remembers everything, but cares about nothing. Things slide off *Xīwàng's* back like *baiju* tossed in a drunk's face. The only way to keep hope alive was to let the world move without letting it interfere. The monks that founded Hope had dedicated their lives to providing hope while the world itself descended further and further into the madness of the Dragon Wars and the unpleasantness that followed.

Crow's fingers traced the whole of the stone wall and found nothing but whispered memories. He stepped back and scowled. There had to be a way in. If anyone in the city would know where to find the Beast, it would be the monks of Hope.

He hadn't come this far to be stopped by mere stone.

He reached out with his senses and felt the cold stone. His mind pushed aside the stories and visions and dug deeper. The stoneness of the wall gave way to increasing emptiness. Crow pushed deeper until he saw the first pinprick. Soon the world was filled with pinpricks of light, each vibrating in mad intensity. He didn't completely understand exactly what he was looking at, but he knew how to make it do his bidding.

His mind gently pushed one of the vibrating things. Crow was no aetherist, but he knew enough to know what he was looking at was intensely tiny. In addition to being able to see very slightly into the future, the dragon in the North had given him a kind of magical power. The stone wall, immense though it was, was essentially the same thing as the knife that had exploded earlier. It was matter and all matter was made up of the tiny pieces.

Crow nudged one of the buzzing things and watched as it collided with another buzzing thing. Soon they were all buzzing and knocking against each other. A final push set the pieces atwitter. The air in the alley buzzed and hummed. He'd never tried anything this big before, but like the dragon had said, "Magic can create a gold statue or remove a mountain."

The humming in the air turned in a deep basso thrum, the kind of thing the kids in clubs like to listen to. That music always gave Crow a headache; he was more of the traditional music kind of guy. He slowly backed away from the thumping door. Once the reaction started, it was almost impossible to stop it.

Thunder and smoke rippled down the alley. When the dust cleared, Crow found himself staring through the black and white *paifang* into an exquisite garden. He pinched himself to make sure he wasn't dreaming. The *paifang* was an archway to another country, one that shouldn't be in the middle of an alley in one of the many worst parts of Croatoa.

He stood and stared at the garden and wondered where the golden light was coming from. The garden reeked of calmness and peace - promises too vague to be disappointing when they don't show up. Felix Crow calmly stepped over the rubble of the old stone wall and into the garden. He didn't need calmness and peace. He needed information and this was as good a place to start as any.

2 | It's Just Chan

The crowd was a rambunctious, roiling mass of bodies chanting and yelling. *Baiju* and *bidi* smoke and sweat mixed with the smell of roasting *jùxíng jī*. The great birds were a favorite at any event and at the Fights they were a standard. The food and drink and smoke laced with magical drugs kept the crowd alert and attentive, but it was one man in the center of a pentagonal structure that held everyone's attention.

The man was dressed simply in plain gray robes and a conical dǒulì on his head. He stood perfectly still as a pair of men dragged a limp body out of the ring. Money changed hands as the man calmly let the world pass around him.

His name was Chan. Just Chan. He may or may not have had a family name, but the world of Aluna knew him as Chan. He was a favorite in the fights; a beloved predator that everyone wanted to love, but no one completely trusted. They watched him out of the corner of their eyes, like people watched snakes and scorpions that looked like they might get too close.

The truth was, he was less of a threat than anyone would have guessed. Even though he was dangerous, it was only to those who attacked first. Chan was also a badass, but he was a gentle badass.

Where Crow trended toward the darker side of his nature, Chan embraced his better nature. That didn't mean he was a pushover, though. Because sometimes to encourage the better nature, it was necessary to dance with the darker nature.

Once a month, downtown Croatoa was shut down for the Fights. They weren't random street fights with thugs sparring with each other or punks knifing strangers in alleys; those kinds of fights happened during the day. Croatoa's famous - or infamous - Fights were legendary. The Fights were ostensibly a spectator sport, but in a world where most people looked at fighting as the highest form of sport and expression, they were viewed as the art of the people and things tended to get out of hand.

Fighting was at the very heart of Croatoa. After the Dragon Wars, the idea of being able to take care of oneself through violent means took hold. The people elevated it to an art form and thousands of distinct styles had emerged over the turns: varying drunken styles, high-flying kicking styles, grappling, punching. Fighters learned quickly how to integrate new information into their skill-sets or they learned how to kiss the mat.

Chan was widely regarded as one of the best to ever walk into the ring. His first fight was the stuff of legends. At eighteen, he wandered into the fights as a young punk with nothing to lose and everything to prove. Chan won that night, barely, but he bested every opponent that walked into the ring. He himself would describe his victory as luck, but he also liked to define luck as the intersection of skill and opportunity.

He watched patiently as a pair of assistants dragged an unconscious fighter off the matt. Blood trails from the man's broken body glistened under the magical arc lights. The crowd roared. Some roared for the money they'd made, others for the money they'd lost. The man being dragged off the mat had been a heavy favorite to break Chan's winning streak. Remaining undefeated for over a hundred fights meant every young raptor in the city wanted a shot at Chan. To beat him would be like beating Chi You. Just like the god of war, though, Chan remained steadfastly unbroken.

"Who would like to be the next to challenge the almighty Chan?" the announcer asked the crown. "Surely there must be a warrior somewhere out there. Someone capable of dealing with the man in the *d□ulì.*"

Chan remained still as a murmur rumbled through the crowd. He had all night. If no one challenged him, the pot would be smaller, but rich nonetheless. Rich enough to live on for a while.

"Remember!" The announcer yelled. "Beating Chan also means beating all his opponents."

Chan breathed in and let the air out slowly. His pulse never changed. Some would claim that a sign of a psychopath, but Chan had spent a lifetime learning to fight and win. Emotion got in the way of a clean, precise fight, so he excised it from himself.

He practiced the traditional preset patterns and forms, but also liked to explore new ways to cripple his opponents. Out of this miasma of traditional training learned at the feet of the masters of yore and hard-won knowledge from growing up alone on the streets of Croatoa, Chan had fused together a system that made sense for him and his abilities. The result of that fusion was a fearsome fighting system that blended the best of the traditional with the brutality of fighting for his life in alleys around the city.

Chan wasn't a machine, though. He fought because he was good at it and because he saw it as the highest form of power and art. Some people looked to money to solve their problems or an army of minions to do their bidding, but in Chan's mind the only skill worth having was survival. It was a skill he was attempting to pass onto a protégé he'd recently acquired through a series of unfortunate events.

He watched the crowd distantly as his mind chewed on the problem of finding a pair of missing Earthlings in a city the size of Croatoa. There were millions of people crowded into the city. How then does one go about finding two humans – who, coincidentally looked almost exactly like native Alunans?

"Here comes our newest champion!" the announcer yelled.

Chan watched the crowd surrounding the ring for a sign of who would come next. He'd been here all night, waiting for the perfect opponent. The gangs usually sent at least one of their people to compete, but so far, he had faced nothing more than hobbyists. Not that the gang members were significantly better than hobbyists, but Chan knew the gangs had information. Since he wasn't the kind of person who knew where to find a gang member, Chan did the next best thing. If he couldn't go to the gang members, he'd find a way to make one come to him.

A shuffling of the crowd the left caught his eye. Someone was moving through the throng, shoving people around with wild abandon. The man was a behemoth. He stood head and shoulders above the audience. Chan's first thought was someone must be carrying the man. There was no way a person could be that large.

He looked down at his arms and felt small. Compared to the walking mass of muscle striding through the crowd, the nineteen-hand tall Chan was positively tiny. As the giant walked, the crowd parted around him. Some reached out and patted his back, others held their hands up for a high five. They were looking forward to this giant tearing Chan apart. The crowd that had cheered him on had gone fickle and decided they wanted a new hero.

Such was life, Chan thought. One day you're at the top, the next day the people get bored and look for a new person to follow.

Time slowed down. Chan was experienced at fighting, there was no doubt about that, but he never took it lightly. Especially in the city's sanctioned fights. Here the rule of law was the mob and when thousands are chanting "Kill him", it's almost impossible to ignore. So far, Chan hadn't intentionally killed anyone in the fights. He wore his history like a badge – hundreds of fights, zero intentional fatalities.

Although, as the blood streaks on the canvas pointed out, Chan had little compunction about hurting people.

The announcer started back up. His existence troubled Chan. The man did nothing more than shout. How that could be considered living was beyond Chan, but there were a great many things drifting in the *Tao* that Chan did not know about and did not care about.

A man the size of one of the *Long Wang* strode into the ring. Chan felt the man's *chi* even across the mat. The giant was covered in tattoos that proclaimed his virility and strength, as if such a creature needed help convincing the world he was its master.

Chan sized the man up and found himself lacking. At nineteen hands, Chan was tall. But he was lanky. The beast on the other side of the ring had to be at least twenty-one hands tall and his muscular body had to be almost as much around. His ink also proudly displayed the symbol of the *Qīng Bāng*; one of Croatoa's many gangs. One tattoo on the man's shoulder proclaimed a self-appointed name: Shān.

If ever there was a person who could call himself a mountain, this was it. Chan slowly rolled his joints around and found himself perturbed at the amount of popping and cracking. A lifetime of martial arts was supposed to prevent the noises and slow down the aging process. After all, weren't some of the old Wushu masters supposed to have lived to two hundred?

"In this corner," the announcer said, "is the master of the Vibrating Hand of Death, smiter of Tong Po, the undefeated master of Wushu, Chan!"

The crowd exploded in applause and cheers. Chan faced each direction and bowed to the people. His world became muted. He saw them cheering and raising their fists, but he didn't hear them. He turned back to face his opponent. The giant stood still and calm, like a rock in a windstorm. The man's face was expressionless, save for a hint of disdain in his eyes.

The announcer wore a sparkly red *changsha*. The jacket was covered in cheap, knock-off rubies that glittered under the magic-powered arc lights. His teeth were white and sparkled almost as much as the rubies.

"And in that corner, the man his own gang calls 'the beast', master of *Shuai Jiao*, the enforcer for the *Qīng Bāng*, the mighty Yánshí!"

Yánshí turned in the four directions and bowed gratefully to the cheering crowd. He tore his shirt off and tossed it into the mass of people. A fight broke out as the fans tried to get their hands on the tattered shirt.

The announcer left the ring and a man in a black and white striped shirt stepped in. Chan often wondered why anyone bothered with referees in a fight that had no rules to enforce. If one fighter threw an illegal strike, it was expected the other would work through the problem in his or her head and deal with the problem. Fighters, after all, must adapt to changing situations and placing rules on a fighter would be like snipping a xi□olóng's wings.

Chan and Yánshí faced off. Each fighter performed an elaborate set of hand gestures that conveyed philosophy, fighting style, and a brief salutation in moments. Chan stepped to the side and extended a fist covered by an open hand – I prefer to act defensively. His hand pulled to his right shoulder as his right foot stepped forward – I will attack if necessary. Both hands snapped in front of his body and his fist cleared the open hand – I will not hold back.

The edges of Yánshí's lips curled up in a smirk. He went through an elaborate series of movements that told the world he was the guardian of the gate and was looking forward to smashing anyone who tried to enter.

Shuai Jiao was one of the grappling styles that had grown up over the turns. It suited Yánshí's frame and reach. While Chan focused his fighting on striking, the mountain had taken a different tack and learned how to tear an opponent apart. Both styles used extensive pressure points and joint locking native to *Chin Na*, but achieved their goals in different ways. Chan preferred to precisely strike targets that would cause his opponents to black out from temporarily stopping blood flow or making it difficult to breathe. Yánshí, meanwhile, would be attempting to tear muscle and tendon.

The referee put his hand between Chan and Yánshí. The

men assumed their fighting stances. Chan relaxed into a narrow position, right foot forward slightly and hands open and out at chest level. Yánshí's right leg slid back and fists up in front of his face.

"Fight," the referee said.

Chan struck first. His training in traditional Alunan martial arts had emphasized the defensive nature of fighting, hence his salutation, but he'd learned over turns that fights were very rarely won from a defensive position. His hand lashed out like his arm was made of firehose being flooded with water. A fist that had punched through bricks hit Yánshí's chest and seemed to keep going.

The monster of a man took Chan's blow like it had come from a child. Chan didn't waste time wondering why a punch that had felled dozens of men didn't work on the beast. He pulled back, hoping to create some distance between himself and the giant, but the big man was far faster than Chan anticipated. The giant grabbed him and easily flung him across the ring. As he flew, Chan chided himself for assuming because he was big, the beast would be slow.

The crowd roared its approval as Chan hit the canvas hard. He managed to roll and avoid the worst of the damage. To defeat the enemy is to defeat yourself, he reminded himself. Preconceived notions lost more fights than won them. He sprung to his feet and took a moment to assess the fight. So far, it wasn't looking good.

Yánshí charged forward. The big man could move like a snake when he wanted to. A terrifying mixture of speed and raw, feral power bore forward. Chan clapped the man's right ear and danced out of the way. The beast stopped his charge and shook his head. There are parts of the body that no amount of strength or training can toughen up. The ears, eyes, and groin are always good choices for dealing with opponents.

Without turning, Yánshí's foot slashed straight out behind him and into Chan's stomach. It felt like being kicked by the *dà jī* on orphanage's farm. The huge birds could pack quite a wallop when they wanted to.

Chan doubled over, but kept his arms out to catch the next attack. The beast spun on his heel and fired a kick at Chan. Chan blocked and dodged to the side and the massive foot cleanly missed his face. With one hand, he kept the foot away from his head while the other slammed an extended middle knuckle fist into the beast's thigh muscle.

The beast staggered. When he tried to walk, Chan could see him favoring his left leg. It wasn't much, but it was a start. That first punch, the one that failed to do anything, proved pure power wouldn't beat the huge man; it was going to take patience and precise strikes to wear the big man down.

Chan took a deep breath and focused his *chi*. There was nothing magical about *chi*; it was just the term the ancients used to represent a high-energy state where the body and mind were working together. Chan needed every bit of help to take down the giant.

Yánshí tried to dart in again, but his damaged leg wouldn't let him run. He had been big, fast, and mean. Chan's strike to the thigh took away the fast part. That left mean and strong. Chan easily dodged the charge and kicked Yánshí in the side of the leg. The big guy went down with a howl of rage.

Chan darted in, twisted, and jumped. A mighty spinning kick flashed into the side of the Yánshí's head. The kick had snapped trees, but the giant was proving to be more of a threat than he expected. Chan was tired and didn't want to risk getting seriously hurt. It would be a fast fight and the crowd might not like that, but there were bigger issues at stake. Like information.

The kick should have snapped the beast's neck. At the very least, it should have broken his nose and probably a couple bones in his face. But it didn't. Yánshí dodged and Chan's foot sailed past the man's face. Chan allowed the force to carry his body around and get ready for the next attack.

He spun fully around and was surprised to find Yánshí struggling to his feet. There was fire in the big man's eyes and a hint of madness about his face. Chan stepped back. Anger was a normal reaction in a fight. Rage kept people fighting long after they'd lost the battle. This was different, though. Yánshí had the look of one of the manic street preachers in the *Nán Zhōngbù* district where the derelicts congregated to let madness overtake them.

Usually people who had trouble walking backed down from a fight, but the big guy got to his feet and stomped toward Chan. He was unsteady on his feet and his eyes were flitting this way and that, like he could see things that no one else could. Yánshí' tried to charge forward again. His bad leg gave out under the strain, but he still managed to grab Chan's ankle.

Before he could react, the beast applied his *shuai jiao*, twisting Chan's ankle and tugging furiously. Chan's leg felt like it was about to come off. The rough mat rushed into his face. He felt the world go fuzzy for a moment. Instinct took over and he kicked back hard with his free leg. His foot hit something and even over the grunting and growling and the roar of the crows, Chan heard something break.

Yánshí's hands loosened just enough for Chan to break free and roll away from the beast. He snapped to his feet and nearly fell back down as his leg screamed at him. It felt like a pulled muscle, nothing serious, but in a fight a pulled muscle could be the difference between life and death. Yánshí was a grappler; once he got his hands on an opponent it was usually all over. It was only the fact that he couldn't move quickly enough to finish the twist that allowed Chan to hobble away.

Chan was a striker. His fists could punch through walls. Earlier in the night, he'd knocked out one person – a fighter from the cold lands – with a single blow. Chan's kicks were legendary. But that arsenal was required mobility and a stable platform to deliver strikes from. For a striker, a damaged leg was an extremely bad thing.

Copper filled his mouth and warmth trickled down over his lips. Chan's tongue delicately probed his mouth and found all the teeth were at least still there, but a couple were moving. He'd be on soup for a while.

Yánshí struggled to his feet, using his hands on his thigh to help him push himself off the ground. Out of the corner of his eye, Chan spotted a small paper packet on the mat. He disregarded it for the moment and focused on the beast. He had only one chance and one shot to make it work or Yánshí was going to turn him into a piece of knot bread.

The big man struggled forward, manic eyes still darting around wildly. Chan shifted his weight to his good leg and took a deep breath. Yánshí was moving slowly, completely focused on grabbing and breaking. He looked like he'd forgotten all the rules of protecting himself in a fight. Every stumbling step forward exposed a myriad of targets.

Chan quickly processed the best way to end the fight. The correct kick to the jaw would likely snap the giant's neck. That wouldn't do. Yánshí was *Qīng Bāng* and Chan needed information they might have. Dead men don't give up information. Chan needed to hurt the beast, though, beat him thoroughly and leave him completely at his mercy.

That left a few attacks. Chan chose one and relaxed. Yánshí lurched forward. Before he could steady himself, Chan struck. His bad leg bent at the knee and raised. Yánshí saw the knee come up and his arm moved down to block it. Chan jumped off his good leg and kicked straight out. His foot slid neatly past Yánshí's blocking arm and slammed up between his legs.

Every fighter knew exactly how it felt to kicked in balls. The pain was crippling. It wasn't uncommon for a man to collapse and writhe in agony, rolling in his own pain vomit. Thus, every fighter learned very quickly to protect himself. A good distraction was necessary to open the gates.

Yánshí stopped dead in his tracks. The madness in his eyes disappeared as they rolled back into his head. His skin turned ashen and his legs collapsed together. A tiny sound escaped his lips as he fell to knees.

Chan landed with a stumble and nearly fell into Yánshí. He caught himself and finished the beast with a clumsy blow to his head. They fell to the ground with Chan's elbow on Yánshí's throat. As the light faded from the beast's eyes, Chan noticed the paper packet on the mat again.

"Where's The Beast?" Chan asked. "Where are the Earth people?"

Yánshí groaned and whimpered, but didn't answer. The final blow took too much out of the big man. The tension drained out of the giant's body. Chan wanted to scream. Then he wanted to punch the guy again. Kevin would be disappointed. Chan rolled off Yánshí's body and sighed. The poor boy was getting far too used to being disappointed.

He pulled himself to his feet and limped over the giant's body. There, on the mat, was the small packet. Chan picked it up and looked at it, ignoring the referee holding his hand in the air and the crowd chanting his name. *"Tiāntáng de fěn,"* he whispered to himself. "What is Heaven's Powder?"

3 | Dragon Lady

The ends of Huizhong's dark hair were pink tinted gray, a leftover from her time in Croatoa working in the Clock Tower. The city was noisy and dirty and stank of bad ideas and dark alleys where predators roamed unchecked. She described Croatoa as *Dìyù* come to life; a living, breathing example of what not to do.

She shuddered slightly as a bit of memory wafted across her brain. It was only her ongoing attempt at centeredness that let her push the memory aside and focus on cleansing her mind of the horrors she'd seen and done.

Huizhong sat cross-legged in the middle of a forest clearing and focused on removing the bad person she had became from the good person she was supposed to be. But, like the smells of the city, the bad didn't wash out easily. She felt tainted by it, like Croatoa had soiled her very soul.

All along the edges of the clearing were towers of neatly stacked, barely balanced rocks. Huizhong felt like those towers. All it would take is a gentle nudge to push her over into oblivion. She closed her eyes and tried to calm her stormy mind.

Huizhong wanted to rebuild herself after the Clock Man died. The death of Chenming Zhang was a net positive – less evil in the world – but she felt she had become as bad as he was. When he fell out the window at the top of the Clock Tower a part of her sighed in relief, but a thought nagged at her constantly. For everything she'd done: infiltrated the tower, infiltrated the Beast's gang, killed a few people, nearly consigned Felix Crow to a slow, miserable death, she felt like a part of her soul had been stomped on and put back in place upside down.

Did the ends truly justify the means? Or was she as bad as Crow and Chenming Zhang? After all, she wasn't exactly innocent in Zhang's death. Before he fell, Huizhong had been actively exploring ways of killing him. To get closer to the Clock Man, she'd joined up with his inner circle and done the terrible things inner circles do.

When Chenming Zhang finally died, Huizhong ran from Croatoa and came back to the forest to rediscover herself. Everyone said Nüwa dwelt in their churches and places of worship, but Huizhong only ever felt Nüwa's presence here in the forest. Specifically, in this clearing. Mab and the rest of the Furious Fae never claimed the great goddess lived here and maybe that was why the sense of her was so strong. No books, no rules, no chanting monks, just the peace and quiet of creation calmly doing its thing.

Xiǎojiě was shining her weak silver rays through the trees, casting long shadows across the clearing. Some people preferred the radiance of *Dàjiě*, but Huizhong felt Little Sister's light was less obtrusive. Big sister lived up to her name.

Eyes closed, Huizhong forced her mind to calm itself. She thought of the still waters of the lake she had grown up next to, so calm the surface looked like glass. She felt her hair brush her cheek as the breeze played with it. Slowly, her mind became as calm as the lake and light as the breeze.

Then the vision started again. It was yet another thorn in her spiritual side, a vision of death and blood and horrifying things no one should experience. Each night when she closed her eyes to sleep, the vision took hold. Even in her dreams, she fought to close her eyes and roll into a mental ball to avoid seeing the images.

Maybe it was Nüwa, maybe it was someone else, but whoever was sending the vision was insistent. So far, Huizhong had managed to avoid seeing the details of the vision as it played out in her head night after night. And night after night, the vision came back. Tonight, Huizhong was determined to calm herself enough that she could explore the vision and remain detached from it.

It started as it always did; she was walking through a long passageway with Felix Crow. He was edgy and irritable, even for his already edgy and irritable personality. Someone was behind them. In her mind, she turned to see who it was, but all she saw was a tall man in a *d□ulì* that covered his eyes. He was wearing rough clothing made of canvas. Crow was wearing his trench coat and hat. They were following something, something young and male. Whatever it was, it felt tremendously powerful. The follower felt dangerous, like getting too close to a downed magic line. Then the vision degenerated into skeletons and blood and fire.

"Your friend Crow is an interesting thing," a deep, rumbling voice said from behind her.

Huizhong's eyes popped open. Part of her wanted to snap and lash out for interrupting the vision. The other part knew neither of those things was a good idea. Instead, she touched her neck and remembered.

"He's not my friend," Huizhong said.

The voice moved around the periphery of the forest. A sound like silverware lightly clattering followed its movements. Then, as if someone flipped a switch, the clattering sound stopped. "You treated him like a friend. A special friend."

She felt like he was hunting her. In truth, he probably was. It was his way. "That was part of the job and you know it."

Huizhong's face burned in embarrassment. Of course, he would know about ... that. How could he not? But he didn't have to remind her of her shortcomings. "Do not fret, child," the voice said. "Human mating rituals are beneath my concern."

The voice moved around the periphery of the clearing. He was so silent, Huizhong never knew where the voice would come from next. Even though she'd conversed with him before, she couldn't get over how such a large being could move so silently. It must have been eons of predatory evolution and centuries of practice.

"Then what does concern you?" Huizhong asked.

"Power," he said. "The same thing that drives you drives me. We are not all that different, physical aspects aside."

Huizhong brushed a stray hair out of her face and leaned back to look at the stars. "The only power I want is the power to find a nice bed and sleep in it forever."

This time the voice came from left. "I, too, enjoy sleep. But sleeping forever would be a waste of a life."

"Are you going to wander around the forest all night?" Huizhong asked. Her mind was still too much of a mess to deal with his games.

The forest fell silent. The usual chittering calls of insects and muted chirping of the tiny dragons stopped suddenly. A primal part of Huizhong's mind tensed. When the forest critters went dark it meant something dangerous was lurking nearby.

If they only knew, she thought. If they could only understand exactly what was skulking around in the woods.

"I will never understand how you manage to do that," she said.

The forest exploded. One moment it was deathly silent, the next a huge blur sped at her. Huizhong didn't even have time to get her hands up before she was face to face with a dragon as black as the night itself. The creature's eyes were glowing amber, as if lit from within by very fires that powered its breath. Fangs that could rend a person in two glowed in Little Sister's faint light.

The multitude of whiskers on its snout pointed up in the air and bounced gently as it made a series of short growls. The dragon chuckled to himself, pleased with his ability to hunt and kill. "Do what?" he asked.

Huizhong's flight response faded from her body even as adrenaline was still surging through her veins. Dragons were odd creatures; undoubtedly intelligent, but their intellect was far different from humans. The fact that humans had fought a war with these creatures and fought it well spoke more to numbers than any intelligence or skill on the humans' part.

She took in a deep breath and tried to calm her raging heart. "Turn off the forest like that," she said a little more breathily than she would have liked.

The dragon coiled around himself. Normally, dragons in this part of the world had long legs and majestic wings that made humans want to drop to their knees and worship them, but the big creature before her didn't fit that bill. He had short, stubby legs. While he had wings, they were smaller than the normal Northern dragon, more evolutionary leftover than functional. He looked like a three-hundred-hand-long snake that someone had added wings and short legs to.

He cocked his enormous head to the side and bared his fangs in dragon-y grin. "Trade secrets, my daughter," he said.

Huizhong's heart was still caught in her throat. He thought it was hilarious to burst from the forest like that and even though he'd done it dozens of times before, the mere thought that a massive, fire-breathing, apex predator could move that quickly and quietly still filled her heart with dread. Not that she'd ever let him know that. She gulped hard and asked, "Care to share the secret?"

His breath was a fetid mixture of sulfur and whatever he'd hunted for dinner. "Humans cannot understand interconnectedness well enough for me to teach you. The wholeness of everything is a delicious myth. When you have seen everything, you will see that it is nothing. It may seem as the nothing is all there is, but buried beneath it all is everything. We have learned to be part of everything and embrace the nothing. Of course, none of this means anything to you since you still think you've seen everything."

There it was again, that general air of superiority he had. Huizhong bit back the urge to remind him who had pushed who to surrender in the Dragon Wars. "Then why are you here, Ao Shun?"

"You reek of magic," Ao Shun replied. He took a deep breath, inhaling the world through his nostrils. "It clings to you and seeps out of your human pores. Magic does not often cling to people. Whatever you sought to do is not finished."

She clenched her fists and released them. Dealing with dragons was always frustrating. They were so tuned into the world, they had trouble understanding those who were not. Since they couldn't comprehend not being tied to the world, they assumed everyone was in on the same secrets they were.

"I didn't seek to do anything," Huizhong replied. "I did what you told me to do: infiltrate the Clock Tower, report everything I found, and find a way to eliminate Chenming if he became too much of a problem. And let me tell you something, watching the Clock Man fall to his death felt wonderful. I can still feel his thoughts in my head and I'm glad he's dead. I just wish you hadn't sent Crow."

Ao Shun grunted and growled. His dragon-y grin reappeared in a mass of sharp fangs. "Your boyfriend was the best choice. Just ask Mab."

"I did!" Huizhong shouted. The words echoed faded into the trees like lizards before Ao Shun's bulk. "She told me she was opposed, too! And he's not my boyfriend!"

"He means something to you," Ao Shun said. "And his job is not done yet. The *Tao* still has plans for him."

"No," Huizhong said. "Absolutely not. There is no way that man is that important."

"You humans still think you have control over the world," Ao Shun grunted. "You can't even control yourselves or understand why you do what you do. We dragons have learned to glide along on the *Tao*. Why can't you?"

Huizhong contemplated that. It was the dragon version of the one hand clapping question. "I don't think it's in our nature," she replied. "We don't go quietly into the dark night; we go screaming and crying and yelling."

"But you go nonetheless," Ao Shun said. "And into that dark night you must go. The *Tao* is calling for you and your boyfriend. He'll need your help or he'll be in a world of trouble."

She slumped and sighed. Getting through to the dragon was nearly impossible; his ego and alien intellect always got in the way. "He is not my boyfriend. And let him get himself in trouble. My throat still hurts when I think about him and I still taste him in my mouth."

"You are obviously still thinking about him," Ao Shun said.

Huizhong stuck a finger in Ao Shun's face and was about to tear into him when she realized he was right. Crow might be a rogue, and a violent one at that, but he wasn't without his charms. And it wasn't Crow's hands around her throat that kept her up at night; it was the feeling of Chenming's fingers digging through her mind. She could still feel the sensation of utter helplessness as she watched her body obey The Clock Man's commands.

It was Chenming Zheng that commanded her body to attack Crow, just like it was Ao Shun's request that sent her in his path in the first place. The rage in Crow's eyes as he lifted her off the ground and nearly choked her life out was understandable, even if it was misplaced.

"Let us say our relationship is complicated," she told Ao Shun.

The dragon grunted. "All human relationships are complicated because you humans never admit what you want. You have strayed too far from your animal nature."

Huizhong clamped her mouth shut and closed the part of her brain that wanted to explore her own animal nature. Serenity was what she needed right now. It wasn't easy to be used and it was even harder to come back from it. Almost everyone used her. Ao Shun used her to get close to the Clock Man. Those strange men that worked for the Clock Man used her to lure Crow. Chenming Zheng used her body as a puppet.

Out of all of them, only Felix Crow hadn't used her. He nearly killed her twice and happily stole her *bidis*, but he never used her. Which begged an interesting question. "Why would the Clock Man even think about remotely controlling people? And why would he do what he did to himself?" she asked. "He had everything he could ever want. Yet he became a monster both mentally and physically."

"Has it occurred to you that maybe the Clock Man wasn't operating independently? That maybe Chenming Zheng had outside help that influenced him and guided his decisions. In all the thousands of turns of Clock Men, how many have tried what he tried?"

Facts and histories and statistics flooded Huizhong's brain. In going undercover at the Clock Tower, she'd been forced to learn the entire history of those mystical men who control and regulate the magic that powered Aluna. "None," she said. "Some went crazy and one blew a hole into the Dreaming Lands, but none of them tried what he tried. Chenming was a disaster."

Ao Shun grunted and snorted. He coiled around himself and grinned his dragon-y grin. "Why do you think it was that a Clock Man would tinker with controlling people's minds, then?"

Huizhong started to answer, but realized her rationalizations rang false. She'd conditioned herself to think Chenming had gone mad; that kind of thing happens with Clock Men from time to time. But his actions, while revolting, weren't the actions of a madman. There was intent, deliberate and bold, behind his actions. From the armless, headless torso floating in glass to the little dragon that was nothing more than a set of wings hooked to a tiny brain, everything Chenming had done was intentional.

"I ... don't know," she said. "It doesn't make any sense."

"You don't understand the reason," Ao Shun said, "because you don't understand the question. You are wondering why Chenming Zheng wanted to control people like he did. Perhaps it wasn't Chenming that wanted control. Perhaps he was simply an agent for someone else."

She sighed. "Are you trying to solve a mystery from halfway around Aluna?"

Ao Shun raised himself up to dizzying heights and stared down at her. "The machinations of humans mean as much to me as why insects do what they do."

"Glad to know we're so important," Huizhong said. "If that's the case, why do you care what Chenming was up to?"

The dragon lowered himself until his snout was almost touching her nose. "Two reasons. One, he was a Clock Man and that means magic. Dragons are always interested in magic. Two, I fear what sent Chenming spiraling down wasn't human. I am curious and scared. I enjoy curiosity, but I do not like being scared. Finding the solution would satisfy my curiosity and allay my fears. I'd examine the problem myself, probably far better than you could, but I would be an obvious interloper in Croatoa. You will go in my stead."

Terrible visions of a half-man, half-machine Clock Man and his menagerie of animated body parts filled her Huizhong's head. Fingers wrapped around her throat and constricted. Fingers dug through her mind and made her watch as someone else controlled her body.

Then there was the vision of Crow and whoever that man with him was. And was there a boy? There was something in the vision about a boy. Then there was nothing but fear and pain and fire.

"Why would I ever want to go back to that horrible place?" Huizhong asked. "What's in it for me?"

Ao Shun's fangs shone in the weak light when he grinned. "You will never know peace until you answer your questions."

All the energy and peace she'd found in the forest drained from Huizhong's body. A tiny part of her, the one she didn't want to admit existed, leaped in joy at the thought of going back there. She beat it down with sheer willpower, but still it sang its happy gējù. "The answers are in Croatoa, aren't they? Buried somewhere in the Clock Tower. How am I supposed to get back there? It took weeks of walking."

"The Fae have packed your bags. I left you a personal present. Use it as you deem fit. Your flight leaves at dawn. There is one other thing before you go."

She didn't want to meet eyes with him, didn't want to leave her peaceful enclosure where everything was safe, but once Ao Shun spoke, it was best to listen. "What?" she asked sullenly.

"There is something there that you must bring back to me."

Huizhong glared at him and almost vibrated with rage. "Are you going to tell me what it is?"

Ao Shun snorted and she nearly choked on the reek of sulfur on his breath. "I do not know what it is. But you will come across and it and know what it is. Bring it to me."

Rather than cursing up a blue streak – which would have been childish, but fun – Huizhong rolled her eyes and said, "I'll do my best."

4 | Out Of Place

Kevin awoke to the rattling, basso rumble of a pit bull in deep slumber, the chirping of little dragons outside his window, and a deinonychus chirping and whistling back. It was the usual racket that split the silence of a small place outside of Croatoa. Of all the menagerie, Kevin felt the little dragons were the strangest. Aluna, from what little he knew of it, thought the dog was the strangest thing.

In a world of scales and feathers, a furry thing that wasn't human was an oddity. The deinonychus, a creature that hadn't lived for millions of turns and had never existed on Aluna to begin with, was more readily accepted than the dog. Kevin supposed it had to do with the fact that humans, no matter what planet they found themselves on, needed to feel special and another thing with hair freaked them out.

At eleven turns old, Kevin thought far too many deep thoughts.

It wasn't really his fault, though. Not long ago he was a normal boy with normal parents doing normal things like watching TV and building spaceships with Lego pieces. Then…

He clenched his fists and choked back anger. The chirping and whistling of the deinonychus gave way to a stuttering hoot as the dinosaur eyed a bright green little dragon. Kevin wished he could be more like Tina; the dog could sleep through the end of the world. But, no matter how many times Chan tried to encourage that level of *níngjìng*, serenity always slipped through Kevin's fingers.

"Dino! Hush!" Kevin yelled. He tossed a little toy dragon across the room at the dinosaur.

Dino's snout snatched the dragon out the air. Amber eyes whirled and fixed on Kevin's prone form. The dinosaur's tail twitched and long claws clicked on the bare wood floor.

Happy chirping noises echoed around the room and soon six feet of late Cretaceous predator was flying across the room.

The dinosaur landed on the foot of Kevin's bed and collapsed next to Kevin. Human fingers stroked downy feathers. "You need to sleep later, buddy," Kevin said, scratching the back of Dino's skull.

Dino rolled over onto his back and put his feet in the air. Six-inch-long claws happily clenched and unclenched as Kevin scratched under the dinosaur's chin.

A slow thumping sound meant the dog was waking up, too. She was always the last to drag herself out of bed. Kevin turned his head and saw a graying muzzle open in a huge yawn. Dino heard the noise and leapt off the bed. He skittered to a halt in front of the dog and nuzzled her.

"Good morning, Tina," Kevin said from the bed. She responded with a grunt and sigh.

Kevin sat up just in time to see Tina and Dino nose to nose. The old dog gave the dinosaur a quick lick on the face before settling back down again. "You two are far too happy to see each other," Kevin said.

While the dog and the dinosaur said good morning to each other, Kevin focused on what Chan called his *chi*. He didn't completely grasp what Chan meant when he said *chi*, but there were a lot of things Kevin didn't understand about Chan. Or Aluna. Or what he was doing here.

Kevin knew two things with absolute certainty, though. His parents were here on Aluna somewhere and Chan had promised to help him find them. He also knew he had a latent ability to make things happen. Call it magic, luck, *chi*, whatever; Kevin had turned a stuffed deinonychus toy into a living, breathing dinosaur.

It was, unfortunately, a feat he hadn't been able to replicate. Chan, crazy warrior ascetic that he was, assured Kevin if he could do something once, he should be able to do it again. The path forward, Chan said, is sometimes not obvious. Sometimes, one must clear one's mind to understand that the difficulty lay not in the road ahead, but in the head of the person on the road.

Kevin closed his eyes and pushed away the chirping of the dragon lizards and the noise of the animal friends and clicking of claws and found the tiny, peaceful world inside himself. His breath slowed and pulse lowered. He dove into that space and swam.

He would be hard pressed to explain what the tiny world was to anyone. It was both there and not there, real and not real. Rather than dwell on the details of how it worked and what it meant, Kevin did what any eleven-turn-old would do and ignored that part of the problem. The world seemed to work just fine without him understanding it.

While he swam in the light he saw snapshots of the world. He supposed these were pictures of things that had happened or would happen or were happening right now, but he wasn't completely certain. Again, it didn't really matter. It worked and that was good enough.

A picture of that nice Mrs. Chow flashed across his mind. She was scowling at something, but he couldn't see what. Chan said she was the head of a *san ho hui* – a triple union society. That didn't sound like a bad thing to be, but Chan said it was a nice way of saying she was head of a criminal enterprise.

Kevin didn't see a problem with being the head of a criminal enterprise. It sounded exciting.

Other pictures popped in and disappeared. A woman talked to a dragon. A man in a long, black coat wearing a hat walked through an alley. Chan's snarl as he hurled a *dao* at something. Skeletons. Chains. Darkness. An explosion of power.

Then everything was okay.

He gasped and opened his eyes. The pictures weren't always pretty, but he'd never seen anything that felt so ominous. Kevin shook his head, but the image of the skeletons wouldn't go away. Nor did the sense that everything was fine;

it was as it should be.

The door to Kevin's room opened and Chan appeared. He looked like Hell. Kevin rolled his eyes and mentally corrected himself. Chan looked like one of the many Alunan hells. Perhaps *pò bízi dì dìyù*. The Hell of Broken Noses seemed apt considering the state of Chan's face.

"What happened?" Kevin asked.

The Wushu master's body sagged. He'd always told Kevin emotions got in the way of victory, but it looked like he was riddled with guilt. His gravelly voice and drawl, normally straightforward and powerful, felt weak. "I failed you again."

Chan slid to the floor and slumped his shoulders. From the blood on his face and the dark bruises around his eyes, he had to be in pain. But it wasn't the physical pain that worried Kevin. Chan was incredibly tough on the outside; he'd once been kicked in the head by a hopper and kept right on going. Everyone else that got kicked by the one of the giant lizards was out for the count, but not Chan.

Something about Chan looked broken, though, like he was physically and emotionally drained. "You've been at the fights," Kevin stated.

Chan nodded. Tina stretched and slowly walked across the room until she collapsed with her head in Chan's lap. He stroked the dog's fur and smiled. The normal fire in his eyes was gone. "I was looking for information and money. I got the money, but the information eluded me. All I found was a tiny envelope with Heaven's Powder written on it."

Kevin knew Chan hadn't given up on his promise. Months ago, Kevin was a normal kid on Earth. Then the ghosts showed up. His family tried to capture and evict the ghosts with a candle and a jar. The plan worked well; the ghosts were captured. But they weren't ghosts. They were Alunan guardians sent by Chan and possibly others. By capturing the guardians, Kevin's family had allowed the Beast – whoever or whatever that was – to sneak in and capture

Kevin's parents. He would have been next on the list if it weren't for Chan spiriting Kevin away to this new world.

Now he was a stranger in a terrifying land and his only guide was Chan.

Kevin sighed deeply and wiped a tear from his eye. After six months on Aluna, his old life had started to fade into the background. Every time he thought about his parents the past came crashing back into him. He nodded and tried to smile, but his voice was choked when he asked, "What does that mean?"

Chan shrugged and continued running his fingers through the dog's fur. "I don't know. Probably some kind of drug. Croatoa is rife with them. It is odd that a fighter would take drugs, but he was *Qīng Bāng*. Some people take everything they can to escape from reality."

"Reality can be a crushing place," Kevin replied.

"It can," Chan agreed. "But I'll take a real thing over a fake thing any day of the week. Fake things will trap you forever in a prison without walls. Reality may beat you down, but you can always get back up."

Kevin nodded and the hint of a grin formed at the corners of his mouth. "And find a way to punch reality in the face."

Chan chuckled. "I thought I detected something different about you the last time we trained."

"What, yesterday?"

"If you're going to do something…" Chan started.

"Do it all the time and as best you can," Kevin finished. His parents may be missing. His only friends may be an aging dog, a dinosaur, and this strange mystic, but he had learned to appreciate what he had.

"You enjoy the training," Chan continued. "That's good. But you need to be sure you don't let your anger overcome you. You're already showing signs of becoming a great fighter. It's a pity you didn't start training earlier."

"I was ten!" Kevin said.

"Exactly. Starting you at four or five would have been

better."

Kevin slouched back on the bed. Dino hopped up and cooed in his face until Kevin stroked his feathered head again. For a moment, everyone was silent and Kevin's mind calmed down. "When did you start?"

"I don't remember. I was so young all I can remember is training."

"Do you ever take time off?" Kevin asked.

"Never. When I'm sick, I find ways to work around it. When I'm injured, I change my training to work with the injury."

"That's a sad life," Kevin replied. "Back home... Back home, taking breaks from school meant I went back in with renewed vigor."

Chan pondered that for a moment. "What did you study?"

"Ugh," Kevin replied, remembering the endless classes. "History, geography, math, science. We were working on the solar system when I ... when I came here."

"It must have been a different solar system from ours. You only had one star."

"Yeah. We called it the sun. Kind of a lame name. Some people liked to call it Sol."

"It would be strange to live in a place with only one star," Chan said. "*Dà Māmā* and *Xi□o M□qīn* have been all I have known. Big Mother gives us light, Little Mother takes away shadows."

"We also had TV and computers and the Internet."

Chan's eyebrow raised. "What are those things?"

"TV is like your vidders. Computers and the Internet were something else entirely. They were like machines that think and they were all connected together. They could talk to each other, share things, talk to people all over the world." Kevin's face fell. Another thing he'd likely never see again. "Why did you bring me here, Chan? You said something about the beast, but I still don't know what that means."

Tina rolled over and put her feet in the air so Chan could scratch her stomach. The old dog had taken a liking to him and she never failed to bring a smile to his otherwise dour face. "I needed to save you. There's a group of women in the North; they call themselves the Furious Fae. They know things, things they shouldn't know, but do. I've been working with them. Their leader, a woman called Mab, set up the guardians in your house. I don't know how she knew to do it, but she knew."

"Guardians?"

"You would see them as *jīngshén*. Spirits. Ghosts, I think you call them."

Kevin's mind thought back to the last night in his house. His mother threw a jar with ghosts out the door because she was terrified of them. He raced after the jar and found the ghosts staring sadly. "They weren't ghosts after all," he whispered. His dad was right, they weren't a threat. "They said the beast was coming. You said the beast was coming. What is the beast?"

"The Beast is a crime lord in Croatoa. No one knows what he looks like or where he lives. He hides well, but in a city the size of Croatoa, disappearing in the crowd isn't difficult. He is bad news, but either no one can find him or no one wants to find him. He is dangerous, though, I know that well enough. Mab decided to get you out of there before he could get to you. We handled it poorly, but it was absolutely necessary to get you out of there. I had hoped to get there before The Beast took your parents, but other events took precedent. I am truly sorry."

"Sorry?" Kevin hissed. "You're sorry? My parents are gone, probably forever and you're 'sorry'?"

Chan shrunk. His eyes focused on the dog lazing happily next to him. "I did not listen as well as I should have. I felt the more immediate threat was here and wasted time getting to you when the guardians sensed a presence. Had I left immediately, things could have turned out differently."

Kevin wanted to scream. He wanted to tear the world apart and force it to make sense. He wanted to go home. He wanted his mom's tacos and his dad's laugh. He wanted his friends. His fists clenched. Dino's eyes opened and stared at him in fear. The air crackled in the room.

Tina sat up and whimpered. Chan stared in wonder. Kevin's eyes glowed bright blue. A stuffed toy dragon rose and floated in midair.

"Who is The Beast, Chan?" Kevin hissed.

"I don't know, Kevin. No one seems to know."

The dragon exploded in a flash of light. Bits of scale leather and stuffing floated slowly to the floor like all of Kevin's hope. All the angry energy dropped out of Kevin and he flopped backward on the bed. "Why is this happening Chan?" he whispered.

Chan patted the dog's head and stood up. "Again, I don't know. But I might know someone who can help. Do you remember the man you met when you first came here? The man at Mrs. Chow's?"

Kevin nodded. "Big guy. Hat. Jacket. Looked like hell. It must not have been his best day."

"He doesn't exactly have best days, but you definitely didn't catch him on a good one. He was a student of mine once. He is undisciplined and violent, but he has a way of finding things. Perhaps we should take a day off; I think it's time we talked to Felix Crow."

5 | No Hope For The Wicked

Crow turned around and looked back at the alley. Fifty feet behind him the alley was a gray place that reeked of desperation and flop sweat. Ahead was nothing but green grass and *Dà Māmā's* golden light. In the center of the garden was a pagoda with a golden statue of a man in a lotus pose. The garden of Hope was serenity with neatly trimmed foliage. Crow smoothed his jacket and adjusted his hat before deciding he didn't really care how he looked. The alley was more his style. He was more comfortable with degenerates and desperados than he'd ever be with people who would live in this sanctuary. There was truth in desperation that could never be found in serenity.

He sighed and stalked forward into the monastery of the monks of Hope. The sooner he beat the information out of someone, the sooner he could get home to his little dragons and a nice bottle of *baiju*.

The trail blended neatly with the environment in a kind of *fēng shu*⬚ run completely amok. Everything flowed so perfectly from the natural to the man-made that it was almost impossible to determine where the world ended and the monastery began. Some people would find hope and calmness in a place like this. Crow was disgusted. He lit a *bidi* and glared at the garden.

"What do you seek here?" a voice whispered in his ear.

Crow took a deep drag from his *bidi* and exhaled the sweet smoke in a giant cloud. "Information."

"This is a place for people looking for hope. If you want information, try a library."

"The kind of information I need isn't in a library. If it was, I wouldn't have knocked on your door."

The statue's eyes opened and focused on Crow. "You call that knocking?"

"You call yourself a monk, golden boy? You look more like a trinket they sell to tourists down at the Buddhamart."

The statue's eyes narrowed. "There are many kinds of monks, just like there are many kinds of assholes. You are but one kind of asshole. I am but one kind of monk."

Monks, Crow thought derisively. He couldn't understand how an entire order of people dedicated to slinging nonsense could be so accepted. They didn't do anything but meditate. They didn't say anything useful. Why were they still around?

He dropped his *bidi* on the ground and crushed with his boot. "Are you the kind of monk that has information? Or are you just the kind of monk that's read a lot of fortune cookies? Because I'm the kind of asshole that needs information on the Beast."

"What makes you think I know anything about a beast?"

Crow shook his head. "Not a beast, The Beast."

"What is this 'The Beast'?"

The statue smoothly rose to its feet. Crow expected to see a point where the gold paint had rubbed off the priest's body, but he was uniformly gold. "Wise men seek to avoid the beast," the monk said, "not seek to find it."

"So, you do know about it."

"I know the beast that lurks in the hearts of men."

Crow clenched his jaw. This was worse than dealing with Chan. At least with Chan he had some idea that conversation would eventually go somewhere. "Do you just sit here all day thinking of new and exciting ways to talk like a fortune cookie? Seriously. What would you say you do here?"

The priest's eyes burned into Crow. They weren't angry eyes, they were the cold eyes that the derelicts got when they'd seen the faces of gods. When someone thinks they have all the answers, threats to the sanctity of the equation are not tolerated. "I am the caretaker of Hope," he said. "And you have defiled it."

Crow threw a thumb over his shoulder. "What? That thing? That *paifang* was old and falling apart anyway. All I did was give it a nudge."

"Your presence is an affront," the priest said. "I walled this place off myself, to stave off the corruption. Now you have allowed it to penetrate my sanctuary."

A quick bit of mental math made Crow suck in air between his teeth. "That would mean you've been here a while. What, over three hundred turns? You're pretty spry for someone that old."

"When one has hope, one needs nothing more."

The monk stalked forward like he was made of liquid. He moved more like a predator than a human. Crow slid his left foot back and put one hand on his belt buckle and the other on his chin. He could make inanimate things explode, but he could never make living things explode. He was no expert on the matter, but he suspected it had to do with the way flesh and blood where constantly changing while rock stayed pretty much the same. If something is already changing, knocking the tiny bits of it around won't do much good.

Crow held his ground as the monk stalked toward him. "What about *baiju*? How can you have hope when you have no *baiju*?"

At the top of the stairs leading to the dais, the monk leaped into the air and did a flip. He came down smoothly. His legs crouched to absorb the impact, but he was back upright in a heartbeat and stalking toward Crow.

"So, tell me about this hope thing," Crow said, slowly stepping to the side.

"There is no hope for you," the monk replied.

Crow chuckled. "Funny. I just said the exact same thing to another guy not too long ago."

When he was six feet away, the monk darted forward. He stopped on a *yuen* and fired a rapid punch straight at Crow's head. Crow's gift of prescience gave him enough time to fire his own punch. Crow's punch was slightly faster and his arm nudged the monk's arm out of the way.

To Crow's surprise, the monk easily dodged his punch

and kicked at his crotch. Crow ducked back, pushing his hips away from the attack. The monk's foot grazed the front of Crow's pants. A twist to the right and raised knee blocked the monk's kick.

Rather than immediately strike back, Crow pulled back a few feet and analyzed the situation. The monk stayed where he was. Whatever gold coloring was tinting the monk's skin still hadn't flaked off. Either he had some magical paint that could withstand a lot of punishment or the man really was gold.

The monk flexed. The muscles all over his naked body rippled. He assumed a classical Hun Gar pose, low to the ground with a wide stance. Crow dropped into his own stance, something he'd modified from what Chan taught him. His right leg slid back and his knees bent. Closed fists covered the lower part of his face.

Crow winked and blew the monk a kiss, but the golden monk wasn't going to be easily baited. The monk looked still and relaxed. Crow forced his mind to clear. At an unseen signal, the monk attacked. A flurry of punches and the odd kick almost overwhelmed Crow. He resorted to keeping his hands up and continuing to move. The rapid-fire combinations overwhelmed Crow's innate ability to see attacks coming, but his natural reaction time helped.

A fast punch from the monk nearly took Crow's nose. Crow deflected the punch and saw an opening. Chan loved to say luck was the intersection of skill and opportunity, and Felix Crow was feeling very lucky. The monk dodged the punch by leaning to the side, which was exactly what Crow was expecting. Rather than pull his hand straight back, he hooked the back of the monk's head and pulled it forward into a waiting knee.

The monk's hands crossed in front of his face and caught Crow's rising knee before it could hit. Crow flicked his foot straight out into the monk's waiting groin.

It wasn't a powerful kick, more an afterthought than

anything else, but it doesn't take much to smash a testicle. The monk deflated. To his credit, he kept his feet under him and his arms up to block another attack. Crow nodded and smiled. He jabbed twice at the monk. The golden man absorbed the first jab on his forearms and deflected the second one.

The monk's back arched and he lashed out with rapid right punch. Crow sensed the Drunken Eight Immortals strike and deftly blocked it. Before he could get his own punch in, the monk moved to Hiding Dragon Leaping Snake. His left hand struck out at the same time as his right foot. Crow hopped back, spun, and slammed a rear kick into the golden man's chest.

The monk's strikes were smooth, picture-perfect representations of how the ancient masters had developed their punches. Crow could tell The Golden Monk of Hope had centuries of practice. He'd likely spent endless hours in horse stances and refining his strikes. Against a *mook yan jong*, the monk was unstoppable. But the wooden man didn't move and he didn't strike back. Wooden dummies are predictable; Felix Crow was not.

The downside to becoming an absolute master of a single style was the monk was so focused on his own style that he could not comprehend anything outside of that system. He may have been perfect at Hun Gar, but every system has its flaws and an observant opponent can exploit those holes. That was the downside to the classical styles of fighting; everyone already knew them. Locking himself away from hundreds of turns of fighting arts hadn't done the golden monk any good.

Crow concentrated on smothering the monk's hands before they could become weapons. He closed the distance and kept himself close to the golden man, using elbows and knees to keep the man off balance. Every time the monk tried to use his hands, Crow blocked the punch with an elbow and kneed him in the rib or thigh. Soon, the monk's stance was weak and he couldn't use his legs to generate power. His punches became hesitant and slow.

In the end, the monk's legs were unsteady and his hands couldn't close into fists. Crow waited until the golden monk was at his weakest point and kicked him hard between the legs. The monk whimpered and crumbled to the ground.

"Now," Crow said, flicking a bit of fluff off his jacket. "About The Beast. A book in a pawn shop told me you'd know where to look. Tell me what you know and I'll walk out of here."

The monk's eyes were unfocused when he tried to look at Crow. A small tear dripped down his face. "If I say, 'no'?"

"I'll kick you in the balls until my foot gets tired," Crow replied. He pulled a long, double-edged dagger out of his jacket and flashed it in the monk's face. "Then I'll cut your swollen nuts off and make you eat them."

Whatever hard edge the monk had left fled him. "The beast is the reason this temple was sealed off."

Crow squatted down next to the golden monk. "That was a long time ago. Are you saying there's another one of you running around?"

The monk shook his head. "No. Not like me. Not by a long shot. You'll find out, though. You'll find out just before you die and I'll laugh about it."

"After I cut your dick off you're going to be laughing like a school-girl."

"You don't have a clue what you're up against, Crow. If you want to die, go ask Fei Long about The Beast."

"Am I going to have to kick his ass, too?" Crow asked. "It's getting to be a pain fighting everyone I meet."

"Fei Long will not fight you. The Beast will certainly kill you. I can die a happy man knowing you will be miserable until The Beast rips your heart out. There is no Hope for you, Crow."

Before Crow could say anything else, the Golden Monk of Hope bit down hard and smiled. A strange grin crossed the man's face. His eyes rolled back into his head and his body tensed. Then, all the slack fell out of the monk's body. Crow wondered if the monk had truly found serenity in death. Then he remembered peace and serenity come from *baiju*, not superstitions.

Crow sat down in the grass and stared at the naked monk. Something was nagging at him. One of the things that had made him an effective police officer was an uncanny ability to pick up on small things. Perhaps that was why the dragon chose to imbue him with magic that let him see attacks slightly before they came.

Perhaps the dragon just thought it was funny.

He replayed the entire incident in his mind, from the moment he walked in until the moment the monk killed himself. Everything seemed normal until an oddity hit him. The monk claimed to have sealed off the Monastery of Hope hundreds of turns ago. But the monk, in his dying words, had used Crow's name.

How would someone holed up in a sealed-off monastery for over five hundred turns know anything about Felix Crow?

6 | Flight Plans

Huizhong adjusted the bag over her left shoulder. The strap ran across her body and ended on her right hip. The bag bounced on her thigh as she shimmied this way and that, deftly avoiding the throng of people putting their own bags over seats or fidgeting in the narrow aisle. Her seat was 21A. Not the best, not the worst.

"Sorry," she mumbled as the bag that contained all her world possessions brushed against an old lady.

The woman looked at her with glassy eyes and nodded before leaning her head back and closing her eyes. Airship travel was slow, but better than busses. The old lady's clothes, bright and cheerful pieces that felt like tropical breezes, clashed with her tired eyes. She'd likely come from one of the eastern provinces where everything was green and warm. Beautiful places, but a long flight from the north, and an even longer flight from Croatoa.

Huizhong panged for the quiet solitude of her forest. Clean, cool air and the scent of the *sōngshù* trees. Even Ao Shun stalking among the trees would be preferable to the din and hot air of bodies packed into the gondola. She clenched her jaw and pushed forward to her seat. 21A was a window seat. Staring at the world from a few thousand feet up might be as much solitude as she was likely to get. It wouldn't be the clearing and Nüwa's voice would be drowned out by announcements and talking, but it would have to do for now.

As she passed row nineteen, a young man glanced up at her then looked away. His head snapped back toward her. He cocked his head to the side and gave her a strange grin. Huizhong nodded, but refused to smile. Smiling would indicate she was interested and the only thing she was interested in right now was pretending the world wasn't pressing against her.

21A was occupied. Her one chance at freedom was staring out the window and someone was already sitting in her seat. She unzipped a pocket on her vest and pulled out her ticket. The sign above the seats clearly said 21A was the window seat, yet there was someone already in it and it wasn't her.

Huizhong reached across the empty seat and shook the man in it. She tried to keep her voice even and calm, even though she wanted to scream. "You're in my seat. You need to move."

The man didn't respond. For a moment, she thought he was dead, but his head rolled over and he looked at her distantly though hazy eyes before going back to *Mèngjìng*. She desperately wanted to be in her own dream world, away from everyone, and this asshole was taking her seat.

She shook him again. "Move. Please."

He grumbled something and twisted in his seat. Her seat. He didn't even have the common decency to put up his tray table. An empty tea cup and discarded food wrappers covered the tray.

His head flopped against the wall of the airship with a thump. He farted, a long and dizzyingly loud explosion of toxic gasses. Huizhong balled her fist and looked around. There were too many people around to get away with clobbering him and, in his state, it probably wouldn't do much to him anyway.

She settled for lightly slapping him, hoping the shock would rouse him long enough to get him to move. "Move. Now."

Nothing happened. "I'm calling the porter," she said loudly. "You'll be kicked off."

"Could you hurry?" a voice said behind her.

A tall man in an immaculate suit glared at her. He tapped a time crystal on his wrist. "You're holding up the line," he said.

"He's in my seat," Huizhong said. She realized it sounded ridiculous as soon as she said it. It was like being in youth school and telling the teacher one seat was better than another. In this case, though, the other seat was better.

"Take his," the man. "Or get off. I don't care. Just move."

Huizhong's temples buzzed. She cursed herself for not disappearing into the wild. She cursed herself for listening to Ao Shun. She wanted to tell the man in her seat to die in a fire, but causing a scene and getting kicked off the airship wouldn't help things. The sooner she got to Croatoa and figured out whatever her brain was wondering about, the sooner she could get home.

She slid into the empty seat, but refused to sit in it on general principle. Her seat was by the window. She made sure to "accidentally" hit the man in the window seat with her bag as much as possible. Even after everyone else had sat down, the man in her seat remained steadfastly asleep.

"You need to sit down, ma'am," a steward told her.

"There's been a mistake," Huizhong said. She shoved her ticket toward the steward. "This man is in my seat."

The steward took the ticket from her and examined it. Huizhong fumed. He looked at the numbers over the seats. Huizhong resisted the temptation to yell at him to hurry up.

"Excuse me, ma'am," he finally said.

She eased past him and stood in the aisle once again. Finally, someone would get this oaf out of her seat. She watched as the steward shook the man. When he still didn't move, the steward handed Huizhong her ticket back and said, "You'll need to take the aisle seat, ma'am."

"I bought a ticket for the window seat," she replied.

The steward was a veteran on these flights; he'd seen every bit of nastiness people could summon from themselves and learned to let it slide off him. His face remained neutral. "I understand that, ma'am, and I do apologize. But the ship is leaving and you need to take your seat."

"He already took my seat."

"You'll need to take his, then."

"I bought a ticket for a window seat," Huizhong

reiterated.

"As I said, ma'am," he replied, "I understand that. But the ship is leaving and you need to either take your seat or book a different flight. The next flight to Croatoa leaves tomorrow morning."

Huizhong wanted to press the issue. She almost demanded to speak to his superior. She came extremely close to simply leaving the airship. In the end, a desire to have the flight be finished overcame her desire to stare out the window for twelve hours.

Gods above. Twelve hours in the aisle. It was better than sleeping in the airship dock. She sat down angrily in the seat and glared at the steward. "Thanks for nothing."

"You'll need to stow your bag, ma'am," he replied before moving further down the aisle.

She squirmed out of the bag and rose to put it in the overhead bin. The bin was full. Of course, it was. Huizhong slammed the door shut and looked around for any open spaces. Behind her a stewardess was shutting the bins as she worked her way up the aisle.

Huizhong spotted an empty space and almost got her bag in before the stewardess slammed it shut. She pulled her fingers out of the way just in time. "You need to take your seat, ma'am."

"I just need to stow my bag," Huizhong said. "The other man, the steward, he told me to put it away."

The stewardess nodded absently. "These bins are full."

"There was a space right there," Huizhong protested.

"You need to take your seat, ma'am. Your bag will fit under the seat in front of you."

"I-," Huizhong started.

The stewardess finally looked at her. Dark eyes looked Huizhong up and down and seemed disappointed. Huizhong idly tried to smooth her hair and adjust her old vest and skirt, but it was a lost cause. She pointed at the bin and tried her best to smile.

"The airship will be leaving momentarily," the stewardess said. "You need to take your seat. Now."

The air flowed out of Huizhong's sails. She slouched and slunk back to her seat with her tail between her legs. The seat was hard and she couldn't get comfortable. When she leaned forward to put her bag under the seat, she found another bag already there. Her row-mate had apparently decided he needed not only her seat, but also more legroom, so he took the window seat and stuffed his bag in front of her seat.

At least the stewardess had kept going down the aisle and wouldn't pester her about the bag. She hid the bag behind her feet and did her best to not think about twelve hours in this uncomfortable seat with no way to move her legs.

A deep thrumming sound rippled through the cabin as magic poured into the engines. She looked past her slumbering row-mate and saw the ground-crew releasing the lines that held the massive ship to the ground. The airship gently lifted into the air and eased forward slowly.

The higher the ship rose, the more Huizhong relaxed. She wanted her seat, but the trip was underway and that meant she was growing ever closer to a bed. The hotels in Croatoa ranged from opulent, gold and jade bedecked affairs to flop-houses adorned with vermin. Somewhere in the middle would do nicely. She leaned her head back, closed her eyes, and thought about a warm bath.

"You'll never get him to move, you know," a voice said.

Huizhong growled. She was just about to relax. "What?" she snapped.

"That guy. He's not going to move the entire flight."

She glared at him. From his baggy canvas pants to his T-shirt with a man in a d☐ulì with electricity flying out of his fingers, he looked like every worthless punk she'd met in Croatoa. In ten turns, he'd be frying tarantulas for a street vendor and going to the fights to cheer on some other fighter looking to get himself killed. If he was lucky. More likely he'd be living in an alley and eating bugs and lizards.

"Fine," Huizhong said and closed her eyes again.

"He's blissed out," the young man said.

Huizhong opened her eyes and glared. It was the same guy from earlier, the guy with the fire in his eyes that had grinned at her. Something in his tiny little brain had told him to come talk to her. She had thought the seating arrangements couldn't make things worse, but this *tā mā de báichī* had found a way.

"I'm taken," she said. "Big guy. Very bad temper. Likes to hurt guys that talk to me."

She closed her eyes again and tried to drift off.

"I hope he doesn't hurt you," the guy said.

This time, Huizhong didn't open her eyes. "Only guys that talk to me."

"That's messed up. No worries, though. I don't like girls, so I'm not a threat, right?"

She looked at him again, up and down. "No," she said. "You're still a threat."

"Your guy should bliss out. He sounds like he needs it."

Something clicked in Huizhong's mind. "What does that mean, bliss out?"

"He got so high, he touched the heavens. He found bliss."

Huizhong stared at him and waited for more information, but it wasn't forthcoming. She sighed. "What does that mean? How did he find bliss?"

"I like your hair," the guy replied.

Everything clicked into place. This guy wasn't trying to pick her up or join the three-thousand-hand-high club, he was just another whacked out user from a city that cranked them out wholesale. "That's nice. I need to get some rest."

"You look like you used to be someone and then decided to be someone else. But you were always that someone. The someone else is the mask."

Huizhong's blood boiled. "You don't know a damned thing about me. Get lost."

The words stung. Not because they were lies, but because

there was a huge nugget of truth to them. The woman she was when she had her pink and gray hair would never have put up with this *tā mā de báichī*. She was strong and self-assured and wouldn't have worried about Clock Men or ethics or fucking Felix Crow. That woman would have taken one and told the rest to screw off.

"Your aura is magical. Do you want to bliss out?" the young man said.

No. No bliss for the wicked. No hope for the wicked. Nothing good for the wicked. Huizhong felt her pink-haired self laugh at her dark-haired self. *Weak*, she thought. *Weak and small and indecisive.* Her dark-haired self laughed at the impetuous pink-hair. The back and forth in her head made her feel older than her late twenties. Too much mileage. Everything made her feel old, though. People called her a classical beauty, and even that made her feel old.

"No," she said. "I do not want to 'bliss out'. I don't even know what that means. All I want to do is sleep."

"Far out, lady," the guy said. He gently set a small paper packet on the armrest of her chair. "That will help you sleep just like that guy. You'll be able to feel the magic in the air. It's like making out with the *Tao*."

The guy gave her a lopsided grin and headed back to his own seat. Huizhong stared at the packet on her armrest just like she stared at the *xiēzi* that hid under the fallen trees in her clearing. The paper packet was tiny, not much larger than half her pinkie finger. Its surface was clean save for a few words: *tiāntáng de fěn*.

"What the hell is heaven's powder," she mumbled to herself before depositing the little packet in a pocket on her vest.

She settled back in her seat and reflected on the steward, the stewardess, her row-mate, and that guy from a few rows back. All in all, not the easiest day of Huizhong's young life. "This job is going to kill me," she whispered.

7 | History Lesson

"Fried tarantula?" Chan asked, holding a stick out to Kevin.

Kevin looked at the sickly thing and shook his head. Its eight legs were curled under a bulbous body and his young mind reeled at the idea of eating a spider. "No. Please," he replied.

Chan broke a pair of legs off and popped them in his mouth. His expression went from hopeful to exuberant as he chewed. "Are you sure?" he asked, motioning at the vendor cart behind him. "Wong here makes the best fried tarantulas in Croatoa."

"Thank you," a man standing behind the cart said.

"No, Wong," Chan said. "Thank you. Can I get two more?"

Chan looked back down at Kevin and motioned at the dead arachnid. Kevin closed his eyes and shook his head rapidly. He slowly backed away from Chan until he nearly tripped over Tina.

"Just two more, I guess," Chan said. He opened the pouch on his hip and pulled out a pair of battered yuen.

Wong bowed slightly as he presented two more tarantulas to Chan. "On the house, Master Chan. You had an excellent fight last night. I won a lot of money off you!"

Chan graciously accepted the spiders and held one out to Tina. The old dog sniffed at the tarantula before taking a tentative bite off the critter. She chewed slowly, almost thoughtfully. Her next bite took the rest of the tarantula out of Chan's outstretched hand.

While she chewed, Chan presented the remaining spider to Dino. The dinosaur, who had never met food he didn't like, snatched the tarantula from the stick with a happy chirp.

Neither tarantula lasted long. Both animals eyed Chan's

remaining tarantula greedily. Chan smiled and pulled two more legs off his spider and ate them. "See, they have good taste," he told Kevin.

"They're animals," Kevin said as if that explained everything.

Chan smiled under his omnipresent *d☐ulì*. "You're an animal, just one that stands upright and refuses food. Don't knock animals, though; they don't have the same issues we do. An animal doesn't worry about how it looks or sounds, it just does things. They're the ultimate Taoists."

Kevin looked at the dog and the dinosaur, both happily begging for another treat and couldn't help but smile. They slept with him every night, protected him, and loved him unconditionally. Now they were in love with a man who might give them more snacks.

All around them, the throng of humanity was moving down the streets of Croatoa. Every now and then, someone would look up from a book or look down and notice the animals. Dino, a deinonychus, was the first thing they noticed. He looked like a big bird with colorful feathers and gigantic claws on his feet. He was the more energetic of the two, hopping and chirping happily. Tina, an aging black and white pit bull, sat calmly and slowly wagged her tail back and forth.

Most people were fascinated by the dinosaur. Dino fit in perfectly with the rest of their world, nothing more than a big bird. The dog was another story, entirely. A man scurrying to work fumbled his cup, spilling the contents all over himself and the sidewalk when he saw the dog.

After six months here, Kevin was used to the reaction. He tried to make a sign that said "Don't Panic", but Tina always found a way to get it off. Since then, he learned to ignore the people or laugh at their reactions to the dog.

Something always bothered Kevin about that, though. According to his school, humans and apes had a similar ancestor and, at some point, the two species evolved along different paths. There weren't any apes on the planet, though.

"Chan," Kevin asked, "how is it that humans came to be on this planet? They didn't evolve here."

Chan's smile faltered briefly, but returned as he ate some more of his spider. He motioned everyone along. It was still a long walk to Mrs. Chow's and having a story to tell would ease the time.

As they walked, Chan spun his own tale from school. "You're very observant, Kevin. Humans aren't native to this planet. Aluna was a world of dragons before we showed up."

"Like the little dragons?" Kevin asked. Like every Earth schoolboy he'd been taught dragons weren't real.

"No, the real deal. Some over a few hundred hands long. I've never met one, and I've been told they're all extinct now, but I don't always blindly trust what people tell me."

"Trust, but verify," Kevin said, nodding.

Chan squeezed Kevin's shoulder and smiled. He'd never been a father and never would. His life had been dedicated to the perfection of fighting and had little room for anything else. But he found he was drawn to the boy and relished his achievements. "Exactly."

"If they once ran the planet, how did they go extinct?"

"Humans came to this planet a couple thousand cycles ago and soon ran into the dragons. The first humans here were wizards and witches. Spell casters. They ripped a great hole through reality and ran into Aluna. From here, you can go back and forth. But from Earth the hole is shut."

Kevin grabbed Chan and stopped him. His eyes were full of hope and Chan knew exactly what question was coming next. "Wait," Kevin said. "I can go home?"

"I pulled you off Earth because I'd heard the Beast wanted you dead. I can only assume he still does. On Earth, you'd be helpless."

"Go kick his ass!" Kevin shouted. "You're Billy Badass, go find this Beast and beat the snot out of him!"

Chan didn't know who Billy Badass was, but he got the gist of the conversation. He frowned. "It's not that simple,

Kevin."

"What's complicated? You find this Beast guy and pummel him. Then I can go home, right? I can...see my friends. And take Tina home. And...," Kevin said, tears welling in his big eyes. "I miss my home, Chan. I'd miss you, but that's my home and I miss it. And I want my parents back. I just wish... I just wish none of this had happened."

Chan stiffened. A lifetime of driving emotion out had left him unable to handle other people's emotions. Some would say it was his upbringing, but he wouldn't say he had a bad childhood. He loved the *wuxia* novels and comics of martial artists saving the world and wanted to be just like them. The real world wasn't like books or comics, though.

Kevin pushed into him and wrapped his arms around Chan's waist. Tina whimpered and Dino chirped sadly. Unsure what else to do, Chan wrapped his arms gently around Kevin. Together they stood in the middle of the sidewalk while magic pulsed through wires overhead and people scurried around them.

"For what it's worth, Kevin," Chan said. "I'm sorry. I promised to find your parents and I will."

"Can I go home then?" Kevin asked.

"It takes an enormous amount of power to open a portal, but it can be done."

"But it *can* be done?"

"Yes," Chan said quietly. "It can be done."

Tina nosed at Chan's leg. When everything was said and done, he'd miss the dog far more than he ever thought possible. It was such a strange creature, all fur and teeth, but she never failed to bring a smile to his face.

"We need to go, Kevin. I'd like to find Crow before he's had a chance to drink himself into oblivion."

Kevin dried his eyes and nodded. "Crow's an alcoholic?"

"He likes to drink. A lot. But he is, at his heart, a good man. And he is very good at finding things."

"Think he can help find my parents?"

"Felix Crow found his way into the Clock Tower, the most heavily guarded place on Aluna, and killed the Clock Man. If he can do that, he can find your parents."

They continued walking down the street. Moving through crowds of people trying to get to work or trying to get home after working all night. All the magic in the world flowed right through the heart of Croatoa, harnessed and processed in the hundred-plus-story spire called the Clock Tower.

Kevin's eyes watched the world with a hint of Chan's training. He sized people up as potential threats and moved out of their way if they looked like problems. Chan watched the boy and marveled at how much he had changed in the six months he'd been on Aluna. At first Kevin was fascinated with the glowing scripts etched into walls and the little dragons perched around the city, then he started looking at the city through the eyes Chan had taught him to use.

Chan felt proud that the boy had matured so quickly, but he also missed the carefree Kevin who wanted to see and touch everything.

"What's a Clock Man?" Kevin asked.

"All the energy on Aluna is made from the magic in the air. I don't know exactly how it works, but centuries ago the first Clock Man found a way to take the latent magical energy and start a fire with it. After that, things grew rapidly."

"Magic? Like what I do?"

"Similar," Chan said. "You have Earth magic. Earth magic is mostly concentrated in the hands of a small group of people. It's reckless magic; very different from what we have here on Aluna. Our magic is predictable; yours is chaotic. When it pops up on its own, it usually gets snatched up by the same people who already have all the magic. Sometimes, though, someone like you comes along and changes the rules. It's your reckless magic the Beast wants."

Kevin mentally chewed on that. It was a lot of information to compress into a short statement. Not only did it imply a lot about Earthlings, it spoke volumes about his own abilities. He looked at his hands, trying to see through the skin and find where the magic lay.

"You won't find it in your hands," Chan said. "There's something about you, some little thing that's different from other people, but it's not in your hands."

"Just like *Wushu*," Kevin muttered.

Chan's heart swelled. Kevin was often closed-off and distant. Considering his recent history this wasn't too surprising. To hear that he had learned and internalized Chan's lessons was wonderful. "Exactly like *Wushu*. You may punch with your hands and kick with your feet, but it's the entire body that drives those strikes. Magic, as I understand it, works along similar lines. It's not a singular part of you; it's the whole you."

"I blew up that stuffed dragon this morning, didn't I?"

"Yes," Chan replied.

"I wish I knew how I did that. I wish I could make it happen when I wanted to. Then I could find the Beast and take care of the problem."

"They say the Beast has powers, too. He also has a penchant for roasting people alive in barrels."

Kevin had no response to that. The mere idea of roasting people took him back to the ovens of Earth in the 1940s. He shivered at the thought about being cooked alive. "Why don't the police arrest him for that?"

"The police in Croatoa aren't exactly the best people. Felix was a cop once; he's the kind of person the police force creates."

"Drunk?"

Chan chuckled. "And violent. Most people avoid the police for that very reason. Calling them is like calling up a *yǔnjìngshé*; you'll probably get rid of your pest problem, but the snake will kill you eventually."

"No offense, Chan, but this place is a mess. When you can't trust the police and people are getting cooked in barrels, something is really wrong."

"That's right. That's why I teach you everything I can. When problems arise, the only person you can really trust is yourself."

They rounded a corner and walked down Huo Yuanjia Avenue, Croatoa's main street. It bisected the city right down the middle. On weekends the avenue was quiet, but during rush hour like now it was just as packed as the rest of the downtown area. People all over the city referred to the district as the Ch'uan district as a little play on words.

Sandwiched in between a bar called Tears of Heaven and another called The Jade Dragon was a non-descript wooden door with No Admittance painted on it. Chan knocked twice and took a step back. He stayed perfectly still.

A slat opened and a voice said, "We're closed. Drinks and dancing are tonight."

"I see you have still not learned your lesson," Chan replied. "Tell Mrs. Chow, Chan is here to see her."

The slat slammed shut and Kevin and Chan heard locks being furiously slid aside. The door opened and a large man in a shirt covered with pictures of strippers bowed deeply. "Please forgive my foolishness, Master Chan."

Behind the man was a short hallway. A woman's shriek echoed down the hallway and out the door. "Is she okay?" Chan asked the door man.

The large man bowed his head in shame. "Unfortunately, yes. This is how she treats us when she's in a bad mood."

"What triggered that bad mood?" Chan asked.

"Who knows?" the man said. "All I know is one moment she's fine, the next she's busy shredding everyone in her path. She is the mistress, though, so her word is law. Besides, she pays well."

Chan put a hand on Kevin's shoulder and nodded to the boy. "We are here. Let us hope Felix Crow has drunk himself into oblivion."

"And hope we can avoid Mrs. Chow," Kevin replied.

8 | The Curious Fei

Fei Long was a specialist. In a world of generalities, with people flitting this way and that, Fei Long did exactly one thing: he specialized in knowing. He spent his days assimilating information from any source he could find. A tiny bit of data here, an overheard conversation there. Isolated things combined in his head until he alone had the full picture of the world around him.

He would say he wasn't special, that anyone could do what he did, but the people who knew about him would strongly disagree. Not everyone had the time, patience, or ability to juggle the vast quantities of uncoordinated information the people of Croatoa didn't even know they had.

In another place or time, Fei's abilities would have been utilized to find information about foreign enemies or locate insurgents before they could strike, but Aluna had been unified under a sort of disconnected government for centuries and there was no need for such things. Thus, a master spy became an information broker for the only groups that could pay for his services: the vast criminal underworld of Croatoa.

Fei was also unique in that he was the only person in the whole city who was untouchable. All the criminal houses used his services and none would risk losing his abilities.

Felix Crow was adept at finding. Where Fei Long found information, Crow found things. He had a knack for figuring out which thug to strangle and which one to threaten. Oftentimes, though, he found things simply by wandering around until he bumped into them.

Crow found Fei sipping tea in a run-down tea house near the docks. The place was made of wood that was old when the first nail penetrated it, but the tea house bore the weight of centuries easily. Like a person who grows old and decides to finally wear a lot of purple, the tea house had been painted, stained, sanded, and reworked so many times that it had finally given up trying to be cool or popular. By being tragically uncool, it became cool to be seen there.

Fei Long was leaning back in his seat with his eyes closed. There wasn't much of a crowd in the tea house, but a faint din echoed around the room. Crow spun a chair around and straddled it, staring at the old man in the fineries sitting across from him.

"Fei Long," Crow said.

The old man's eyes didn't open, but he did afford Crow the barest of nods. Fei held up a finger and put it to his lips. Crow started to speak, but Fei shushed him quietly.

Crow motioned to the bartender, a bear of a man with scars over both eyes to indicate he'd seen something he shouldn't have seen and was smart enough to keep quiet about it. The big man raised what was left of an eyebrow and pointed at an array of teas behind him.

Crow slumped in his seat. It was late afternoon and he was stuck in a tea house. In this part of town there should be some *baiju* or at the very least some Tears of Heaven. The Tears always gave him heartburn, but tea gave him a headache. He waved his hand and the bartender shrugged.

Fei Long's eyes were still closed. Crow sighed. The old man didn't respond except to twirl a finger around his long mustache. Crow sighed again, louder this time. Fei still didn't move or open his eyes. For a moment, he wondered if the old man was dead. That would be just his luck: an old guy dies in a place where there's nothing to drink and he'd have to wait for the police so he could give a statement. He had enough friends on the force that it wouldn't be too much of a problem, but it would take time and he didn't feel like waiting.

He drummed his fingers on the table. Fei raised an eyebrow, but didn't open his eyes. Crow's fist clenched. He could always beat the information out Fei. Of course, if he did that he knew he'd pull down the ire of every crime family in Croatoa.

That would also cause problems, so Crow resorted to drumming his fingers harder and looking around the tea house. A handful of regulars huddled over teas made of gunpowder and dragon scale herbs mixed with the dark tea that the teahouse was known for. Sitting at the bar was a couple that looked far too perky to be from this part of town. They were talking animatedly about their jobs on the other side of town and how fun it was to be here with the real people.

Crow hated them immediately. They came to the dark streets, his part of town, and talked about how incredibly neat it was to hang out with real people at a real tea house. They'd be long gone before the sun went down and the real darkness poured into the streets. Desperation – and the people who worked the docks for a pittance were desperate – creates a reality the expensive people could never understand.

Back during his days on the force, Crow had seen dozens like them. Tourists looking for a real experience tended to find reality had a nasty bite. He found them in alleys, dismembered and violated. If they were lucky, it was in that order.

One of the regulars was watching the couple a little too closely. As the tourists waved their hands around, a glint of purple metal caught Crow's eye. He cursed his luck. Fei Long was still meditating on whatever it was that information brokers meditated on, so Crow decided to entertain himself. He walked over to the table the regular was sitting at it and dropped into an empty seat across from the man.

This close, the man smelled of sea breezes and the fetid stench of *jīnqiāngyú*. The huge creatures were tasty, but their oil clung to the fishermen who caught them and the dock workers that unloaded the ships. From the scars on his hands and face, Crow guessed this man was a dock worker.

"Rough day?" Crow asked, leaning close.

The man threw a glare that could peel paint. "*G□nkāi!*"

"Already taken a piss," Crow said.

"Then how about you go fuck yerself," the man growled. "I'm drinkin' mah tea."

Crow's hand was a blur as he snatched the cup of tea from in front of the man. He leaned back in his seat and licked the splashed tea from the palm of his hand before taking a sip. The gunpowder and dragon scale herbs burned the roof of his mouth. "Now I'm drinkin' ya tea".

The man glanced down at the place where his tea used to be and then back at Crow. His bushy eyebrows furrowed. "Give it back," he growled.

"Make me," Crow said with a grin.

Picking fights with people in bars was a time-tested technique among the Croatoa police; if they couldn't find a way to arrest someone legitimately, they'd find an excuse like assaulting an officer. Crow drained the cup of tea and pounded his chest to keep the foul stuff down. He belched and slid the cup back across the table.

"Who do you think you are?" the man asked. He pushed the seat back and stood up.

Crow remained sitting and stared up at the huge man. "Crow," he said. "Felix Crow. And you are?"

The man's eye twitched. Massive, scarred hands squeezed the table until it creaked. While he stood shaking in anger, Crow noticed a tattoo on the man's chest. A circle with cross and square in the middle. Uncolored for now. Unfortunately, that symbol changed things.

"My name is fuck off."

"Well, Mr. Off," Crow said. "You may not know me, but I know a couple things about you. Wanna learn something today?"

"The only thing I want learn is what your guts look like."

Crow concentrated on the part of the table the man was gripping. Tiny things moved in the old wood. It was slow movement at first, but soon the little things were smashing into each other. The table vibrated, legs rattling on the wooden floor. The man stepped back slightly, just in time for the table to explode.

Every eye in the place turned to stare at them. Crow could feel stares burning into the back of his head, but he refused to break eyes with the man in front of him. He smiled and motioned at the chair. "Now, how would you like to learn something?"

The man sat down hard on the chair, a look of shock growing across his face. "How?"

Crow spread his arms wide and grinned. "I'm Felix Crow," he said. "That's how."

The man started to ask a question, but Crow held up a finger. "Now, I'm going to tell you two things that are going to change your afternoon. One, I know you're with the *Qīng Bāng* and I don't care. I have no quarrel with your organization. They might have a quarrel with you if you wind up mugging an important man's kids, but that's beside the point. And that leads us to lesson number two. Did you know Hoqwua has a bunch of kids? From everything I've heard, they're rich idiots. But, hey, at least they're rich, right? I'd happily be an idiot if I could be a rich one."

"Hoqwua," the man said. "As in the Hoqwua?"

"The very same." Crow scooted his chair closer to the man, close enough to whisper in his ear. "The man made has a complete lock on *Lóng gāng*. So much of a lock, that the only people that can wear purple metal are his family. They say he's the richest man in Croatoa. You know what I say? I say he's the richest guy on Aluna. You don't get that rich by being a nice guy. The man has an army. But, more importantly, he has two kids and they're sitting right over there wearing purple rings with his signet on them. Do yourself a favor, find another pair of rich idiots to rape and murder. I guarantee you those two are off limits."

The man gulped and nodded. Crow rose from his chair, straightened his coat and tipped his hat to the man. Fun as it would have been to threaten the man or take him out back and beat the shit out of him, the last thing he needed was a problem with the *Qīng Bāng*. The Green Gang guys got pretty surly when one of their own got worked over. People who crossed them wound up gone.

Fei Long was watching him, but Crow was angry enough to want to push the old man's buttons a little. It was a little game he played when he was bored or angry or frustrated. Or, well, anytime. Felix Crow was a man of many talents, not all of them savory, but his greatest skill was the ability piss people off.

He walked to the bar and slapped a twenty yuen note on the polished wood. "Please tell me you have something to drink here."

The bartender motioned again to the wall of teas arrayed behind him.

"No," Crow said. "Something to drink. Something not tea. Something that will burn away the pain of the modern living."

"Oolong," the bartender said. "Best tea for upset stomach."

Crow took in the bartender's smirk and rolled his tongue over his teeth. He liked messing with people, but didn't like it when they did it to him. "*Baiju*," he said. "Or anything of the 'dancing with Yi-Di' variety of liquors would work nicely."

"Yi-Di does not dance," the bartender replied, still smirking. "Yi-Di lounges on his bed surrounded by many beautiful ladies who keep him well supplied."

"Look, pal, I don't care how the god of alcohol spends his free time, I just want some of his nectar."

"Ask the ladies. Supposedly they milk his nectar."

Crow gripped the bar top and did his best to reign in his cool. "That's not the nectar I want."

The bartender casually wiped and polished a small glass. "Then why ask?"

"Look, pal," Crow said. "I just saved three lives: Hoqwua's kids and that *Qīng Bāng* underling over there. And I did it without starting a fight or tearing up this place. Do you have a drink or not?"

"My table is broken," the bartender said. "You owe me a new table."

Everything was a negotiation in this part of town. Crow hated negotiating. In his eyes, it was a waste of time. People would have a lot more free time in their lives if they just accepted things at face value rather than trying to come to an agreement on something as trivial as a drink.

"Fine," Crow hissed. "I'll get you a new table."

"It had better be a nice table."

"For a drink, I'll steal you the best table in town."

The bartender dropped below the bar and rooted around. Crow thrummed his fingers on the bar and fidgeted. When the bartender stood up, he put a dark blue bottle on the bar and grinned at Crow. "Finest in Croatoa."

"Seriously?" Crow asked. "I've seen derelicts turn that stuff down. That's the stuff you drink when you don't have any other choice."

"Do you see any other bottles of *baiju* around here?"

Crow didn't relish the taste – or the heartburn – but he desperately wanted a drink after meeting with freaky golden monk. He dropped his head to his chest and shook his head. "How much?"

"Twenty yuen."

"For the bottle? That's highway robbery."

"No," the bartender said. "Twenty yuen for one drink. One hundred for the whole bottle."

Fingers drummed harder on the bar. Crow seethed and wondered if this was all worth the effort. He could go home right now, feed his little dragons, and forget this whole quest. He looked around and saw jaw-droppingly stupid people spending money on overpriced tea. This town needed a purge, a cleansing flame to wipe the slate clean of tea drinkers and Hoqwua and Green Gangs. Maybe when it was all gone, he could rest.

He slammed an extra eighty yuen on the bar and reached for the bottle. The bartender slid it back, just out of reach.

"The best table."

Crow's hand moved like a snake and snatched the bottle from the bartender's hand. "The best."

Fei Long was waiting with a sly grin when Crow plopped down on his abandoned chair and set the bottle on the table. "Forget something, Crow?" he asked.

Crow looked around and found a blue bottle sitting on the table. It would rot his guts, but it would numb the world. "Not that I can see."

"Do you need a glass?"

"Not really, no," Crow said. He unscrewed the cap and took a deep swig out of the bottle. The cheap *baiju* felt like fire pouring down his throat. The flames eased the world's fingers from his throat.

"You have a problem, Mr. Crow," Fei said. He sipped his tea delicately, like an effete snob.

"Just one?"

"Some would say you are drinking yourself to death," Fei Long said. "I would argue you're not really alive as it is, so what is the problem? No, I'm referring to a lack of information. You want to find The Beast."

"How do you know my name?" Crow asked.

"It is my business to know things, Mr. Crow. Information is what keeps me alive and safe. I know, for instance, that you have been looking for someone that prefers to remain unfound. Turn over too many stones and you will eventually be stung by a *xiē*."

"Then you do know how to get to The Beast. Where is he?"

Fei Long leaned his elbows on the table and twirled his white mustache like a villain from one of the old street plays. "Information is power, Mr. Crow. It is a weapon. If you know how to aim it, you can destroy worlds."

"Just like my burps."

"I have made it my life to learn things, to know things. Those kids at the bar, you are correct, they are Hoqwua's children. They are fools, yes, but they are talkative fools and in my line of work, talking in public is just like giving me money."

Crow raised an eyebrow and took another swig from his blue bottle. "What were they talking about? Dad's business interests?"

"Trade secrets, Mr. Crow. I only divulge information when I'm paid for it."

"Well, we're pretty screwed then. I just gave my last hundred *yuen* to the bartender for a bottle of *baiju* that probably cost 5 *yuen*."

Fei Long chuckled. His high-pitched laugh was like the schoolgirls giggling over the latest street show performer. "I am not interested in your money, Mr. Crow. You do not have enough wealth to be interesting to me. My services are not for the faint of heart or the light of coin. But, perhaps, an exchange can be arranged."

Crow took a long pull from the bottle. The world was receding slightly around him. It wasn't gone entirely, but its edge was dulled. "What kind of exchange?"

"I know a great many things, but there is always more to learn. The kids talking at the bar thought they were sharing a secret. Two people can only keep a secret if one of them is dead. Or if one of them is alive and the other is missing."

Fei sipped his drink and set it down. He adjusted the cup so the designs lined up perfectly with the magical axis. "I am speaking of Alyssa Zhang, missing since her father fell out of the hundredth floor of the clock tower. There was also a young lady known only as Huizhong. And, of course, you. Many people disappeared when Chenming Zhang died, but no one seems to know why."

Crow flashed back to the hundredth floor of the clock tower. A head and torso, stripped of all limbs, silently screaming in a bath of green goo. And the little dragon that was nothing more than a head and a pair of wings flapping mindlessly. Among all the terrible things he'd seen in the

Clock Tower, that floor was the worst. Then there was the old Clock Man himself. Chenming Zhang had stripped parts of his own body off and replaced them with shining metal. A monster come to horrible life.

"I don't know why, either," Crow replied.

"When I don't know something, it feels like a feather tickling my nose. It's a constant irritant that won't let me rest until I find out what I'm missing."

Crow burped. "That sucks. Are you going to tell me where to find The Beast?"

Fei waved his hand in front of his face. "I don't know where to find him and that's the one piece of information I absolutely do not want. People who know how to find The Beast either work for The Beast or are killed by The Beast."

"Then what am I doing here? Other than buying overpriced *baiju*, I mean."

"You are here because the Golden Monk told you to come here."

Crow chuckled. "You know about him? I'm impressed; I only met him a couple of hours ago."

"Do you know what information is, Mr. Crow?"

Crow nodded and smirked. "Things that are happening. People doing things. Stuff like that."

"Information is a weapon," Fei said. His gray eyes sparkled in excitement. "Wars are won and lost on information alone. And I control it all; save a few pieces. One, as I've already said, I don't want to know. The whereabouts of The Beast shall forever remain a mystery to me and I am quite happy to keep things that way. Another bit you don't know, but we'll get to that later. You have, locked away in that addled brain of yours, a piece of information that I would like to know. I'd like to propose a trade. Information for information."

Crow watched Fei twirl his mustache and recognized the nervous twitch of someone desperate. However calm the man might seem from the outside, something was going on inside his head. "You don't know where The Beast is?"

"No, but I know someone who might."

The *baiju* was searing inside of him, a calm lake of fire in his belly that burned away the horrors and worries. "What do you want to know?"

Fei paused. Again, Crow's police instincts kicked in and told him the man was hiding something. The old man's eyes narrowed and he leaned in close. A lifetime of seeking out information had taught him to be wary of who else might be listening. "I want to know who hired you to kill Chenming Zhang."

Crow didn't hesitate. He held no allegiance to her and it's not like he was betraying her. "Alyssa Zhang."

The gasp could be heard around the bar. Fei caught himself and sat back in his chair like he'd just gotten the best sex in the world. "Why didn't I guess? It was so obvious all along. I thought she was working with you to kill her dad, but you were working for her all along. Why did she want him dead? Did she know what he'd become?"

"Nope," Crow said. "Information for information. I told you something, now you need to tell me what you know."

Fei looked horrified at the idea of giving away information, but he had made a bargain and the only way he could stay alive in a place like Croatoa was if everyone adhered to the bargains. "There is a man that lives under pier 22. He says he knows how to find The Beast."

"Wonderful," Crow said with a sigh. "That's your information? There's a derelict under the pier that says he knows something. You know what? You're an asshole and I hope one of the families decides to have you killed."

"I assure you, his information is valid."

"How could you possibly know that? Did you confirm it with someone else who knows where The Beast lives?"

Fei's hands went up and his eyes got wide. "Pardon me?"

"Pardon you? Screw you," Crow hissed. "You're wasting my time."

"Under Pier 22 a man with one red sandal who goes by the name of Jolan can point you to The Beast. Jolan is in deep hiding because he used to work for The Beast. As I've already told you, you either work for The Beast or you're killed by The Beast. Ask him and tell him Fei Long wishes him well."

Fei Long slid his chair back and rose. Crow smirked and set his bottle down on the table. "Leaving so soon?"

"We have exchanged information, our job here is done."

Crow shook his head. "No so fast, old man. I still have questions."

"You have nothing left to offer me."

"You still want to know why Alyssa wanted Chenming dead, don't you?" Crow leaned back in his chair and grinned. "I mean, a big-time information broker like yourself shouldn't have any trouble finding that out, right?"

Fei hesitated. He hated leaving things unknown. Of all the people in the city, only one had the information he desired. The knowledge wouldn't bring money, but like all collectors he had to possess the thing he missed. "What do you want, Crow?"

"No Mr. Crow? I'm disappointed."

Fei glared. His already beady, black eyes got cold and hard. "What do you want, *mister* Crow?"

"How did the Golden Monk know about me? He said he was sealed in *Xīwàng* for a few hundred turns, yet he knew who I was."

Fei sat back down and adjusted his brocade *changshan*, easing the long jacket under his legs. "I went first last time. It's your turn. Why did Alyssa Zhang want her father dead?"

"She said he had found a way to control people, like take over their heads and wear them like flesh puppets. She wasn't kidding. Zhang could remotely control people. He mostly hid out in his tower and screwed around with dismembered corpses but, no kidding here, he could take over people's minds. Outside of the tower he had to use a wire, but inside all he had to do was think. That girl you mentioned,

Huizhong, Zhang took her over and made her fight me while he was fighting me himself. Mind control, Fei, that's why Alyssa Zhang wanted her father dead. She wanted that knowledge erased."

Fei's brow furrowed. He sat back in his chair with a deep, dissatisfied sigh. "Mr. Crow, it is now my turn to express sincere displeasure at this tall tale. I saw the pictures of the Clock Man from when he hit the ground, so I'll buy your tale of dismembered corpses. But there is no way to control people's minds."

"There is and he did it. That's why she wanted him dead."

"Perchance, do you know how he did it?"

"Don't get greedy, pal," Crow said. "Information for information. You still need to tell me how the monk knew me."

"The Golden Monk." Fei sighed. "How is he?"

"Dead."

Fei gasped. His hand covered his mouth and the color drained from his face. "You killed the Golden Monk?"

"He attacked me. All I did was knock a little too loud for his liking." Crow paused and reflected on the meeting. "Actually, you know what? I don't think he liked me very much. He pretty much attacked right away. He said the Temple of Hope was sealed off because of The Beast."

"They say the Golden Monk's job was to maintain Hope for future generations, thus he was forbidden to leave and was required to protect his temple. Why he was aware of you, I cannot say. Nor can I say why a being as incredible as the Golden Monk would fall to the likes of you."

"I'm pretty spry when I get my blood going." Crow stood and bowed slightly to Fei Long. He would have relished smashing the bottle of cheap *baiju* over the man's head, but that would be too risky even for him. "Thanks for the info, old man. I hope I never meet you again. Pier 22, Jolan, right?"

Fei nodded, still deep in thought. Whether the old man was thinking about Alyssa Zhang or the Golden Monk, Crow didn't care. He had the information he wanted.

"Come to me, wee beastie," Crow whispered to the tea house. "It's time for your reign of terror to end and mine to begin."

9 | Lonely City

Huizhong woke with start when the airship touched down. She was twisted in her seat and every part of her body ached. Her fitful slumber, punctuated with strikes to her elbows when the stewardess pushed the drink cart up and down the aisle, had left her more groggy and irritable than rested.

She opened her eyes slowly and found her row-mate stretching. A giant grin covered his face. As he ran his hands through an unruly mop of blonde hair, she thought he was kind of cute in an assholish sort of way. Then her neck cracked and popped and she remembered it was because of him that her whole body ached.

"Good morning, sunshine," he said brightly.

Huizhong closed her eyes and resolved to steal his purple ring. "You're in my seat," she said.

"Yeah, sorry about that. I was dozing off and no one else was here, so I took it, you know. I hate the aisle. No big, right?"

She assumed he meant no big deal, but at that moment, in her condition, it was a big deal. "I hate you," she said and immediately regretted it.

To her surprise, he smiled and laughed. His face was completely devoid of worry lines. She was in her late twenties and was already feeling old. He was probably older, but there wasn't a sign that he had ever had to worry about anything in his life. Huizhong retraced her mental steps and realized that, yes, she did hate him even as she wished she could be more like him.

"Tell you what," he said. "Let me buy you something to eat. It's been a long trip and I am starved. You like fried stuff? There's a place near here that serves great fried stuff."

Huizhong wanted to tell him to eat a dick, but her

stomach was rumbling and there's no better meal than a free meal. "It's not a date," she said.

"On my honor," he said. He made a strange set of signs across his chest. His finger drew downward in a right arc, then back up and downward in a left arc. He finished with two rising arcs.

She cocked an eyebrow. At first, she thought he was drawing a magical symbol or some sort of talisman, but the final strokes changed her mind. "Why did you just draw fire on your chest?"

"Because I'm so hot," he said and laughed. "Nah, it's just something I picked up. Fire's supposed to be dynamic, you know? Strength and persistence; that's me in a nutshell."

Huizhong sat up, straightened out in her seat and did her best to stretch. "I guess that would make me water."

"Oh, man," he said. "The low point, eh. You totally need to eat some fried stuff. That'll perk you right up."

"Food would be good," she admitted. Ao Shun and the Furious Fae hunted and grew their own food. It was good and wholesome, but bland. She also never got over the idea that the meat had been in a dragon's mouth. Something with flavor, something really bad for her, would taste wonderful right about now.

"Cool, man. Hopefully they'll have some *xiā*. You've got to be near water to get those little guys. Out in the desert it was all lizards and birds and stuff, I'm dying for something with more legs than me dropped in a batter and fried."

Anything sounded better than roots, nuts, the odd fruit, and whatever Ao Shun decided to share. And a nice plate of *xiā* would fill the bill. She reached out her hand. "Sorry if I came off as rude; I'm just tired and hungry. I'm Huizhong."

He took her hand and shook it firmly. "Jonal."

"That's an interesting name."

"My family's from out in the desert. Huizhong. That's usually a boy's name, isn't it?"

She brushed her hair behind her ear and nodded. "My

folks weren't into gender roles. They thought if they named me wise and loyal, I'd be wise and loyal."

"Are you?"

"Not really, no. It seems their experiment failed. What does Jonal mean?"

He shrugged. "I don't think our names mean anything. My brother was Jolan, I'm Jonal. I think my parents were lazy."

"Well, it's a nice name," Huizhong said.

The crowd of people pushing their way off the airship had thinned out. Jonal blushed when he realized his bag was under her seat. "Man, I totally screwed up, didn't I? I am so sorry."

His personality was so different than what she expected, that Huizhong couldn't help but smile. "Don't worry about it. A boat can't always sail with the wind; an army can't always win battles."

"See," he said with a huge grin, "you are wise."

"I had good teachers."

They walked out onto the airship field and the whole of Croatoa came smashing back into Huizhong. The city stretched to the East while the ocean stretched to the West. From here, everything looked peaceful and serene. Even the Clock Tower, rising like a hundred-story needle into the sky, looked peaceful. Was it really only six months ago? It seemed like the last time she was here was in another life.

Croatoa, for all its vile filth, had a grip on her. She loved to hate the place. The city, like the people that lived in it, put on a face for visitors that was rarely seen for people who lived here. A normal tourist getting off the airship would head straight North and soon be in the gilded part of town. Her hovel wasn't far from here, in the southern part of the city that never saw the pleasant face of Croatoa. Her part of town saw the drunken, angry face of the city as it shrieked and whined, hopped up magical drugs and madness.

It was amazing to her. A city of millions of people all

going about their business without noticing anything around them. People passed each other on the streets and barely batted an eye when the person they used to see on the way to work was found dead and half-eaten in an alley or roasted alive.

She'd walked the streets when she was last here. Late at night, when the city was slumbering or too hammered to be mobile, she walked around and tried to feel anything other than the crushing expanse of the city. Even when it was quiet, Huizhong could never hear Nüwa's voice. It felt as if the goddess had left Croatoa to its own quiet, lonely destruction.

Even now, just stepping off the airship, she felt alone. All around her, stretching for gōngl□ in every direction were people, but Huizhong never felt connected to any of them. Save one, and he was not someone she wanted a connection with. Somewhere, out in that sprawling metropolis of sweat and decay, were answers she desperately wanted. She'd have to get into the Clock Tower to find them. And that likely meant seeking out Felix Crow.

"Food?" Jonal asked.

Huizhong shook away the memories and nodded. "Please. Lead on."

Jonal crooked his arm at the elbow. She blushed and wondered if twelve hours on the airship made her smell as bad she felt, but slid her arm through his anyway. They broke from the rest the travelers and headed down the tarmac. A guard held up his hand to stop them. Without acknowledging him, Jonal held up his hand and tapped his ring. The guard bowed and let them pass without incident.

Huizhong looked back at the guard as they passed and found the man had gone back to watching the rest of the people walking. "How'd you do that?" she asked. "Those guys don't have a sense of humor."

"Or decency," Jonal said distantly. "They're a necessary evil, though. It would be a better world if everyone could get along without control, but most people need the leash to stay in line."

She shook her head and wondered how a guy who would take a seat and put his bag under someone else's seat could have the *gāowán* to talk about other people staying in line. In the interest of food, she decided to drop it. "But how did we get past him?"

Jonal patted her arm affectionately. It felt patronizing, but she couldn't say exactly how. "He recognized what kind of trouble he could get in. Power has its privileges."

"Power?"

"My family is, uh, rich. My great granddad started mining and found this purple metal. It proved to be immensely popular. Since he was sitting on the only place on Aluna with it, he had total control over the distribution. Over the turns, my family has expanded into all kinds of trade. We are royalty without all the tedious parts of having to listen to people."

"Let me see that ring," Huizhong said.

He held it up and she looked closely at it while they walked. It was beautiful. Tiny flecks of pink, nestled safely in deep purple, glistened in Dà Māmā's bright light. Something about the ring seemed almost alive, like it was full of magic that had once breathed and stank and spoken with gods. It was made from woven strands, expertly intertwined; poetry in pink and purple metal.

"Like it?" Jonal asked.

"It's amazing," Huizhong admitted. "I've never seen its like and I've seen a lot of things."

"This is one of the special ones. We employ a man who does nothing more than make these," Jonal said as he admired the ring. "He is both an artist and a scientist. Ah, here we are."

Huizhong looked up from the ring and found a gleaming green vehicle in front of her. Bits of jade and gold accents highlighted the sleek lines, drawing the eyes from the huge engine and down the rest of the car. The whole thing hummed slightly. A man stood at the back door and bowed when Jonal and Huizhong approached.

"Where to, sir?"

Jonal didn't break stride, but that winning smile of his flashed and he happily grasped the hand of the man in the black uniform. "It's good to see you, Lo Pan. How has Croatoa been treating you?"

Lo Pan flashed the barest of smiles and nodded slightly. "It is good to see you, too, sir. Croatoa has been keeping me busy, but I am happy to serve the family."

"My brother?"

"We located him this afternoon, sir. Fei Long was less than enthusiastic about divulging his whereabouts."

"Oh, Fei, you old *húndàn*," Jonal said with a sad smile. "I trust Fei is still breathing."

Lo Pan bowed. "Of course, sir. He is an unpleasant man, but I followed my orders. Shall I take you to your brother now, sir?"

"Is he moving around a lot?"

"No, sir. He appears to stay in place under a pier by the docks. I have been watching him; he doesn't leave."

Huizhong listened to the back and forth with a curious ear. Something pinged inside of her mind, a tiny warning bell that everyone who lived in the big city learned to pay attention to. That little paranoid warning told her something wasn't right. She did what Ao Shun had taught her and stayed quiet.

"Excellent work, Lo Pan," Jonal said. "This young lady, by the way, is Huizhong. I took her seat by accident and have promised her some dinner to compensate."

Lo Pan looked her up and down with a hint of distaste on his face. He had expressionless eyes, dark and lifeless that sent a chill up Huizhong's spine. He hesitated slightly before bowing to her and turning back to Jonal. "With all due respect, sir, your ticket was for first class."

Huizhong absently patted down her hair and adjusted her skirt. She felt vaguely offended that the driver would assume she wasn't in first class, but given her condition understood the assumption.

"The stewardess in first class was a... How shall I put this?" Jonal asked.

"Say no more, sir."

"It would have been an uncomfortable flight. Let's just leave it there. Some people don't know when to let things go."

"I will have the situation taken care of before your return flight, sir."

Jonal grinned again. "Thank you, Lo Pan." He shot a glance at Huizhong and smiled. "Sorry, I shouldn't be talking like this, let alone wasting your time. Lo Pan, to Mrs. Chow's, if you would be so kind."

Lo Pan bowed and opened the door. Inside, Huizhong found luxury that was every bit opposite from her clearing in the forest. The seats were made of the softest material she'd ever felt and there was enough room to fit at least another four people. When Jonal closed the door, the outside world ceased to exist. There was a faint vibration and the car pulled smoothly off the tarmac.

10 | Chow Time

Mrs. Chow hugged Kevin tightly and sat on the floor to scratch Tina's ears. Chan shrugged and chuckled to himself before wandering off to the bar. Dino put his head on Kevin's shoulder and cooed sadly. Kevin scratched him while he watched Mrs. Chow contentedly talking to the dog. Something about the situation seemed strange to him and like all kids his age, he had trouble holding his tongue.

"Mrs. Chow?" he asked quietly.

She looked up with a face wet from pit bull kisses with a huge smile on her face. "Yes, dear."

"Um, I hope this isn't, um, bad to ask. What is a criminal enterprise?"

Mrs. Chow's smile faded even as her fingers kept working away at Tina's ears. "Where did you hear about criminal enterprises?"

"Am I in trouble?" Kevin asked, lowering his eyes.

"Not at all," Mrs. Chow replied. "I am just wondering where you heard about such things and why you would think I know anything about them."

Kevin glanced up and although Mrs. Chow didn't seem happy, it didn't look like her ire was directed at him. That could mean it would be directed elsewhere and even though he didn't want to get into trouble himself, he didn't want anyone else getting in trouble, either. "Never mind," he said. "It was a dumb question."

"There are no dumb questions," she replied. She glanced at Chan and a scowl crossed her face. "Only dumb people who should know what to not talk about."

Mrs. Chow rattled off a long string of what sounded like curses in Chinese. From his six months here, he'd picked up a lot of the language, but didn't consider himself fluent. Fluency requires an understanding of the culture that made the language. Kevin understood a lot of the words, but not the underlying meaning behind them. For instance, Mrs. Chow used words phrases like "*cào n☐ z☐zōng shíbā dài*" and "*n☐o cán*" that seemed to mean something to her, but meant nothing to him.

"Oh," Kevin said.

Mrs. Chow yelled something to the cook behind the bar. Kevin picked up the words *miàntiáo* and *dim sum*. His stomach rumbled at the thought of noodles and dumplings. "You live with interesting people, Kevin. It's inevitable you'll hear things like 'criminal enterprise'. That's what small-minded people say about smart people like me. Would you want to go to a job every day and sit in a small room and take notes?"

"Sounds like school," Kevin replied.

"Exactly! Do you like school?"

Kevin shrugged. "Sometimes it's okay. Sometimes I just want to do what I want to do. I don't really care about what happened in England in 1066. No one does."

"I didn't go to a school. My school was the streets. I don't know what England is and I don't know what 1066 is, but you know what? It doesn't matter. I've got this place and I can take care of myself and I've got a lazy cook that I have to yell at, but he makes good food. The best education is learning what you need to learn when you need to learn it. The best jobs are the ones where you do what you need to do to be happy. People believe I'm a criminal because they can't understand why I don't want to sit in an office all day and make someone else richer. I provide services that are in great demand even if other people have decided they're wrong. I'd rather help people and if they want to pay me for that, then that's great."

Kevin nodded. While he lacked an understanding of the nuance of what she said, the words made sense. Why should he have to do what everyone else thought he should do? What good was school if someone like Mrs. Chow got this far without needing it?

"So, a criminal enterprise isn't a bad thing?"

"People are going to tell you all your life that this, that, or the other thing is bad. They only say things are bad because they don't like them and want to make sure no one else does, either. Good and bad are entirely up to you to decide."

The cook, a grumpy-looking man in an immaculate apron carefully handed a bowl of noodles to Kevin and a plate of dumplings to Mrs. Chow. She nodded and said, "*Xièxiè.*"

He bowed and mumbled, "*Shì de qíngfù.*"

Mrs. Chow's emerald eyes danced in the light. Kevin got the impression she wasn't always a happy person, but Tina's fur and muffled grunts seemed to delight the little woman. She held up a dumpling and let the old pit bull sniff at it. The dog wrinkled her nose and took a tentative bite.

Dino, never one to let a bit of food escape his attention, skittered across the floor and jabbed his snout at the plate. Mrs. Chow slapped him on the nose. His feathers ruffled, but he seemed to get the message and waited patiently.

Eventually Tina decided she wanted more and her gigantic maw of a mouth took the rest of the dumpling in one gulp. "Now you, whatever you are," Mrs. Chow said to Dino.

Unlike the dog, the deinonychus didn't hesitate. He snatched the dumpling from her hand and skittered across the floor until he felt he was safe. Kevin watched them both eat with a smile on his face.

"Where did you get the dog?" Mrs. Chow asked.

"My parents found her at an animal shelter when she was a puppy. She's been my best friend and my protector."

"What about the bird thing over there?"

"He's a dinosaur. They're all extinct now. At least on Earth. I don't know how I made him, but the night my mom and dad disappeared, I was terrified and felt like I needed someone to keep me safe. What better protector than a predator?"

Mrs. Chow slowly rose and helped Kevin to his feet. "You have a pair of remarkable protectors. Plus, you've got Chan teaching you. You'll be safe."

Kevin sat at a table and happily ate his noodles. They weren't what he'd grown up with, but he was young and adapted rapidly to his changing environment. While he ate, he watched Chan and Mrs. Chow talking. Chan was his usual immobile self, but Mrs. Chow's hands were all over the place. She was an animated speaker, something Kevin found amusing.

Chan spoke of Mrs. Chow as someone to be feared, but she was always nice to him and he had trouble being afraid of her. Besides, she always gave him food and she liked Tina. The old dog seemed to like her, too, and dogs were supposed to be good judges of character.

Kevin was slipping noodles to his protectors when shouting echoed down the hallway. Chan and Mrs. Chow turned. A look of horror crept over Chan's face while Mrs. Chow's face darkened. The shouting intensified.

"Let him in!" Mrs. Chow shouted.

A loud bang replied. Kevin jumped and Dino put himself between the boy and the hallway. For a moment, nothing moved. The air felt heavy, tangy. Kevin tasted a hint of magic on his tongue and wondered what was going on. Chan was muttering something and something and shaking his head. Mrs. Chow was screaming something in Chinese that didn't sound too happy.

A man in a long, black coat and wearing a hat with a wide brim walked through the hallway and into Mrs. Chow's like he owned the place. He had a swagger in his step and a mischievous glint in his eye. "Sorry about the door," he said as he sauntered to the door. "Put it on my tab."

"Crow, don't you know how to knock?" Chan asked.

So this is the legendary Felix Crow, Kevin thought. He didn't look like much, a middle-aged guy with a bit of a paunch and a waxy complexion. But those eyes told a different story. Even from where he was sitting, Kevin could tell by the way the man scanned the room that he'd been in some scrapes.

He'd met this man once before. Shortly after he came to

Aluna, Chan had brought him here to meet Mrs. Chow. Crow had shown up, looking more or less like he did right now. From what he remembered, Felix Crow seemed like a nice enough guy, even if he was scary looking.

Crow's eye landed on Dino and a grin crept across his face. He turned from the bar and headed toward Kevin. Tina glanced up from her place on the floor and wagged slowly, tail slapping the floor. Crow stopped in his tracks. "What does it mean when they do that?"

"It's called wagging. It means she likes you," Kevin replied.

"Ah, good," Crow replied. "I'm a likeable guy. We've met, haven't we?"

Kevin nodded. "A while back. Right after I got here."

"Ah, yes," Crow said thoughtfully. "Sorry if I wasn't on my best behavior then. I'd just been entombed for a couple weeks and was starving. Also, I had just killed the Clock Man."

Crow held out his hand and Kevin shook it. "Kevin Kindig," he said happily. "You've already met Tina and Dino's around here somewhere."

"Right. The dino-something-or-other. Felix Crow, by the way."

"I know who you are," Kevin replied. "Chan talks about you a lot."

"Don't trust everything Chan says," Crow said. "He's prone to making up stories about me."

"He says you can find anything."

Crow chuckled and set his hat on the table. "Well, kid, I don't know about that, but I usually manage to find trouble pretty easily."

"Can you find my parents?"

Mischievous eyes glittered. Crow grinned a sly grin that made Kevin both like the strange man and scoot his chair back at the same time. Suddenly all the stories made sense. The man in front of him might be able to find his parents, but how much damage would he cause in the process? Still, he was running out of options. "How much?"

Crow cocked his head to the side and peered closely at Kevin. That gaze reminded Kevin of all the times the police would give their "Don't get out of line" talks. That look, the half-angry, half-intense glare was something every cop Kevin had ever seen could pull off. It must be something they learned in the police academy.

"How much?" Crow replied. "For what?"

"Finding my parents," Kevin said. "They're out there somewhere and no one knows where."

"Whoa there, buddy. What makes you think I can find them? Or that you can afford my services? No offense, pal, but I don't work for free and I don't work cheap."

"Name a price," Kevin said.

Crow opened his mouth and closed it again. "Let's back up a bit. How do you even know they're here?"

Kevin pointed across the room where Chan and Mrs. Chow were bickering about something. "Chan says some group of women told him to find me and my parents, but he didn't get moving quickly enough and someone called The Beast got hold of them first. Chan's been looking, but he can't find them. I like Chan, but he says you're the best at finding things. So, how much?"

Chan stalked over with a grim expression on his face and put a hand on Crow's shoulder. "We need to talk."

"I am talking," Crow replied without looking at Chan. "Negotiating, actually. My friend here is looking for The Beast. By a strange bit of luck, so am I."

"We will find him ourselves, Crow," Chan said quietly. When he was pissed as hell, Chan's already gravelly voice took on a basso tone that made him sound as dangerous as he looked. His southern accent also kicked in. It made him a strange sight to behold; a man dressed in traditional garb, but with an accent that was anything but traditional.

"I'm busy, Chan," Crow replied. "We are going to figure

out a way to make this mutually beneficial."

Chan leaned in close to Crow and wrinkled his nose. "You are drunk."

Crow leaned his chair back and spun around on one leg until he faced Chan. "You make that sound so lurid."

"It is still early. It is not even dinner time and you are drunk."

Crow chuckled and grinned. "So, you're buying dinner, then? I mean, I already bought the drinks, right? I even drank them for you since you don't drink. I think that means dinner is in order."

"I thought you two were friends," Kevin chimed it.

"We are," Crow said. "Well, allies at the very least."

"Allies?" Chan asked.

"Allies in the war against boredom. And beasts. And The Beast. Shall we share some information over dinner? I don't know about you guys, but I've been busy already."

Chan sighed and shrugged. Kevin covered his mouth and laughed. Chan might have been an amazing fighter, but he just got schooled in tactics by a drunk guy. Chan turned toward the bar and held up three fingers.

"He owes me money!" Mrs. Chow yelled. "I'm not going to feed him until he fixes my door."

Crow looked over at Kevin and winked. "That door was ugly anyway," he told Chan. "It needed to come down."

Chan started to repeat what Crow said to Mrs. Chow, but closed his mouth and sat down instead. He fidgeted in his pocket and placed a small paper packet on the table. It was an attempt to prove he'd been looking for The Beast and not just sitting around.

"Heaven's Powder, eh?" Crow asked. "You never struck me as the trashy, gutter drug type."

"I found this at the match last night. The last man I fought had this on him. Do you know anything about it?"

Crow reached into his jacket and pulled a fistful of similar packets out. He tossed them on the table and motioned to

Chan. "A new street drug," Crow said. "It's been popping up everywhere."

"Are you taking it?" Chan asked.

Crow shook his head and looked serious. "I don't do drugs," he said quietly.

"I did not suspect that you truly were," Chan replied. "But I had to be sure."

"What are those?" Kevin asked.

Crow slid an empty packet across the table to Kevin and tapped another one. "Drugs, kid. Nasty stuff. I ran into a guy earlier that took this stuff. He was a skeleton in reeking clothes. Do yourself a favor, stay away from this stuff. Drink all you want. Smoke all the time. Hell, fight with people over trivial things, but stay away from this crap."

"Sage words, Crow," Chan said.

"Did you just roll your eyes at me?" Crow asked.

"I have no idea what you are talking about."

"There!" Crow said. "You did it again. You rolled your eyes at me."

Chan bristled and lowered his head so his eyes wouldn't be visible under the d□ulì. "I assure you I did no such thing."

Crow laughed. Kevin watched in wonder as the two verbally sparred with each other. It was clear from listening to Chan over the months that he held Felix Crow in some esteem, but to see them interacting it became more obvious that they were friends and had been for a long time. The two men couldn't be more different – Crow was shorter and stocky, Chan was lean and lanky; Crow loved life; Chan fought to suppress it – but they got along well.

"What say you, young man?" Crow asked.

Kevin rolled his eyes in response and Crow laughed again. "You're doing a good job with him, kid. Ol' Chan here might eventually develop some emotions."

"To the task at hand," Chan said.

Crow raised a glass about half-full of some colorless liquid and said, "I'll drink to that."

Chan stared at him with a dour look on his face. Crow grinned and downed the glass, wincing as the liquid hit his stomach. "I meant we should get back to the task at hand."

"I know what you meant," Crow replied. "Fine. Let's get back to boring old drugs and crime. Here's what I've found out while you were fighting: very few people seem to know how to find the The Beast. He's out there somewhere, but no one's talking. That, in and of itself, is strange. I've met plenty of people like this guy and they love it when everyone is talking about them. The Beast, though, is a different matter. He hides in the shadows. I think I might have someone who can find him, though. Fei Long said there's a guy that lives under Pier 22 that knows how to find The Beast."

"Fei Long said that?" Chan asked.

Crow poured himself a drink and downed it. "Yep. Pier 22. Name's Jolan. I figured after lunch, I'd take a look under Pier 22 and see what Mr. 'I Know The Beast' really knows."

"Hello!" a voice called out. "I would like some fried things."

A man with a mop of blond hair and a dark-haired woman on his arm barged into the place like he owned it. "Tourists," Crow mumbled as he stared at the newcomer.

Mrs. Chow didn't seem happy to see the new couple, or their emotionless bodyguard, but she deferred to him in a way neither Crow nor Chan had ever seen her do. People who walked into her bar usually got the authentic Mrs. Chow treatment: good food served with a side of attitude and shrieking at the cooking staff.

Crow's eyes were blurry, but he could swear he'd seen the couple before. He couldn't place where or when he would have been in a position to meet them, though. In fact, he couldn't picture the two of them together in his head, yet there was something about the two of them that tickled his brain.

"Do you recognize them?" Chan asked.

Crow shook his head. "Kind of, but mostly no."

Mrs. Chow motioned the new arrivals to a table toward

the front and bowed before leaving. "Did she just scamper?" Crow asked.

Chan grunted. "Mrs. Chow does not scamper."

"I'd swear that looked like a scamper," Crow said. "What about you, kid? Did that look like a scamper to you?"

"She scampered," Kevin said.

"See," Crow told Chan. "That was a scamper."

"I repeat, Mrs. Chow does not scamper. She exits gracefully and rapidly."

"Whatever, Chan," Crow said. "I know a scamper when I see one and she definitely scampered."

Chan pursed his lips. "Why would Mrs. Chow scamper?"

"She looked afraid to me," Kevin said.

"Mrs. Chow has no reason to fear anyone in this town," Chan said.

"Because she's the head of a criminal enterprise?" Kevin asked.

Chan grunted again and Crow laughed out loud. "Exactly!" Crow said. "What kind of head of a criminal enterprise fears anyone?"

Chan turned in his seat and stared at the newcomers. The man talked incessantly, waving his hands around and gesturing wildly. "I cannot see a reason to be afraid of anyone at that table."

"Maybe you're not looking at the right thing," Crow said. "Maybe you don't know enough to be afraid."

"Possibly," Chan said. "But there seems to be nothing special about any of them."

Crow wanted to push the issue, to keep the debate going. Not because he thought he could change Chan's mind, but because he was bored and needed the entertainment. Mrs. Chow, looking peaked, dropped three bowls of noodles piled high with fried things on the table before disappearing without saying a word.

"She's scared," Crow said as he wrapped a long noodle around his chopsticks.

But scared of what? he asked himself.

11 | Family Affair

Chan watched Crow talking animatedly with Kevin and wondered if he'd made the right choice. The boy was at an impressionable age and Felix Crow was not someone to be emulated even by adults. Crow's life was a mixture of violence, an almost preternatural ability to solve problems, and sheer dumb luck. Where Chan had dedicated himself to his art, always seeking the ever-elusive perfection, Crow had gone around his problems or chosen to mask them with the acerbic veneer of *baiju*.

The dog and the dinosaur followed close behind Crow and Kevin, never letting the boy out of their sight. It was incredible that the two animals were so loyal to the boy. Native Alunan creatures – *ni□o lèi* and *páxíng dòngwù*, mostly – didn't have affinity for each other. The *ni□o lèi* would stick together long enough to hatch eggs high in the treetops, but once the eggs hatched the feathered creatures would separate again. For the *páxíng dòngwù*, the idea of a home was probably alien to them. They skittered around on the ground and crept into any hole they could find. Even the dragons kept to themselves. Presumably, dragons mated, but no one had ever seen it happen. Dragons, like *páxíng dòngwù* and *ni□o lèi*, didn't seem to enjoy each other's company very much.

Only the little dragons seemed content with others of their kind, but they seldom worked together. A *qún* might consist of a dozen little dragons. When threatened, each of the dozen little dragons went in a different direction.

Seeing the dog and the dinosaur so tied to Kevin still boggled Chan's mind. They even slept in his room. There was some unspoken connection between the three of them, but Chan couldn't figure out what it was.

"What are those?" Kevin asked, pointing at a set of purplish bars that blocked off a cavern in the distance.

"Some kids kept getting lost in there, so Hoqwua put up a gate to keep people safe."

"Who's Hoqwua?" the boy asked.

"A very rich man," Chan said. "And, apparently, a good person."

Crow chuckled. "I doubt he's a good person, but he is rich."

At Pier 22, Crow slapped Kevin on the back and hopped onto the crimson sands of the beach. The boy laughed and followed. Chan brought up the rear, marveling at the strange prints the dog and the dinosaur made. He had to duck his head to get under the pier, but the ceiling got higher the further along he walked.

Under the pier, the persistent reek of the ocean filled the air. Chan's nose wrinkled when the smell of fish and rot hit him. Above them, the air smelled clean and tidy. Down here, the air smelled like a slow descent into madness.

"Crow," Chan called out. "Do you know where we're going?"

Crow didn't look back. He shook his head and pointed forward. Chan started to object, but the man kept going, chatting with Kevin and pointing animatedly at unseen things. Crow was not the type of person to worry even though it was painfully obvious to Chan that the people under the pier would happily gut them and eat them if the opportunity presented itself. Chan took a deep breath and relaxed, trying to ready himself for the attack he knew had to be coming.

The pier was long and one of the widest at the beach. In the summer months, when the air was warm, the wood above would creak with the weight of visitors. It was rumored the edge of the pier was a special place. If lovers proposed to each other at the edge of Pier 22, their vows would never break. Chan felt it was nonsense, but he still panged for the day he could try it himself.

If Fei told the truth, it wouldn't be too hard to find Jonal. In the darkness, the red sands took on a crimson hue. Things moved in the shadows. Ahead, Crow and Kevin were still chattering away. The boy should be nervous down here. Anyone should be nervous in this place. If the top of the pier was where people went to live forever, this was where they went to die forever.

From time to time, Crow would stop and peer closely at some derelict. Most ignored him. A few lost souls snarled and waved feebly when Crow got in their faces. One managed to get to his feet and lumber forward. Crow deftly placed himself in front of Kevin and dropped the man with a single blow. Chan noticed the punch was strong and correct. Part of him was disgusted with Felix Crow, but another part, the part that had taught Crow to fight, was pleased at his former pupil's abilities.

Crow dropped and looked at the man's feet. He snorted and rose to his feet, continuing a conversation with Kevin like nothing had happened. The boy seemed happy and relaxed. Chan's heart was a lump in his chest. If it hadn't been for The Beast, Kevin would still be safe in his home rather than exploring the dank underworld with a man best known for killing a Clock Man.

Chan followed behind them. He told himself he was protecting them from the rear, but in truth he didn't feel comfortable inserting himself into the conversation. Crow could talk for days about nothing. Chan could happily go days without talking at all.

Lost in his own thoughts and pondering the philosophical ramifications of not talking, Chan almost ran into Crow. A stray chirp from Dino woke him from reverie just in time. He reached a hand down and stroked the dinosaur's feathers, receiving a contented coo for his efforts.

"Jolan," Crow said a little too loudly. "I need information and you're going to give it to me."

In front of Crow, curled and wrapped in discarded linens, was what was left of a man. At some point in the past, the man must have been tall and powerful, but now he was little more than a skeleton covered in the *h□iz□o* that was always washing up on shore. The man had apparently tried to eat the rubbery plant, but eating *h□iz□o* was like trying to chew rubber.

"Hey," Crow said and kicked the sleeping figure. "Wake up."

The figure didn't move. Crow reached down and shook it, but still the slumbering skeleton remained steadfastly asleep.

A low growling noise rose slowly. The quiet murmur of the people living in the shadows quieted. Chan had never heard anything quite like the sound. His scalp itched and a chill ran through his spine as some long-forgotten bit of genetic code told him the sound was not friendly and he should run.

Chan looked furiously around for the source of the growling noise before his eyes finally alit on Tina. The dog was up and sniffing the air around her. The fur on her back was standing up and her teeth were bared. Rather than wagging back and forth, her black tail drooped behind her.

"What's wrong, Tina?" Kevin asked.

"What's going on?" Crow asked.

"She doesn't like someone or something," Kevin said.

Crow looked at Chan and shrugged. "Is she going to explode?"

Kevin stroked Tina's head and got the dog to calm down a bit, but she kept growling and looking around nervously. The hair on the back of Chan's neck went up and he got the distinct feeling something was watching him.

Dino stalked in and chirped. His head was low. The long claws on his back legs dug deep grooves in the dank sand as he flexed them. A long, trilling whistle rolled under the pier as the dinosaur sniffed. The two animals continued searching the air for something.

Chan instinctively took a step back. All his experiences with the two creatures had been pleasant, if frustrating sometimes, but their demeanor reminded him of the *dà jī* when the big birds got spooked. Unlike the *dà jī*, the dog and the dinosaur were predators. The birds would run from a threat. The dog and the dinosaur looked ready to attack anything that moved.

Around them, the air grew colder. The derelicts under the pier disappeared into the shadows. Crow cocked an eyebrow and did his best to look unperturbed, but Chan could feel the deep worry coming off the man. Crow had died in the Clock Tower. Died and came back to life with power he couldn't explain. Chan brushed the world, but Crow felt it deep in his bones and the look on his face said bad things were afoot.

Something moved past them, invisible, but still tangible. The air grew heavy. It felt like the desert when the storms were coming.

Then, as soon as it started, the sensation left. Tina and Dino relaxed slightly, but still looked around and sniffed at the air.

"What was it, girl?" Kevin asked.

She licked his face and wagged her tail feebly. Whatever happened still had her spooked, but she relaxed enough that the fur on her back went down. Dino chirped a few times before shaking his feathers and wandering off.

"Any idea what that was, Crow?" Chan asked.

Crow shook his head slowly. "No clue."

Kevin scooted closer to Chan and shivered. The boy had his arms wrapped around himself and a panicked look in his eyes. He looked up at Chan and gave a wan smile. "Sorry," he mumbled, but didn't move. "That felt weird."

"It felt strange for me, too," Chan said. "Crow?"

Crow shrugged and shook his head. "It felt … familiar, but I don't know how."

"It felt familiar," a voice said in a sing-song voice. "Ooooh. We're so scared of the dark."

Chan turned, ready to face the drugged-out remnant of one of the pier's denizens. Instead, he found a young man with long, blond hair and a young woman at his side. Behind them stood another man in dressed in all black.

"Piss off," Crow snapped. "We're busy."

"Busy leaving," the man said.

Chan slowly moved in front of Kevin, placing himself between the unknown and the boy. A quick look around showed him the dog and the dinosaur were watching the man warily. "It is best that you leave. We do not have any quarrel with you," Chan said.

The blond man stepped closer to Chan, his swagger visible even in the semi-darkness of the pier. Chan kept his face neutral. "You must be the legendary Chan," the man said slowly. "The famous master of the fights. I don't know what you're doing here, but it's time for you to get back to the streets my boy."

"Boy?" Chan asked. His fists clenched and released. He could feel the tension rising. His mind automatically started plotting the next several moves. Fighting, in Chan's mind, was like a rapid-fire game of *xiangqi*. He planned out his moves well in advance of the first strike, but always had several back-up plans in mind.

From the way the man was sauntering, Chan knew he thought he was safe. Not the kind of safe that comes from being able to take care of oneself, the kind of safe that comes from knowing others are watching out. That meant the real threat was the man in the suit.

"Yes," the man said. "Boy. You are the best in town, but Lo Pan there is the best in the world. Would you like to see what he can do?"

Chan looked over the man's shoulder and took a close look at Lo Pan. The bodyguard was completely attentive and completely at ease. His posture looked like someone who was capable and self-assured. "Not particularly," Chan said.

"I'd like to see what he can do," Crow said, walking forward. Chan held out an arm to stop him. Crow had been a talented pupil, but something about Lo Pan said he was well out of his league.

The man stepped back slightly and smirked. "You must be Felix Crow. I've heard about you. Killed the Clock Man by pushing him out a window. There aren't any windows here, Crow."

"Crow?" the young woman said. "What are you doing here?"

Crow's head snapped toward the voice. His eyes were hard, but he was still doing his best to look calm. "Do I know you?"

"You don't remember me?" she asked.

"Shut up, Huizhong," the man said. "I didn't bring you here to talk to the rabble."

"Huizhong," Crow said quietly.

"Well, this is happy little reunion," the man said. "Tell you what; I'll leave her here with you and take that man in her place."

"Can't have him," Crow said. "Not until he talks."

Lo Pan took a step forward. The man raised his hand and the bodyguard in black stopped in his tracks. Chan caught a glimpse of Crow out of the corner of his eye and heard him mutter, "Shit."

"I don't think you understand what's happening here, so let me explain in no uncertain terms," the man said. "I am going to take that man on the ground behind you and there's nothing you can do to stop it. Let me tell you a story about how bad things are going to be for you if you don't step aside."

He paced and waved his arms wildly as he talked. A hint of madness in his eyes told Chan the man was a habitual drug user who didn't want to admit it to himself. "See," the man said, "if I were to have you killed – and Lo Pan would happy to kill you, right Lo Pan? If I were to simply say the word nothing, absolutely nothing, would happen to me. I could say a word and your pathetic little worlds would end."

Lo Pan nodded and locked eyes with Chan. There was a challenge in his stare as if he'd be happy to fight even if no one asked him to. Out of the corner of his eye, Chan saw Crow slowly back away. That wasn't like Crow, but Chan didn't have time to worry about it now.

"First," the man continued. "Lo Pan is going to destroy – destroy! – the legendary Chan. I wish I could record it somehow. Maybe I'll commission someone to write a book about it. *The Fall of the Legend*. Has a nice ring, right? Anyway, after Lo Pan is done with Chan here, he's going to go through Mr. Crow back there.

"When all that is done, and it won't take long, not long at all. When it's all done, Lo Pan is going to pick up that stinking waste of a person behind you and take him back with us. And you will have died protecting someone you don't even know."

He rounded on Chan and caught a glimpse of Kevin hiding. "A boy!" he said and pointed. "Well, tell you what, boy, I can kill you first or kill you last. What will it be?"

The man pulled a dagger from behind his back and showed the black blade to Kevin. Chan felt the boy cringe, but he also felt a crackling intensity in the air. The fight had been engaged and whether the man knew it or not, he was in grave danger.

Chan held up his hands and tried to defuse the situation before the world exploded. He thought back to the exploding dragon this morning and knew the boy wasn't disciplined enough to control the power coursing through him. "Kevin," he said quietly, "please do not do this."

"Do what?" the blond said. "Pee his pants?"

He grabbed Chan's wrist and tried to pull him away from Kevin. Chan's hand was a blur. It seemed like he twitched more than moved, but in a moment the man was on his knees with his arm twisted and pulled. "Walk away," Chan said. Storm clouds grew in his eyes.

A black blur streaked toward Chan. He barely had time to register Lo Pan had moved before the bodyguard kicked him in the side of the head.

Chan's grip on the blond man faltered. He turned to face

the larger threat, already planning his tactics. The man was a complete unknown, fast and strong, but Chan had plenty of experience at dealing with unknowns no matter how fast or strong they were. Out of the corner of his eye he saw the blond man climb to his feet and stalk toward Kevin.

If he turned to save the boy, Lo Pan would kill him. Chan had little doubt in his mind the bodyguard would be more than a match for Crow, so he had to deal Lo Pan before he could do anything else. He also knew the blond man would happily sever Kevin's soul from his body or Kevin's uncontrolled magic would bring the pier down on them all.

"Crow!" Chan shouted as he parried a series of rapid-fire punches from Lo Pan. "Help Kevin!"

The bodyguard was fast and experienced. Chan's fists found their target, but Lo Pan's fists did, too. Soon, both fighters backed off to re-examine their tactics. As they stalked around each other, Chan noticed the blond man holding the knife at Kevin's throat. Crow's eyes were focused on the black blade, and he was heading toward the man.

A loud noise stopped everyone in their tracks. It sounded like staccato thunder. Chan wasted a glance around and found Tina, her teeth bared making the loudest noise he'd ever heard an animal make.

The blond man snorted and grabbed Kevin by the hair. He held the knife back, ready to slam it into Kevin's throat. The boy was terrified beyond belief, completely frozen as tears dropped down his cheeks. Crow would never make it in time.

Chan had failed.

Before the blond man could kill Kevin, the noise stopped and was replaced by a snarl that sent chills up Chan's spine. Tina launched herself forward faster than the old dog had any right to move. Her teeth bared, she slammed into the man's crotch and clamped her mouth shut.

The blond man squeaked, then whimpered, then screamed as the dog turned her head from side to side and snarled. A little part of him found the dagger still in his hand

and drove it in the dog's side. She let go with a whimper and backed away.

Before the blond man could stab her again, a mass of green and red feather leaped on him. Dino's huge claws slashed at the man's face and chest. He screamed anew as strips of his flesh flew away. As the blood leaked out of him and shock took over, the dinosaur hissed in his face. The man's hands started to move up, desperate to protect his face from the onslaught.

Dino looked briefly back at Kevin, as if he was making sure the boy was okay. When he turned back, his jaw opened wide. The man whimpered when he saw the rows of teeth in the dinosaur's mouth. Chan watched in horrid fascination as Dino ripped the man's throat out and chirped happily.

Time sped back up. Kevin rushed to Tina's side and held the dog. She collapsed and licked his face feebly. The boy's tears and plaintive cry spurred Chan back to the world. He turned to find Lo Pan sprinting away and counted himself lucky.

"Chan!" Crow shouted. "Stop him! These are Hoqwua's kids. If he escapes, we are completely fucked."

12 | Staunch

A desperate cry from the boy shook Huizhong from her panic. Jonal took her to dinner as he promised and then insisted he follow her under the pier. Lo Pan followed behind her. She got the sense that something terrible was afoot, but couldn't find a way to shake the man or his bodyguard. Then they were under the pier and something dark slid through reality. The dark thing left her shaking and thinking of Ao Shun. When the dragon wanted to hunt something, he was silent; so silent the animals didn't even know he was there. But when he wanted to show off, he radiated power. Whatever moved past them felt like that, only more distant.

She focused on the sense of power and tried to find her own. It didn't feel like she was going to be raped, murdered, and her corpse left under the pier for the forgotten to feast on, but whatever was going to happen didn't feel right.

Then she saw Crow and was disappointed that he didn't recognize her immediately. Of course, why would he? The last time he saw her she had gray hair with pink accents and was dressed like one of the local courtesans. She was a different woman now. A sparkle hit his eye when she said her name and that was enough.

But the world exploded before she could continue. Jonal was ripped apart by the strangest animals she'd ever seen. A man in *d□uli*, the same man from her dreams, fought Lo Pan, and everything went to *Diyu*.

Though her ears were ringing from the screaming and the terrifying noises from the animals, she distinctly heard Crow yell something about Hoqwua. The man in the *d□uli* took off like a shot and left her shaking. The plaintive cry of a young boy cradling one of the animals kicked her brain back into gear.

She took a tentative step forward, unsure of what would

happen. No one attacked her. No one yelled. Huizhong ran to the boy and skidded to a stop on her knees. What she saw broke her heart.

The boy was young, ten or eleven at the most and was cradling a mass of black and white hair. She tentatively reached out her hand and touched the animal. It was soft and smooth, but from the sounds it made it was obviously in pain. The hair on its side was sticky with blood. Jonal's dagger had likely punctured a lung.

She looked at the boy, peered deeply into his eyes and said, "My name is Huizhong. Will you trust me?"

The boy looked back at Crow and over at the other strange creature. He wiped a tear from his eye and nodded. "Kevin," he said quietly. "This is Tina. She's a dog. From Earth."

The world spun around Huizhong. Like most people who travelled in magical circles, she knew of Earth, but never imagined how strange it must have been. To see it in the flesh was mind blowing. The dog, the bird thing, the boy; they were all far out of place. The boy was obviously terrified.

"Kevin, I know a person who might be able to help," Huizhong said.

"Chan said I shouldn't go anywhere without him. He said it was dangerous."

"He was right to say that," she replied, "and you're right to believe it. But we need to get help for the dog. I don't want you to go anywhere, okay. I want you to stay here and trust that I'm trying to help you."

The boy thought about that. He looked so lost and terrified, she wanted to hold him and tell him everything would be okay. Crow was busy dragging Jonal's mangled corpse into the shadows. The dog wasn't large, but was big enough she knew she couldn't lift it on her own.

"Crow," she called out. "I need your help."

"Just a minute," he said without looking at her. He finished dragging Jonal's body into the shadows and knelt by the corpse. A moment later he stood up and pocketed something before joining them in the sand.

"We have to get this animal to a *Zhìyù zhě*. I know a man nearby, but I'll need help carrying him."

"Her," Kevin corrected. "Tina's a girl."

Huizhong flashed back to the dog ripping into Jonal's crotch without a moment's hesitation and wondered if she would have the wherewithal to do the same. "Tina," she said. "That's a pretty name."

Kevin nodded and kept stroking the black-haired dog. "Her full name is Sistina. That's the Italian name for the Sistine Chapel in Rome."

She understood some of the words, but Huizhong had no idea what half of what the boy said meant. "I know a man nearby who might be able to help Tina. Do you trust me?"

The boy looked her up and down and nodded slowly. "Why were you with that man?"

"It's a long, strange story. All you need to know is he bought me dinner and made me come down here with him."

"So, he's not a friend?"

"I never met him before this morning when he took my seat on the airship."

The boy blinked and nodded. Huizhong's eyes fell on the dog. Her breath was labored and she was making high-pitched sounds with every breath. The wound in the dog's side was still bleeding. It wouldn't be long before the poor animal bled out.

Crow stood over them and shook his head sadly. "We can't move her. That wound's too deep."

He knelt and gently stroked the dog's head. A hint of sorrow in his eyes made her wonder if he was remembering some horrible event from the past. The day hadn't started out well, and it wasn't looking like it was going to end well. But the fight must go on. That's one thing Ao Shun drilled into her: never quit.

She rose to her feet and nodded. "I'll be back. Keep

pressure on the wound so she doesn't lose too much blood. With a bit of luck, I'll be back with help in a few minutes. Do you think Hoqwua has any more people in the area?"

"Even if he did," Crow said, "it wouldn't matter. That kid's body will be devoured long before anyone knows he's missing."

"Are there scary animals down here?" Kevin asked. "Animals that eat people?"

Crow started to say something, but changed his mind. "Sure, kid. Animals. Don't worry, they won't mess with us."

Huizhong heard them talking as she ran. Eventually the pier gave way to the light and the light gave way to the streets. She should be happy to be free of that place, but all she could think about was something completely unique on Aluna was dying because a rich kid thought he could do whatever he wanted.

At least the bird thing was still down there. Whatever that thing was, it shredded Jonal. She shuddered as she saw him fall over and over again. The bird thing had claws and teeth. It must have been a horrible way to go. Being eaten alive was always one of her fears.

Her feet clattered along the sidewalks as she dodged the thin crowds. The docks were never a popular place to come and the people who worked there were on the ocean or hiding out in one of the warehouses that dotted the dock.

She rounded a corner and nearly got run over by a carriage drawn by a shiny blue *Wěidà de xīyì*. The creature hissed at her and the man on the seat shook his fist at her anger. Huizhong mumbled a brief apology and kept running.

The streets flew by in blur of dodging pedestrians. To escape the traffic, she ducked down an alley and immediately had to jump over a woman passed out in the middle of the way. Under normal circumstances, Huizhong would have stopped to see if the woman was okay, but seeing people passed out was the new normal and she had to get help for the dog.

She exploded back into the sunlight and stopped to catch her bearings. Gong-Detian had smiled upon her; Huizhong found herself right across the street from where she wanted to be.

A hop in her step, she almost danced across the narrow street until she stood in front of a small shop with a sign out front that read "Sun Simiao: *Zhōngyī*". Some people felt Sun's approach to medicine was unorthodox, but very few would claim it didn't work. On one side of Sun's shop was a run-down pawn shop and the other a shop boasted the best spells money could buy.

Huizhong pounded her fist on the door of Sun's shop and waited. She tapped her foot. A passerby told her he could show her a good time. She replied by telling him she could show him a foot between his legs.

While she waited – Sun was no longer a young man – Huizhong looked through the windows of the pawn shop. It was the typical den of a scavenger of human misery: trinkets, baubles, and dreams sold at a massive discount, but one item caught her eye. On a pedestal, all by its lonesome, was a book.

Something about the book called to her. It whispered promises of truths hidden from mortals and where to find dragons. The book had to be some sorcerer's prize piece; even at this distance, she could feel the power flowing off it. She wondered how it came to be in a pawn shop and how the Clock Tower personnel hadn't seized it.

For a moment, she thought about throwing a rock through the window and freeing the book from its captivity, but shook her head and cleared the thought away. It would have to wait. Unfortunately, she had bigger problems at hand than a book.

The business on the other side of Sun's was likewise closed. Unlike the pawn shop, the sorcerer's shop felt empty and barren. She would hardly consider herself a sorceress, but enough time in the forest with Ao Shun had taught her to sense magic. A sorcerer's shop should feel otherworldly and magical, this one felt dead.

"What?" a voice cracked.

Sun Simiao had passed old a very long time ago. Now he qualified as archaic. He was bent over and wore glasses so thick Huizhong could barely see his eyes. Sun may have been old, but his mind was as sharp as ever.

"Sun," Huizhong said, "I need your help. There's a … a creature that needs your help."

When he looked at her, she could see the faint trace of a smile form on his leathery lips. "Huizhong? Huizhong, my dear, it is you. Where did you go? You've missed our tea time twenty-four times. Wherever did you go?"

She took his hand and smiled, remembering the hours listening to Sun spinning yarns about the Croatoa of his time, before the gangs rose to power and the city fell to its own dark heart. They met when she had twisted her ankle and was limping past his practice. He draped a foul-smelling leaf of *Èmó zh*□*o chá* on her swollen ankle and told her a tale about how the sorcerer next door taught himself to use magic. When Sun was done talking, the Devil's Claw tealeaf had worked its natural magic and her ankle was fine. He sent her away with a smile and an adamant refusal of payment. He had everything he needed, he told her. She needed her money more than he did.

Huizhong went back the next day to bring Sun a flower and wound up spending hours talking with the old man. When she left Croatoa, it nearly broke her heart to leave without saying goodbye to Sun, but the city was in turmoil and the police were looking for anyone with answers. Since Croatoa's police force had a reputation for being less than pleasant, she packed a bag and disappeared.

"I had to leave, Sun. I had to get away from here. I'm sorry I couldn't say goodbye."

Sun craned his neck and looked up at her with a cocked eyebrow. "You left right after Chenming fell out of the Clock Tower."

Huizhong bit her lip, unwilling to delve into her role in

the Clock Man's demise.

"I knew him when he was young, you know. Brilliant doctor back in his day. I trained him. He was the best student I ever had. Speaking of which, you said something about a patient. A creature, if I recall."

Panic rolled back in. The animal was strange and vicious, but it had put its own life on the line to save the boy. "Yes, Sun. There's a – what did he call it? – a dog. It's an Earth creature. It's been stabbed and it's dying."

"An Earth creature, eh? Well, I'd like to see one of those. I take it time is of the essence."

Huizhong wanted to stay and drink tea, but the little boy's tear-filled eyes drug her back. "Yes, my friend, I'm afraid it is."

"Well, then. I suppose we'll have to hurry."

An upside to Sun's longevity was he had helped countless people over the turns. Since he rarely asked for payment, half the city felt it owed him a favor. They walked down a block and found a carriage drawn by two huge *xīyì*. The scaly creatures may have had short legs, but they could run like the wind. They burst through the city and deposited them under the dock in only a few minutes.

"Now," Sun asked, adjusting his glasses and leaning on his walking stick, "where is the patient?"

Huizhong pointed under the pier. From out here, it looked safe enough, but the things that used to be people still made her skin crawl.

"From Earth, you say?"

She nodded.

"Should be easy to find then. Come along, Huizhong. Help an old man through this *z□zhòu* sand."

As they walked under the pier, cold eyes followed them. The eyes belonged to the things that called this place home and usually an old man and a young woman would be food and entertainment, but the *yíqì* held back.

Even here, Sun had treated people. They knew him, or at

least of him, and stayed out of his way. Much to Huizhong's pleasant surprise, the walk under the pier was uneventful. The eyes continued to watch them warily, but no one made a move to attack.

"Sun Simiao," Crow's voice called out. "You know Sun Simiao? I may have to take back some of the bad things I've thought about you, Huizhong."

She blushed, then shook her head sadly. It was Crow's way to play the role of the buffoon to cover up his perceived failures. "We met shortly after I moved here. How do you know him?"

Crow shrugged. "It's complicated."

"I saved him after he rolled over on *Línzhōng kānhù xiē*," Sun said.

Huizhong whistled. The little buggers weren't common, but their stingers packed a venom that hurt so much, some people tried to kill themselves to end the pain.

"He was drunk at the time," Sun added. "The *baiju* killed the Deathwatch's pain. Now, I take it this is the patient."

Sun struggled to kneel next to Kevin and Tina. Huizhong steadied him and he patted her arm once he was down. He smiled at Kevin and gently touched the dog's side. "You are amazing," he said as he stroked her fur. "Truly amazing."

"Can you save her?" Kevin asked. "She said you were a doctor."

"A healer," Sun said as he gently touched the dog's wound. She whimpered, but didn't try to bite him. "Doctors fix things. I heal things."

He rustled around his bag and pulled out a small bottle of foul-smelling oil and gently dabbed it on Tina's side. A large bluish leaf covered the oil. "Hold this here, please," he told Kevin.

Kevin's hands shook as he held the leaf in place. Huizhong put her own hands over his and met his eyes. Sun muttered to himself in an archaic tongue. The leaf started smoking as whatever medicine was in it mixed with the oil and the wound. He pulled a bandage out of his bag and wrapped it around the wound, holding the smoking leaf in place.

"The wound was very bad," Sun said. "I've never worked on a dog before, so I'm hoping my medicine will work for her."

"Thank you, Sun," Huizhong said.

"Don't thank me yet," he replied. "If she survives the night, she'll be fine. Be careful moving her."

Huizhong and Crow helped Sun to his feet. He looked at them both with a strange expression on his face. "Good luck," he said. "You're going to need it."

The dog's whimpering stopped and her eyes closed. At the very least, the pain was ebbing enough that she could rest. Kevin stroked her head. The boy still had tears brimming in his eyes, but at least he'd stopped shaking.

"Thank you, sir," Kevin said.

Sun smiled gently at him and nodded. "Thank you, my friend. I've never met a dog before. Keep her comfortable. Come, my dear. Walk an old man back to his ride."

13 | Pan Fried

Chan sprinted hard after Lo Pan. If Crow was right, and he usually was about things like that, they could all be in grave danger. Hoqwua was well known. Even Chan had to admit no one rose to Hoqwua's level of power without breaking more than a few rules.

Lo Pan was close. Chan caught glimpses of the black uniform as Jonal's bodyguard sprinted toward a car parked next to the beach. If the man in black made it to the car, there would be no way Chan could catch him. Cars weren't uncommon in the city, but their cost put them well out of reach of common people and Chan fell well into the range of being a common person.

The bodyguard leapt and slid neatly over the hood of the car. In the setting sun, the car shimmered like a beautiful beast. For a moment, Chan thought his quarry would escape, but luck was on his side. Jonal, like all rich people in a place full of poor people, was terrified of being robbed of what he had stolen from others. The doors to the car were locked.

Lo Pan patted his pockets as Chan grew nearer. He reached into his pocket and pulled the keys just in time to catch Chan's flying kick right in the lips.

Chan landed easily and stared down at Lo Pan. There were no words to waste in the fight. One man wanted to report back what he had seen and the other wanted to make sure that didn't happen. Neither of them were big on talk, anyway.

Lo Pan wiped a bit of blood from his lips and rose to his feet. Chan waited patiently. He could have pressed the attack and leaped on Lo Pan, but his desire for a fair challenge outweighed that. Chan was many things, but he was not a man to kick people while they were down. He might kick them to the ground or break legs so they couldn't stand, but he refused to kick them once they were down.

Crow wouldn't have hesitated; he would have dived at Lo Pan and used every advantage to win the fight, but Chan was not Crow.

Lo Pan tried to dart around Chan and get into the car, but Chan couldn't allow that. Lo Pan looked around, seeking an easy escape. All he had to do was turn and run, but Chan would have followed him to the ends of Aluna. Besides, there was that desire to see if he was truly as tough as he liked to think he was.

Chan put his right fist inside of his open left hand and bowed. The salutation wasn't as complicated as the one he used at the fights, but so much of the fights required showmanship. In Chan's mind, a salutation was a salutation, no matter how formal it was. Here, on the red sands stained black and greasy from countless ships and loads of fish, a formal salutation was unnecessary.

By bowing first, Chan had put himself in the position of host of the fight. It wasn't quite subservient, but it deferred a bit of respect to his opponent. Chan had seen fights where both fighters had refuse to bow first for fear it made one of them look weak.

In Chan's mind, it didn't really matter who bowed first; it only mattered who remained standing last.

His left leg slid back smoothly and his arms extended in front of him. Chan's fighting style had evolved over the turns from the fiery kicks of his youth to the calculated strikes he was known for now. Against Lo Pan, an unknown opponent, Chan chose to focus mostly on rapid-fire punches and assumed a stance that would allow his strong right hand to be closer.

Lo Pan spat a wad of blood into the sands. He smiled and slid into his own stance. Unlike Chan's loose body, Lo Pan tightened up. His hands, open like claws, came up to cover his face as he put most of his weight on his back leg.

Yáng z☐ è Style, Chan thought and nodded. Lo Pan would

focus on vicious, linear attacks designed to knock an enemy off balance and keep him there. As Chan's old teacher once said, though, that made *Yáng z□ è* predictable. An experienced fight strove to avoid predictability.

This was not to say *Yáng z□ è* stylists were bad fighters; they were a fearsome group. Part of their routine practice was spending most of their free time practicing by punching anything and everything. Now that he had occasion to look, Chan saw Lo Pan's hands were a mass of callouses and enlarged bone. The *Yáng z□ è* stylist had spent time practicing his Iron Hand techniques.

If Lo Pan would be *Yáng z□ è*, Chan decided to be the Crane. Where *Yáng z□ è* charged, the Crane danced.

Some of Aluna's martial arts were based on watching animals fight and emulating their techniques. *Yáng z□ è* were large beasts with huge claws and teeth. When they attacked, the huge creatures charged into the fray and attacked with everything they had. The attack was devastating if the enemy wasn't ready for it or couldn't react quickly enough to get out of the way.

Crane style, on the other hand, emphasized mobility and precision strikes to soft targets. While Lo Pan was focused on punching and shredding, Chan would be focused on moving out of the way and doing his best to strike small targets that hurt.

Lo Pan struck first. He went from neutral to full attack in the blink of an eye. Chan barely had time to dodge before the next strike followed the first. *Yáng z□ è* fighters were famous for combinations. Chan dodged the first strike, parried the second strike, and barely blocked a low kick. The block staggered Lo Pan and cut his attack short.

Chan hopped to the side, emulating the hop of a crane that dodges a gator in a stream, and snapped a fast, high kick to Lo Pan's ribs. The bodyguard leaned to the side as one of his ribs cracked. A look of surprise and anger crossed his face.

Lo Pan was the undisputed master of fighting in a place

where most people don't know how to fight. Croatoa was a different beast than the pomp and circumstance that he was accustomed to in Hoqwua's headquarters in the mountains. He was an enforcer, and his skills were non-trivial, but slapping around cooks and miners was a far cry from fighting someone like Chan.

Chan waited until Lo Pan was leaning far to his left and holding his side. A quick knife-edge kick to the side of Lo Pan's knee dropped the bodyguard to his knees. He looked up at Chan with a face filled with horrified wonder. For all his faults, Lo Pan genuinely strove to be the best martial artist he could be and he had just come face-to-face with one of the best in the world.

"I like to find teaching moments whenever I can," Chan said calmly. "You rely too much on strength and aggression. A fighter, a good one, must be ready to change to suit the needs of the conflict."

Lo Pan's eyes narrowed. He struggled to his feet and stood on wobbly legs. Chan nodded and cupped one fist in an open hand as a salute. He didn't think it was smart for Lo Pan to continue the fight considering his damaged knee, but he could respect the will to go on.

"You don't have to do this, you know," Chan said. "There is no dishonor in quitting now."

Lo Pan flexed his knee. A loud pop exploded from the damaged joint as the knee reseated itself, but Lo Pan could put weight on it again. "This is far from over," he snarled.

Chan bowed slightly and slipped back into his fighting stance. "As you wish. Attack when you are ready. I'll be waiting."

Lo Pan growled and raised his fists. The damaged leg slid back so he could keep his good leg forward. His stance was narrower than before. Even though his knee was better, he couldn't handle the deep stances of his *Yáng z□ è* style. Chan noted the man had adapted and wondered if it was his words or if the bodyguard was better than he suspected. He decided to assume Lo Pan was more skilled than his first attack would suggest and resolved to end the fight quickly.

A small crowd gathered around and watched the two men square off. Chan was well-known in Croatoa, but Lo Pan was not. Anyone who would challenge the master of the fights was interesting, if suicidal.

Lo Pan adjusted quickly. He pushed off with his back leg and turned the momentum into powerful roundhouse kick that caught Chan by surprise. The bodyguard's foot sailed neatly into Chan's jaw and spun him around.

"Maybe you should do more than just wait," Lo Pan said with a sneer. "I heard you were the best, but I have to admit, I'm not seeing it."

Chan adjusted his chin and had to admit the man was faster than he thought. It was time to end this. He raised his head and focused gray eyes full of storm clouds on Lo Pan. "Then it is time for your next lesson."

The fists of Chan were something of a legend in Croatoa. Over time, stories had evolved that said he could punch through stone walls and his fists were so fast there had to be dark magic involved. Chan allowed these stories to continue because they made his opponents wary and wary opponents were easier to beat. In truth, he had never punched through a wall. But he was very fast and there was no magic at all involved in that; it was endless practice and a passion to become faster and stronger that pushed him.

His strike was so fast it didn't even create a blur. One instant his open right hand was out in front of his body, the next it was smashing into Lo Pan's nose. He felt the cartilage give way as the palm of his hand pushed Lo Pan's head back. In the past, he had been taught a solid strike to the nose could kill an opponent by pushing bits of bone into the brain. Chan had done the strike on enough opponents to know it was unlikely to kill anyone, but that didn't mean it didn't hurt.

He slid to the side, deftly avoiding a clumsy punch and set about destroying Lo Pan.

A solid blow to the nose enraged the sinus cavities. The eyes water and the sudden swelling makes it hard to breathe. Lo Pan reeled back, holding his hands to his nose. Chan didn't hesitate to continue the attack. As Lo Pan dealt with the after effects of his broken nose, Chan took advantage of the fact that the bodyguard's hands were on his face and landed three punches in rapid succession to the man's stomach.

Lo Pan doubled over from the rapid-fire assault. Chan expected the change and smashed a fist into Lo Pan's kidney. When the bodyguard's back arched from the pain in his lower back, Chan hammered the man's upper back. That pushed Lo Pan's head back down just in time for Chan's knuckles to slam into the side of Lo Pan's head.

The bodyguard reeled from the onslaught and desperately tried to figure out where to put his hands to block the next strike. Chan's fist hit the Lo Pan's temple and the strength left Lo Pan's body.

Lo Pan dropped to his hands and knees in the sand. Chan thought about driving kick after kick into the man's body, but opted instead to wrap his fingers around Lo Pan's throat and shove him into the car's hood.

Lo Pan looked terrible. Blood was streaming down his face from his broken nose. His sinuses were clogged up and working overtime to figure out what was wrong, leaving Lo Pan to suck in air through his mouth. One shoulder dropped and he was having trouble standing even as he leaned on the car.

Chan put his face near to Lo Pan's and whispered in his ear. "That is why I'm the best."

"They'll be here any second," Lo Pan said. His grin told Chan everything he needed to know; the man was unhinged and dangerous.

Chan released Lo Pan and backed slowly away from the car. The threat was neutralized. Even though Crow had asked for it, though, Chan refused to kill a man for doing his job. "Who will be here?"

Lo Pan spat a wad of bloody mucous and grinned. One of his front teeth was missing and another was at an odd angle. "You think you're safe, that you know the underground. There's something down there and it can't wait to come back up."

"You are not making any sense," Chan replied. "There is nothing under Croatoa but bedrock and sand."

Lo Pan's laugh was wet and full of malice. "The war never ended, Chan."

Chan stepped closer. "What war?"

"The only war that mattered," Lo Pan said.

Something brushed past Chan's cheek with a slight hum and whistle. An arrow embedded itself in Lo Pan's chest. Even though Chan couldn't see it, he was certain the arrow was pinning Lo Pan to the car. He started to move around until he could see if the bodyguard was pinned to the car, but a strange sight stopped him cold.

Attached the arrow was a long tube connected to a tiny box with two flashing lights on it. In his head, Chan heard Crow scream at him to run. Chan took one last look at the arrow with the strange box and ran as fast as he could.

Behind him, an explosive mix of lubricants and pent-up magic exploded into the air with a force that knocked Chan to the ground. He twisted his body around to face the remains of the car and found only Lo Pan's legless torso slowly dangling off the hood.

Chan rose and looked around rapidly. The crowd was a mixture of shocked face and pointing fingers. Non-sanctioned fights were a rarity, cars were a rarity. Exploding cars were unheard of. In addition to the crowd, the police would likely be on their way soon and Chan had no desire to tangle with them.

While the crowd was focused on the remains of the car and Lo Pan's crispy torso, Chan slunk away down an alley. He was enough of a celebrity that the police would soon come knocking on his door, but he at least had a head start.

Hopefully it would be enough time to gather up Kevin and keep him safe.

He found Kevin sitting with Tina. Chan would admit he wasn't an expert on dogs, but she didn't look good. At least someone had treated the wound. Crow and the girl were talking, both pointing animatedly this way and that.

"Someone just blew up a car," Chan said.

Crow turned to him and rubbed his temples. "Blew up what?"

"A car," Chan said. "A very nice one."

"This town is going to Diyu in a bucket," Crow said. "It must be the way the sisters are aligning. Everyone's going nuts."

"That's a myth, Crow," the girl said. "This place is always crazy."

"Be that as it may," Chan said, "it seems like things are getting worse. By the way, who are you?"

Crow motioned at the girl and said, "Sorry. Huizhong, Chan. Chan, Huizhong. He taught me to fight and set me up to take down the Clock Man. She tried to kill me a couple times."

Huizhong looked shocked and Chan raised an eyebrow. What Crow had said was technically correct, but as usual was lacking details. While it was true Chan had persuaded Crow to kill Chenming Zhang, there were other elements at work.

"That is not true!" Huizhong said. "I wasn't trying to kill you. It was Chenming."

Crow nodded and held up his hands. "Okay, sorry, guys. Look. We've got bigger problems than history. What car, Chan?"

"A large, very nice one. A bomb on an arrow took it out."

"Was it green?" Huizhong asked.

"Yes, with jade and bronze accents."

"That was Jonal's car. Who would blow up his car?" Huizhong asked.

"I told you this town was going crazy," Crow replied.

"Did you see who shot the arrow?"

Chan shook his head. "No, I was focused on the fight. It did not occur to me to look for archers."

"Well, shit," Crow said.

"We need to find a place to lay low," Huizhong said. "Someone will come looking for anyone with information about the car."

"We could stay here," Crow said. "No one comes down here."

"No thank you," Chan replied. "We will find a safer place."

"Okay," Crow said. "You find a safe place. I need some answers and there's only one person I can think to ask. Unfortunately, I already traded my best information."

"Mind if I join you?" Huizhong asked.

Crow looked her up and down and shrugged. "Sure, I could use some company. Do you have a problem with beating information out of an old man?"

"Not after today," she replied.

"Good, it's settled then. Chan, find us a hole to hide in. Huizhong, let's go thump an old guy."

14 | Not So Furious Fei

Crow watched Fei Long's windows shake. Silhouettes flitted back and forth inside the information magnate's apartment. Crow's best guess put the count inside at four. There was Fei Long himself; he was the silhouette that always had its hands up. Pleading, Crow guessed. Of the remaining three, there was a silhouette with a limp. That had to have been the leader. The other two silhouettes were at least a head and a half taller and waiting until the limper directed them before they did anything.

Whatever the direction was, it didn't seem to be a good one for Fei Long.

"Fei must have screwed up royally," Crow mumbled.

"Why do you say that?" Huizhong asked.

She was sitting next to Crow on the balcony of an empty apartment across the street from Fei Long's shrine to information. They'd watched Fei Long's apartment since just after *Dà māmā* and *Xiǎo mǔqīn* had set. It was one of those rare Alunan nights when the mothers were in enough alignment that both set around the same time. The sisters, *Xiǎojiě* and *Dàjiě* hadn't risen yet, but the forecast was for both of them to be full within the next couple days.

Most of the turn, there was at least one star or one moon in the sky, but for the time being darkness swept over the land.

"He's untouchable," Crow said. He fished in his pocket for a flask and a box of matches.

Crow hesitated before lighting his *bidi*. The shades were drawn in Fei's place, so it was unlikely he'd be seen. The little match flared up in a tiny conflagration. He quickly dumped the still-lit match over the side of the balcony and inhaled deeply.

"Untouchable?" Huizhong asked.

"He runs information for most of the local gangs. Information is more valuable than money. Since information is what wins wars, knowing where the rivals are going to be in the morning is huge leg-up when it comes to setting up hit-squads. Go here. Look for this guy. Kill him."

Huizhong reached across and took the *bidi* from Crow. He glared, but didn't push the issue. She took a deep drag and handed it back to him. "If he's untouchable, why is someone beating him up?"

The big silhouettes were busy kicking the snot out of something on the floor as the smaller silhouette looked on. Crow shrugged. "He must have talked to someone he shouldn't have. The gangs accept him and put up with his *lā shɑ* as long as he works for all of them. They don't like it, but they put up with it. If he went outside the alliance, they're gonna be disappointed in him."

"Should we help him?"

"Nah," Crow said and waved the lit *bidi* dismissively. "If we bust in on them, we'll be in their crosshairs. It's better to let Fei take his licks. Besides, he'll be more willing to talk after they're done."

"If he's still alive," Huizhong said. She snatched the *bidi* from his fingers and took another drag. "It looks like they're trying to kill him."

Quick fingers pulled the *bidi* back before she could react. Crow screwed it between his lips and pulled another from his jacket. He lit the new one and handed it to her. "They don't want him dead; he's too important. This is just a message to remind him who's really in charge. He'll be up and about in the morning."

Huizhong leaned back and kicked her feet as she smoked the *bidi*. The air was warm and moist, sea breezes caressing the city like an overly jealous lover. Overhead, the power lines crackled quietly to themselves as green and purple pulses of magic flowed through them. Someone, somewhere, was using that magic to turn on a lamp or cook a *xiyì* for dinner. The constant murmur of the city wafted up, but it was muted. It wasn't her clearing, but it was more peaceful than any other place she'd found in the city.

They watched one of the silhouettes pull another silhouette to its feet. The limping silhouette pointed a finger and shook it wildly. "It looks like they're almost done," Crow said. He tossed the edge of his *bidi* off the ledge and stretched his legs. "As soon as they leave, we'll pay Fei a little visit."

Huizhong took another deep drag and tossed her *bidi* over the edge. "Think he'll feel like talking?"

"Probably not."

"Are we going to give him another beating?"

Crow snorted. "Wouldn't do much good. I was thinking about a knife."

She pulled a short dagger from the small of her back and held it up. In the dim light of the evening, the deep ebon blade glistened purple and green. "Will this work?"

Crow glanced at it and smiled. "Nice. Dragon stone. Where'd you get that?"

Huizhong shook her head and wondered what she'd gotten herself into. Finding answers was one thing, cutting them out of someone's flesh was something else entirely. From what she'd heard, Fei Long was hardly a good person. That didn't necessarily justify cutting him up or her thrill at the idea of it. She wondered what kind of person she truly was. What kind of person shrugged her shoulders and looked for a knife when the opportunity to slice bits off someone else arose?

Felix Crow was more damaged than any soul should ever be and she was destroying herself trying to save him. Or maybe that guy on the airship was right. Maybe she really was the person who reveled in being the bad woman who always got what she wanted, no matter the cost. Could it be that all the time in the forest wasn't finding her true self as much as burying her true self?

"A ... friend made it for me. Kind of hand crafted, if you

will."

"Would that be the scaly friend up in the forest?" Crow asked. Huizhong stammered something indistinct even to her. How could he know about Ao Shun? Dragons were in deep hiding. Their pride had been hurt in the dragon wars and they didn't suffer losses gracefully.

"Oh, don't look so shocked," Crow said. "When you drugged me – thanks for that, by the way – I slipped between life and death and wound up in that forest. A dragon talked to me and a woman shot arrows at me. I don't know of many people with dragon stone blades and since you said someone made it for you, that means it's new. Not a whole lot of dragons these days."

Huizhong leaned her head in her hands and wondered how her life had gotten so off track. "They're mostly gone," she said. "Hiding out. For what it's worth, I'm sorry. I was doing what I thought was right. Ao Shun, the dragon you saw in your vision, he sent me to infiltrate the tower. They're extremely sensitive to magic and he felt something strange. Magic is everywhere. It's all interconnected. We get the slightest hint of what they feel. Ao Shun felt a vibration and didn't understand it. Something strange. He's thousands of turns old, Crow. Thousands. And he felt something he didn't understand."

Crow chuckled. He had a way laughing at the most inopportune times. He would say he found the joke stitched into the innards of the universe, but Huizhong felt Crow was just a jerk sometimes. "That something he didn't understand was busy sitting at the top of the Clock Tower and tearing things apart."

"Yes, but why?" Huizhong asked.

"Because he was crazy?"

She turned to face him and found that glint of intellect reflecting in his eyes. For all his many faults, and Felix Crow had a lot of them, he was not stupid. "How many times has a Clock Man lost it that late in his tenure? Plenty of them lose it in the first few turns-"

"It's a tough job," Crow interjected.

"Yeah, but Chenming went bonkers, what, eight turns into his term? That's unheard of."

Crow chewed on that. A Clock Man served a ten-turn term of regulating the magical flow through the power lines. They had complete autonomy on how they went about doing that task and some wondrous machines had been created by Clock Men throughout the turns. The job was constant – twenty-six hours a day, eight days a week for ten full turns. The stress was immense and some cracked under the pressure. If a Clock Man was going to break, most had a psychotic episode between two and three turns into their term. A few made it to five turns before their brains cracked. Eight turns was atypical in the extreme.

"I can see that big brain working, Crow," Huizhong said.

"You saw what he had become. Maybe he'd lost his marbles turns ago. How long would it take to do what he did to himself?"

"Granted," Huizhong said, "it would take a lot of time to learn how to remove flesh and replace it with metal and vidders for eyes, but do you want to know what keeps me up at night?"

"Sexy thoughts of me?"

Huizhong snorted, unwilling to accept or admit the fact the Felix Crow occupied her thoughts more than he should. "I named my buzzer Felix, but it was for a different guy. No, what keeps me up at night is the idea that Chenming Zhang hadn't gone crazy. I think he was perfectly sane."

"The guy had a limbless man kept alive in goop in his workshop," Crow snarled. "He'd cut a little dragon down to a brain, a pair of eyes, and some flapping wings. In what world is that sane?"

"Hear me out," Huizhong pleaded. "Yes, he was unbalanced- "

"Unbalanced?"

"Unbalanced. Something was wrong with him, but it was physical. All the Clock Men have been … different. You can't do what they do and be normal. The job has serious physical and mental tolls. Do you know how long the average Clock Man lasts when his term is up?"

Crow shook his head. Like everyone else, he tended to forget about the men who channeled magic into their day-to-day lives, the caretakers of the world. Once their terms were up, Clock Men disappeared and no one cared.

"Two turns," Huizhong said.

"Two turns?" Crow asked. "That's it? I thought they lived forever on a *mùch□ng* or something."

"That's dead pets, Crow," Huizhong said. "Remember, I used to work at the Clock Tower. It was undercover, but I was there for two turns. I learned a lot about the history of the Clock Men. Most barely last two turns after they retire. A lot die within half a turn. A few make it to three turns. The job is a death sentence and everyone knows it; that's why we put up with so much from them. Without their skills, the whole world would fall apart. Did you know they had a new Clock Man in place within thirty minutes of Chenming Zheng falling out the window?"

"I figured there'd be a succession plan."

"The point is, Crow, Chenming knew he was going to die. He was a physician before he got picked to be a Clock Man. Clock Men have almost unlimited funds available; Chenming had skills. I think he was chopping animals and people up to save himself. The brain control stuff is what I can't understand."

Even as she said it, she felt Chenming's dirty fingers in her brain. But there was something else there, too. A presence that wasn't human. She'd always chalked it up to Chenming being crazy, but that's not what it really felt like. It felt alien, but somehow familiar.

"If he wanted a new body, it would be easier to steal one than make a new one."

"But he already had a new body. Remember that mechanical thing he turned himself into. He was at home in that. Chenming didn't want someone else's body, he spent too much time on his own to want to leave it. He was brilliant physician by all accounts; he could have made himself look however he wanted, but he made himself into an automaton that could think."

Crow lit up another *bidi*. Huizhong could see the wheels turning in his head. Finally, he nodded and looked back at her. "Are you sure you're not an investigator?"

She smiled and blushed. It was one thing to convince herself that crazy story had some merit, but to hear someone like Crow, who'd been a cop and was legendary for sniffing out missing things, think it had some merit felt amazing.

"No, I'm not," she said.

"I could use a partner," Crow replied. "If you ever find yourself out of work and feel like digging through the muck of this fine city, look me up."

Across the street, three silhouettes left the room. The fourth one, the one they assumed was Fei Long, didn't get up. "We should probably go check on Fei. He'll need a drink after that beating," Crow said.

*****

Fei's apartment building was decorated in red jade and gold. It was a not-so-subtle reminder that he and the rest of the people that lived there were important. Most places were bare stone or wood, sometimes inlaid with colorful rocks, but Fei's was opulent to the point of being gaudy and ostentatious. Huizhong shook her head as she peered around the spacious common area. It was bedecked with watercolor paintings from lost masters and statues carved from rock brought over the sea. Everything about it seemed desperate to prove how much better the denizens of the building were than the rabble on the street.

"Remind me to steal that dragon statue on the way out,"

Crow mumbled. He pointed at a smallish statue of a Southern dragon in flight.

"This place could use less stuff," Huizhong replied. "I've never seen so much gold in my life."

"Do you want me to steal something for you, too?" Crow asked, looking around. "It doesn't mean we're dating or anything. How about that statue of Ho Hsien-Ku over there?"

The tiny statue was solid gold with inlaid gems. The gems, sparkling in red and black glory, didn't appear to serve any purpose other than taking up space. "Why would I want a statue of the Immortal Maiden?"

"Who wouldn't?" Crow asked.

Huizhong walked toward the stairs and did her best to ignore the horrific explosion of golds and reds around the room. "I'll pass," she said.

"Suit yourself," Crow replied. "But I think it's a nice piece."

At the front desk, a nebbishy man in an overly tailored *changsha* glared at them. He pursed his lips when Crow smiled and waved. As he started to his feet, Crow signaled he should sit back down. "It's okay," Crow called out, "I'm with her."

The desk man stood up ramrod straight and narrowed his eyes. His fidgeting fingers gave away his nervousness. In a place like this, he'd been told over and over the renters were in complete control and he was unsure of what to do. First there were those strange people earlier and now this odd couple. Tomorrow, that man on the tenth floor was going to get a strongly worded letter from the management.

"We're all good," Crow called back as he struggled to keep up with Huizhong. "We'll send for you if we need anything. And I promise, we'll keep it down."

Huizhong strode up the ten flights of stairs like they were nothing. Crow kept up, but she could hear him breathing behind her. At the landing on the tenth floor she stopped and waited. There was a single door made from swirling blue and gold metals with a plain plaque that read "*Zhù n□ mèngxi□ng chéng zhēn"*. She paused and pushed a stray lock of hair out of her face.

"Jackass," Crow said. He was leaning on the railing at the top of the stairs and looked sweaty and peaked.

She looked at him and cocked an eyebrow. He shook his head and pointed at the plaque. "Who puts that on their door sign?"

"What's wrong with 'May all your dreams come true'?"

"The bad dreams," Crow said and reached for the door.

Huizhong grabbed his hand before he could touch the cold door. "Blue and gold metals," she said.

Crow shrugged and reached for the door again. Again, she stopped him. "What?" he asked.

"Blue and gold metals don't ring a bell for you?" Huizhong asked. She dropped his arm and looked carefully around the landing. Her forehead furrowed in concentration and then her nose winkled in frustration.

"What are you looking for?" Crow asked.

She kept looking around the floor. "Blue and gold. Immortality and God consciousness? I don't know who made this door, but whoever did it, they did a marvelous job. I guarantee you the door is protected."

Crow peered intently at the door, but couldn't discern anything special until his keen eyes noticed something out of place: the door had no keyholes. It was obviously meant to be a one-way portal. From the cold, smooth metal to the lack of a doorknob, the door defied expectations.

He closed his eyes and focused on the metal. Something in the door pushed back against him. Crow shook his head and reached out, touching the door with whatever power had been granted him. Rather than pushing through like he usually did, he stroked it gently. The surface felt smooth, smoother than anything he'd ever felt. It was almost like it wasn't there. When he pressed the door, it pressed back. The harder he pushed, the harder the door pushed back.

Crow took a deep breath and pushed as hard as he could.

The rebounding force smashed into him and sent him flying across the room. He hit the back wall hard and felt his lungs deflate. He tried to suck in a breath, but his body didn't want to respond.

Huizhong rushed across the room and knelt next to him. She held his face in her hands. "Breathe, Crow!" she shouted.

His eyes glazed over and rolled back into his head. Huizhong slapped him. Crow's head lolled to the side. She shook him, yelled at him, slapped him again. Finally, she closed her eyes and pressed her lips against his. A stray bit of magic shocked her lips and Huizhong jumped back. She shook her head and pressed her lips against his again. She sucked in air until she felt like her lungs were going to explode. Her lips sealed against Crows and Huizhong pushed all the air she could into his lungs.

Crow coughed and rolled to his side. Huizhong collapsed on the floor and slapped him on the back as he coughed. "I told you it was protected."

He waved a hand at her wildly and coughed some more. In between fits, he managed to squeak out, "You … were … right."

"You didn't believe me?"

Crow pushed him upright and chuckled hoarsely. "Kind of did."

She shoved him and smiled. "Well, believe me, it's protected."

Crow nodded. "Never felt anything like that. Felt so smooth, I wasn't even sure it was there."

"Any bright ideas on how to get in there?"

"Sure. The door's impenetrable, so we'll have to go around it."

Huizhong shook her head. "Okay Zhang He," she said.

Crow raised an eyebrow and cocked his head.

"Zhang He," she reiterated. "Famous navigator. Sailed around Aluna. Famous for finding a way around the Impenetrable Reef of Lao Tsung."

Crow nodded slowly, clearly not understanding. "Yes," he said. "That guy. Lang Zhe."

"Zhang He," Huizhong said. "Did you not go to school? Never mind. Point being, how are you going to find a way around the door? In case you hadn't noticed, this place is a fortress."

Crow started to stand up and stumbled again. "Help me up," he said.

She stood up and offered him her hand. With a bit of effort, mostly on her part, he was upright and leaning on the wall in no time.

Crow reached into his jacket pocket and pulled out a pack of *bidis*. He offered her one, but she shook her head, so he screwed it between his lips and lit it with a shiny lighter. After a deep drag and satisfied exhale, he said, "Back when I was still on the force we got called into check on a guy suspected of dealing synthetic *hailuòyīn* out of his apartment. It was a shitty place in the south valley, all grungy and covered in graffiti. Kind of like my place, now that I think about it. They built those places back before there were rules for how to build apartments."

He took a deep drag on his *bidi*. Huizhong motioned for him to continue. "And this would have what to do with our door problem?"

Crow ignored her question and kept on telling his story. "We found the guy's place easily enough. It had this massive iron door inlaid with all kinds of pictures of historical events: the Dragon War, the treaty, the fall of the first Clock Man and the rise of the second. It was an amazing artifact and here it was, stuck being used as some drug dealer's door.

"Then it hit me. I knew this door; I'd seen it in a museum a turn or so ago. It was rumored to be the impenetrable door of Shang Tzun, but I couldn't be certain. Still it looked like a door Shang Tzun would have. One of my guys, a real brain with an eye for antiques, confirmed what we'd heard. This guy had somehow managed to get hold of a sacred door and use it to protect his burgeoning drug business."

"Never underestimate a junkie," Huizhong said.

"Exactly, especially when money's involved," Crow replied. He was looking around the edges of the door, studiously ignoring the door itself. "So, there we were, four hardened badasses standing around with our dicks in our hands because there was no way we were going to break that door."

"That's a lovely image."

"It was a party, let me tell you. Four cops out for blood, stopped by a damned door. We were pissed. We tried the battering ram, but we may as well have been hitting that door with chopsticks for all the good it did."

Huizhong tried to picture Crow as a police officer, but the image didn't gel. Four cops trying to break through a door and failing made her laugh, though. "Did you let it go?"

Crow peered carefully at something just outside the door and snapped his fingers. "Of course, we didn't let it go, we were cops. Croatoa cops don't let anything go. Finally, our smart guy came up with a plan."

"The brain?" Huizhong asked.

"The same," Crow replied. He stepped back from the door and stood in the middle of the landing. His eyes closed. His features went slack.

Huizhong debated stepping behind him to catch him when the door's protection shoved him again. To her surprise, though, the door didn't push him away. "We went after the weakest link in the system. The door was the toughest, so we had to circumvent," Crow said. "Always go for the weakest link. It's a life skill."

The frame around the door exploded. Huizhong jumped. Even though the sound of the explosion was nothing more than a series of loud pops, it still took her by surprise. Crow smiled that crazy smile of his at her and mumbled, "Sorry. Should have warned you."

"It's okay," she replied. "It just startled me."

"It's about to get worse," he said.

"Worse? How?"

Crow motioned at the door. "That thing is a massive hunk of magic metal. Right now, it's balanced, but that won't last long."

Huizhong glanced at the faint light shining through the edges of the door. Her heart thudded in her chest. "That's going to make a lot of noise when it falls and hits those tiles, isn't it?

"Oh, it'll make enough noise to wake all the dead in *Dìyù*. Probably crack a few of Fei's pricey tiles, too."

The door moved. At first it was barely perceptible and Huizhong dismissed it as a trick of the light, but the more she watched it, the more it looked like the door was moving back and forth. "Should we stop it?"

He shook his head. "No way. We'd need an army of people to catch and lower that thing."

The movement became more pronounced. Her heart thudded, wondering each time the door swayed if it was going to fall. Each sway went a bit further than the last. Huizhong found herself holding her breath in anticipation. The door took its sweet time, though. In some ways, it was worse than torture.

By the time the door hit a tipping point, Huizhong exhaled and wondered how long she'd been holding her breath. Finally, the wait was over.

The door fell slowly, like it was one of the Tai Chi practitioners in the park working through Dragon and Crane. Unlike the Tai Chi practitioners, the door made an enormous racket when it fell over. Fortunately, the apartment complex was used to catering to extremely wealthy people who didn't appreciate questions.

Crow walked through the now flattened door and stopped just inside Fei's luxurious apartment. A curious look swept over his features and vanished into the Ten Courts of Hell. He held up a hand and said, "Wait."

"Why?" Huizhong asked as she stepped onto the door.

"This is terrible," Crow whispered.

Huizhong stepped slowly onto the fallen door and looked around. "What? What's terrible?"

"Fei's got the worst taste in decor I've ever seen. I mean, I like nudes as much as the next guy, but this is on a whole other level. Also, Fei himself is a bloody mess. But mostly it's the decorating. On the plus side, I think we've got a safe place to hide out. Stay here, I'm gonna grab that punk Jolan and cut some answers out of him."

15 | Spill The Beans

Jolan threw up.

It was the vomit of someone trying to expel his entire life in a mass of rot and stench. Like all long-term addicts his diet consisted of whatever he could find to eat whenever he managed to remember to eat it. In Jolan's case, it was mostly sand and some other things best left unidentified.

He was on the floor of Fei Long's apartment, alternatively curling into a ball and stretching out. It was worse when he stretched out. Not only was it possible to see the whole skeletal figure when he was stretched out, but he did a better job with projectile vomiting all over Fei's expensive, bleached *zhu*-wood floor.

Crow stepped back and frowned. It was hardly the first time he'd been in the company of addicts, but on the police force they were usually dumped in a cell and forgotten. Jolan had information, though, and made him less a prisoner than a guest that needed to be nursed back to health.

Jolan coughed up something straight out of Diyu and moaned. His eyes rolled back in his head and a line of drool trailed down his filthy, battered face. He curled into a ball and whimpered for a moment before he started snoring.

"Fucking addicts," Crow said with a sigh.

Huizhong crossed her arms and glared. "He's in a lot of pain."

"I'm in a lot of pain. Do you smell this stuff? Between Fei Long's blood and this idiot's puke, no one is going to be able to move into this place for months. They're going to need to call in a sorcerer just to get rid of the stench."

Huizhong brushed black and white pillows off the pure white couch and sat down with a deep sigh. "At least the furniture's comfortable."

"Yeah, ol' Fei Long loved money and feeling important.

He didn't even die on his comfy couch."

She raised an eyebrow, but didn't say anything.

"There's a lesson in there somewhere," Crow continued. "I'm not a hundred percent certain what it is, but there's a lesson there."

Huizhong shook her head and brushed hair out of her face. She looked exhausted. Her whole body slumped in the couch and she laid her head back. "There doesn't need to be lesson, Crow. It could all be random."

"No, I'm sure there's a life lesson in here somewhere," Crow said. He paced around the room and examined the trinkets Fei Long had collected in life. The information broker had a penchant for jade goddess figures. Crow held up a statue and showed it to Huizhong. "Chuang-Mu."

She rolled her eyes. "It would figure that man would keep a statue of her. I seriously doubt she did him much good."

"Even goddess-like powers have their limitations," Crow said with a smile. He looked around. "Ah, that's the lesson. For all his power and wealth, Fei died inches from his comfortable couch. The goddess of the bedroom wouldn't help him. None of these goddesses helped him."

"Why should they? They don't owe us anything."

Crow grinned and pointed at Huizhong. She raised an eyebrow. "Yet we pray to them anyway. We burn incense and say prayers and, in the end, we die inches from their images with holes our bodies while they watch."

Huizhong covered her mouth and laughed. "That was the most melodramatic thing I've ever heard."

"Thanks," Crow said. "I used to practice it in my mirror."

"Still the same old Felix Crow," Huizhong replied. "Not taking anything seriously."

"I take things seriously," Crow replied.

"When you take things seriously, I wind up getting choked."

Crow opened his mouth and held up a finger, but no words came out. He took off his hat and ran a hand through his hair. He started to say something again, but again couldn't think of the right words. Yes, he had choked Huizhong. Yes, he had wanted to see her lips turn purple as the oxygen in her blood depleted.

"I wish I could say I was sorry about that, but you did knock me out and leave me to die sandwiched between two slabs of stone."

Huizhong lowered her head and stared at the floor. "I'm sorry about that. I was deep undercover and had gotten orders that you were to be neutralized. I had no idea someone switched my medicine or that you'd wind up one of Chenming's playthings."

"You were supposed to kill me?" Crow asked.

She nodded slowly. "Chenming's head guy, Robinson, he knew you were sniffing around. He wanted you alive. It was Ao Shun that wanted you dead."

Wheels turned in Crow's head. The whole situation didn't make sense. Why would a Southern dragon stuck up north want him killed and then, when he did die, somehow resurrected him and sent him back with the power to make things go kaboom? "Ao Shun is the dragon from the North, right? Lives in a forest, hangs out with chicks with bows and arrows?"

Huizhong nodded. "Her name is Mab. She's nice when you get to know her."

"I must not know her," Crow mumbled before continuing. "Unless her idea of being nice is shooting arrows at people. That dragon, Ao Shun, brought me back to life. Why would he want me dead?"

"Because you're an asshole?" Huizhong asked.

Crow shrugged his shoulders and grinned. "I am, indeed, madam. I am indeed. Still doesn't explain why a Southern dragon is hanging out up North. Let alone why he would want me dead. I take you think it was this Robinson character that was behind the whole thing?"

Huizhong shook her head. "He didn't have the brains or

the drive. Robinson was completely loyal to Chenming Zhang. He was Chenming's *dāpèi g□u*; loyal to a fault."

"He looked like someone who was reincarnated from a lap lizard," Crow replied.

"Robinson never had a single original thought in his life," Huizhong said. "He was the living embodiment of everything that is wrong with the world."

Crow let out a long whistle. He often wondered if he wasn't as good a person as he wanted to be. Then he decided he was happy lurking on the sidelines and doing the odd nefarious job if the money warranted it. Even at his darkest moments – those times when it's too early to get up, but far too late to go to bed – he never thought of himself as being evil.

"It's not often you hear someone described like that. Loyal lap lizard. Heh, heh. That's your reward for being a lackey; the world remembers you in the worst possible way. What happened to him, by the way? I'd like to kill him, but no one seems to know where he is."

Huizhong shrugged and closed her eyes. "I got out of town as quickly as I could after Chenming died. We left the building, you went one way, I went the other. That was the last time I thought about Robinson."

Crow paced around the room, examining statues and Fei's dubious taste in decoration. He stopped suddenly and peered around the room with new eyes. "Did you realize all these women are naked? I think Fei had a thing for the ladies."

"Following your train of thought is giving me a headache," Huizhong moaned. She stretched out on the white silk couch and dangled her feet off the edge.

"Sorry, kiddo, this is how I think," Crow replied as he paced around the room. His mind was a whirlwind. There were too many things going on that he knew had a connection, but he couldn't figure out what they were.

"No wonder you live alone," Huizhong replied.

"I have my little dragons."

"They probably ignore you. Nüwa knows I'm trying to."

The discussion was interrupted as Jolan groaned and tried to sit up. Crow stared at him, a malicious grin on his face. Huizhong sat up and watched. "How do you want to play this?" she asked.

"I can handle it," Crow replied. "You look tired."

She shook her head. "Exhausted, but no way. Because of this guy, that boy might lose his friend."

"Good cop, bad cop?" Crow suggested.

"Trite. Everyone does that. How about I sit here and look menacing?"

"Bad cop, bad cop," Crow replied. "I like it."

"Bad cop, worse cop?" Huizhong asked.

Crow grinned and nodded before turning his attention Jolan. "Well, good evening shit head."

"Where...," Jolan stammered.

Crow cocked an eyebrow, but didn't say a word. He had enough experience to know the best way to interrogate a suspect was to get them off balance from the get go. Jolan looked around with a dazed look in his eyes. "Where?" he asked again.

"Where what?" Crow asked.

"Am I?" Jolan asked. His eyes were wild. Crow knew the withdrawals would be kicking in soon and he'd be reduced to jabbering, wailing sack of waxy bones.

"I'd like to say you're safe," Crow said, "but that would be a lie. Your brother wanted to kill you. I'd like to cut you up. She's on the fence, but I suspect she wouldn't mind killing you. You smell like *lā sh*□. You look like *lā sh*□. And, to make things even worse, the shakes are about to hit you like the fist of an angry god."

Jolan's eyes slowly focused on Crow. The man was a complete wreck, a broken piece of detritus that still managed to look somewhat like a person. "What ... want?"

"I want to peel the skin off you layer by layer. I want to cut your eyelids off. I want to cut your lips off. I want to do a lot of things. Because of your dumb, drugged up ass people are a dead. Granted they weren't good people, but they're dead. See that young lady over there? She'd love to gut you. I have other plans, though."

Crow put his hands in his pocket so his coat would flow out behind him and stepped toward Jolan. "A boy may lose his best friend because I went to talk to you and your dumb shit brother showed up with other plans. Your brother's dead, by the way. I suspect some of your former buddies have eaten him by now. Never could understand cannibalism, but when you're hungry a meal's a meal."

Some of what Crow said penetrated what was left of Jolan's mind. He held up his hands defensively and nearly fell over from the effort. "No," he stammered. "Not fault."

"Not your fault?" Crow asked. "Every piece of *lā sh*☐ drug user I've ever met has had the exact same story. Not your fault you're a waste of flesh. Not your fault you got hooked on poison. Not your fault you're dying and there's nothing you can do about it."

Crow pulled a wicked looking knife from behind his back and showed it to Jolan. "Do you know how much blood is on this dagger?"

Jolan shook his head. The realization that someone wanted to cut parts of him off had temporarily woken his mind. His eyes were wide and twitchy. Crow knew the shakes were starting. Once they hit full-bore, Jolan wouldn't be able to do anything but vomit and scream. The rumors on the street said Heaven's Powder withdrawals were soul crushingly bad.

"It's killed no less than two dozen men. I used to be a cop here. We were worse than any of the stories on the streets. The stories on the streets were stuff told by survivors. Now, you don't have long and I have something to ease your pain if you're willing to talk."

Crow dug in his pocket and produced a small paper envelope. "Heaven's Powder. I picked it up off a guy under the pier earlier today. Don't know if it's any good, but it's all you've got. Or, you can go through the shakes. They're only supposed to last a week or so. When they're done, I'll start cutting parts off you."

Jolan got on his hands and knees and scrambled toward Crow. His eyes were locked on the little packet. "What do you want?" he asked.

Crow kicked him in the teeth when Jolan got too close. The man scrambled back, but his eyes remained on the envelope. "Information," Crow said. "About The Beast."

Jolan stopped and looked at Crow. He shook his head violently.

Crow wondered what it was about The Beast that an addict would rather suffer withdrawals than talk. Heaven's Powder was new when he left the force, but they had picked up a few people who'd been habitual users. Police procedure was usually to let someone sober up before their real problems started and the junkies got to deal with a police department that had no love for law breakers.

"I was a cop, you know. Back in a better life, I was a member in good standing of the greatest street gang in the city," Crow said. "We brought in the first *Tiāntáng De Fěn* addict, he looked like every other junkie on the streets. Within a few hours, he was hurling himself against the cage and screaming for a taste. By the end, he'd peeled strips of flesh off his own face. Cannibalism, madness, pain. That's what you're in for.

"What do you think your skin will taste like? Whatever you were eating under that pier or something worse than long pork?"

"Crow!" Huizhong said.

Crow ignored her. He was back in his happy place, pushing around victims until they cracked and gave up everything. "When it was all over and his face was a bloody mess and his finger nails were stuck in the muscles, do you know what he said?"

"Crow!" Huizhong repeated.

Jolan stared in silent horror. He was rich kid, raised in pomp and circumstance by people who didn't even understand the meaning of pain and he was far, far out of his league.

"He said it was better to be in pain than what he was feeling when the drug ripped his soul out. Back in those days, we had sorcerers on the payroll. They weren't the happy sorcerers who would conjure up riches or love; these guys were mean. The one in my precinct was known for the work he did at Qincheng. Remember that one? The one where a latent psychic dreamed too hard and the world fell apart. Wang Chi went in there and cleaned up the mess. No one else would do it. They say he made the two hundred prisoners explode rather than deal with them.

"Well, ol' Wang Chi took a look at the room our man shredded himself in and refused to enter it. The *chi* was corrupted beyond repair or some such thing. All I know is Wang Chi wasn't afraid of anything; but he refused to go into that cell.

"My point is: you think you're feeling bad now. Just wait. Or tell me what I want to know and I'll slip you a little extra time off your life. You can keep getting hopped up on daddy's money until the summer suns boil your brain."

Jolan threw up again. Crow sighed and wondered how someone who lived under a pier could find so much to eat. Junkies, by and large, didn't do the best jobs of taking care of themselves, and food was usually way down on their list.

"This is going nowhere," Crow said. "We need to secure him. As soon as the shakes start in earnest, he'll start talking just to make the pain go away."

"No," Jolan said, wiping vomit from his chin. "It's already bad enough."

Crow looked at Huizhong. She shrugged. "Up to you," she said.

"I think we should secure him anyway," Crow said with a

glint in his eye. "I knew a guy that taught me some amazing ways to secure people. He runs the ropes over at Núyì."

"The bondage club," Huizhong said.

"You know it! Great. Yeah, he ties women up for money and they apparently love him for it."

Huizhong rolled her eyes and started to say something, but Crow was on a roll.

"Anyway, he used to specialize in something of a lost art. You know how it used to be that you couldn't be convicted of a crime until you confessed? Well, he was one of the guys that helped people, uh, confess to crimes they may or may not have committed. His specialty was tying people so that no matter what they did, it was painful. People would confess just to get untied and thrown in a dank cell."

"You know some charming people," Huizhong replied.

Crow smiled and pointed at Jolan half passed out on the floor. "He taught me a few tricks where it makes it feel like no matter what you do, your arms are going to pop right out of their sockets."

"No," Jolan said. "I'll talk."

"We could also cut his balls off," Crow continued. "It's not subtle, but I've found if you do one then threaten the other, people tend to talk."

"I'm glad I'm a woman," Huizhong said.

"Paper cuts on the nipples work wonders," Crow said. "Those work pretty well for guys, too."

Huizhong wrapped her arms around her chest and groaned. "You do know he said he'd talk, right?"

"I'm just thinking out loud," Crow said. He spun on Jolan and menace crept into his voice. "Because if this g☐uz☐izi doesn't tell me what I want to hear, I want him to understand what he's buying himself."

Jolan flopped on his back and rubbed his eyes. His hands twitched and spasmed. When he opened his eyes, they were wild. He was having trouble looking at any one thing in the room for more than a moment. "What do you want?" he asked in a shaky voice.

Crow squatted down in front Jolan and patted his head. "Tell me where to find The Beast."

"Under the Clock Tower," Jolan said. "That's all I know for sure. There are tunnels under there and he hides out in the darkness. I never saw him, but his voice will rattle your brain."

"The Clock Tower?" Crow asked. He turned to Huizhong. "Are there tunnels under the Clock Tower?"

She shrugged. "I've only heard rumors. But it's possible."

"See," Jolan said, pointing at Huizhong. "I've told you what I know. Can I go now?"

"Sure," Crow said and stabbed him in the throat. "See you later."

As the light faded in Jolan's eyes, a calm expression washed over him. All the tension in his body left and he fell backwards. The throat wound was serious, but survivable, but it was the way the knife pierced the spinal column that paralyzed the man. He smiled a curious, melancholy smile that said Crow's knife didn't condemn him to death, it freed him from life.

Crow shook his head and spat on the corpse. "Let's get this cleaned up before the others get here."

16 | Huizhong Xīdú

Huizhong closed the door to her room and leaned against it. Whether it was to keep everyone else out or just to keep herself upright she couldn't say. She sighed, clenched her fists, and bit her tongue. Dealing with Crow was just as much of a pain in the ass as she remembered it was. Screaming, no matter how much she wanted to, wasn't going to help things.

She looked around the room and shook her head slowly. Crow was right – damn him – Fei Long may have had an unnatural knack for gathering information, but he couldn't decorate a room to save his life. Huizhong wasn't a firm believer in *feng shui*, but even energy would have trouble moving in this room.

The bed was massive. For a master bedroom, it would have been huge, but in this tiny back bedroom the gigantic bed with the black silk sheets and blanket was so big it was almost oppressive. And circular, too.

Above the bed were black and white paintings of naked women cavorting with demons. For a moment, Huizhong thought about turning around and going back out to the living room. But, for all the chintzy horrors of the room, it was quiet and she needed the silence and the space to pull her head together.

Outside of the room, outside of the apartment, the city was alive. In the room, she felt insulated from the frenetic energy of the world. It wasn't her forest, but it was better than nothing.

She kicked off her shoes and gripped the floor with her toes. The wood was warm and smooth. Hints of life still echoed through the pale planks, faded now and overcome with whatever passed for life energy in Fei Long's love den.

Part of her wanted to avoid the bed, unsure of what she'd be sitting on, but Fei didn't look like the type to entertain ladies very often. Besides, the fastidiousness of the room made it look like the sheets were sterilized or incinerated immediately after Fei did his dirty deed.

Huizhong sat on the bed tentatively. To her surprise, it didn't come to life and try to take advantage of her nor did it feel rock hard. It was comfortable. Firm, yet still soft. She laid back and stared at the ceiling while she tried to remember when she last got to lie in a bed. It had to have been before the flight. That meant nearly a full day. Out in the forest with Ao Shun and the Furious Fae, a bed was nothing more than a cot.

She should be exhausted beyond belief. The airship ride alone should have pushed her over the edge, but the rest of the day proved to be even harder. Yet, here she was, staring at the ceiling while her mind refused to calm itself.

Huizhong tried to force sleep to come, as if she could go to sleep by sheer willpower alone. But her mind was having none of that; it sped along and refused to be shut down. Images flashed through her head – Jonal's shock of blond hair, the thankful look on Jolan's face as he died, the horror in the boy's eyes as he held his dog.

To say it had been a long day was a gross understatement. At least lunch had been good.

Finally, after a short eternity of staring blankly at the ceiling, she sat up and decided a walk might calm her jittery-jattery brain. The city she loved to hate was just outside and down a bit. Huizhong wasn't familiar with this part of town, but there had to be something nearby that would serve her a drink.

Money. She'd need money. She patted her vest and found a few bills. While she unfolded them to count out her cash, something fell onto the bed. Huizhong looked down and found a small paper packet with *tiāntáng de fěn* written on it.

"Heaven's powder?" she asked the packet. "Where did you come from?"

Then the morning came back to her. The flight. Jonal "blissed out" and that young man with the funny hair putting this packet on the armrest of her seat. She held it up to the light and shook it. Maybe that's what the kid meant about blissed out. Heaven. Bliss. Heaven's powder blisses people out.

Huizhong had never done drugs – legal or illegal – in her life. Her parents believed in traditional medicine. Heal the whole person, don't just treat the symptom, her father used to say. Whenever she got a fever, he took her to the local *Zhōngyī*. The man would poke her and prod her and ultimately give her a cup of steaming hot green tea.

And, as if by magic, Huizhong would feel better.

At the time, she thought the green tea was the medicine and even tried to use it whenever she got sick when she was older. After a particularly nasty bout of fluid lung, her local *Zhōngyī* explained that it was never the tea – although the tea was good for the body. It was always the powders and herbs that were dissolved into the tea.

Maybe this stuff worked the same way. Jonal didn't seem at all affected by being blissed out for the whole flight. His brother was an obvious addict, but she didn't have to go the full route. One time couldn't hurt. Maybe Heaven's Powder would help her relax and get some sleep.

She gently tore open the packet and peeked inside. A fine, white ashy substance was in the packet. It didn't look dangerous. In fact, it looked an awful lot like the powdered Shui Fong root that every *Zhōngyī* in the world seemed to have.

The only question remained how to take it. Surely it couldn't be injected. Jonal didn't have track marks anywhere that she could see. Snorting it or smoking it would have raised a few eyebrows on the airship, yet somehow or another Jonal had tuned in and dropped out.

When the answer hit her – obvious in retrospect, but fiendishly well hidden – Huizhong slapped her head and groaned. Green tea was ubiquitous in Croatoa; people drank more green tea than anything else.

She snuck out of her room and nearly stubbed her toe on a statue blocking her path. Huizhong covered her mouth and limped to the kitchen to start some hot water. Crow was sacked out and snoring on the white sofa. His perpetual smirk was gone and, for once, he looked innocent. Chan and Kevin were in their own rooms.

A quiet chirping sound startled her. Huizhong turned to find the bird-lizard creature watching her. Its amber eyes glinted in the faint light of the room. After seeing what the thing could do, she kept her distance from it. Chan and Kevin insisted the thing was safe, but those claws on its feet still terrified her.

"Shoo," she hissed.

It cocked its head and let out a low trilling sound. Feathers ruffled and it tapped its huge claws on the floor.

"Shut it, dinosaur," Crow snarled. "I'm gonna turn you into a pair of underwear."

That's right, it's a dinosaur, Huizhong thought. An ancient creature brought back to life by whatever magic that boy had. The boy unlocked an instinct in all of them, a desire to protect him. She didn't know his whole story, but anyone who could conjure life out of thin air was someone worth taking care of.

The dinosaur chirped again, sounding distinctly huffy, but it snuck back into the boy's room and disappeared. Huizhong slowly let out a breath.

"Why are you still awake?" Crow asked.

Huizhong looked over at the couch and found he hadn't moved. In the darkness, she couldn't be sure, but it looked like his eyes were still closed. "Getting some tea. Too much excitement today. I can't calm down."

"Fei probably has some *baiju*," Crow mumbled.

"Tea will work."

"Suit yourself," Crow replied, "but *baiju* is better than any tea."

She snorted and continued to the kitchen. "That's just because you're a drunk."

"I'm not drunk now, therefore, I am not a drunk."

"Sounds like something a drunk would say," Huizhong replied.

Crow rolled over on the couch and pulled his jacket around him. On the nights that *Dà māmā* and *Xi□o m□qīn* both set, the nights got cold. "It is something a drunk said."

"Which drunk?" Huizhong asked.

He didn't reply. Soon she heard him start to snore again and headed back to the kitchen. Fei Long was a meticulous housekeeper. Everything had a place and everything was in the right place. The forced neatness of it made it seem like the apartment was the end result of demonic summoning.

As the water boiled, Huizhong thought about where she was in the world. Sure, not everyone could become the head information gatherer in the city, but what was she doing with her life? The one time she was genuinely happy was in the forest and here she was making tea in an apartment decorated with tastefully muted paintings of naked women.

Things could be worse, she thought to herself, *I could be one of the models for the paintings and know someone like Fei Long was staring at my naked body all day.*

The tea pot's hissing brought her back to reality and she quickly took it off the burner before it started screeching and woke up everyone. The hiss faded to a sigh that matched Huizhong's sigh. She poured a small cupful of boiling water and mixed a spoon of dried green tea into it.

With a final glance at the naked women and the graffiti tag on the wall, she walked back to her room.

Her tea was steaming when she stared into the open the packet of Heaven's Powder. It may have been her frayed nerves, but Huizhong could swear she heard a faint hiss and growl coming from the powder. She sniffed it before dumping the powder into her tea. It smelled like the spices and warm flat bread from her youth.

The effect of the powder hitting the tea was anticlimactic. After the hiss and growl, Huizhong expected something more than the powder dissolving. She didn't know what she expected, a burst of magic or a cloud shaped like a skull like in the vids she watched growing up. Instead, the powder spread across the surface of her boiling water and melted away into nothingness. It was a bit disappointing.

She sniffed the tea briefly, but the spices and flat bread were gone. The way her day had been going, the kid on the airship probably gave her some fake stuff and she was about to drink *xiē* poison.

"Enough stalling," she told herself. "Bottoms up. Time to either get some rest or go visit Ho Hsien-Ku."

Huizhong closed her eyes and sipped the tea.

It tasted exactly like green tea. Good green tea, the kind the rich people keep for themselves, but green tea nonetheless. *Maybe it will take a while,* she thought.

At least the tea was good and it was already calming her down. Or was that the Heaven's Powder? No matter. She wandered around the bedroom, examining books that Fei would never read again and touching the dead man's statues of gods and goddesses in all kinds of sexual positions.

The man had a thing for sex, she thought as she pondered a statue and wondered how two people were supposed to do...that.

As she sat on the edge of the bed examining the statues, she sipped the tea. Soon, without her even noticing the time passing, Huizhong looked down and found the cup empty.

Still she didn't feel the effects – whatever they were – of the drug. She put the statue down on the bed stand and got up to look at another one. Again, she was stymied by what she saw. It was sex, but not as she knew it. Some people would look at the statue and immediately be turned on by it, but all Huizhong could think was how much her lower back would hurt. The risk of neck damage was remarkable.

The statue came into sharp focus. Every little detail, the impurities in the paint, the actors in the statuary scene, the pores on her hand, was magnified and intensified. She looked closer and closer at the statue until she found tiny pinpricks of light dancing in nothingness.

Huizhong gasped and reached out a hand to touch the statue. It still felt like smooth jade, but she felt like she was also touching its very essence.

The world around her shimmered and danced. Her mind reached out and found the whole of the universe waiting for her, singing an endless song of creation and destruction.

"Beautiful," Huizhong whispered. "So beautiful."

There, standing in the middle of the universe and finally comprehending the depths and layers, Huizhong made a choice. In the face of everything, nothing seemed to matter. Not her indecision about who she was, not Crow, not Chan, not Kevin, not even the dinosaur. They weren't things that were separate from the universe, they were part of the universe in the same way she was part of the universe and their individual decisions and actions didn't matter.

Nothing mattered. Everything was running at the whim of the whole.

Wait. That couldn't be right. If that were correct then nothing would be anything and anything would be nothing. She shook her head and tried to ignore the eternal rhythm of the universe. She closed her eyes and thought back to Ao Shun.

What had the dragon said about the universe? It was everything and nothing and under the nothing was everything. He said they glided along the *Tao*.

The *Tao*, the underlying principle of the universe. Opposites constantly swirling and colliding and being reborn.

Ao Shun didn't say dragons were of the *Tao*, he said they glided along the *Tao*. The dragon knew what the universe really looked like and had learned to look beyond what he saw on the surface. Huizhong closed her eyes again and sought out a single vibrating pinprick light. When she saw it with her mind, it was much clearer. Instead of a single thing, it was lots of little things. Balls constantly orbiting other balls in a miraculous display of clock making on an incredibly tiny scale.

But it was still surface strata. She pushed closer and closer until the balls resolved to their pieces. Then those pieces resolved to pieces so small she could change them just by looking at them. At deepest depth, she found the quantum universe, a place with completely different rules than even the pinpricks of light adhered to.

Another universe buried under her universe. And likely another one under that. Then another one under even that. And they were all dancing to slightly different tunes.

Suddenly, everything made sense. Everything was interconnected and things that happened influenced other things in a rippling effect. But it wasn't that what happened didn't matter. No, it only appeared that way. It was that reality rewrote itself based on what happened, so it always appeared that nothing mattered.

There wasn't a plan, there was a constant stream of changes and collapsing realities that made it look like there was a plan. Much in the same way that insects could perform what looked like complicated rituals, but were really nothing more than a series of simple rules strung together.

In the universal scheme of things, nothing mattered and everything mattered. Yin and yang. Creation and destruction. A whole universe built on the binary concept of this and that. Duality was so much more than Huizhong had ever thought. It wasn't just male and female, alive and dead, great and small. It was real and not real. It was there and not there.

She smiled and collapsed back on the bed. As she stared up at the hand-carved ceiling, Huizhong felt she finally understood things. Matter, doesn't matter, whatever. All choices were inherently fine because the interaction of things was rewritten to make it okay.

That was the true path of the *Tao*: it wasn't non-action, it was a realization that any action that followed the *Tao* was okay and, therefore, wasn't worth the stress of worry. Going against the Tao was like going against the ocean, only on a much larger scale. From there, she understood what the ancients had said bout *Wu Wei*. Non-action didn't mean do nothing, it meant flowing with the eternal energies of the *Tao*. It meant stop fighting. Be natural. Be yourself. With a satisfied mind for the first time in months, Huizhong closed her eyes and slept the sleep of the wise and innocent.

In her dream, she glided on the Tao.

17 | Awakenings

Chan had a habit of going from completely asleep to completely awake. He understood other people could spend time in bed, relishing the slow process of waking up and greeting the morning. That wasn't how he was, though. The sun came up and Chan was immediately, irrevocably awake.

He climbed out of bed and resolved to find some tea for breakfast. He wasn't much of an eater. His master and his master's master and so on down through the ages had instilled in their students a very simple, but easy to misunderstand, rule: Food is fuel.

Chan wasn't linear enough to think the rule meant no fried tarantulas, but unless he was actively hungry he rarely ate. Right then, his tank was full.

He crept silently out of the room and looked around Fei's living room. Crow was still stretched out on the couch, snoring quietly. Huizhong's door was closed. Chan put his ear to Kevin's room, but heard only silence. Usually the dog was snoring, but considering her wound he wasn't surprised she was quiet.

The living room was huge and mostly empty. Apparently, Fei Long had a thing for art, but not much else. It boggled Chan's mind that anyone would need such a large space, but the sparsely furnished room would work to his advantage. He moved to an area far away from any doors and set about his morning workout.

Chan was no longer a young man. In fact, he'd seen the tail end of youth disappear into the sunset decades ago. He wasn't old, but the only thing that kept him on top was constant practice. His art had ceased to be an art and had become a way of life. Fighting drove him to stay in shape, to eat well, to read philosophy, to teach. Anything and everything to make himself a better fighter.

He knew he didn't have much more time left in his fighting career. There were always young raptors wanting to rule the flock and it was only a matter of time before one of them clawed his eyes out. Better to retire of his own volition than to be forcibly retired.

Every morning, without fail, Chan practiced. He'd learned from a series of masters and taken what they had taught him and fused it into a practical, lethal system. That system required only that students learn it and, most importantly, practice it.

Chan started with his salutation. His first master, Xiang Shao had taught him the salutation shows respect for both the opponent and the practice. Of course, this was the same master that decided to teach Chan how to take a punch on his birthday. Chan showed up to his surprise party at the orphanage with two black eyes and a wide grin.

The salutation was rich in meaning. The hand positions symbolized mind, body, and spirit; the legs moved lightly, as if treading on rice paper. After the salutation was ended, Chan decided to practice his form blindfolded. He scanned the room and found nothing that would work as a blindfold, so he closed his eyes and went about the form's movements.

Xiang Shao was a firm believer in the power of touch. In addition to being able to manipulate the world, he swore skin provided more information than eyes. The old man could feel things that young Chan could never see; a faint hint of breeze moving in front of a punch, the way the floor shifted as someone moved about. Master Shao's tutelage was all about how to feel one's way through a fight. It was a rite of passage to finish Master Shao's form blindfolded in a strange room. The first time Chan attempted the rite, he broke his foot kicking a metal pole and was out of training for the better part of a month.

He eventually learned to feel his way around a strange space, a skill that had helped Chan innumerable times.

Over the turns, Chan had fused pieces of dozens of forms

into his own form. He kept his eyes closed as he felt in circles with his feet. Once he was sure there wasn't anything in his way, Chan struck. If anyone had been awake and watching, it would have looked like Chan's arm glimmered slightly. His punch was fast enough that most people would never see it coming.

He pulled back into a cat stance and felt around with his toes again. This time he ranged further out and his foot brushed a stray piece of furniture. Chan turned, pulled back, and released a flurry of kicks. The first kick was aimed at an imaginary opponent's knee. The second snapped between the opponent's legs. The final kick rose straight up into the imaginary opponent's nose.

When the kicks were done, Chan again pulled back to a cat stance and felt around the room. The entire form followed the principle of attack, defend, and pull back to assess.

As he continued the form, Chan's senses expanded to the world around him. That, Master Shao had taught, was the key to doing the form blindfolded. The way sound echoed could tell if something was nearby. A faint hint of breeze could mean something had moved. He gently stroked the floor with his bare feet, sweeping away threats that could be stepped on or slammed into.

His speed increased as his focus increased. Soon, Chan would pull into a cat stance and explode back out of it. When an opening was available, the form taught, it was imperative to strike and strike hard.

At the end, Chan opened his eyes and found Huizhong watching him. She had a cup of tea in her hand and a curious look in her eyes. "How did you do all that with your eyes closed? Didn't you worry about hitting something?"

Chan was naturally shy around people; Crow, Mrs. Chow, and Kevin were the only ones he really allowed into his life and even most of them were kept at arm's length. "I studied," he said and immediately worried he came off as condescending. "What I mean to say is, I had a teacher who encouraged me to study."

Her eyes were large and sparkly in the morning light. Something about them made Chan think something had happened. He was hardly an expert with women, even though there were always throngs of them at the fights who wanted a piece of the champion. Chan kept his distance and disappeared into the crowd, not sure of what to do or say to them.

"Who was your teacher?" Huizhong asked as she settled onto the sofa. She curled her legs underneath her body and set her tea on the arm of the couch.

Chan shook his head, pushing thoughts and questions out of his mind. "I've had several. They all taught me something. The form I was just doing was a variation of Master Xiang Shao's Hunting Crane form. It emphasizes contraction and expansion."

"I noticed that. Toward the end, you were moving so quickly it took me a moment to understand you'd even moved at all."

Chan blushed and bowed his head to her. "Thank you. If I had known I would have an audience, I would have done more. Perhaps a more fluid form from Northern Dragon style."

"As far as I could tell, it was perfect," she replied. "But I would like to see the Northern Dragon style form someday."

Chan's heart swelled. "Northern Dragon style forms emphasize similar movements; retreat then counter-attack from a different angle. Personally, I think the form implies that Northern Dragons are duplicitous in nature."

"They are," Huizhong replied.

"She'd know," Crow said groggily. "She lived with one. A real jerk of a dragon, too."

"Back from the land of the dead, I see," Huizhong said and sipped her tea.

Crow sat up and looked around the room like he couldn't figure out where he was. He looked worse than usual, but

Chan had to admit he hadn't seen Crow in the morning in many turns. Age and *baiju* had taken a toll on the man. His face was puffy and his eyes were shot through with red lines.

"Are you okay?" Chan asked.

"Fine," Crow said and flopped back down on the couch. "Never better."

Huizhong rolled her eyes. "You look like *lā sh*□, Crow. Mother *baiju* isn't doing you any favors."

"She's dulling the world-weariness in my soul," Crow replied. "Or something like that."

"Your problem...," Chan started.

"There's only one?" Crow asked.

Chan sighed and wondered if Crow was legitimately trying to kill himself or if he was just so far gone that he didn't realize what he'd become. "Your problem is you have spent so much time with the bad people of the world, you have forgotten there are still good people out there."

"I was a cop, now I find things," Crow said. "Cops rarely see the best of the world. No one ever calls the police when there's fresh tea and pastries; cops only get called when the world has turned to *lā sh*□. No one ever asks me to find something good. I spend my days looking for cheating husbands and missing money. Good people don't pay my bills; bad people do. And most people fall into the bad category when there's anything of value on the line."

"That's a seriously messed up philosophy," Huizhong said.

"Say what you will, it's an ethos," Crow said. "So, what were we talking about? Dragons? I met a dragon in a dream once. He was a jerk."

Chan cocked his head to the side and held up a finger. He wanted to continue the conversation, but the weeping sounded like Kevin and that could only mean one thing.

He bowed his head to Huizhong and Crow and rose. "Something is wrong," he said as he headed toward the door to Kevin's room.

Crow leaped to his feet faster than he should have been able to and followed. Chan opened the door and the sound got louder. It was definitely a young boy's cry. Inside, Kevin sat cradling Tina's head in his lap. Dino was behind them both, his feathered head propped on the boy's shoulder. Tears were streaming down Kevin's face as the dinosaur chirped and trilled quietly.

In a voice that was barely above a whisper and reeked of pain and loss, Kevin said, "She's dead. She was trying to protect me and now she's dead."

18 | Elegy For A Foreigner

When he was a young man, before he started on the police force, Felix Crow spent some time palling around with the gangs in his neighborhood. They were strictly low-rent, small-time gangs, focused mostly on staying alive in Croatoa's poorer neighborhoods. Crime was rampant and even a small group increased survivability significantly.

Crow had a tendency toward violence and propensity for hurting people. Growing up in an orphanage had taught him to take what he needed and Chan had taught him to fight. Unfortunately, neither of those things taught him any kind of ethics. He was inches from becoming one of the *Jiē Mógu*□ – the street devils that die young, violent deaths – when an old man with a cane and a beard to his knees opened a monastery in the neighborhood.

A new place meant the possibility for new things, so the gang went in one night with the intent of stealing everything that wasn't tied down. They found an empty room with two candles and the old man floating in a lotus position a few feet off the ground.

Even in Croatoa, a floating man was an odd sight. Magic existed, and most people knew about it, but it wasn't terribly common. Anyone with magic used their skills to escape the *Pínmín qū*, not come back to it. Crow and his two friends – Jackie and Feng - stopped and stared at the man with a kind of wonder in their eyes.

"*W*□ *de tiān a*, that *hāhuā gōngz*□ is floating," Feng said.

"You've got a flair for the obvious, *Mótuō Chē*," Crow said. "Of course he's floating."

Poverty breeds fantasy, a desperate need to escape the real world that left people behind. It was far easier to explain the world in supernatural terms than to ascribe the bad times to a vast array of choices made and kept. Anything out of the norm could be best described as the work of any number of *mógu*□ – devils – that worked incessantly to bring pain to the world.

"People don't float down here, *hāhuā gōngz*□, he's some kind of *mógu*□," Jackie added.

Crow didn't buy it for a second. "*Mógu*□ are supposed to be filthy rich with all the things they've stolen."

"So," Feng asked. "What's your point?"

"Look around you," Crow said. "This guy doesn't own *lā sh*□. How can he be a *Mógu*□ if all he owns are a pair of candles?"

The logic seemed to mollify his compatriots somewhat. Of the three of them, Crow was the accepted smart guy and the others tended to accept his intellect.

"Maybe he's a new *Mógu*□, and he's here to steal everything," Feng said.

"Or maybe he's not," a voice said.

Everyone jumped. Knives came out as the small gang looked around for the source of the words. The floating man was still sleeping, so there had to be someone else.

"Who said that?" Jackie asked the empty room.

The floating man continued floating, completely unconcerned with the world around him. His face was impassive. Not even his clothing moved. He could have been a floating statue for all the movement he made.

"I said it," the voice said again.

This time, Crow's keen eyes saw the smallest hint of movement on the floating man's face. "He said it," Crow said, pointing at the floating man.

Feng and Jackie slowly approached the man. They were halfway across the room when the man's eyes opened. Inside those brown orbs was a serenity Crow had never dreamed possible. It had never occurred to him that he could spend his days being serene and content in the face of crushing poverty and rampant drug use. Rather than constantly scrabbling for the next thing, he could relax and let the world go by.

"Why are you here, old man?" Crow called out.

"Why are you?" the man replied.

Crow's face turned red and a lump formed in his gut. Had the man kicked up a fuss or threatened to call the cops or just stayed quiet, none of this would have been an issue. But rather than looking worried or threatened, the man seemed completely nonplussed by kids with knives. And that left Felix Crow in a strange place. The idea of telling the truth – that they had come to steal anything and everything – made him feel petty and weak.

"We want your money, pops," Feng said.

"Yeah," Jackie chimed in. "Give us the loot. Riches, old man. Where are the riches?"

"The only riches here do not sparkle. I can share them with you if you'd like. You can take everything I have to offer and I will still have everything I have," the floating man replied.

It happened so quickly, Crow wasn't certain anything happened at all. One moment the floating man was watching them, the next he was on his back and Feng's knife was in his stomach. Even then, the monk didn't scream or even look like he was in pain.

"What the fuck?" Crow yelled. "He said he didn't have anything."

Feng yanked the knife out of the monk's stomach and shoved it in Crow's face. "You don't know shit! He said he had riches but wouldn't share them."

Crow raised his hands and spoke as calmly as he could. "He said his riches don't sparkle, that he could share them and still have them. It was a riddle."

"It wasn't funny!" Feng yelled. He pushed the tip of his knife closer to Crow's eye.

"Yeah!" Jackie said. "Riddles are supposed to be funny. He was playing us and got what he deserved. Hey! Feng! Now that you've killed that guy, maybe the Green Gang will take us."

"Shut up, Jackie. I killed him, not you."

Crow rolled his eyes and, not for the first time, wondered how his life had come to this. "He was talking about knowledge, *bái chī*. No sparkles. He can give it away but still keep it."

Feng's beady eyes darted around the room, but the knife never wavered. "You're the *bái chī*."

"It's still not funny," Jackie added.

"Riddles aren't supposed to be funny," Crow said, "they're meant to make you think."

"You know what I think?" Feng asked. "I think you're weak and stupid, *bèn dàn*. I think we don't need you in our gang."

Crow rolled his eyes. "Some gang," he said. "We kill floating guys for no reason? I don't think I want you in my gang."

Feng growled and pushed the tip of the knife right under Crow's eye, just barely breaking the skin. A single drop of blood dripped slowly down his face. The knife was in Feng's right hand, Jackie was behind slightly and to the left. Chan taught Crow to assess the situation as much as possible and make sure no one was left in a position to keep up the fight.

Crow twisted slightly, pulling his face out of the way and slamming his right hand into Feng's outstretched arm. At the same time, he used his left hand to fold Feng's arm at the elbow while he snapped a kick straight up between his legs.

As Feng crumbled, Crow turned his attention on Jackie. A vicious punch to the nose rocked Jackie's head back. Before the blood could even flow from his broken nose, Crow stepped slightly to the side and kicked into the side of Jackie's knee. The kick took Jackie completely off-guard and he started to fall even before the pain hit his receptors.

Crow turned back to Feng. The man was on his knees, holding his balls and whimpering. A roundhouse kick to the face drove him backwards until his skull bounced off the bare concrete floor.

Jackie was prone on the floor. Tears welled up in his confused eyes. He never was the brightest bulb on the marquee and couldn't understand why his friend Felix Crow just crippled him. But Crow was beyond such trivialities now. He was an empathetic man and, even if he didn't always care, pangs of guilt would keep him awake at night. The sight of an old man who had offered to share wisdom, dying in a pool of blood just because his hophead friend didn't understand something, forced Crow to evolve.

He knelt next to the dying man and whispered, "I'm sorry."

The old man had some strength left in him. Even as his life leaked out on the floor, the man grasped Crow's bicep with vice-grip like force. "You have started a path today, and I am happy to have helped you along as your friends have helped free me from this frail, old body."

His eyes locked on Crow's and stayed there as the fire inside slowly faded. When there was nothing left, Crow closed the man's eyes and walked to the nearest police station. As he filled out a report of a dead man and the murderers, a recruitment flyer caught Crow's eye. He couldn't hack it as a criminal, maybe the other side of the law would work better.

Life and the endless pursuit of dulling it had taken their toll on Felix Crow, but he never forgot that moment when his life changed and the amount that change cost. As he stared down at an old dog that had given her life to protect her boy, he wondered if he would ever have the same commitment that she did.

Tina's body was wrapped in whatever cloth they could find in Fei's apartment. She was unique on the planet, so it seemed fitting that her funeral shroud would be unique, too. Even through the haze of misty eyes, Crow wondered where Fei Long managed to find sheets with naked women on them and whether or not the dog would find them somehow appropriate.

He couldn't say how he came to be the first to speak, nor

could he say why he felt such sorrow at the death of an animal that he barely knew. All he knew was he felt empty inside. He stared at the floor and started speaking, telling whatever came to mind.

"Over the turns, I've managed to do all manner of terrible things," he said. "There are times when I feel I have wasted a new life that was given to me long ago, but I still manage to keep on. Yesterday, something terrible happened. Some bad people died, but it's not enough to balance it all out.

"When I was young, I ran roughshod over the world, like I was Hundun after a three-day bender with YI-DI. I was always confused about what my life was supposed to mean. Then I saw a man die. Not just any man – I'd killed several people by that time – but a special man. A man who wanted me to do something better with my life. I … believe. I believe he wanted to go. He'd walked his path and wanted me to start a new path. Maybe it led to the *Tao*, maybe not, but it was a new path and that was good enough for me.

"I so wanted to bring that man back to life and learn his secrets. But, in the end, I've learned two things: one, there is no coming back to this life and two, he passed his ultimate secret on without so much as moving a muscle.

"You see, we all take paths and make choices and not all of them work out well. Sometimes the choices help others, sometimes they help us, and other times our choices amount to nothing. But the path always moves forward."

Crow cleared his throat and downed a glass of *baiju*. He wiped the mist from his eyes and chuckled to himself. "I think my choices should serve as a warning to everyone else."

Nervous, detached laughter responded, as if everyone else knew they were supposed to laugh, but couldn't manage to get their hearts into it. Crow accepted the polite laughter by raising his glass and bowing his head.

"That wasn't the secret," Crow said. "The secret was we're all on a path whether we want to be or not. When you find yourself at 3am standing outside a strip club and holding your broken nose it might not seem like a path, but it's a path.

"Death will come for everyone. That's the sad fact of life. You have a lot of choices: follow the path or ignore the path, be rich and stupid or create something amazing and die in obscurity. Some people..." Crow paused to stroke the sheet-wrapped body of the dog. "Some people get the choice to choose their own death and those are the people we should look up to with jealous eyes.

"Yesterday, Tina gave her life to protect someone else. She didn't realize she was giving up her life; all she knew was there was a threat and she was going to deal with it. Perhaps that's the pack mentality, the unending desire to protect the pack – to protect home – at all costs.

"And that's definitely something to look up to with jealous eyes. For not everyone gets the chance to have their death mean something. Most of us will die in our beds or falling off cliffs or getting into drunken brawls and nothing will come of it.

"A strange animal that has never been seen before on this planet found a home and a pack and died to protect that pack. And that's a death that means something."

Crow absently wiped his brow and took another swig. The small bundle, wrapped in naked women, was all that remained of her physical body, but lives are so much more than bodies; they expand and touch other lives and form a collective. Lives remain in that collective, even after the body has decayed.

Kevin, tears streaming down his face, leaned into Huizhong. Crow felt a deep emptiness coming from the boy – after all, he'd felt the same thing himself many a time. Late at night, when the *gu□zi* rang and wanted to party with their fangs and horns, he reached out and felt nothing out there but the faint echo of a dying man's last words: *You have started a path today.*

Started and restarted and restarted again in an endless iteration of failing and getting back up.

"Thank you," Chan said. He put his hand on Crow's shoulder and fixed him with a serious stare.

"What?" Crow asked.

Chan looked around the room like he was worried someone was listening in. "We still have problems. Jonal was not working alone, he was here for his brother. Also, while I was fighting Lo Pan, someone shot him with an arrow. I would very much like to know who did it."

"You know," Crow said, remembering a hazy memory that didn't seem all that important. "I saw a couple of Hoqwua's other kids yesterday at a tea house. It was strange place for rich kids to hang out. I just assumed they were slumming it, but what if they were after Jolan, too? Or up to something else."

Chan nodded sagely. "That is a distinct possibility. Hoqwua has a long reach. We should watch ourselves. Kevin must never be alone. If one child of Hoqwua worked for The Beast, there's a fair bet the others have too."

"*Aiya*, maybe Hoqwua is The Beast. He's certainly got the drive," Crow replied.

"What do we do now?" Kevin asked.

Crow's heart skipped a beat. The boy had snuck up on Crow and Chan without either of them noticing. Months of training with Chan had apparently paid off, he was silent as the night breezes coming off the ocean.

"What do you mean?" Crow asked.

Kevin pointed at the wrapped body. "With her. Do we bury her?"

"Burial is extremely rare on Aluna," Chan said. "Tradition dictates we burn her."

"Is there any way to bring her back to life?" he asked. "I mean, there's magic here. Can't that magic bring her back?"

Crow grunted as he settled onto one knee. "I won't lie to you, Kevin, there is magic that can bring people and other things back from the dead. I've seen it work myself."

The boy's face lit up. Hope settled into his eyes. "Can we

do it?"

"It's illegal, but I know people who can do it and I strongly recommend against it," Crow said. "Once a person dies, all their energy – the stuff that makes them who and what they are – vanishes into the *Tao*. You can call it back, even stuff it back into its old body, but the results are always catastrophic."

"It was used as a torture technique for especially heinous crimes," Chan added.

"Why is it catastrophic or torture?" Kevin asked.

"As the energy dissipates and blends with the Tao, it grows," Chan said.

"It would be like shoving your feet in shoes that are four sizes too small and walking around town," Crow added. "There are other things, too. The times I've seen it done were terrifying. The energy that came back desperately wanted to get back out. We had a case many turns ago where a man was accused of killing women, but we could never find the bodies and had to throw the case out. I got a tip from a girl I knew to go check out an abandoned school.

"The guy was a murderer, but he was also a budding wizard. He'd kill women, absorb their power and use it to reanimate their bodies. Then he stuck their energy back in so he could keep torturing them. He had them all in cages, all shrieking because it was too much to bear to be stuck in a body once they'd become energy. That's one of the reasons we tend to burn bodies here; less chance of some *dà mó tóu* deciding to torture the dead by bringing them back."

"I am sorry for your loss, Kevin," Chan said, "but what he is saying is true. It would be an act of unspeakable cruelty to bring her back."

Kevin's face fell, but he nodded. "She was my last touch of home."

Huizhong wrapped her arms around him, but he didn't relax. Crow could see the signs in everything the boy was doing. His body was rigid, fists clenched tightly. He recognized himself in the young boy who just lost his safety net. Unlike Crow, though, Kevin was extremely dangerous. His latent magic ability was downright frightening.

Dino nudged the boy and chirped. Kevin's hand idly stroked the dinosaur's feathered head.

"If you ever need a home," Huizhong said, "just find me and I'll make you a home."

Kevin nodded again, but the rage was still burning in his eyes. Too much had been taken from him for the boy to ever be the same again. He closed his eyes and took a deep breath. As he slowly let it out, some of the tension leaked from his body.

"Can we take a walk?" Kevin asked Chan. "I need to be anywhere else right now."

"Of course," he replied. "Is Dino coming with us?"

"Yes, please," Kevin replied. His voice sounded hollow, even to Crow's jaded ears. "We're a pack of two now."

19 | We're Missing Something

"That is odd," Chan said.

Under the brim of the *d☐ulì*, Kevin could see his furrowed brow. Chan was rarely confused; he was one of the most plan-oriented people Kevin had ever met. And that included Kevin's great-grandmother who needed detailed notes in fifteen-minute increments to even go to dinner.

"What's wrong?" Kevin asked. He and Chan had decided to wander the city while Kevin tried to put his broken heart back together. The noise and tumult of Croatoa wasn't helping his mood, but it was taking his mind off Tina.

Chan pointed at a small, dusty storefront. "That was Chung Li Soo's shop. He had been there for decades. I was here only a few months ago and he gave no sign of retiring."

Kevin shrugged. "Maybe he moved."

"People like Chung Li Soo do not move. Their shops are part of their power. In order for magicians to move after they have been in one place for a long time, they have to find another magician to take their place or the magic in the store becomes restless."

"Restless?" Kevin asked.

"Magic needs someone to control it or it becomes unstable and dangerous. Sorcerers amass vast amounts of magic and it becomes part of their stores. Chung Li Soo knew this and would never leave his store without setting someone else up in there."

"Could he have died?"

Chan peered through the dirty window and shook his head. "All his things are still there. He was old, probably a few hundred turns, but in magician terms that is not that old. When magicians of Chung's power pass away, the Clock Tower sends a team to collect their belongings. Magic saturated things are bombs once the magician that controlled them has passed."

"Bombs?" Kevin asked.

Dino trotted up to the window and cooed softly. Chan reached down and scratched the dinosaur's head idly as he peered through the glass. "His books are still here, too. No magician leaves without his books. Something is not right here."

Chan walked to the next storefront and knocked on the door. An old lady invited him in. Kevin started to follow, but Chan held up a hand. "Please stay here. I will only be a moment."

The door clicked shut and left Kevin and Dino standing alone on a street corner, wondering what to do next. He leaned against the wall and watched people passing by. The city was truly a spectacle. Croatoa wasn't a gem, but it was carved out of magic and that made it amazing in Kevin's eyes, even if it didn't look like a place on a different planet.

All around him, the city hummed. Even at night, people went about their business as if the crackling magic powerlines were nothing special and the art that shifted and changed on the walls was perfectly normal. It all still boggled his mind.

From the maps he'd seen, he knew Croatoa was on the southern tip of one of the great continents. To the north, desert stretched out, but here in the city it was humid and breezy. Trees that looked just alien enough to remind him he was on a different planet pushed against buildings that would have been at home in any city on Earth.

When he was younger, Kevin had a fascination with sci-fi books. He'd sneak them off his dad's bookshelf and read them when no one was looking. Alien worlds were supposed to be these shimmering, organic-looking things where it was difficult to tell what was built and what was grown. There was supposed to be neon everywhere. It was supposed to be high-tech and filled with robots.

Instead Croatoa was surprisingly pedestrian. The magic signs were neat, but the overall look of the city was so normal it was almost boring. People came and went; they sold things and bought things and watched fights and vids of old plays.

He stood on the street corner while Dino chirped and chittered and watched things. He'd always been a good observer. His teachers liked to say he could learn from just watching things. Maybe it was true. All Kevin knew was he was good at seeing things other people missed.

For instance, a thin purple tendril was idly floating down the street. This was odd enough, but what made it strange was everyone else on the street either didn't see it or didn't care. Kevin looked back down the street, hoping to find the origin of the strange sight.

There were too many people and there would be no way to see a building over a mile away. No wait, a few *li* away.

Kevin leaned on the stone walls and picked at his nails. He'd seen tough guys do the same thing in Earth movies and wanted to project just the right amount of cool.

He was in deep cool mode, studiously ignoring the world while taking it all in, when a thought hit him. How did he know there was a building a few *li* away? Worse yet, how would he know the purple tendril came from that building?

Kevin stared at the purple tendril as it delicately touched people on the street. They didn't even notice it was happening. How could someone be touched by a purple tendril and not notice it?

"Chung Li Soon has not been seen in weeks," Chan said. "He went to sleep one night and no one has seen him since."

Kevin motioned him over and pointed down the street. "Can you see anything odd down there?"

Chan peered down the street and nodded slowly. "The woman with the tiny dragon on her shoulder? That is normal. Many people keep tiny dragons as pets."

"No, the purple tendril thing."

Chan looked, but finally shrugged his shoulders and looked back at Kevin. "There is no purple tendril thing out there."

"It's touching people on the street. They don't feel it, but it's happening. I swear, I'm seeing this, Chan! What is it?"

A serious look crept across Chan's face. He stopped looking down the street and gazed hard at Kevin. "Touching people?"

"Yes, yes! It's touching them on the head and then moving on."

Without a word, Chan grabbed Kevin and pulled him down the street toward an alley. He clucked his tongue and Dino came loping after them. The dinosaur looked disinterested, like he'd rather be hunting the people on the street, but followed along.

"Chan," Kevin said. "What's going on?"

Chan clamped a hand over Kevin's mouth and whispered, "Shh. Not a sound. Tap me if the tendril gets close. I will explain later."

Together they watched the street pass by from the comfort of their dark alley. Kevin's sharp eyes kept a lookout for the tendril and he gasped slightly when he first saw it. It didn't seem to have noticed them. As people passed under it, the tendril gently touched their foreheads before moving on.

It passed the alley and Kevin let out a sigh of relief. Whatever it was, it had Chan spooked and he didn't spook easily. His sigh turned into a gasp as the tendril backtracked. It hovered at the end of the alley like it was looking at them. Kevin felt weighed and measured. He glanced behind him and found nothing but a wall. They were trapped.

He tapped Chan and felt the master tense. Another first for Kevin.

"Don't move," Chan whispered.

The tendril stopped in the middle of the alley and turned slowly in place. Kevin stopped breathing and refused to blink. Behind him, he could feel Chan turn into a statue. The tendril floated in space, undulating like a neon snake.

Kevin figured it had to be a drone of some kind. He'd heard of drones on Earth, robotic aircraft that could fly without help from people, but this thing was like no airplane he'd ever seen. Up close and not moving, the tendril was more like a fat snake that expanded and contracted its way through the air.

He was certain the thing could hear his heart pounding. It floated and looked around like an animal that knows something's there, but can't figure out where. Finally, it slowly backed up and moved out of the alley.

His lungs were burning. Kevin had to force himself to breathe again. The glowing snake was bad enough on its own, but the effect it had on Chan chilled Kevin to the bone. Whatever the thing was, at least it was gone.

Kevin slowly turned and looked at Chan. The master's lips were set in a thin smile. He searched for anything in the master's eyes that would tell him what to do, but Chan's whole focus was down the alleyway.

Dino rubbed against Kevin's hand. He stroked the dinosaur until Dino let out a loud chirp of satisfaction. Everything stopped. Chan and Kevin both peered down the alley. When the neon snake reappeared, Kevin wanted to scream.

It moved slowly and purposefully down the alley, heading straight at them. Kevin tapped Chan over and over, but the master didn't respond. They looked around the alley and found they were completely boxed in. That thing was going to get them and it wouldn't be good.

Without warning, the tendril darted forward until it hovered right in front of Kevin's face. Kevin tensed, uncertain of what to do. The tendril stretched out until its tip hit Kevin's forehead.

Then, as quickly as it appeared, it disappeared into nothingness.

Kevin looked around, mentally checking behind things, but couldn't find the tendril anywhere. It was just gone. "Well, that wasn't so bad, right?" he asked quietly.

Chan's face was serious and he had that glint in his eye

that he got before training. "Get ready to run. I hope I am wrong, but if I am right we are in a lot of trouble."

"What?" Kevin started. Before he could finish the thought the air crackled and pulsed around them.

Kevin's hair stood on end. Dino hissed and let loose a scream that set his teeth on edge. Distantly, he felt Chan step back. The master was flexing and releasing his fists, getting ready for battle.

Chan's head was down, eyes invisible under the brim of his *d□ulì*. His body was relaxed, but ready. It was the state he constantly drilled Kevin on being in. A relaxed fighter focuses on fighting his opponent; a tense fighter fights the opponent and also fights himself.

"Combat magicians," Chan said quietly. "I will do my best to distract them, you must run."

A loud popping noise announced the arrival of the first of the combat magicians. Kevin dropped low, unsure of what else to do. Everything slowed down.

The combat magician had glowing green eyes, barely visible under his d□ulì. He was dressed like one of the monks from downtown – the guys that were always screaming about how the world was coming to an end. There was fire and madness in his eyes, like he'd seen something that shorted out his brain and left only twisted remains.

The magician oriented himself and looked straight at Kevin. He didn't waste time raising his arms or performing elaborate gestures with his hands; he just closed his eyes and the wall behind Kevin and Chan erupted.

Two more pops and, barely visible through the dust cloud, two more magicians arrived. They worked as a team, standing in a triangle and focusing their energies. Kevin felt the air turn rancid as the magic was sucked out of it and bent to the will of the combat magicians.

Dino was the first to react. He leaped at the first magician. The look on the magician's face turned to horror as huge claws on Dino's hind legs slammed into him. Whatever magic they were working stopped immediately as the leader went down in a mass of feathers and teeth. His cries went from surprise to pain to a gurgling sound as Dino's teeth found his throat.

Chan took advantage of the confusion to run toward another magician. A lifetime of constant practice and training had made him fast, but the combat magician was faster. Chan threw a punch and was amazed to see it hit nothing but air.

The man countered with a punch of his own. Chan barely managed to block it before the next fist was flying at his face. Every time he tried to counter-strike, the magician calmly stepped out of the way and punched Chan somewhere else. It was like he could sense was a strike was coming and got out of the way before it even fired.

The magician took advantage of Chan's discontent. A mighty backhand swatted Chan aside.

Chan rolled with the blow and came up on his feet. Already the side of his face was swelling, but he didn't back down or cower. He'd been hit harder in the fights, but there he expected it and was prepared. The combat magician wasn't a big guy and there was no way he should have been able to generate so much power from a simple strike.

The remaining magician focused his efforts on Dino, who proved to be much tougher game. Humans have natural weapons that are good for grabbing, smashing, and crushing. Deinonychus was a biological killing machine, honed to perfection in a world filled with other killing machines. Dino also had the advantage of being completely unique on the planet and that uniqueness gave him an edge over a combat magician that had only ever fought humans.

Dino was lower to the ground than humans, standing only waist high to the magician even though from tip of nose to tail, he was almost 40 hands long. For such a large creature, he moved with amazing agility, hopping and leaping back from the magician's array of kicks before charging forward and snapping at whatever he could.

Attacks that worked on humans simply didn't apply when it came to Dino, but that didn't mean the combat magician didn't try. He tried a punch that would fell any human and found his arm grasped tightly in a mouthful of razor sharp teeth.

While Dino held his own, Chan focused on changing his tactics. If the magician could sense attacks before they came, Chan had to find other ways to attack. He watched carefully as the combat magician dodged his punches and decided the man relied too heavily on his magic and not enough on his skills. Every time Chan threw a right jab, the magician dodged to the right. He was probably seeking easy access to Chan's dead side so he could land a crippling blow, but Chan had learned to keep his guard in place.

Chan threw a right jab that was so fast it should have been invisible to any normal person. Just as he expected, the magician dodged to the right. Chan faked high, forcing the magician to deal with a second punch, but he kicked out with his right leg at the same time.

The magician dodged the second jab just in time to feel Chan's foot hit the side of his knee. A hideous popping sound escaped from the man's leg before he fell to his other knee. To his credit, the magician didn't make a sound as Chan dealt him a crippling injury.

Meanwhile, Dino still had the other magician's arm in his mouth and was trying to rock his head from side to side. Instinct told him to destroy the enemy's limbs rather than immediately kill it; that way the food was still warm when he started to eat. The other magician finally got a chance and used it to kick Dino in the side of the head. It drove dinosaur teeth into his already mangled arm, but hurt Dino enough to make him let go.

He took advantage of Dino's momentary disorientation to help his fellow combat magician to his feet. Both magicians did their best to back away from their attackers. Their eyes were still hard and focused, though, jaws set resolutely. They glanced at each other and shared the realization that they weren't going to escape.

Together they closed their eyes. Before Chan and Dino could finish them off, the air seemed to change around them. Kevin felt it first and even though he wasn't trained, he recognized something was amiss. The air felt charged and heavy, like it did before the sky exploded and the rains hit.

He focused on the feeling and rode it back to the source. The combat magicians aimed to detonate every single thing in the alley and hope the resulting explosion would take care of their problem even as it killed the magicians themselves.

Kevin felt power rise inside of himself. At first it felt like butterflies in his stomach, then there was a sense of being one with everything. When he felt the siren song of oneness, Kevin reached back to the first combat magician and then over to his partner.

"Duck," Kevin yelled.

Chan didn't wait for an explanation, but he knew the dinosaur didn't understand. He threw himself at Dino and prayed the beast would realize he wasn't a threat. Before Dino even knew what happening though, the alley exploded.

Power flowed out of Kevin's small body and poured into the two combat magicians. They were caught completely off-guard and unused to chaotic Earth magic. They would have brushed off traditional Alunan magic, but the Earth variety overwhelmed their defenses. The effect was just like what happened when someone touched a magic powerline.

The first monk's arm blew off. The second one's good leg exploded in a mass of red and pink. Kevin's chaotic magic continued to work them over. Limbs exploded and eyeballs popped as the energy surged through their bodies.

In the end, there was just the ammonia and ozone smell of renegade magic mixing with the burned bodies. Chan tentatively approached the nearest one and nudged it with his toe. When he didn't get a massive surge of magic pushing through his organs, he knelt and examined what was left of the body.

Kevin stepped forward slowly, terrified not only of the combat magicians but of what he'd done to them. It was one thing to blow up a stuffed dragon, but these men were humans.

"It was not your fault," Chan said without looking up. "You are not a murderer. You were protecting yourself from someone who intended to do you harm."

"How do we know that?" Kevin asked. "We never asked what they wanted and they never said a word about their goals. These guys could have been cops for all we know."

Chan dug around the corpse, seeking anything that would tell him who these men were and what they wanted. Warrior monk clothes had a lot of pockets and the uniform of the combat magicians was far more complicated.

The buttons on Chan's dead guy were fused shut. Chan grabbed the man's tunic and pulled. The material eventually gave way and exposed the man's bare chest. Chan pointed at a tattoo on the dead man's torso and said, "There is something strange about these markings. That tattoo means he's untouchable, but it doesn't look quite right. He's Green Gang, fairly high up in the organization, too."

Kevin looked down and the still-smoldering corpse and wondered if the man's heart exploded or if it was just the trauma of having his legs blown off that killed him. His face was still covered by a mask, leaving only his unfocused eyes staring at nothing.

"I killed him," Kevin said. "I killed them both."

A sense of power came over him. For the first time since he walked across time into Aluna, he felt like he wasn't struggling to keep up with the world. He didn't feel like he was hiding behind Chan and Dino and anyone else who would rescue him.

Chan kept rooting through the dead man's pockets. "They would have killed us," he said.

"I know," Kevin said, a hint of joy rising in his voice. "But

I got them first."

Chan looked over his shoulder and noticed the glint in Kevin's eyes. He recoiled slightly, but recovered quickly. "I don't think we are safe yet. These guys are with *Qīng Bāng*. Their brothers will want to know what happened."

"Bring 'em on," Kevin said.

Dino stood next to Kevin and twitched his long tail. Chan looked concerned, but Kevin couldn't understand why. He did exactly what Chan had always taught him to do; Kevin took care of himself and he did it on his own.

20 | Chow Down

Madam Chow's was a different experience at night.

For instance, during the day she was Mrs. Chow. At night, when the bar was hopping and the *baiju* was flowing, she became Madam Chow. Everyone wears a different face, acts a different way when the situation calls for it. In her case, she wore a whole new persona that matched her bar.

During the day, her bar was a quiet, inoffensive place. Even local businessmen and healers found their way to her doorstep in search of solitude and legendary noodles. At night, however, Madam Chow's was far from quiet or inoffensive.

Stylized gang signs, carved into the walls and burning with green and purple magic, matched the stylized gang members and hangers-on that frequented the bar at night. Various alcohols flowed, easing the transition between people who merely wanted sex and the people having sex in the bathrooms.

Madam Chow was a firm believer that everyone should have drunken toilet sex at least once in their lives. She might have been a dangerous woman, even an unpleasant woman at times, but Madam Chow had her plusses.

Felix Crow had spent the better part of the night alternating between watching the crowd with wistful longing and allowing Madam Chow to keep refilling his *baiju*. To call him drunk would be a criminal understatement. Crow had transcended drunkenness in the way Buddha had transcended the physical body.

He was one with the booze.

"Why do you do this to yourself, Crow?" Madam Chow asked him. She had to yell to be heard over the music.

Crow looked around, trying to lock onto whichever of the several Madam Chows had asked him a question. His mind was so far gone, he wasn't entirely certain which one had spoken, but the one on the far left seemed nicer than the others.

"Do what?" he asked.

Madam Chow pulled a chair from a nearby table. The young man sitting there started to say something, but recognized her and immediately backed down. She sat, ramrod straight with her ankles crossed and shook her head; the portrait of demure beauty. Behind the façade, though, lurked the heart of a killer. In a way, wondering about Crow drinking himself to death was nothing more than professional courtesy.

"You're killing yourself," she said. "I don't want it to happen in my bar. Moving bodies isn't cheap."

"It is when you know the right people to call," Crow replied. "Want their numbers?"

"I have my own people. They're professionals."

"My people are professionals," Crow said. His head was lolling from side to side as he talked, making the seven Madam Chows into fourteen Madam Chows. He pointed a finger at her and asked, "Did you know there's a guy? He does this kind of thing. I think he said he feeds the bodies to the guys under the piers."

"That's a myth, Crow. No one under the piers eats people."

Crow shook his head sadly. "Nope. It's true. I've seen it happen. When I was on the force, we had to go under pier 9 to, uh, talk to a guy."

Madam Chow shook her head and chuckled. "You mean beat him."

"Well, I'm not going to lie, yeah we beat his ass half to death," Crow said. "Point is, he was a bad guy. We found him eating a kid."

Felix Crow felt the weight of the world come crashing down on him. Kevin, the poor lost soul that he was, lost his one final link to the world he knew when some rich punk stabbed his dog. He sagged in his seat and took another shot. At that point, he was so far gone no amount of alcohol could make him drunker or further dull the pain.

"That was you?" Madam Chow asked. "That guy always made me nervous. He was like a *xiē* with its stinger pointed right at me. I almost had him taken out myself."

Crow smiled a lopsided a grin. His eyes couldn't focus on much, but he could see a glimmer of ... not really friendship, but at least comradery in her face. "Just serving and protecting."

Madam Chow held up her hands and snapped her fingers. A waiter appeared and handed her a clean glass before vanishing into the club again. Madam Chow reached across the table and poured herself a shot from Crow's mostly empty bottle.

She downed the glass in a single gulp slammed the glass back down on the table. "I supposed I should thank you for that. You saved me some money and time."

Crow nodded. "A lot of people thought we went too far on that one, but I say leave kids alone."

Madam Chow poured another shot and raised her glass to toast him. It took a few tries, but Crow finally managed to clink his glass with hers. "To the suffering of the destroyers of innocence."

They each took a drink and looked across the table at each other. "It's the only part of the job I miss," Crow said sadly. "Mostly we were thugs with fancy uniforms, just another street gang, really, but I do miss kicking the *lā shǐ* out of bad guys. Did you know, I once pissed in the empty eye sockets of a child rapist? True story. There was a girl missing and we found her in his place. She was a mess, but we saved her. Rather than put this guy on trial, we took him to a warehouse. I carved out his eyes and pissed in the sockets. How screwed up is that?"

"Is that why you left the police?"

"Why? Because I pissed in some guy's eye sockets? No,

but it was the first time I looked at myself and wondered what I'd become."

Madam Chow lowered her eyes. A faint hint of sadness danced across her face. "We all make choices, Crow. While those choices make us what we are, they're not always easy pills to swallow."

"Don't take this wrong way," Crow asked, "but why this sudden interest in me?"

"I was watching you with that boy the other day. He looks up to you and I wanted to make sure you weren't going to screw it up."

Crow chuckled. "See, that's the Mrs., uh, Madam Chow I know and love to hate. Don't worry, I'm not planning on actively screwing up the kid."

Madam Chow moved her hand dismissively. "Thank you for your time, Mr. Crow."

Without another word, she rose from her chair and disappeared into the crowd.

Crow's brow creased as he tried to understand what just happened. The gesture was obviously a signal of some kind. He was still here, so it wasn't a signal to slit his throat or lead him into the cellar. Crow's vision was blurred and he was having trouble keeping his eyes open, but training egged him into looking around the bar.

Two men, hard cases by the look of them, on either side of room waved at him. Crow squinted, trying to force his eyes to focus. Minor details escaped him, but one of the men seemed to have a scar across his face. Unable to figure anything else out to do, Crow waved back.

The noise was giving him a headache. He knew he should go back to Chan and Kevin, go back to Huizhong, but he couldn't get his mind to issue the right commands to his body. His limbs felt like lead. Whatever kind of *baiju* Madam Chow served had a kick to it.

His bladder urged him on. It had been full even before that foul temptress brought her delightful nectar, now it felt like it was about to burst. With a mighty surge of discipline that would have impressed even Chan, Crow struggled to his feet. The world swirled and bobbed, but the table held him steady.

Food. He needed food if he was going to keep drinking. Bathroom first, then food. He staggered through the densely-packed crowd. Faces laughed and danced around him. No one paid any attention to his unsteady gait until he bumped into a man with a pinched face and squinting eyes.

Crow caught himself on the bar, but the man collapsed to the floor. A bag slid across the floor and the man scrambled to grab it before anyone else could pick it up. He wore a nice, well-tailored suit made of *Xīyì* scales and crisp *mábù*.

"Sorry, buddy," Crow slurred. "Nice suit. Let me help you with that."

The man hugged the bag to his body and pushed himself away from Crow's outstretched hand. "I'm fine, you drunken oaf," he spat.

"I may be drunk, but ... well, okay, I am an oaf. Still, let me help you up."

The man pushed himself further away, a look of panic in his eyes. "No," he said, climbing to his feet. "I'm fine. See, I'm fine."

"Okay, pal. Okay," Crow said as he adjusted the man's suit jacket. "Anyway, sorry. If you'll excuse me, I need to drain Doctor Lizardo."

Crow pushed past the man and hurried to the bathroom. A strange thought pinged around his slow mind as he urinated. The man with the bag seemed out of place. Everyone else was drinking, smiling, having a good time. But the man with the bag seemed tense and edgy.

No matter. Lots of people got tense in crowds. Ever since being sandwiched between two hunks of stone, Crow himself had developed a fear of being closed in. Maybe that was it; the guy just didn't like crowds.

If he didn't like crowds, though, what was he doing in

Madam Chow's at night? The place was always packed with wall-to-wall sweaty people talking too loud and jostling each other about. No one came here without drinking.

Crow shook his head and tried to clear the cobwebs. The couple having sex in the stall behind him wasn't helping, but he'd feel guilty if he told them to keep it down. It's not like he'd never been in their position. Drunken toilet sex was one of the main attractions at Madam Chow's and everyone knew that.

Something Chan said penetrated Crow's mind. Lo Pan had exploded. Not a lot of explosions in Croatoa. Every now and then a stray bit of magic would kludge up a transformer and give everyone an impromptu fireworks display, but actual explosions were rare. Rare enough that police were all over it. One of Crow's former partners confirmed the cops had rounded up more than the usual suspects. In holding rooms all over the city, gangsters were getting worked over for information they likely didn't have.

Explosion. Kaboom. Lo Pan was detonated by some kind of sizzling stick bomb. Usually one doesn't strap stick bombs to arrows and shoot them at chauffeurs. Usually stick bombs were carried in satchels. At least that's what Crow had figured out during the case of the miners.

Satchels. Bags.

"Oh, shit."

Crow zipped up and ran out of the bathroom, tossing an apology and a warning to the couple in the toilet stall to hurry up and get out of the building. He heard them accelerate just before the door slammed shut and he found himself back in the noisy bar.

His mind was still stupefied with *baiju*, but he pushed it aside as best he could and scanned the room. The man with the pinched face had disappeared into the crowd. Crow cursed, a long stream of profanities that would have made even YI-DI blush.

"What's wrong, Crow?" a voice asked. "Run out of *baiju*?"

He turned to find Madam Chow next to him. She handed him a fortune cookie, another insult no doubt, and started to turn away.

A commotion erupted on the floor. People packed in tight were being jostled about. The man with the pinched face was running toward the door and shoving people out of the way. As he ran, he kept screaming "*Qīng Bāng y□ngy□u Croatoa!*"

"The Green Gang doesn't own Croatoa," Madam Chow said. "I do."

A bright light caught Crow's eye and his heart sunk. He flipped his jacket out and spun around to grab her in a bearhug. She could be pissed off at him later. As they fell to the floor, a sound like Guan Yu growling erupted.

The next few moments were confusing. Madam Chow was trying to say something, but he couldn't hear her over the ringing in his ears. He rolled off her and put his hands on his ears to stop the noise. All around him was acrid smoke and the distinct smell of burning flesh and human hair. People's mouths were open, screaming in fear and agony. One woman pulled herself toward the door by her fingertips. Crow watched in horrified wonder as she dragged herself along with a lost look on her face, leaving a trail of blood from her severed legs.

He hated himself for it, but Crow sat up and looked around the room. The damage to the building was minimal. Pinched face had set off the bomb in the middle of the floor and most of the explosion was absorbed by bodies. Directly around the area where the bomb went off were the remains of the people closest to the blast. It was a bloody mess punctuated by severed limbs and crying people.

Madam Chow touched Crow's shoulder as she sat up. The look on her face was pure horror. In time, she'd muster her army and go after *Qīng Bāng*, but for now she was content to be terrified.

The ringing in Crow's ears slowly ebbed off and was replaced by the sound of screams. He decided the ringing was preferable to a club's worth of sobbing and screaming. Crow climbed to his feet and helped Madam Chow up. "You need to get out of here," he yelled over the din. "The police will be here soon."

"What about you?" she asked.

He fixed her with his best goofy scoundrel grin. "I was one of them and left on good terms. I'm hoping they remember that."

Madam Chow smoothed her long, red dress and adjusted her hair. "You should come with me. There are more ways in and out of my bar than ways for YI-DI to get drunk."

She grabbed his hand and tugged, but Felix Crow remained planted to the spot. "They have information. At least I'm hoping they do. Someone needs to pay for your bar." He grinned again and tipped his hat to her. "Without this place where will I find noodles to throw up on people?"

"You're not a completely loathsome man, Mr. Crow. Good luck. Don't forget your fortune."

Madam Chow took off at a good clip, rounding up her employees and disappearing through any number of secret exits. The bar was a honeycomb of different ways in and out and Crow had no doubt she and her staff would be safe.

He chose to walk out the front door and wait for his former compatriots. Anyone who could move was high-tailing it out of the area, but Crow stood still, hands behind his back at a normal parade rest. He might not be a cop anymore, but remembered the drill.

All around him, people limped off into the darkness rather than deal with Croatoa's notoriously difficult police force. Crow understood the cops' violent streak in a way none of them ever would. It was a tough job keeping a semblance of order in a city effectively run by gangs and the police usually didn't have time to play by the book. Add in a corrupt judiciary and virtually non-existent government, and all that was left was a group of people who enjoyed smashing heads in the name of safety.

Crow looked around and noticed something strange. Painted on the front door of Madam Chow's building was the ideogram of the *Qīng Bāng*. Just like in Fei's apartment, though, the drawing was crude and made several amateur mistakes that would be obvious to anyone familiar with the Green Gang.

The first police showed up in one of the few police cars in the city. It was decked out like the police themselves, clad entirely in black. There was no siren, no lights, nothing to let the world know it was coming; the police preferred the element of surprise.

Crow held up a hand, greeting whoever was in the car. All four doors opened and police in full armor stepped out. The first one, a woman with piercing green eyes headed straight at him.

"Crow, Felix," he said as clearly as he could. "DN38416. Assigned to Commander Shu Mong in the Northwest quadrant. Retired."

Her fist barely registered in his drunken brain. All he remembered was a blur, then a sharp pain. His head hit the stone walkway and bounced then everything went black.

21 | Information Extraction Techniques Part 2

Crow came to face down and drooling on a metal table. He groaned and tried to scratch his nose, but his hands wouldn't move. It wasn't the first time he woke up to a body that didn't feel like moving. *Baiju* could be a cruel mistress sometimes. His head was throbbing, but at least the metal table was comfortable even if it was a bit wet.

He opened his eyes and found the light too bright to deal with. People talk about red-hot pokers in the eye, but that's probably worse than what light felt like. Crow never had red-hot pokers jammed in his eyes, but he had done it to others and the screams made it sound like extremely uncomfortable. The light in his eyes was more like a stabbing sensation in his brain than a fire.

Stabbing he could deal with. Crow had been stabbed plenty of times in the past and managed to walk away from each one. He slowly opened his eyes and moaned when the light hit them. It wasn't as bad the second time, but it still wasn't fun.

By the third time, all he had do to was blink a lot and the pain eventually subsided, leaving him staring at an over-bright, blurry room. He decided there was nothing to worry about and closed his eyes again. Maybe when he reopened them, the room would be darker and his arms would work again.

A voice jolted him awake. "Are you going to lay there all day, *jièyān*?"

The night came crashing in around him. *Jièyān* literally meant quitter, but the only people who used it like that were cops. Being called a *Jièyān* was an insult slung around from academy on. No one quit the police force in Croatoa; they died on the job. The police protected their own, so even the retirees who killed themselves with mega-doses of *yāpiàn* were still listed as casualties of the ongoing war against crime.

To quit the police force in Croatoa was tantamount to admitting you were weak.

"Fuck off," he mumbled.

He wondered if the cop in the room was the same lady that slugged him. If that were the case, he had to ask her out. The lady packed a wallop. There weren't many people in the city who could drop him with a single blow.

It was better to be jerk in the beginning of the interrogation. Croatoa police loved intimidating people and couldn't handle it when suspects didn't show the proper fear.

"Are you going to fuck off? No, wait. Don't fuck off. Go get me *kāfēi*," Crow said. "That's it, fuck off and get me *kāfēi*."

He heard a snort from the same corner of the room where the voice had come from. "You can get your own damned *kāfēi* from the comforts of your very own prison cell. I'll make sure to send you my used grounds so you won't have to settle for the swill they serve in prison."

Crow slowly turned his head and found the owner of the voice sitting in the corner. He couldn't make out her face, but her voice certainly sounded familiar. "That's very kind of you. Are you sure you're a cop?"

"More than you ever were."

Details slowly resolved themselves, enough that Crow could see long hair. "I'll have you know I busted more crims before breakfast than you do all day."

"That's because you woke up in bars filled with crims. That's cheating."

"I woke up in lots of different places," Crow replied. "Bars were just more convenient than gutters."

Long, brown hair pulled back behind her head. Crow forced his eyes to focus on the face, but all he could find were piercing green eyes. He shook his head, remembering a woman with piercing green eyes and a furious punch. "Are you the one that punched me?" he asked.

"Dropped you, you mean? Yes, that was me," she said.

Crow chuckled. "You hit like a bitch."

"A badass bitch. Flattened your drunk ass," she said.

"Is that why I'm handcuffed to this table? Because you're such a badass that you can drop me with one punch?"

She laughed and shook her head. "You should know the answer to that, Crow. Shu Mong should have taught you to never leave a crim unchecked. And you, dear boy, are quite the crim."

Crow sat up and did his best to get comfortable. It wasn't an easy task with the cuffs digging into his wrists. She apparently followed protocol and locked the damned things as tightly as she could. He gave an experimental tug and found his hands were secure. "How am I a crim?" he asked.

"Blowing up a bar. Pushing Chenming Zhang out of a hundredth-floor window. Do those ring a bell?" she asked.

"I didn't blow up anything and last I heard Chenming fell," Crow replied. "I heard he had some, uh, body issues or something. Besides, I was nowhere near the tower when he fell."

She stood up and straightened her uniform jacket. Her green eyes bored into Crow. She walked calmly to the table he was chained to and took her time opening a large envelope. Her eyes didn't leave his as she pulled a series of photographs out and examined them. "Hmmmm," she said quietly.

"Who are you, anyway?" Crow asked.

"Chief Inspector Josette Faubus," she replied without looking up. "This is a particularly nice one. I like the way the light catches your features."

"Well, morning glory, it seems to me you don't have any evidence, so if you'd be so kind...," Crow said as he held up his cuffed hands.

Faubus slapped a picture down on the table. It showed Crow, slightly emaciated and looking manic, walking out of the Clock Tower with a crowd of other people. "Care to explain this?"

Crow glanced at it and slid it back across the table. "I like to learn about history. Got anything interesting? Maybe you in your underwear?"

She slapped down the rest of the photos, leaving just enough time between each one to let him glance at them. He saw himself talking to the guy at Mrs. Chow's just before he detonated the bar. Another picture was of him talking to the *Qīng Bāng* gangster at the tea house. Yet another showed him choking the druggie in the alleyway. A final one showed him standing in front of the *Qīng Bāng* sign outside of Mrs. Chow's, just before the police showed up.

Crow flinched each time a new picture hit the table. He wasn't worried about what he'd done, he was concerned that someone had managed to follow him without being seen. Something was terribly wrong and, somehow, he'd picked up a powerful enemy.

"Fake," he said calmly. "I know a guy that can make any image look real. Seriously, he could even make you look good."

Faubus bristled at the comment and Crow knew he had her number. Pissing people off was a gift he had and it served him well. He didn't have anything against the woman, she seemed competent and was doing the exact sorts of things he'd be doing in her place, but he needed information and the best way to get people to slip up was to piss them off.

"Fake?" she asked. "That's the best you can come up with?"

"Sure they're fake. Can't you tell?" Crow said with a leer. "Of course, you look like a rookie, so it's understandable. Then there's that whole, uh, less than attractive woman thing you've got going on. Look, I get it, you need a slam dunk so the Chief will get off your ass, but you don't have to be so bitchy about it. Besides, I'll bet you've faked things yourself, if you know what I mean."

She was around the table faster than he expected. With his hands cuffed he couldn't block the punch that slammed into the side of his head. A deep buzzing sound reverberated around his skull. Crow wasn't a *yīshēng*, he wouldn't even know where to begin healing a body. He wasn't even a *zhōngyī* with an encyclopedic knowledge of herbs and medicines, but he knew a solid blow to the side of the head and accompanied ringing wasn't a good thing.

"You really should have started with my legs or balls," Crow said. "Too much risk of losing consciousness when you start with the head. Didn't they teach you anything at the Academy?"

"They taught me to never trust a *jièyān* cop," she replied and punched him again.

Crow pulled himself back upright and glared at her. "Damn, girl. You don't have to be so mean."

Faubus growled under her breath and looked like she was going to hit him again. Instead, she adjusted her uniform and stepped around the table again. For the moment, Crow was reasonably safe. He knew Croatoa Police protocol was to eliminate any crims the officer felt were unredeemable within the first five minutes. She might beat him up, but she likely wouldn't kill him.

He focused on the metal in the handcuffs and set the little glowing dots in motion. From the corner of his eye, he could see Faubus pacing and hear her muttering to herself in a deep Western accent. He spared a moment to wonder if she moved to the big city to get away from small town life and wound up a cop or if it was always planned.

"What's your alibi, Crow?" she asked, trying to change her tactics. "Convince me you weren't involved and I'll let you walk. Mess with me and you'll spend the rest of your days locked up far away from your beloved *baiju*."

"Okay," Crow said, "how about this; what reason would I have for blowing up Mrs. Chow's joint or pushing Zhang out of a window? I find things, not destroy things."

"Are you trying to tell me you've never killed anyone or destroyed anything?" Faubus asked.

"Of course not. I was a cop, just like you. And just like

you, sometimes I wound up in situations where things or people got broken. It's part of the job. But it's a job I don't do anymore."

She picked up a folder and flipped it open. Crow immediately recognized it as a case file and he hoped it wasn't the one he thought it was. Faubus set it on the table and slid it to him. "Is this why you don't do the job anymore? Shu Mong said you were great once, but after this girl died you lost your zest for being a cop."

Crow stared down at the dead eyes of a girl not more than ten or eleven turns old. No one knew for sure exactly how old she was because, like so many of the kids on the streets of Croatoa, no one bothered to remember them. Being remembered, it would seem, was only for important people.

In the picture, there was a hunk of rotting, splintered wood shoved through the girl's heart. Her eyes were wide open, but there was nothing lurking behind them.

"Zeola," Crow whispered. "She went missing. I stumbled across her purely by dumb luck. She was being chased by sex traffickers or some damned thing. Had a bunch of wires in the back of her head. I tried to talk to her, but she bolted like a damned little dragon with a piece of stolen food. When I finally caught up to her, she was holed up in a run-down house that junkies had been using for a toilet. Whoever was chasing her decided it was easier to blow up the house than deal with the police. I jumped on her, tried to shield her from the blast."

A pregnant pause hung in the stale air of the interrogation room. "And wound up killing her."

"Yeah. That was when I decided I'd seen enough of the bad side of humanity."

Faubus pulled up a chair and sat across from Crow. Her eyes searched his for something, but he couldn't guess what from her inscrutable gaze. Remorse? Sorrow? It was a long time ago that Crow killed a ten-turn-old girl and he was long past the grieving stage even if her face was usually the last thing he saw at night.

With enough *baiju*, at least he could pretend Zeola was smiling.

"Interesting," Faubus said.

Crow tore his eyes away from the photo and that fateful night when the man who once gouged the eyes out of a rapist and pissed in his eye sockets decided he'd finally seen too much of himself. "What's interesting?"

"Well, you mentioned wires in her head. It's not in the report. Not that I think you're lying, but why would that not be listed?"

Crow flipped through the report until he came to coroner's report. She was right, there was nothing about wires in the back of the girl's head. He looked up at Faubus and found a human behind the green eyes, dark uniform, and badge. He shrugged. "I made damned sure to make the report as accurate as possible; it was my last one, after all. The only reason to leave anything out of a report is to be able to deny it happened later."

Her brow creased. "I'll buy that." She flipped through the pile of photos from earlier and slid the one of him standing outside Mrs. Chow's across the table. "These are real, by the way. I've had them authenticated by dealers on both sides of the law. That said, what do you make of the symbol?"

Crow glanced at it and knew exactly what to say. "Whoever made that was not *Qīng Bāng*. I worked with some of the gangs in town and *Qīng Bāng* guys are adamant about their tagging. There's no way they'd blow up a bar that everyone goes to and put up a half-assed tag like this; they're into extortion and the odd mugging. Blowing things up isn't their style."

"Maybe they're branching out."

"The Green Gang is the biggest gang in the city, aside from the police. They got that way by doing just enough to keep themselves from getting into too much trouble, not by bombing bars. There are neighborhoods in Croatoa where the people will go to the *Qīng Bāng* before they'll go to the police."

Faubus's shoulders sagged. She looked beaten down, like she'd been carrying the weight of the world on her back for far too long and someone dropped another problem in her lap. She straightened up, balled her fists and slammed the table as hard as she could. "Don't screw with me, *jièyān*. You and I both know what's really going on."

Crow jumped back and nearly tore his hands off at the wrist. Faubus could go from good cop to bad cop and back again like an expert. He had to admit, she was far from a rookie. Her eyes were full of fire again. Instinctively, he knew it was just a trick to get him off balance and keep him there; he'd used the same tactics on countless crims over the turns. But what really panicked him was when she walked over to the vidder on the wall and unplugged it.

The vidder was a report of sorts, and as he'd just pointed out, the only reason to keep something out of a report was to deny it later. He furiously focused on the little pinpoints of light that made up the handcuffs, willing them to move. The cuffs might take his hands off when they blew, but there was no way he was going to be beaten to death in an interrogation room.

Faubus faced him just in time to see the cuffs explode. Her eyes went wide and her mouth dropped. Crow staggered back and kicked the chair out of the way. He was just about to kick the table into her when she held up her hands and smiled. "So it's true. You can make things explode."

"Yeah. Just not people. It's a long story."

"Magic usually is."

"Look, I know what you're thinking, but I had nothing to do with Mrs. Chow's."

She shook her head. "I know. We've had the lab tests for a while now. The explosion was created by run of the mill explosives; nothing magical about it. We also dusted your hands while you were passed out; no residue on your fingers."

"Then why bring me in?" Crow asked.

"Sorry about the subterfuge."

Crow flexed his fists and wondered what game this was. Standard procedure when a crim broke free was to sound the alarm, but she hadn't made a move toward the big button on the wall.

"Subterfuge?" he asked.

"The ruse. Look, I agree with you. We got word from on high that you were to be apprehended and held. No one knew why. Until tonight, no one figured you in Chenming Zhang's death. But, from what I saw of the guy, if you pushed him out that window you did the world a favor. His corpse was snatched up before our guys could analyze it and we were politely but firmly told his death was Clock Tower business and we were to keep our noses out of it. This mess with the Green Gang tonight, too, is odd. No one else wants to think about it, but it doesn't make any sense. It doesn't match their operations, a bunch of their guys were there when the bomb went off, and no one, not even the Green Gang wants to mess with Mrs. Chow. Another anonymous tip told us they're expanding their operation. We lost an officer last week; he had a crudely drawn *Qīng Bāng* tag cut into his chest. It had the same mistakes as the one on Mrs. Chow's. What is going on Crow? You're out there on the streets, what have you seen?"

Crow relaxed, but kept ready. She could be leading him on. Healthy levels of paranoia kept him safe and he still didn't entirely trust her. "The same thing as you; nothing. Whatever's going on is deep. And why would anyone point the police at me?"

"You tell me. What have you been up to?"

He thought about that. The whole truth – looking for The Beast to kill him and take over his operation – was probably not the best thing to share, but an information exchange could come in handy. "I've been looking for The Beast."

She cocked her head to the side and covered her mouth to stifle a laugh. "He's a myth, Crow. There is no Beast."

"He's real," Crow insisted.

"If he's so real, how come no one knows where he is or what he looks like? No pictures, no reliable witnesses, nothing. He's a ghost because he doesn't exist. Our best guys figure he's a whole bunch of other guys trying to scare the criminals into not getting too out of hand."

Crow shook his head. He could throw out names like Fei Long or Jolan, son of Hoqwua, or even the Golden Monk, but he still didn't entirely trust Faubus. She could very easily be playing him or worse, setting him up to confess to something he didn't do. "I assure you he's real. That's all I can say at this point. It may be immaterial, though."

She crossed her arms and peered at him with those green eyes of hers. Crow felt like a bug on a stick, but didn't back down. "Immaterial how?" she asked.

"Look around you. You were ordered to bring me in and probably make sure something happened to me. Someone's been trying to pin an increasingly violent campaign on the Green Gang. Doubtless, there's information dropping into their laps, too. Someone is trying to pit the two biggest gangs in the city against each other. You've got a new drug on the street, too."

"Heaven's Powder," she replied. "We've seen it. No one knows where it comes from. We've grabbed a couple dealers, but they don't know where it comes from. The stuff shows up on their doorsteps and no one ever demands payment for it. Drug dealers are getting powerful stuff to sell and never have to pay anyone back for it."

"Strange behavior, even for drug dealers."

"Maybe we should compare notes, share information," Faubus said.

"Sorry," Crow replied. "I work alone. I might need to do things that are less than legal and it wouldn't help having cops showing up and making people nervous."

"Okay, Crow, I get it; you don't trust me and I don't entirely trust you. For the time being, *jièyán*, I'm going to give you the benefit of the doubt."

"That's downright neighborly of you," Crow said. "Can I go now?"

"Almost. There's still something else I need you to do."

Crow chuckled. "Sorry, I'm not feeling up to sex on the table and the handcuffs have already come loose."

Faubus rolled her eyes so hard, Crow wondered if she could see her brain. "Not sex, *báichī*. If I want to get laid, it's not going to be in this room and it's not going to be with you."

She let the statement hang in the air. Crow was unsure of how to respond, but managed to avoid saying something to make things worse.

"I need you to hit me," she finally said.

"Kinky. But not one of my many fetishes."

"*Aiya! Dàsh☐gè!* I need you to hit me so you can escape without getting me in trouble."

Crow held his hands up and showed her the cuffs still on his wrists. "Can you take these off?"

She shook her head. "It would look suspicious."

"Okay. Remember, you asked for this."

As Crow strode toward her, Faubus shook. She held up her hands and said, "Wait."

Crow held back. Truthfully, he was relieved. For all the terrible things he'd done in his life, punching an unarmed woman wasn't one of them. "What?"

"Keep me in the loop if you can." She closed her eyes, took a deep breath, and pointed at the side of her head.

"Will do," Crow said and dropped her.

22 | Decisions

Kevin sat on Fei Long's couch and stared around the room with eyes filled with wonder and hatred. He missed his life on Earth. He missed his dog. He was in a room filled with trinkets, ceramic images of gods with big breasts these people worshipped, and posters of women with big breasts.

Fei Long had a thing for breasts.

At his age, Kevin didn't understand the allure of breasts, nor did he care to understand. He wanted his dog back. He wanted his life back. He wanted to go home. But more and more he wondered if there even was a home to go back to. After months of looking, Chan still hadn't found his parents and it was looking more and more like they weren't going to be found. Alive, at least.

Dino was curled in a ball, chirping in his sleep as he hunted something. Maybe the dinosaur had the right idea. Just like Kevin, Dino was a creature out of place on this planet, but he seemed content to do what he did wherever he happened to be. Tina was like that, too. Kevin wiped a tear from his cheek and choked back a desire to smash something. He wanted so desperately to be like them, to be content, but he couldn't.

Chan had tried to teach him for months about the dangers of constantly wanting things. The want becomes a need and the need becomes a driving force. Desire rises and creates a hole in a person, straight through their hearts, minds, and souls and the only thing a person can think about is getting that thing. Then, after desire has overtaken reason, the wanted thing is attained, but it's never enough to fill the hole.

Crow's philosophy of drinking and being generally happy seemed more reasonable, but from what Kevin had heard, the top of that mountain was a rugged one. And Kevin got the feeling Crow only seemed happy. Deep down inside, he too was full of holes. He just filled his holes with alcohol.

Chan stormed out hours ago. The man was hard to read, but he looked extremely pissed off. A pissed off Chan was a dangerous thing to have around, so Kevin didn't even try to stop him. Crow staggered out a while later after all the *baiju* in Fei's apartment was gone.

Huizhong stuck around, though, and he was thankful for that, even if she did seem preoccupied. Of the three adults in his life now, she seemed the most normal. Chan was driven by ascetic perfection, a way to fill some hole in his heart that he might not even know was there. Crow was just a mess all the way around.

But Huizhong, with her dark hair with the pink tips had a certain wisdom about her. She seemed on the edge a lot, though, like she couldn't quite figure out what to do with herself.

They sat in the living room, six feet apart physically, but thousands of *li* mentally. He was being generally pissed off at the world and she was reading a book from Fei's bookshelf. If he was reading the lettering correctly, the book was about the odds of something happening.

Maybe it was a gambling book. Kevin's dad had taught him poker when he was in the third grade. He took to the game naturally and quickly learned about the subtleties. It was a game built off a mixture of lies and truth and Kevin had learned the lesson well enough that even his teachers had trouble telling when he was lying. They joked that he should become a politician, but giving speeches and making laws didn't suit Kevin. He didn't want that kind of life. He wanted action and adventure. Kevin used to sneak books off the bookshelf in the living room and read them while his parents were sleeping. Most of the titles didn't mean anything to him, nor did the authors, but certain things caught his eye. His father had a complete collection of books about a stainless steel rat. It turned out there was no metal rat, but the stories were amazing, anyway. Kevin didn't want to rule, he wanted to live like James diGriz.

He just didn't know if he was smart enough to do that.

None of the books around Fei Long's apartment looked as interesting as books about James diGriz, which did nothing to improve Kevin's mood. Honestly, there was nothing to do here and it was boring. He'd always assumed other planets would be exciting and there would be chases and action and gunfights with bad guys.

Other than the brief encounter with Jonal yesterday, Kevin's life was pretty boring. He got up and walked to the window. Outside, the suns had gone down and only Little Sister had risen. The city was lit up and twinkling contentedly. A whole new world and, day to day, there was absolutely nothing exciting happening.

"It's pretty at night, isn't it?" Huizhong asked from the couch.

Kevin shrugged his shoulders. "It's pretty nice, I guess. The magic is neat."

He caught her reflection in the glass as she stood and came to join him at the window. Her hand touched his shoulder and Kevin felt somewhat connected again. His own parents had been huggers and friends. Chan was a good guy, but he was physically distant.

"This is the biggest city on Aluna," Huizhong said. "It's a terrible, wonderful place. They say almost four million people live here."

Kevin sniggered. "You should see New York sometime. There's no magic, but there are almost ten million people there. We went there once on vacation. Tokyo was nice, too. That's almost fourteen million."

Reflected in the window, Huizhong looked at him. At ten turns old, Kevin was over fifteen hands tall, almost as tall as Huizhong herself. "Seriously?" she asked.

Kevin nodded sadly. "My own town had almost a million. There are a lot of people on Earth. Nearly seven billion."

"It must be incredible. I can't even fathom being around

that many people."

"We had movies that would fill walls and games and schools and …," he trailed off.

"You miss it," Huizhong said quietly.

He sniffed and wiped a tear from his cheek. He tried to speak, but nothing came out, so Kevin nodded sadly and tried to pretend he wasn't crying.

Huizhong put her arm around his shoulder and pulled him close. He leaned into her and tried to be strong and smart and let nothing bother him, just like Chan. But he wasn't Chan and he probably never would be. The tears flowed and soon he found himself sobbing in her arms and not caring one bit what anyone thought. He was supposed to be at home, in bed, worrying about school and games and toys and, yet, here he was, staring out at a city he shouldn't even know existed while his parents were out there somewhere and no one could find them.

He let it all go and embraced the sorrow in his soul while a woman who claimed to know a dragon held him. Claws clicked on the tile floor and soon Dino was nuzzling him and chirping.

"Huizhong," Kevin finally asked when the tears dried up, "do you really know a dragon?"

"I do," she said softly. "Ao Shun. He's a big, black dragon up north."

"Can he breathe fire?"

She chuckled. "Maybe. I've never seen him do it, though."

"What's he like?" Kevin asked, trying to imagine a big, black dragon. In his mind, he pictured a proud dragon with his head held high and wings extended.

"Wise. Dangerous. He's a hunter and something of a philosopher. I guess if I ever lived to be that old, I'd start acting like a philosopher, too."

Kevin looked up at Huizhong and wondered what her life must have been like. She palled around with dragons, so it had to be interesting. "How old is he?"

"He never gives a straight answer, it's all 'as old as the stars' or 'old enough to not ask so many questions', but I'd guess he's a couple thousand turns old. Sounds old to us, but apparently he's one of the younger dragons on the planet."

Kevin tried to understand what living over two thousand turns meant. It was such a big number he couldn't even begin to understand it. His grandfather had died when he was ninety of so. Compared to two thousand turns, being ninety was a drop in the bucket.

"That's old," Kevin said.

"Old for a person, maybe," Huizhong replied. "Not so old for a red Gingko tree. Even less so for a dragon."

"It's all relative, huh?"

Huizhong released him and pointed out the window. "Out there are millions of people all trying to do whatever they need to do to get through the day. Some of them are hard-working people building houses and stores, others are selling drugs, still others are investing other people's money and keeping the profits. They all make it somehow. Some work harder than you or me, some barely lift a finger. Everything is relative. And all that matters is whatever you do makes you happy and doesn't hurt too many other people."

Kevin nodded, not entirely certain he understood everything, but the gist seemed to be there was no absolute right or wrong in Huizhong's world. In a way, she reminded him of Mrs. Chow. Even though they'd chosen different paths, both women held a similar view of right or wrong. Chan, on the other hand, had very absolute ideas about what was right and what was wrong.

Crow seemed to inhabit his own little world. He was like chaos with a coat and hat, yet things always seemed to work out for him.

"What do you do here?" Kevin asked.

She looked at him like she didn't understand. "What do you mean?"

"Like, for work. How do you make money?"

"That's ... complicated," Huizhong said.

Kevin bristled. All his life he'd heard adults say things were too complicated for kids to understand, but he understood more than anyone gave him credit for. "Try me," he said.

"Well ... okay. This city controls the flow of all the magic in the world. That's both a good and bad thing. There are some people up north that I work with who are worried that the Clock Tower has too much control. They've taken it upon themselves to keep an eye on things."

"Is that where the dragon lives?" Kevin interrupted. "Up north?"

"Yes. Ao Shun lives in the north even though he's a Southern Dragon."

"Why?"

Huizhong started to reply, but stopped herself. What was a Southern Dragon doing up north? It got awfully cold up north and Southern Dragons were supposed to hate the cold. "I don't know," she replied. "He's never said. Anyway, I work with a group of people, and Ao Shun, to make sure no one gets too much power over magic."

Kevin watched her intently, wondering if she was finished or was just pausing to think more. "You know, you still haven't said how you get paid."

"Oh," Huizhong said. "I don't get paid."

"Why do you do it if you don't get paid? We had a philosopher on Earth who said, 'If you're good at something, never do it for free'."

The corners of Huizhong's lips curled up and her eyes twinkled. "I guess I do it because I believe in the cause. No one should ever too much control over the way things happen. People need to control their own destinies, so we sometimes step in to do things that need to be done."

"Is it dangerous?" Kevin asked.

"It can be. Some of the Furious Fae have met Nüwa prematurely, some have been caught and executed by people who don't want anyone watching what they're doing."

"So you're basically spies," Kevin asked. A huge grin crossed his face as he thought about a life of intrigue.

"Kind of. We also try to stop things before they get too out of hand. That's how I met Crow, actually."

Kevin nodded slowly, still not quite getting what she meant. Was it killing people or was it something more mundane like watching and waiting?

"What were you doing when you met Crow?"

"Trying to figure out what the last Clock Man was up to. I was supposed to infiltrate his inner-circle and report back. Hours turned to days, days turned to weeks. The next thing I know, I'm in all the way and have only the most basic idea of what was going on. Crow was the one who broke up that mess. After I got him killed."

Kevin almost asked what she meant when Huizhong said she got Crow killed. It had to have been a figure of speech. On the other hand, when he first met Crow all those months ago, the man did look he'd just risen from the grave.

"What was going on?" Kevin asked. "What was the mess Crow broke up?"

Huizhong hesitated and Kevin could tell she didn't really want to talk about it. She swallowed deeply and said, "The old Clock Man was a man named Chenming Zhang. He was a brilliant man, but something happened to him. He started … changing his body. He cut off his own legs and replaced them with metal piston and rods. His eyes were vidder cameras, and so on. The worst part was, Chenming had figured out how to take over someone's mind and make them do what he wanted them to. That's the part I can't understand. Why take over minds?

"Crow was hired by someone to kill Chenming Zhang. It's all shrouded in mystery because Crow doesn't talk about his jobs and Chenming is dead. No one knows the whole story and likely no one ever will. I was there, though, and saw some of it with my own two eyes. Chenming Zhang was a madman.

Crow did the world a favor."

Kevin pondered all this and wondered if Aluna wasn't crazier than Earth. There, he'd be just another kid in a world ruled by grown-ups. Here, though. Well, that was something worth considering. "Did you know there's no magic on Earth?" he asked. Without waiting for her to answer, he added, "It's true. Chan said so. I guess there's still some, but a small number of people have it. They hoard it. I have it, though. I made it work on Earth. I made Dino real. He used to be a stuffed toy dinosaur, but now he's real."

"I've heard that," Huizhong said, "but I've never been to Earth myself. Very few people go there anymore."

"I lived there. Chan's been there, too. That's where he found me."

A strange look came over Huizhong's face, like she couldn't quite believe what she was hearing. "Chan's been to Earth? How?"

"I don't know," Kevin said rapidly. "My house had ghosts in it, but they weren't really ghosts, they were protectors. Someone put them there to keep an eye on things because the Beast was after me. My dad captured the protectors, but my mom threw them out of the house. As soon as they were gone, something happened. Chan was there, though."

Huizhong's brow furrowed as she tried to follow Kevin's staccato speech. "I knew about the protectors. We call them *Jiānhùrén*. Guardians. They don't guard so much as watch, but I guess that's a kind of guarding, too. I was there when Mab created them, but she never told me what they were for. Or who."

"Yeah, me," Kevin said happily. "This Mab guy…"

"Woman," Huizhong corrected.

Kevin barely broke his stride as he continued. "Woman, right. This woman sent them to keep an eye on me. They couldn't stop the Beast from taking my parents, though. I think there was something else in the house when I left, but Chan says we were alone. If I knew then what I know now, I could have saved them."

They fell silent for a moment as each pondered things. Huizhong rubbed her temples, trying to stave off a headache. Kevin's energy finally dropped off and he yawned and rubbed his eyes. "What time is it?" he asked.

"It's ... uh," Huizhong replied. She looked around the room, but couldn't find a clock. "I'm guessing it's about ten or so."

Kevin yawned again and his whole body shook with the effort. He hugged Huizhong and stroked Dino's smooth feathers. The dinosaur looked up and shook his head. "I need to get some sleep, come on Dino."

Kevin waved one last time and slunk into his room. As soon as the door was closed and the lights were off, he straightened up and moved to the window. Outside, the city was slowly shutting down for the night. He knew from experience that plenty of people – bad ones especially – would continue their patrols well into the night.

Since he didn't have to go to school and even Chan seemed to be ignoring their usual morning lessons, Kevin had taken to staying up late and watching the city. Each night, he told himself that tonight would be the night he'd sneak out and see the night up close and personal. It couldn't be too dangerous; he'd have Dino with him and the dinosaur had more than proven a good companion to have around.

He heard a door click shut and assumed Huizhong had gone to bed. If he was going out, he would have to make sure to be back before anyone noticed. The window would have been an ideal way out, but he'd still have to sneak back in from the lobby and a boy and a dinosaur wandering around at night would definitely draw attention.

It was the getting back in that had stopped him every time. For all the madness of this place, Kevin didn't want to disappoint Chan. The man had been a father figure and taught him and gave him a home. If Chan knew he'd snuck out at night to see the city all alone, it would worry him that Kevin would do it again. So, he had to figure out how to get in and out without being seen. Crow would have a way, but he was off drinking some more and wouldn't have wanted to help anyway.

There had to be a way in and out without getting spotted, but Kevin couldn't come up with it.

For the time being, Kevin stared out the window and wondered where his parents were. They were out there somewhere, but the city was huge and spread out. It would take an eternity to find them. Maybe a master sorcerer could find them, but Kevin knew he was far from being a master sorcerer. Making a guy explode was great fun, but it was hardly mastery.

He watched a figure dart from shadow to shadow and wondered if it was one of the bad guys out doing bad things. Anyone who slunk around in the shadows had to be up to no good. Kevin watched the figure closely until, as it was speeding through a well-lit area, something made it stop. The figure looked around cautiously and the light hit its face just right.

Kevin scratched his head as Huizhong sped off into the night.

23 | Chan Goes To War

The attack on the street was bad enough, but when the *Qīng Bāng* blew up Mrs. Chow's bar, they crossed a line. Chan was only peripherally involved with the gang life in Croatoa, but he knew enough about the world to know blowing up bars and using combat magicians in the middle of the street against a boy was pushing the boundaries too far.

If the Green Gang wanted a war, it was a war they would get. Chan was only one man, but he had skill and an indomitable will on his side. It took a lot to raise his ire, but when it was piqued he would move the heavens to smash everything in his path.

It wasn't well known in Croatoa, but Chan fought to keep his mind stable and sane. He had a ruthless edge and found that fighting in a controlled environment allowed him to express his dark side without endangering anyone who didn't want to be endangered. No one who'd spent his life learning how to hurt people didn't have a dark side.

Chan's Wushu training was anything but pleasant. His many teachers all had one thing in common: a desire to push a student to the edge and see what happened. When he was first learning, that was just the way training was delivered. To learn how to deliver a punch, a five-turn-old Chan had to learn how to take one first.

And so it went.

Wushu training on Croatoa focused on the combative aspects of martial arts. There were *taolu*, of course, but the goal of practicing forms was simply to get better at destroying opponents. Some schools focused on training exclusively for the fights or the supposed philosophical aspects of the martial arts, but Chan was trained to do two things: hurt people and survive the encounter.

Since Chan's training was combative in nature, he was

taught from a very young age how to handle weapons and armor. Not all fights were fair and not all took place on the streets. Even on the streets, any tool that could shift the balance was considered fair game.

Chan studied sticks and staves and knives and *kwan dao* and even metal fans. But his favorite tool for fighting – aside from his fists – was the *dao*. Some students felt the *jian* was the superior weapon due to its light weight, dual-edge, and stabbing capabilities, but Chan always felt more comfortable with the single-edged broadsword. He felt there was an elegance to slicing that stabbing lacked.

His sword had no name. Unlike many of the warriors on Croatoa, he felt no need to personalize the weapon. Personalization came from letting the blade become an extension of his body.

He hefted the *dao* and felt the weight of ages in it. The blade was forged hundreds of turns ago, and was passed down from master to student as each master retired. Legend had it that the blade had tasted dragon blood, but Chan knew from experience how many of the legends were fanciful stories. Even stories about Chan himself had reached the point of epic tales, legends woven by drunkards and just as easily dismissed.

For instance, Chan had never killed three men with a single blow. His record was two.

The *dao* gleamed in the late evening light. For all its life and bloody history, the blade still looked new. Experience and history took over Chan's mind. He stepped back gently and drew the sword to guard position. It was appropriate to greet the weapon. He hadn't had need to draw the blade in many turns and his body needed to remember how to handle it.

As he moved through the *taolu*, Chan allowed himself to focus on how he got from point to point, rather than worrying about the cuts. His sword *sifu*, Fan Li, taught him to tear apart the *taolu* and look for the things that happen between the things happening.

"Most students," she told him, "will never progress beyond the strikes and slashes of the *dao*. Those are the obvious things, the things any idiot can reproduce with a little training. What sets mastery apart from talented amateurs is looking between the slashes and the strikes of the dao. What happened to make the *taolu* move from this point to that point? Those transitions aren't random; they are there for a reason."

Chan nodded, not entirely certain he understood, but willing to learn and explore.

Fan Li moved like a *dúshé*. Her body undulated in ways a body shouldn't be able to move. When she wanted to strike, her *dao* moved as fast as any fang. In the early days of training with her, she used to regularly cut his cheek just to prove he wasn't as fast as he could be.

She was as lithe as any dancer and deadly as any *xiē*. "You must always move. I cannot stand toe to toe with a man and hope to beat him by strength alone. My strength is my technique and my ability to be where I need to be when I need to be there. Those are the transitions you should seek, Chan."

The *dao* was a smooth silver blur as she arced it around the room. The seven-hand-long blade weighed almost a full *jin*, but she made it seem weightless. "The trick is to keep it moving," Fan Li told him. "It takes time to make a heavy *dao* move, but once it's moving, it will flow like water. Transitions will get you from where you are to where you want to be."

As usual, Fan Li ended the lecture by stopping the sword a *li* from his face. "As always, control. Never cut anything you don't want to cut. Control the blade or it will control you."

Chan closed his eyes and felt the blade in his hand. It became an extension of his body, a razor-sharp part of him that should move as readily as any limb. He started slowly, remembering the complex series of movements that Fan Li taught him. As his rhythm increased, he broke from her *taolu* and improvised his own. He felt the change in position of the sword and knew where he needed to be to let it taste blood.

He focused on moving, constantly changing from tall to short, near to far until the *taolu* was complete improvisation.

He ended the *taolu* with the blade exactly one *li* from a statue of Xuanwu. The god seemed to smile at him, pleased with the demonstration.

Chan bowed and said, "*W□ huì gěi n□ róngyù, Xuanwu.*" *I will bring you honor, Xuanwu.*

He was never much for prayer, though it was comforting to think there were others out there who were more powerful and had sway over the world. By telling Xuanwu he would bring him honor, Chan made a promise to the one god martial artists tended to revere without begging for assistance. Like most of the things he'd done in his life, he wanted to know it was him doing them and not the gods influencing his hand.

Along with the sword came the armor. Speed was his best armor, something Fan Li was happy to point out, but it never hurt to put a little extra space between his flesh and pointy things that wanted to pierce it. A chest plate supposedly made from dragon scale, forearm and hand protection made from tanned *wěidà de xīyì* scales, and a mask molded to look like the face of a *yaogui*. The *Qīng Bāng* were superstitious criminals; the face of a demon should give them pause enough for Chan to take their heads.

He placed his *d□ulì* back on his head and wrapped a black cloak around his shoulders. His pockets were full of dirty tricks – smoke bombs, pointy *ji li*, and a handful of short daggers. The *dao* was last, sliding neatly into his belt.

It felt good to know there would be no quarter in this fight. The night fights in the Ch'uan district were entertaining, but Chan felt he had to hold back too much. Tonight, he would either return a hero or gaze upon Nüwa's visage in the afterlife. Either way, he was satisfied.

Chan barely recognized himself in the mirror. His stormy gray eyes bore through the reflection. From top to bottom, he looked like a *mógu□* come to take the souls of evil.

Yes, tonight would be a good night and the *Qīng Bāng*

would learn what happened to people who pushed Chan into a corner.

The Green Gang had hangouts all over Croatoa. No one knew for sure where their headquarters was, or even if such a place existed, but a tea house not far from the docks was well-known *Qīng Bāng* gathering place. It wasn't large, but he didn't need a torrent of blood to send a amessage.

*****

Chan stood outside of the tearoom and watched the six gangsters laughing and joking inside. A man on the street corner was deep in the arms of *Tiāntáng De Fěn*, watching with blank eyes and drooling on himself. Another reason to despise the Green Gang. It was bad enough they were blowing things up, but they were also slowly poisoning the city.

He touched his sword and slowed his breathing. Against six men even someone with Chan's skills had to be perfect. Ancient *taolu*, things hidden from average people, taught methods for dealing with multiple, armed opponents. *Sifu* Li had taught them to him and taught them well, but it was still up to the practitioner to find place to stick the blade and know when to transition from one opponent to the next.

Chan walked purposefully toward the door. As he passed the man with the blank eyes, he heard the man mutter something. He knew he should ignore it and keep walking, but Chan was a man of principle and he considered ignoring someone to be rude. "What was that?"

"Autograph?" the man asked.

"I apologize, but I cannot sign an autograph right now. I have pressing business. Perhaps another time."

The man on the ground seemed to accept this and went back to staring at the world through dead eyes. Chan afforded him one last glance before gently pushing open the door to the tea house.

As he entered, time seemed to stand still. Chan knew this was just his brain kicking into high gear in anticipation of the fight, but it was a welcome effect to see the world slowed down. At first no one noticed him or paid him any attention. He took a moment to scan the room and make note of the positions of each gangster.

His presence didn't go unnoticed for long. All eyes turned to face him. Some were curious, others shocked. The demon face mask didn't have the exact effect he'd been hoping for, but it would work for now.

Immediately to his right a man sat at a table sipping tea and playing *mahjong* alone. Chan's practiced hands drew the *dao* and sliced through the man's neck.

The blade was extremely well-maintained. Even though he never carried it, Chan kept the weapon oiled and sharpened. It was so sharp, the man playing *mahjong* didn't even register that his head had been severed. His head rested atop his shoulders like it could come to life any time.

A chair shrieked as someone pushed back from a table. Chan deftly switched position to deal with the new threat. His foot sent the table slamming into a man trying to pull a knife from his jacket. His legs twitched and Chan twisted back long enough to grab the head from *mahjong* man before it could fall.

Time seemed to slow down for him. Chan was so used to fighting that facing down even the toughest opponent barely got his adrenaline moving. Against five people, though, his *chi* was singing. Everything took on an ultra-sharp clarity. His eyes caught details most people would miss: the man in the back of the tea house stepping back in measured steps was a worthy opponent, the man and the woman in white suits reaching for hand axes winked at each like long-term lovers before turning their attention to Chan, and the large man at the back with the wobbly knee and broken nose grinned at the thought of vengeance. Yánshí was back

Chan flipped the table he'd kicked earlier up and into the air. As his body twisted the coiling strength of the dragon stance roared to be unleashed. He unwound and kicked the table face-first into the man who was still trying to reach into his pocket.

The table hit the man hard, pinning his hand to his pocket and shattering his nose. Chan knew from experience a broken nose was hardly a fight ender, but it hurt and swelling made the eyes tear up. He took advantage of the time to toss a smoke bomb at the large man with the wobbly knee before turning his attention to the couple.

When he first walked into the tea house, Chan thought his demon mask was a failure. From the wary looks on the couple, though, he knew it had struck a nerve. The couple worked well together, communicating silently in the way only long-term couples have. Their axes were small, with short, stubby handles and gleaming heads. Those axes were weapons; no woodcutter would use such a short handle and the meatpackers preferred larger blades.

The woman moved first; a feint meant to draw Chan into engaging with her. He remained steadfastly resolute instead of taking the bait. Just in time, he sensed movement and realized the man had swung around behind him while Chan was otherwise occupied.

Rather than waste time taking them on sequentially, Chan kicked forward at the woman, catching her in the midsection and folding her in half. The man received a powerful hammer fist to his groin at the same time. Chan twisted and the *dao* slashed at the heavens before descending to the underworld and taking the woman's head with it. Chan controlled the arc of the sword and worked with it, allowing it to continue around and back to the heavens. The man's white suit slowly turned crimson as his life leaked out. A gash from his crotch to his chin first beaded with blood then erupted as his dying body caught up with the deep cut up his body.

Chan heard a commotion and turned to find a man with bits of table stuck in his face struggling to get up. Chan's leg swept the man's hands from under him, slamming him back down just before his foot broke the man's jaw and slammed his head into the floor.

Through the cloud of smoke in the back of the tea house, Chan sensed movement. The smoke from his grenade was thick and blue, a concoction designed by an old master who specialized in disappearing. Chan had kept the recipe, but had changed the delivery mechanism. His old master wanted a small puff of smoke to hide in. Chan wanted something that could fill a room.

Hints of motion were visible through the small empty patches in the cloud. Chan knew going into the cloud would be disastrous, so he stepped back and waited for his quarry to come to him. To his surprise, both Yánshí and the man who knew how to move erupted from the cloud of smoke in tandem.

Each held a stick in one hand and a knife in the other. They attacked as one, forcing Chan to react rather than drive the fight. He circled, doing his best to keep one attacker in front of the other. Eventually, they wised up to the tactic and flanked him.

"Even the heavens cannot plan for the events of people," an old master of Chan's once told him. Seeing both men working together certainly bore that out. He focused on the smaller man, parrying and attacking and trying to break the man's confidence. Every time Yánshí tried to join the fray, Chan kicked him in the knee until he backed off.

With the big man out of the way, Chan focused on the smaller man. The man was fast, unexpectedly fast, like he'd been training for the fights. They clashed together, each blocking the other's strikes until a mutual, unheard message passed between them and they both warily backed off.

"Who are you?" the man asked.

Chan bowed slightly. "Call me *Chéngfá zhě*," he replied, "perhaps you've heard of me."

"Punisher," the man said, rolling the name around his tongue. "What are you punishing?"

"Injustice," Chan agreed. "What, may I ask, is your name."

"My name is of no consequence," the man replied, "but I know a great many people who will be interested in hearing you exist."

Chan lunged, slamming the *dao* the man's chest and cleaving his heart in two when he least expected it. As his life leaked out, the man smiled a bloody grin. "You have chosen a dangerous path, *Chéngfá zhě*. This won't be the last you'll hear from the *Qīng Bāng*. We are everywhere."

The light went out in his eyes. Chan put his foot on the man's chest and pushed with his leg as he pulled the *dao* out of the man. He was a worthy opponent and a skilled warrior. Under other circumstances, Chan would have been happy to meet him over tea.

As Chan pondered the dead man, Yánshí lifted him and casually tossed him across the tea house. Chan rolled when he hit the ground and spun in place to meet the new threat. The big guy wasn't walking well, but he was still a mass of muscle and would have no problem breaking Chan's limbs like twigs.

The *dao* left his hand when he was flying, so Chan threw another smoke bomb. While the smoke was filling the tea house and obscuring Yánshí, Chan reached into his jacket and slipped hunks of brass over his fists.

He had just enough time to prepare before the big guy limped out of the smoke, covering his nose and coughing. Chan didn't hesitate. Before Yánshí could do anything, Chan snapped a kick between the man's legs and kicked his knee. The knee made a sickening crack just before the big guy dropped to the ground howling.

Amazingly, the big guy got back up and tried to get to Chan. His bad leg was trailing behind him with his foot at an odd angle. He hopped and leaned on tables to keep himself moving forward and upright. Chan waited until he was in range and slammed a fist into Yánshí's jaw. The brass knuckles on his hands increased the mass and let the full force of the blow shatter the man's jaw. As the man turned his head to the side, he spat out teeth and blood.

Chan didn't wait to see if he would get back up. He leapt into the air and landed with his knees on Yánshí's chest and pummeled his head until the lights went out in the guy's eyes.

He stood up and surveyed the damage. Of the six people in the tea house when he walked in, only one was left alive, which meant someone could point at Chan. That left Chan in a quandary. He'd only killed one time before and it was a complete accident, but now he had the blood of five people on his hands. He looked around and found a huge mess.

A moan caught his attention. On the floor was the man he'd hit with the table. His face was a terrible wreck, bloody and swollen. He coughed and spat out a tooth. The man's eyes were angry and confused, like he couldn't figure out what happened, but was pissed off about it nonetheless. "Why?" he asked.

Chan's eyes were hard as he glared at the man. "Your people attacked me and attacked Mrs. Chow. This is a warning. Let your friends know *Chéngfá zhě* is coming for them."

"It wasn't us," the man whispered. "We had people there, too."

Chan first reeled at that tidbit, then decided the man was likely lying. He was a career criminal, an animal that couldn't learn to work within the rules. "You lie," Chan hissed.

"He's not lying," a voice said behind them. "It wasn't *Qīng Bāng*. Someone else is out there pulling strings."

Chan rose smoothly, ready to fight the next person that crossed him. Rather than another gangster, he found Felix Crow watching him warily. Crow wobbled slightly, but he had that old manic glint in his eyes that he used to get when he was close to solving a case.

Crow seemed hunkered, almost as if he were hiding from something. He wasn't acting like his normally boisterous self. "What are you doing here, Crow?" Chan asked.

"Saving your ass," Crow replied. "Did you stop to think what would happen if you took on the whole Green Gang?

There are hundreds of these guys and, trust me, pal, it's not a good idea to trifle with them."

Chan glanced back at the man on the floor. He'd likely be okay in a few days, but for now he looked like he just came back from a trip through *Diyu*. The air took on a coppery scent as more blood leaked onto the floor. "My ass does not need saving," Chan replied. "I am quite capable of taking care of myself."

"Look, Chan, you're a smart guy and you're tough as nails, but quit being a dumb ass and listen. What do you think is going to happen when the whole Green Gang decides to come after you?"

"Beat them, just like I beat these members."

Crow rubbed his temples and groaned. "You still don't get it, do you? They won't come for you face to face. They'll wait until your guard is down and drive a dagger into your back."

"My guard is never down."

Chan rose and faced Crow. He could see the little details that told him Crow was nervous: his foot slid back and he put one hand on his chin and the other on his belt. Against a regular person on the street, Crow's stance would look normal and non-threatening, but Chan saw a stable stance and hands in position to defend himself. The former student was preparing for a fight with his old master.

"What about Kevin's guard?" Crow asked. "Is his ever down? Because these guys don't play by the rules of the fights, they play to win at any cost."

Chan lowered his eyes. He was so used to being alone and playing by a strict code that it never occurred to him that anyone would attack a boy just to get to him. Crow kept his eyes on Chan as he walked over to the guy laying on the ground. He stood over the man and stared down at him. "Do you know who we are?" he asked.

The man spat a wad of blood out of his mouth and smiled. "You are Felix Crow. He is Chan, I can tell by the eyes."

Crow stomped on the man's throat and calmly watched as he died gasping for breath. "Sorry, buddy," he said as the man desperately tried to breathe. "I really don't have a problem with the Green Gang and I'd like to keep it that way."

"What are you doing?" Chan cried. He ran over to the man and fussed with his throat, trying to find a way to bring air back into his lungs.

"You taught me that kick, Chan," Crow said. "There's no coming back from it."

"You didn't have to kill him!"

Crow sighed and, just for a moment, looked very old and very sad, like the weight of all his bad deeds had just come to roost on his shoulders. "He knew who we are and would have told his friends as soon as he could. That would have brought the whole of the Green Gang down on all of us. They're already twitchy and looking for an excuse to go after someone."

Chan watched as the man turned blue and clawed at his throat. It seemed an eternity passed before the life finally drained from his body. In the end, the man's eyes turned desperate. He plead for his life in silent, jerking pantomime that everyone understood but no one could do anything about.

"Don't fret too much about him, Chan," Crow said. "He was a hired, uh, enforcer for the *Qīng Bāng*. He specialized in women."

Chan stared at Crow, not quite understanding why the Green Gang would need an enforcer just for women. Perhaps he was gentler than the regular enforcers.

Crow saw the question in Chan's eyes and shook his head. "Sorry, buddy. He was a hired rapist. When a woman went against the gang, they called him in. He specialized in rape and torture. Most of the guys in the gang don't have the stomach for it, but Yang Xinhai here not only specialized in it, but loved it. We had a file on him, but could never prove anything because his victims were all too terrified to talk. The ones that still had their tongues, anyway. He was a bad guy, Chan, and he deserved what he got."

The world fell out from under Chan's feet. It slowly dawned on him that he had just picked a fight with a group of people who employed other people specifically to rape and torture women. He had always assumed *Qīng Bāng* spent most of their time selling drugs or providing protection against themselves for a fee. If they would do that kind of thing, what would they do a young boy?

Chan looked up at Crow and saw, for the very first time, exactly why Crow was the way he was. It wasn't the endless *baiju* that made him seem crazy, it was the things he'd seen and done that had nearly pushed him over the edge. The *baiju* likely kept him nearly sane.

"I understand," Chan said. "And thank you. What else do we need to do here?"

"Sneak out and pretend none of this ever happened," Crow replied. "I was never here. You were never here. We know nothing."

Chan collected his sword and followed Crow out into the darkness. This part of Croatoa wasn't popular after dark. It wasn't an unsafe place – the *Qīng Bāng* kept the bad guys in line because they needed a quiet place where the police wouldn't bother them – but unless someone was part of the Green Gang, there was little of interest here.

As they walked into the dark streets, Chan looked for the man who'd asked for his autograph, but he had apparently moved on. Hopefully, he found a safe, warm place to sleep.

Chan removed his mask and stowed it in a pocket. "If the police knew that man was a rapist, why didn't they go after him?"

Crow watched the alleys and took wide turns around corners to avoid anyone jumping out at him. "You don't move on the Green Gang unless you have absolute proof and a sanction from their leadership to arrest one of their members. They outnumber the police by a large margin."

The idea that the police would have to ask permission from a gang to arrest one of its members boggled Chan's mind. They were the police. Sure, they weren't people you didn't want to be on the bad side of, but they were supposed to take care of the bad guys not work with them.

"Who really runs the city, Crow?" Chan asked.

"The gangs," Crow replied without looking back. "And the Beast runs the gangs. But I think I know where the Beast is."

24 | Huizhong Finds Religion

Huizhong stood in front of the old pawn shop and peered through the window. Through the glass, a book on a pedestal called to her. She was hardly a stranger to magic – living with the Ao Shun and the Furious Fae had inured her to the stranger parts of reality – but the idea that a book could call out to her was odd. Only artifacts that had been in close physical proximity to extremely powerful sorcerers were supposed to contain their own magic.

And this one was collecting dust in a pawn shop.

Her conversation with Kevin pushed her back here. There were simply too many unknowns in this town for her mission to be a success; she needed information. Fei Long might have had all the information she needed, but someone beat the life out of him. That left people who either didn't know what was going on in the world or people who wouldn't talk about what was going on.

So she turned to a book that shouldn't be there. The Clock Tower had the final say on orphaned magical objects and the book behind the window smelled like power. She was no magician, so the spells wouldn't help her, but sorcerers were well-known hoarders of knowledge. Her gut told her the book was important.

Huizhong looked around the abandoned streets and estimated the amount of time it would take to do what she had in mind. Pawn brokers were scavengers of human misery, but they weren't idiots. The shop was full of trinkets and baubles, but that didn't mean there wasn't serious security in place.

Back when she was working undercover in Robinson's little cabal, Huizhong was once tasked with sneaking into a hotel and killing a man by the name of Lothar. The hit was sanctioned by both Robinson and the Furious Fae, each working independently of the other, so she knew he had to be a bad guy. It was her first – and last – assassination and it went smoothly largely due to the preparation she put into it.

Robinson's group had several assassins working for it and they happily took the time to teach the new girl what to do and how to do it. They called it *Bèi pò línghún chū qiào*: Forced out of body experience. It was a phrase that resonated with their black humor.

The problem with the hit was Lothar was adept at creating extremely powerful magical protection. Some said his magic couldn't be cracked. He was susceptible to a blade, just like any other human, but getting past his defenses was thought to be impossible. Most sorcerers create simple shields that have to be forced open, but Lothar thought static shields were as effective at keeping determined invaders out as walls were. Anyone could circumvent a wall, he felt. Walls are right there and any idiot with some free time could examine the wall for weaknesses or simply fly over it.

Lothar took a different tack. His defenses were invisible and fluid. They said five seconds after stepping over his boundaries people died. Huizhong never found who "they" were, but "they" appeared to know their business. Most intruders were turned to bloody messes on hotel room floors, but some were turned inside out. Whatever the death, it always happened at five seconds.

While Robinson's team worked on ways to drop Lothar's shields entirely, Huizhong tried something else. She found a room like the one he was staying in and practiced on getting from the door to the bed and back again in under five seconds.

It turned out to be an effective solution, especially given that the rest of the team never could find a way around Lothar's defenses. When the time came, Huizhong picked the lock on Lothar's room, took a deep breath, and rammed a dagger into his throat. She killed him and made it out of the room in four seconds. She turned around on the fifth second, just in time to see the world flash.

Huizhong never found out why Lothar's magic waited five seconds to kill intruders, but she knew if she'd been there when the light flashed, she'd be dead.

She also never found out why Lothar had to go. That was the problem with working undercover: ask too many question and she would have wound up being food for the things under the pier. Also, just a general rule, assassins aren't told much other than who the target was and what the payment was.

Huizhong walked away from the job a few thousand pieces richer and further in bed with Robinson's group.

The pawn shop likely didn't have the same level of security that Lothar did, but she decided five seconds was probably a safe bet. She peered through the window, looking for anything that could obstruct her path. The shop was packed with junk, but there was a clear line between the window and the book.

She scanned around the window, looking for anything that might indicate a warning, but found only blank glass. It was probably too much to expect the shop owner would advertise what awaited when the glass broke. The fact that it was still intact in this neighborhood indicated that whoever owned the shop was respected enough – or feared enough – to not have to warn people off.

The glass was cool to the touch, but otherwise felt like normal glass. Huizhong wasn't very magic sensitive, so if a security spell was lurking there she might not notice it. Her fingers didn't feel the tell-tale hum of magic, but an advanced enough spell would require a sorcerer to detect.

All around her were empty streets. It wasn't a terrible neighborhood, but she didn't feel like pushing her luck and staying around much longer. She searched the area and found a loose brick that would work for her. A little back and forth and she pulled it free from the wall.

Huizhong paced for a few moments, hefting and tossing the brick in the palm of her hand. When she felt comfortable with the brick, she stepped back away from the glass to give herself time to accelerate. She gave the brick one last heft and launched it like an arrow toward the glass. As soon as the brick left her hand, Huizhong was sprinting and mentally counting.

One, she leapt through the now broken pawn shop window and landed in a roll.

Two, she climbed to her feet and ran at the book.

Huizhong was smart enough to know it was quicker to run in a big circle than to try to stop, grab the book, and go again. At three, she snatched the book from the pedestal and sprinted in a circle back toward the broken window. At five, she flew through the broken window like an arrow. Huizhong landed with a roll and took off down the alleys. The police may or may not show up for something as trivial as a book, but she didn't want to be around if they did.

Croatoa had a deep and abiding love affair with alleys. It sprung from the city's earliest days, back before the first *Wěidà de xīyì* was tamed and the giant lizards were a menace. Back then, traversing the city was always done on foot and dragons were still a very real threat, so the narrow alleys were both convenience and safety measures. As the city grew and first wagons towed by *Wěidà de xīyì* and later cars became more common, the streets grew. But the city never gave up on alleys, even if most people were hopelessly lost after a few turns.

Part of her old life here taught Huizhong to have as many escape routes as possible, so she spent her free time mapping the alleys. It wasn't always pleasant work – the alleys were haven to both lovers of flesh and lovers of chemicals – but she felt it was necessary.

Huizhong clutched the book tightly to her chest and relied on her own internal mapping system to get her where she needed to go. Every few turns, she stopped and looked for the markers she'd left all those months ago. Each marker, carved in the stone with whatever was handy at the time, gave her position. A3f4r, for instance, mean Alley Three (one that ran to the religious neighborhood). F4r meant forward three intersections and turn right on the fourth one.

Her destination was a place most people in Croatoa never admit to frequenting.

At night, the alleys were poorly lit. The occasional torch or glowing insect was all her eyes had to guide her through the morass. More than once, Huizhong nearly tripped over a derelict or a couple having sex on a trash can. She scaled fences and leapt through holes. The whole time she was running, she was absolutely convinced she'd hit a new pothole and break her leg.

Eventually, she exploded out an alley in the Religious District and welcomed the light from torches and magic-powered lamps. The road had a real name, probably remembering a general that fought in the Dragon Wars, but no one could tell what that name was. Most people simply called the Religious District *Shén Jiē*; literally God Street. Some people gasped, others pointed, when Huizhong erupted from the alley covered in grime and carrying a large book in her arms. A man in a nice suit gaped at her before realizing she might be someone he knew and hid his face in shame.

Religion on Aluna was a curious and calamitous affair. The first wave of settlers from old Earth China brought their faiths with them, but lost interest over time. The second wave from the new world brought a new, competitive system of belief. By the time the second group arrived – strange people with pale skin – the original Alunans had largely eschewed religion in favor of porcelain gods. Say a little prayer, burn a little incense, get down tonight.

The only thing that managed to survive the slow fade of religion into nothingness was the concept of the *Tao*. It was an old concept, even when the first settlers showed up on Aluna, and wasn't a religion so much as a philosophy of living. The general gist of the *Tao* was that it represented the way the universe flowed. To flow with the *Tao*, or glide on it like the dragons did, was to attempt to be true to one's nature. Not to be inactive, but to spend less time fighting against the grain.

The new group of settlers that popped onto Aluna brought their own beliefs with them. They spent time attempting to reconcile their rigid beliefs with the fact that they were on a new planet where no one had ever heard of their gods. Or god. To the original settlers, the new settlers were indistinct about how many gods they had; sometimes it was one, other times it was three.

Religious fervor slowly gave way to the horrid reality that they were stuck in a place where dragons were real, magic was real, and they were far in the minority. Faced with the grueling task of simply living, the new settlers eventually gave up religion in favor of not getting incinerated or eaten.

After all, the stories had always said everyone knew of their god. The fact that none of the original settlers had even heard of their god put a damper on the religious fervor of the second group. Fervor is necessary for religion to grow and thrive; it requires true believers and things to worship. Someone had to have an unexplainable experience to convince others and things like that didn't happen.

After all, what good were untouchable, invisible gods in the face of dragons melting people and magic literally moving mountains?

And so religion was pushed by the wayside.

Yet religion still played a part in Croatoan culture even if it had been marginalized. Almost everyone had a personal god or goddess that received prayer and incense, but very few people believed what they were saying had any impact on the world at large. True believers, the ones who sought religious experiences, were considered harmless crazies. And, while no one would overtly judge another for truly believing, it was considered strange behavior.

So, it was no wonder the man buying herbs hid his face; no one wants to be considered a crazy, harmless or not.

Huizhong didn't care about the man in the suit. He could

do what he wanted with whatever gods he felt like and it had no impact on her. The only religion she needed was tucked in her arms. She looked around the busy street until she found a quiet looking spot. It wasn't easy to find one; even this late at night, people that were hankering for something found their way down here.

Voices harangued her as she walked, selling all manner of faith with endless promises of eternal bliss or never-ending horrors. It would seem all she had to do to ensure her place in the afterlife was give up her soul and all her money.

The problem was, she had a better idea of the afterlife than anyone else on the street. Crow had died and come back. The only differences she could see were he was slightly less caustic than he used to be and he hadn't tried to kill her yet.

A mob toward the end of the road caught Huizhong's eye before she could sit down on an empty bench and look through the book she'd just stolen. Mobs weren't uncommon in *Shén Jiē*, but it was rare to find one carrying a man.

She edged through the crowd until she got close enough to see the bright white and red robes of the Sons of the Spider. They were holding a man aloft and chanting something in their strange, made-up language. The Sons made it to the alley Huizhong had just come from and unceremoniously tossed the man into the alley.

In unison, the Sons turned and marched back to wherever it was that they spent their free time. As they passed, Huizhong wondered what crime the man had committed to get kicked out of this place. She knew well enough to avoid talking to the Sons, though; they had a reputation for being less-than-kind to women.

Huizhong pushed the question from her mind and turned to return to her bench. She nearly ran into a man standing directly behind her. "Sorry," she muttered and tried to get past him.

"He was a drug addict," the man said.

That made her take pause. "Why would a drug addict get

kicked out of *Shén Jiē*? It sounds like the perfect place for him. Don't you guys heal people?"

The man was wearing a white cloak covered in mystical symbols. She recognized him as a leader of one of the smaller cults that had been around since long before the Dragon Wars. He was a monk of sorts; a leader in a cult of nature worshippers that peppered their faith with math derived from natural numbers. They called themselves The Protectorate, but they never specified who they were protecting from. Huizhong recognized some of the symbols on his cloak, but the rest were a mystery.

"We heal people who want to be healed," the man said. He waved a hand around the street and grimaced. "These new faiths are young. New ones arise every day. They don't understand the world around them. I try to heal them every day, but it's no use. They think they have all the answers without digging. But, still, I try. It is my duty. These drug addicts, though. They claim to have seen the whole of creation and found it all means nothing. They are beyond redemption."

Something clicked in Huizhong's mind. A faint hint of vibrating things and depth. She shook her head, trying to understand the vision. "*Tiāntáng De Fěn*?"

The man glowered. His faith held a very strict definition of what constituted Heaven and any derivation from that course was considered heretical. "Yes. The ultimate affront. This Heaven's Powder gives a fake idea of the heavens. The only way to Heaven is our path. You cannot snort your way to Heaven."

"Drink," Huizhong replied.

"Excuse me?" the man replied.

"They drink it. Or so I've heard. Mixed in with tea."

The man scoffed and snorted, then dismissed her with a wave of his hand. "However they do it, they are avoiding the one true path. The fact that they endlessly chase the feeling even though they can never catch it again is proof enough that they are not visiting Heaven."

"Couldn't there be multiple ways to Heaven?" Huizhong blurted. She immediately regretted saying it and covered her mouth.

"There is one true path. It's the path the forefathers found when they brought us here."

She knew where this was going and knew it was pointless to continue with him. "Yes," she replied distantly.

"We have services, if you'd like to attend. Even given your gender, you would be welcome. Everyone is welcome."

Huizhong bristled, but kept a fake smile plastered to her face. "Thank you," she said warmly. "I'll see if I can free up some of my time. You know us girls, we're always busy shopping and wasting time."

He nodded sagely. "It is good that you understand that. The first step to wisdom is understanding your limitations."

She touched his shoulder gently and nodded. "I'll see what my boyfriend thinks," she said.

"I'm sure he will be amenable. Peace be with you. Please be careful, there are dangerous people about." He bowed to her and exited without another word.

Huizhong sighed in relief and sat down on the bench. It seemed like every conversation she had with the religious started out normal and descended into chaos in short order. She shook her head and wondered if any of them knew the truth. Or perhaps they all knew the truth and it was different for everyone.

In the long run, it didn't matter.

She put the book on her legs and stroked the cover. Whatever was in there had to be worth it. Things didn't call to her – at least not normally, anyway – but this book called out to her from the moment she laid eyes on it.

The book opened itself and flipped its pages. Huizhong looked on in mild wonder. She'd heard about things like this. Some items that were in close enough proximity to a powerful sorcerer absorbed power day in and day out for centuries. It was rare, but it wasn't unheard of for books to became at least somewhat self-aware over time. Other items that spent enough time in the company of magic became magical bombs, but books seemed to be a special case; they got smart.

When the flipping stopped, Huizhong found herself staring at a richly detailed drawing of a golden man. He wasn't wearing gold, he was gold. He stood in the middle of a garden, arms crossed over his body and a stern look on his face. Underneath was a caption: "The last monk of Hope."

"Hope?" Huizhong asked.

The pages flipped until she came to a chapter entitled "The Hope Monastery."

According to the book, the Hope Monastery was started just before the end of the Dragon Wars. A group of monks left the Boxers in favor of a quieter life where they could be themselves. The monks of Hope made a non-aggression pact with the dragons. In return for hiding wounded dragons in the caves under the monastery of Hope, the dragons protected the monks.

A tickle formed in the back of Huizhong's mind as she read. The Dragon Wars were over two hundred turns ago, but she knew for a fact that there were still dragons out there. Did that mean the monks were still there?

The question was, why would a group of monks make a pact with the dragons? It had to have been for power more than money; monks don't need money. The dragons were plenty rich at the end of the war; they had a tendency to plunder anything valuable when they swept through. As a result, dragons controlled most of the wealth on Croatoa and a person would have to be a *chídùn* to go after a dragon's treasures. But their power waned over the course of the war and if there was one thing dragons loved more than treasure it was power.

It had to be power. "Last Monk of Hope," she said to the book.

The book flipped back to the image of the golden monk.

Huizhong traced his body with her fingertip, noting every line on his serious face. He looked like a stern man, someone from the past who had lived through the fire and brimstone of the earlier ages and it had turned him cold to the world.

There was a saying on Aluna, "Money may make the world go around, but power will stop it."

It wasn't much of a saying, something that sprang up in a more desperate time and resonated with people who felt a severe lack of both money and power. Over the turns, it became part of the Alunan lexicon of sayings along with "Never pet a burning fish."

The fact was, though, just like the idea of never petting burning fish, there had to be a truth to it somewhere, even if that truth wasn't obvious.

"Why would the Monks of Hope need power?" Huizhong wondered aloud.

The pages in the book flipped until three words showed on the selected page. "I don't know."

"At least you're not omnipotent," she said. "I don't know if I could handle hanging out with anything omnipotent."

The book didn't respond. Huizhong chuckled at the words on the page. It had to be tough for something that sprang to life in a magical maelstrom to admit it didn't know everything. She gently stroked the page and felt the book warm slightly.

"Okay," she said. "Why did they call it 'The Hope Monastery'?"

Pages sped by, more than should be in the book, until it stopped on a grainy image of a garden. The picture had to have been one of the first photos taken on Aluna. In it, the last monk of Hope was building a wall, forever sealing himself off from the world.

"Why did he do that?" Huizhong asked.

No pages flipped, but she detected a distinct flare-up on the page. When she looked down, Huizhong saw text write itself on the page.

Before the war, the monastery was considered sacred ground by almost everyone, save the Sons of the Spider and a couple other groups who didn't like the competition Hope offered. People ventured to the monastery to converse with the monks about things they hoped would happen.

Over time, the monks got used to lying to the clientele – they weren't psychics, after all – and learned to exploit their images by remaking themselves into people who could provide a certain truth for a price. There was a rift among the monks. Some of the monks took their vows seriously and did everything in their power to provide some kind of hope, even for the hopeless cases that ventured to speak to them. Other monks became enamored with money and power. They lost their way and wandered far from the *Tao*.

The *Tao* wasn't a vengeful god. It didn't overtly punish the monks that lost their way, but in straying from *Tao*, they found themselves more and more unshackled from their nature. As their greed grew, so did the stories they told their visitors. They promised everything from love and power to riches unending and people ate it up. Money flowed and the monks continued to spin their lies. In a way, they provided hope, but it was nothing more than a veneer wrapped around whatever lies were convenient at the time. Oftentimes, it was a lie provided by a dragon.

The leader of the monks, a man whose name has been erased by time, grew so greedy he himself became gold. Through focus and meditation and the little bits of magic he learned from travelers, he managed to make himself into that which he most adored.

Upon seeing the new Golden Monk, the rest of the brothers and sisters fled the monastery in terror. The Golden Monk was at first curious why they would wish to leave his splendor, but as soon as he tried to eat and realized gold does not eat or drink or breathe, he realized what straying from the *Tao* had cost him. He was gold through and though and there was no way to get back to what he was.

In his shame, he walled off the remains of the Monastery of Hope and resigned himself to meditating until he could be returned to flesh.

Huizhong traced the picture of the Golden Monk with her fingertip. She wondered what it must have been like, hiding out in walled-off monastery while the world grew up around him. All he had to do was open the doors and he could have been free. But again, the Golden Monk strayed from his *Tao* and his magic disappeared along with his body.

Stuck in a metal body and considering himself a monster, the last monk of the Monastery of Hope resigned himself to eternity in an unfeeling, unrelenting prison he had constructed of himself.

She closed the book and shook her head. All that time and the Golden Monk was just hiding out because he felt he was a monster. Her fingers idly traced the cover as she watched the world struggle to find meaning in the miasma of God Street. She closed her eyes and pretended she was in her clearing, mind empty and no pressures.

Hiding.

Maybe it was time to wake up.

25 | Bubble Up

While the *Qīng Bāng* were the dominant street gang in Croatoa, there were several others all jockeying for position in the city's rich criminal history. Violent crime was rare, though. For starters, the city got its fill of violence at the loosely controlled fights, but the gangs tried to keep random violence to a minimum because random violence alerted the police.

So, an uneasy alliance ruled the city streets. All the gangs did their best to patrol the city and prevent anything that would call down the police. The Croatoan Police weren't known for their diplomacy or soft tactics. Besides, police intervention was bad for business.

There were, of course, exceptions to the rule. Sometimes it was a new inductee in one of the gangs who decided to prove himself or herself by attacking a tourist that wandered into the wrong place at the wrong time. Other times it was one of the numerous small-time organizations that usually made their money on illegal mahjong games and synthetic alcohol.

Otherwise, the city was remarkably safe at night, even for a ten-turn-old boy and his pet dinosaur. Provided he didn't wander into the wrong parts of town, decide to explore the alleys, or wind up in the wrong place at the wrong time.

Kevin wandered the streets of Croatoa with Dino at his side. He knew it wasn't the best idea to go wandering around at night, but he couldn't stay in Fei's apartment any longer. The smell of bodies and liquor and Crow's *bidis* all conspired to make the apartment a miserable place to spend time.

It wasn't horrifying so much as it was uncomfortable. He felt there was always someone watching him. They all took turns keeping an eye on him, hovering like protective hens and it made him want to run away and be somewhere else. Safety grated on him. It was one thing when his parents were still around and Tina was still alive; they were reminders of his humanity.

But he created Dino out of sheer force of will and blew up those magicians. And those were combat magicians. For all their skill, training, and power, they were no match for him.

Kevin felt like the most powerful person on the planet and that made him wonder if he even really wanted to go home. Back on Earth he'd be just another kid with too much homework and rules and bed times. Here on Aluna, he was powerful. He could make his own rules.

He walked with his head held high and looked around the city. It took on a different air at night. During the day, it was just another city with bricks and cement and people selling fried tarantulas. At night, the city changed. It got quieter and the graffiti tags drawn in magical paints came to glowing life.

Kevin's command of Alunan Chinese was weak at best, but he could still marvel at the intricacies of the artwork and the way the artists seemed to apologize to each other if their tags got too close together. Some of the pictures made him chuckle: a giant chicken staring down at a town or a lizard smoking a strange looking cigarette. Others made him nervous. There was a tag a little way back that showed a beheaded woman holding her own head in her hands.

He didn't stop to think about the meaning of the art. He enjoyed it for what it was and moved on.

The clack and click of Dino's claws hitting the sidewalk was both annoying and reassuring. Kevin reached out and patted the dinosaur's head. Amber eyes locked on to him and Dino chirped appreciatively.

Kevin wanted to take Dino somewhere fun or buy him something to snack on, but he didn't know where any parks were and didn't have any money on him. The perils of being a kid: no money, no idea where to go. So, they walked and appreciated the glowing wall art.

He was so focused on looking at the graffiti that Kevin didn't notice a shadow slink out of an alley and start following him. Soon another one joined it. Dino kept glancing back, but Kevin didn't notice until powerful arms dragged him into an alley.

Manic eyes, reflecting the light from a sign somewhere, tilted and whirled. "Give it up, little boy," the voice hissed. "We wants it."

"Yes," another voice added. "We wants it."

"And we are going to take it," the first voice said.

Kevin whirled, ready to make a break for the street, only to find a skeletal man wearing what used to be clothes in front of him. Chan's endless hours of training kicked in and Kevin reacted without thinking. His foot smashed the man's testicles. As the guy doubled over in agony, Kevin grabbed the back of his head and drove it into a rising knee. He felt the man's nose explode more than heard it, a sickening, cracking sensation, like breaking pieces of wood over his leg.

Before he could shove the man out of the way, a hand grabbed his shoulder and tugged. Kevin relaxed and went with it. When he felt himself hit the man pulling him, he lashed out with his elbow. A grunt and the hand on his shoulder relaxed.

He readied himself to make a break for it and heard a screech from Dino. Someone behind him screamed in mortal terror. Kevin knew the dinosaur was on top of someone. It didn't matter who it was, claws and teeth were plunging into hot flesh. He took a risk and looked over his shoulder to find Dino standing on someone, flexing six-inch-long claws into his stomach and snapping at his face. The man under the dinosaur had his hands up, desperate to protect himself.

Kevin breathed out slowly and mentally patted himself on the back. Studying with Chan had been difficult at the best of times, almost impossible at the worst, but it had all paid off. He stood up a little straighter and said, "Who else wants some?"

An arm snaked around his body and he felt the cold touch of steel on his throat. "I wants it," someone hissed from behind.

Blood from a broken nose dripped on his shirt. Kevin had forgotten the most important lesson Chan ever taught him: The fight isn't over until the opponent cannot continue. He was big for his age, but Kevin was still a child and he couldn't generate the amount of force necessary to stop someone bigger and hopped up on gods only knew what.

"Get the thing off him," the man behind him hissed.

Kevin struggled, trying to find a way out, but the man was too strong. A life on the streets, a hint of madness, and lots of drugs had hardened him in ways that Kevin's mostly sheltered life was unaccustomed to. He was all alone except for Dino and he was about to die in an alley far from his home.

The knife at his throat moved slightly and Kevin felt the sting of the blade digging into his throat. He panicked and struggled harder but it was no use. Somewhere, deeper in the alley, someone giggled. It had to have been the guy he elbowed.

"Get it off or I'll cut you slowly."

Kevin gulped and felt the blade's sting again as his throat moved. "Dino. Off," he whimpered.

The dinosaur turned to look at him. That brief moment gave the giggling man enough time to dart out of the shadows and kick Dino hard in the ribs. The dinosaur chirped loudly and toppled to his side. Both men jumped on him and held the squirming dinosaur firmly.

"Tasty," one of them said. He was all but a skeleton, used to foraging for lizards and scraps of civilization in the garbage. "We should cook this. We could eat like masters."

"No!" Kevin shouted. "Get off him."

Giggles echoed up and down the alley, punctuated by hisses and chirps from Dino. If Chan had been here, these men would already be dead and nothing of value would be lost. Even if Crow had been here, they'd be dead. But no one was in the alley save a boy who suddenly felt very small and lost and three things that used to be people.

A tear rolled down Kevin's cheek and he wondered if he'd finally meet his parents again in the afterlife. "What do you want?" he asked quietly.

The arm around him tightened and Kevin felt himself lifted off the ground. "We want your flesh. We want your soul."

"Eat him!" one of the men cried out. "Eat him and take his soul."

The other man giggled again. "Eat his flesh. Take his power."

The man he'd elbowed giggled and leaned down to sniff at Dino. The knife pressed harder into Kevin's throat. All around him, time seemed to slow down and details he'd missed before resolved themselves. The two men straddling Dino's thrashing body had sunken eyes and the tattered remains of red and white cloaks. They smiled happily, the grins of predators who have taken down prey rather than the evil grins of malicious villains. Their only joy was the thought of food.

A drop of hot blood trickled down his throat. The knife was so sharp he barely felt it cut him. Kevin concentrated on feeling the knife. He reached out his mind until he felt the metal like it was a living thing. The blood of dozens had stained it, leaking into the blade.

Kevin almost felt as if he was touching the blade with his hands. Surely, he couldn't break it; metal was too strong. But his mind wasn't his hands and metal was no match for the magic swirling in the alley.

The man cutting his throat stopped as the air around them crackled and popped. Unalunan magic arced around the alley in purple and green hues. Kevin felt the world in way he'd never experienced. When he made Dino and when he made the stuffed dragon explode and even when he killed the combat magicians, it was all over in a flash. Those were purely reactive, uncontrolled responses.

But he had learned from the incident with the combat

magicians. Not learned in a way that he could touch or practice, Kevin had learned what Earthly magic felt like when it reacted with the world around him.

Chan often spoke of an esoteric concept he called *Wu Shin* – no mindedness. It was something he said would develop over time when the body's reaction to something became automatic. *Wu Shin* wasn't thoughtlessness, it was moving beyond a need for thought. In a way, Chan explained, *Wu Shin* was trained reaction; the body doing what it needed to do without interference from the brain. The *Tao* of martial arts.

The knife pushed harder into his throat. "Stop this. Stop this. Stop this," the man behind him chanted.

Kevin felt the world bubble up around him. The knife blade turned to sand and fell away from his throat. He felt the man behind him stagger away in fear. The two men straddling Dino got up and backed away. They held their hands up as if mere flesh and bone could stop the onslaught.

The alley lit up with apologies and prayers to broken gods. Even Dino looked around nervously. Kevin grinned. He felt the energy in the alley, became one with it, felt the power as an arc slammed into the giggling man's leg. Bones shattered and blood splashed as he collapsed to his side, screaming and holding a stump with bits of ragged bone sticking out.

Behind him, the man that had held a knife to his throat tried to run. Kevin's power reached out and snatched him up before he could escape. His body bounced off walls as the magic dragged him down the alley and dumped his broken and torn body unceremoniously next to his now legless friend.

"Dino," Kevin said.

The dinosaur slunk forward, uncertain of what was going on and terrified in the face of the storm swirling around him. Kevin's hand patted his head. Through the contact he felt Dino's raging mind. It was primitive, but aware of the world around him. Through the cries and palpable terror, Kevin told his friend everything was okay.

Out of the corner of his eye, Kevin caught Dino look back down the alley. Like these men, the dinosaur was a predator. He killed without moral wrangling; something was either a threat or it was not, food or not.

One man, the man Dino had already attacked, was still standing. Blood from the dinosaur's claws soaked his shirt and his eyes were wild. While the men might feel nothing except full stomachs after killing and eating a boy and his dinosaur, Kevin felt powerful. He wanted to be mean. He wanted to lash out at the world and smash to pieces everyone who had hurt him.

Dino's tail was twitching back and forth. He lowered his head to the ground, then rose again in a strange deinonychus dance. Kevin sensed his agitation at not protecting the flock. There was still a threat out there and it had to be dealt with before everyone would be safe.

"Go," Kevin said.

The dinosaur didn't even spare a glance back at the flock leader. He raced down the alley like an orange and green blur. Powerful legs pushed and Dino leapt with his terrible toe claws extended. A hundred and fifty pounds of pointy parts hit the man at full speed. They went down to the ground together in mass of screams, chirps, and feathers.

When it was over and Dino had ripped the man's throat out, he sniffed the gurgling corpse and shook his body before hopping off and strutting back down the alley. Kevin smiled. Then he grinned. Then he laughed out loud.

Three men wanted to eat him and his friend and now they were all dead or dying. Kevin reached out with his mind and magic found the man who had the knife. Energy rattled its way down the alley to hover right over the man's head. With a twitch of his mind, the boy with the power rammed a bolt of energy through the man's skull.

The remaining man was rapidly losing consciousness. When his leg exploded, it had opened a large vein that was pouring blood onto the ground. Kevin watched as the light faded from the man's eyes.

In the aftermath of the fight, a ten-turn-old boy stared down a dank alley covered with glowing graffiti and felt proud of himself. As the adrenaline wore off, though, the reality of what he had done fell on his small shoulders. He could tell Dino felt nothing about the killing other than a strange sense of duty done. Unlike dinosaurs, most humans feel something when they kill other humans. Killing gets easier with time, but for Kevin it was still a new sensation.

At first, he felt happy. Then, as he looked at the battered corpses, he felt a deep swell of pity and guilt. They had wanted to kill and eat him, but it was emotionless. Kevin started out by defending himself. After the knife turned to dust, he could have walked away, but he wanted to hurt them. He wanted to make them pay for the damage that had been done to his life.

He looked at his hands, but remembered Chan's words, "Magic isn't in your hands, it's in your whole body." Kevin's emotional state bottomed out. His body had killed two people and he stood idly by while his dinosaur ripped a third to shreds.

Chan would have walked away. Crow wouldn't have let it get that far to begin with. Huizhong would have done just enough to keep them from following her. None of them would have done what he had just done and felt proud of themselves. They would have done what needed to be done and moved on.

Certainly, none of them would have smiled and enjoyed every second of it. A dark side, the one thing Chan always warned to him to watch out for, had bubbled up while he wasn't watching. Kevin clenched his fists and resolved to do better in the future.

26 | Meet Up

Crow felt a tickle in the back of his head and stopped at the entryway to Fei Long's apartment and held up a hand. "Something's wrong."

The old tickle was a trick that kept him alive on the police force. He couldn't say if it was psychic or mundane, but every time he felt the brush of feathers against the back of his head, he took heed. Some cops in Croatoa had head tickles, others had feelings in their guts, but every one of them developed a sense that warned them was something wasn't right.

"What is wrong?" Chan asked from behind.

Crow shook his head, both answering and trying to release an answer that his brain didn't want to give up just yet. "Not sure," he mumbled, "but something's not right."

He stepped gently over the remains of Fei's massive door. Behind him, Chan moved like a ghost. That was another of Chan's tricks that Crow regretted never learning. His former teacher had taken on fighting and surviving as a life test. Whereas Crow liked to avoid a fight, Chan seemed to relish them. If it had been possible to pull Chan away from the fights, he would have made an excellent member of the Croatoa Police Force's special units.

The apartment was silent. Huizhong was nowhere to be found. At least Kevin's door was closed; that meant she hadn't taken him on some crazy mission. The lights were dim, so maybe she went to bed, too. He didn't relish checking in on her, but with half the city after them all for one reason or another, it paid to be paranoid.

Crow snuck through the penthouse with Chan close behind. From what Crow could see, it didn't look like there was a struggle. He'd fought Huizhong once before and she nearly got the better of him. Granted, she'd been hooked up to a psychic monster, so there was no proof she was really that good, but the woman he fought was a tough cookie.

Whatever her skills, Crow doubted she'd let herself get taken away without kicking up a fuss. Kevin was the wildcard, though. He might have spent six months working with Chan, but for a ten-turn-old boy that could mean he thought more of himself than he was actually capable of. At the very least, it was probable that Kevin's latent magic would have destroyed something.

"Crow," Chan said, "Kevin's door is closed and I do not hear Dino."

"Right," Crow replied, snapping his fingers, "the dinosaur. That thing should be going nuts right now."

He picked up his pace, but paused when he reached for the doorknob to Huizhong's door. Screw it, he thought and opened the door. The room was empty, clothes neatly folded, and the bed neatly made. It would figure she'd make the bed every morning. Crow knew he should have stopped, called it good, backed away, but something caught his eye. She'd left an empty cup on the shelf next to a porcelain statue of a pair of women on their knees in front of a demon.

There it was, that itch of his again. Who folds her clothes and makes a bed, but leaves an empty cup on a shelf? Crow stepped into the room and took a good look around. At the time that they'd decided on sleeping arrangements he'd half-hoped she'd invite him to join her, but she kept the huge, circular bed all to herself and left him on the couch dreaming about Fei's sexateria.

"What is it?" Chan asked.

"Just curious," Crow said. "Check on Kevin's room, see if he's around."

"You should leave her things alone, Crow. It is not proper to dig through someone else's belongings."

Crow sighed and turned to Chan and nearly jumped out of his skin. The master had put his face-guard back on. In the low light of the room, Chan looked exactly like Zhong Kui or one of the heroes from the pulp novels Crow loved to read. He could almost imagine Chan levitating and shooting electricity from his eyes at some do-badder.

"I'm not rifling through her underwear, Chan, just looking for clues."

Chan didn't move or react. The man looked like a statue and, not for the first time, Crow wondered what he'd be like if he had continued training with Chan rather than joining the police. Probably incredibly disciplined and boring.

"I'm just looking for any obvious clues, Chan," Crow said. He made a fist with his right hand, covered it with his open left hand and bowed his head. "I promise you I'm not going to violate her possessions."

Chan returned the salute and bowed his head. "I believe you."

Crow started to reply, but the big, lanky man turned neatly on his heel and left the room, quiet as a dark *gui*. He waited until Chan was gone and turned back to the shelf and the cup. It smelled faintly of green tea. She made tea last night, so that made sense, but there was a hint of something else in the cup. Lurking under the tea smell was a scent he couldn't place, yet it was tantalizingly familiar. A hint of a spice or something like that.

It had to be nothing. Nothing important, at least.

He set the cup back on the shelf exactly where he found it and turned to the leave the room. Out of the corner of his eye, he caught a flash of white paper against the hard wood floor. Again, odd considering Huizhong's obvious neatness.

Crow reached down to check it out and was almost ready to dismiss the paper when he flipped it over and his heart skipped a beat. It wasn't a simple piece of paper, it was an envelope with *Tiāntáng De Fěn* printed on the front. And the envelope was open.

Then he remembered the junkie in the alley. Under the layers of body odor and alley life, the man had the same hint of spice. "*Tā māde niǎo*, Huizhong," he muttered. "What were you thinking?"

Crow pocketed the envelope and closed her door behind him. He knew he didn't have the moral leg to stand on to lecture her on drugs, but he felt he had to at least talk to her about it. No wonder she wanted the room all to herself; she wanted to dance with the gods.

Outside the room, Chan waited with his arms folded over his chest. "Did you find anything?"

"No," Crow lied. "You?"

"Kevin's room is empty and the window is open. Perhaps the attackers entered through there."

If someone broke in and incapacitated Kevin and Dino rapidly, they could have grabbed Huizhong while she was hopped up on drugs. Crow rubbed his temples. It didn't seem likely that something bad happened here. "I don't think there were any attackers, Chan. I think they left."

Chan unhooked his mask. Gray eyes burned into Crow. "Where did they go?"

"I don't know. Kevin's window was open?"

Chan nodded, but didn't elaborate. Crow sidestepped Chan and looked out Kevin's window. There was a fire escape outside, so it was possible they left that way. He looked along the edges of the window and found what he was looking for: a thin gold wire around the frame.

"There was no attack," Crow said simply. "They left. Kevin probably went out the window with his dinosaur. My guess is Huizhong left through the front door."

"Why do you say that?" Chan asked.

Crow pointed at the window. "The window was magically sealed. Try to open it from the outside and something would have happened."

"Something?"

"I can't be sure what, I'm no security expert, but it was wired up. Probably to do something nasty. Kevin snuck out and Huizhong went to find him."

"Kevin would not do that. I have taught him all about the dangers of this city," Chan said. "Someone took them."

Crow shook his head and gestured around the room. "You're telling me the boy who can make things explode didn't destroy half this building when someone grabbed him? Or that Huizhong didn't kick up enough of a fuss to at least knock over a chair? He snuck out. She left to find him. End of story."

Crow plopped down on the couch with a sigh and wondered what was going on. Chan paced back and forth. The silence in the apartment let Crow's fetid imagination run wild. He'd seen too much of the city to think the boy was sharing snacks with the dinosaur on some street corner. Huizhong could probably take care of herself, but a ten-turn-old boy, no matter how much magic might be lurking in his body, would be out of his league in the city.

"We should go looking," Chan said.

For the first time since he'd known Chan, the master looked worried. Chan had spent his life becoming more and more ascetic, but the boy must have unlocked something in him. "I know you're worried, Chan," Crow said, "but we can't just go wandering around. We need to have an idea of where he went."

Chan's fist cracked and popped as he squeezed it. His gray eyes burned with all the furies of Diyu. "We must do something."

"What?" Crow asked. "Wander around and hope we find him? You trained him, so he's not defenseless..."

"It takes turns to master the arts. You know that."

"It doesn't take mastery to survive. Besides, he's got that dinosaur with him."

Chan nodded slowly. "Dino is a powerful creature. But you well know just how much trouble a ten-turn-old can get into. As I recall, I had to save you."

Crow leaned back and sighed deeply. "I would have been fine."

"You would have been food."

"You know, that event was the thing that made me want

to be a cop. The gangs I could handle, but those alley-dwellers … no one should have to live in a world with them. You know what the bitch of it is? The police didn't care about the *Wàngjìle*. No one cared about them. I got stuck on a detail to stop drugs coming in at the port. Something people wanted and I had to stop it while tourists were getting eaten in the alleys."

"Who was getting eaten?" Huizhong asked from behind them.

Crow leapt to his feet. "Where have you been?"

"Where's Kevin?" she replied.

"You don't know?" Chan asked.

"He was here when I left."

"Why did you leave?" Chan asked.

"I had to get something," Huizhong replied. There was a hint of menace in her voice.

"More Heaven's Powder?" Crow asked.

Huizhong glared at him. "The packet was empty when I found it and stay the *Diyu* out of my room."

"I could smell it in the cup." Crow replied.

"Fine," she snapped. "One of us needed to find out what the big deal was. You're hammered most of the time so it wasn't going to be you. Chan's too righteous and Kevin's too young."

Crow started to say something, but Chan put a hand on his shoulder. "What did you find?"

Huizhong flopped down on the couch and opened her mouth. She started to speak, but stopped herself. After a few false starts, the words flowed out of her mouth like a river. "It's hard to understand. I could see things, tiny bits of the universe. Things so small it's almost like they're not really there at all, but they are there. Little glowing, vibrating balls of light that bounced around. I got the sensation that the universe was constantly rebuilding itself, like it was rewiring everything so that no matter what we did it didn't matter. But that was just a surface thing. I was really looking at the *Tao*, seeing the relationship between everything. It was amazing."

"That's what I see when I make things explode," Crow said. "Bits of the universe. Interesting. So did you find more Heaven's Powder?"

Huizhong shook her head. "No, not interested. That was a one-shot deal. I was after something else."

"What?" Crow asked. "What was so important that you left a kid with powerful magic alone?"

Huizhong dropped a book on the tea table. "This."

The book reeked of magic. Crow felt his mind being drawn into it, subsumed by whatever power it had absorbed. Magic had a distinct quality, almost a taste, depending on who wielded it. The book tasted familiar, but he couldn't place how. It felt like an almost forgotten dream.

The click of claws on the tile pulled him back to Fei's apartment. Kevin, looking somewhat the worse for wear, strode through with fists clenched and a scowl on his face. Dino's feathers were ruffled, but he seemed unharmed, too.

"Going to bed," Kevin snapped as he disappeared into his room and slammed the door.

A wave of relief rolled over Crow. "This is why I never wanted kids," he mumbled as he leaned back into the thick padding of the couch.

Chan quietly crossed the room, completely silent even on the hardwood floors. He tried Kevin's door, but found it locked. Even through the closed door, everyone could hear the window slam shut.

"Is everything okay?" Chan called through the door.

"Sleeping," Kevin snapped.

Huizhong looked guilty, but relieved. "I'm sorry," she said quietly. "I should have waited."

"It is as the *Tao* wills it," Chan said. "What have you found?"

Crow motioned at the book on the table. "Some sorcerer's book," he said.

He sat bolt upright on the couch and peered at the book.

"The Beast," he said.

The book opened itself and flipped through pages until it stopped on a page with a picture of a golden man. He put the pieces together and looked up at Huizhong, slightly aghast, but also impressed. "You didn't pay for this, did you?" he asked.

She shook her head slowly. "The pawn shop was closed."

"This book was the one that pointed me toward the Monastery of Hope. How did you manage to steal it? That pawn shop had more security than any place I'd ever seen."

"I'm fast," she replied with a twinkle in her eyes.

"I guess," Crow replied. "Do you have any idea what this book is?"

Huizhong nodded. "Kind of. It's magic, it's powerful. It may be sentient. It had to have been in the possession of an extremely powerful sorcerer for a very long time."

"Owner," Crow said to the book.

The book didn't respond. Either it didn't understand the command or didn't have it in its index. "Frontispiece," he said.

Pages flipped madly until they stared at the image of an old man in a cloak and dūuli. In the hand drawn picture, the old man's beard seemed to be moving. As they peered closer, the whole picture lit up with movement. Birds and lizards darted among the trees. The clouds moved across a black and white sky.

Crow realized his jaw was almost on the floor. Like most kids in an orphanage, he dreamed of ways out, ways to get some measure of power over his life. That's what drew him to Chan, but before he studied Chan's bizarre, modified *Wushu*, Crow wanted magic.

Magic had been part of Aluna since the first creatures rose from the muck in some tidal pool in the Northeast quadrant. While Chan busied himself in their orphanage by reading *Wushu* pulps, Crow fantasized about magic and the ability to remake the world as he saw fit. It surprised most people who knew him, but Felix Crow was incredibly studious when he wanted to be. Anything that interested him, be it *Wushu* or magic, got his full attention.

"Who is that?" Huizhong asked.

"That is Marcus Hong," Crow said with a sigh. "He died over a hundred turns ago, but people say he lived to be well over three hundred. No one knows for certain just how old he was because they didn't keep the best records four hundred turns ago. He was supposedly the most powerful sorcerer to ever walk the planet."

Huizhong's fingers brushed the page gently. Her eyes shone with reverence. "And this must have been his book."

"It makes sense," Crow replied. "Marcus had a thirst for knowledge. He would have written down everything he could."

"Hmmm," Chan said. "How did a book from Marcus Hong wind up in a pawn shop in Croatoa?"

Crow leaned way back and let the couch absorb him. For all Fei Long's faults and bad taste in decorating, he had impeccable taste in furniture. Crow felt like he was floating, drifting along without a care in the world. The comfort let him think. His big brain turned rapidly, chewing on the problem.

"This book pointed me toward the Monastery of Hope," he said. "I asked for information about the Beast, but all it did was point me down an alley in Crime Alley. When I got there, I found the Monastery of Hope, but the monk already knew who I was."

"Did he ask for an autograph?" Huizhong asked.

"Does blood count?"

"Only if you write your name in it," she replied.

"What happened to the monk?" Chan asked.

"Well, unfortunately we had a bit of a tussle," Crow said.

Huizhong snorted and rolled her eyes. "A tussle?"

Crow nodded and smiled. "A tussle. I kind of blew the door open and he wasn't very happy about that."

"You fought a cloistered monk?" Huizhong asked.

"I really just wanted to talk. He threw the first punch."

Chan's disappointment was palpable. Even from a distance, Crow could feel his old master shaking his head sadly. Huizhong rolled her eyes and sat back on her chair with her arms folded over her chest. "You beat up a monk," she said.

Crow waved his arms around madly. "Have you ever seen monks fight? I swear, all those guys do is practice fighting. Sure, they like to strut around in their orange robes and wax philosophical about how much they abhor violence, but when they're back at the monastery they stand around out back, chatting and punching stone walls."

"How is the monk?" Chan asked.

"What monk?" Crow asked innocently.

"The one you fought," Chan said.

"Tussled with," Crow interjected.

Chan gripped the back of Crow's couch and squeezed. Somewhere, deep inside the couch, wood cracked and splintered. "Fine," he said. "The one you tussled with."

"Oh, him," Crow said. "He's dead."

Crow looked around the room and felt their eyes on him. A part of him got very defensive and another part grew angry. Who were they to determine the right course of action when neither of them were being attacked by an irate, naked gold guy?

"You killed a monk," Huizhong said.

"It's not illegal," Crow replied. "Well, not any more than killing anyone else. There's no *monkicide* or anything."

Huizhong looked at the book on the table and said, "Monastery of Hope."

The book's pages flipped madly until they landed on a picture of a paifang in the middle of a field. The image was good enough that Crow almost wondered if it wasn't a picture so much as a glimpse back in time. Inscriptions covered the face of the stone. Crow recognized a few of them: fire, sorcerers, heavens. Most of the inscriptions were in the old-style writing that no one uses anymore, but even old languages never really die; they get renamed and redistributed.

Huizhong put her finger gently on the text and read out loud, "The Monastery of Hope was built before the end of dragon wars that nearly saw the end of humanity. Originally, the site was a place that aimed to dispense hope in the face of certain annihilation. The monks of the Monastery of Hope eventually intended to broker a peace treaty with the dragons. They sent emissaries to various enclaves in the hope that the war could come to an end and both species could learn to coexist. Unfortunately, as loath as humans are to allow alien intelligence in their realm, dragons are even more so.

"Eventually the tide of war shifted in favor of the humans. Simply put, we outbred them. The Dragon War was a war of attrition and, as large apex predators, dragons only had young every hundred turns or so. That kind of alignment with nature kept their numbers small.

"As the tide shifted, the monastery began to change. The monks returned to their mission of providing hope in the form of tales for weary travelers. Soon, the travelers started paying and the monks learned that money was a good thing to have.

"The head monk, a man whose name is lost in history, became so obsessed with gold that he turned himself to gold. As the rest of the monks fled in fear that they, too, would turn to gold, the head monk decided to look for himself again.

"The purpose of the monastery changed until, one day, the golden monk started a large wall around it. The monk continued until the wall surrounded the monastery. He then set about studiously ignoring the world and focused on his meditation."

"And no one has heard of him since then, right?" Crow asked.

"Not a soul," Huizhong replied. "He's a ghost wrapped in a riddle."

"Are there any ways in or out?" Crow asked.

Huizhong peered closely at the text, lips moving as she read to herself. She shook her head, "No, it doesn't look like it. Probably just the one Crow made when he blew a hole through a wall that had been there for a few hundred turns."

Crow made a spinning motion with his finger in the air. "It was old and falling down anyway."

"It was not!" Huizhong snapped. "If it was falling down, why did you have to use your magic to knock it down?"

"Because I'm lazy?" Crow asked.

"I can't argue with that," Huizhong agreed. "Why would you wonder if there are any ways in or out of there?"

"When I was tussling with the monk…" Crow started.

"The golden one. The one you killed. Tussling," Huizhong interjected.

"It was a tussle to the death," Crow said. "Anyway, he knew my name. He knew Fei Long. He even knew about the Beast. How would a guy holed up in a monastery for a few hundred turns know about all that?"

Huizhong knitted her eyebrows and held up a finger. She cocked her head to the side and leaned back on the sofa. "That's a good question."

"I think there's something that book either isn't telling us or doesn't know about. Someone was talking to that monk. That means there must be a way in and out that we don't know about."

"I can't say for certain, but I have an idea."

"What's that?" Crow asked.

"There's a way in through the Clock Tower," Huizhong replied.

Crow cocked an eyebrow and wondered exactly what it was that she thought she knew. She had worked there for a while, so it's entirely possible she had inside information. "Okay," he said, "I'll bite. How do you know?"

She smirked and Crow caught a hint of the old Huizhong, the one who had seduced him and tried to kill him. The fun Huizhong. "We already know Chenming Zhang came and went as he pleased. He had to get out to gather up all those things and people he was experimenting on. If the administration knew what was going on in his lab, they'd have shut him down for sure. All the entrances and exits of that building are guarded. The monastery is in *Fànzuì Hútòng*, right? No one would notice people disappearing from there and it makes sense that over the turns the Monastery of Hope would have found a way to link up with the Clock Tower. It also makes sense that Chenming would be interested in a three-hundred turn old man. He was obsessed with immortality and would have found a way to link the Clock Tower to the monastery."

"Which would mean there was a way out of the monastery and into the city. You know, just after I got hired to kill Chenming, I met something in an alley behind my apartment. There was a guy trying to get me off the case. That's strange enough on its own – how would someone know that quickly that I was going after The Clock Man? – but the guy had a wire stuck in his head. He sort of fizzled out and then something exploded from a dumpster. The guy died, but I got a nice hat out of the deal. My place isn't too far from Crime Alley," Crow replied

"Wherever the entrance is, it's hidden," Huizhong said, "and I don't feel like digging through alleys looking for a way in. Maybe Chenming's diary will have more information."

"Wait," Crow said, holding up a hand. "What diary?"

"All the Clock Men keep copious notes about their day-to-day lives. I saw Chenming's on his desk before he died."

Crow sat up. The gears were turning in his head as he pondered the situation. Chenming Zhang had contact with the Golden Monk of the Monastery of Hope. Chenming also knew about the request to kill him, which meant he had to have eyes and ears everywhere and a way to contact them without being seen.

"Where is the diary now?" Crow asked.

"The entire hundredth floor of the Clock Tower was

sealed immediately after Chenming's death. I'll bet the diary is still in his lab somewhere."

Crow rose from the couch and held out a hand to Huizhong. "Sounds like we need to visit the Clock Tower. Up for a little trip?"

27 | Spire

Crow stood next to Huizhong, their bodies almost touching, as they stared up at the Clock Tower. Here, magic became reality as an unending stream of Clock Men controlled the flow of magic that powered the city and the planet. The Clock Tower had been in this place for hundreds of turns, but it had grown from the humble beginnings of a hut built by the first Clock Man into a hundred-story tall monolith that tried to pierce the sky.

In addition to the sheer size of the building, it was intimidating in other ways, too. The Clock Men and their tower were heroes on Aluna. Without them, the lights wouldn't burn, the water wouldn't heat, and all the wonders of modern convenience would vanish without a trace. The Clock Tower was a sacred place to everyone on Aluna, no matter what gods they kept on their shelves.

"Are we really going to break into this place?" Huizhong asked. "It's the most tightly guarded building on the planet."

Crow ground out his *bidi* under a heel and nodded. "Not so much break in as walk in. With a bit of luck, no one will notice us. You know your way around the tower; I can lie about why we're doing it. We're a perfect team."

Huizhong looked at him sideways. "Team?"

"What else would you call it? Cooperative effort group?"

She shook her head sadly. "Team it is."

Of the many things people have called Crow – Felix Crow, the infamous Felix Crow, that jackass – no one had ever called him "The attentive Felix Crow". He had trouble sometimes understanding other people had feelings. "Something wrong?"

"No," Huizhong said. "Let's get this job done."

"Hey," Crow said, putting his arm in front of her. "Why do they call them 'Clock Men'?"

She brushed his hand aside and started walking toward the tower. "Didn't you ever study?"

Crow hurried to keep up. "No, why would I? I find it's easier to ask for information when I need it."

Huizhong straightened her back and kept walking, talking without looking back. "Magic is a constant, but you can't send constant streams of power through the lines or they'll burn out. They have to maintain a clock cycle. Tick tock, Crow. Tick tock. That was the bit of great engineering the first Clock Man figured out. Magic pulses down the wires and the Clock Men regulate when each pulse happens."

"Ah. I was hoping for something more interesting. Like a celestial clock or something."

She snorted. "In a way, that's exactly what it is. They're just flesh and blood clocks with engineering skills and a propensity for magic."

"See, when I need an answer, there's always someone around to give me one."

"I'm about to give you an answer full-force in your teeth."

"That's what I love about you; your fiery spirit."

Huizhong stared at him. "Love about me?"

Crow could feel his cheeks redden and wondered if he'd just overstepped some boundary. "I'd like to say it's a figure of speech."

"But you're not going to."

"I'll just say it's a conversation we should have some time when we're not about to break into the most heavily guarded building on the planet and steal Chenming Zhang's diary."

Her face softened and she nodded. "Agreed," she said, holding out her hand. "But you owe me a conversation."

Crow took her hand and shook it. His own palm felt sweaty and clammy to him, especially compared to her warm grip. "I'll even buy you a drink. I know a place not far from here that has the best *baiju* on the planet."

"It's a date," Huizhong said, smiling.

"Great," Crow muttered. "Now we need to have another

conversation. You're buying for that one, though."

Huizhong extracted her hand from his and clapped him on the shoulder. "Come on, old man. It's time to find out what Chenming was really up to."

They walked side by side up the steps to the entrance of the Clock Tower. At the main doors, two men who had obviously been chosen for their size and willingness to shave their hair into Manchu queues glared down at them.

The guards were massive, easily over twenty-one hands tall. The *kwan daos* in their hands were custom built to fit each guard. Each broadsword on a stick was a few hands taller than each guard and weighed in at over eight *jin*, yet the guards wielded them like chopsticks.

Both Crow and Huizhong held their breaths as they approached the doors. She had worked at the tower for some time and disappeared immediately after Chenming Zhang took a nosedive out the hundredth-floor window. Crow was the one who had sent Chenming out the window. If either of them were recognized, the guards would likely shred them on the spot.

"Gentlemen," Crow said as they passed.

Neither guard replied, but the one of the left looked slightly less perturbed than the one on the right. Crow reflected on the guards he'd killed last time he was here and wondered if they had been friends with either of these guys. When people are chosen to be badass guards, do they even bother with things like friendship?

Huizhong stopped in front of the guard on the left and put her hands on her hips. "Are there any tours running right now. We're from out of town and want to see the Tower. When are the tours?"

The guard growled, but didn't answer her. Crow recognized the game immediately and gently pulled on her shoulder. "Come on, sweetie. We need to leave these gentlemen alone. I'm sure someone at the desk will know."

"No!" Huizhong said and stamped her foot. "I want to

know if there are any tours. What good are these guys if they don't know about the tours?"

"Uh, slicing intruders to pieces."

"I am not an intruder. I am a citizen of this planet and I want to know about tours."

The guard growled again and Crow decided it was time to end the game before one or both of them wound up missing body parts. "We can ask at the front desk. Come on, sweetie. Let's get inside before one of these guards cuts us in half."

Huizhong gave one last huff and put her finger in the guard's chest. "You're lucky he's here. Otherwise you'd be answering to me."

Crow grabbed her hand and tugged Huizhong through the double doors. Inside, the lobby of the Clock Tower was a museum of various pieces of equipment Clock Men of the past had created to help them with their tasks. The modern pieces were utilitarian, but some of the early machines were works of art on par with anything hanging in a gallery.

The pieces, machines of varying size and complexity, were created by Clock Men as special projects. Some changed the way magic was delivered, others revolutionized the process. Chenming Zhang's machine – a gold and silver device that could manipulate minds – was nowhere to be found, but the first wireless magic interlocketer was proudly back on display.

Huizhong stepped faster so that she was dragging Crow and made a beeline to the back of the museum. Here, the walls were decorated with pictures of former Clock Men and notes about their accomplishments. Almost no one came back here, so they had the Hall of Faces to themselves. To keep from attracting too much attention as they worked their way down the hall, they pretended to stop and examine the pictures as the security patrols made their rounds.

Near the front of the Hall of Faces, decorated with garlands and flowers, was a portrait of Chenming Zhang. In the portrait, he was smiling and full of life; a far cry from the monstrosity that took over Huizhong's brain and tried to kill

Crow.

They stared in silence at the portrait, each remembering the events of six months ago. When they last saw him, Chenming Zhang looked nothing like his portrait. He had performed surgery on himself, implanting magic and mechanisms until he was more like an automaton than a man. Most automatons can't fight that well or use wireless magic technology to remote control people, but both things were right up Zhang's alley.

"In the middle of the hall is a door," Huizhong said quietly. "We need to wait until it clears out and hope they haven't changed the lock."

"Would that be the door that leads to the storeroom where you drugged me?" Crow asked.

Huizhong glared at him, but the faintest hint of a smile played at her lips. "Among other things, yes."

An old couple walked slowly through the hallway, holding hands and pointing. They stopped at one painting and grinned happily, chattering to each other in near silent Chinese before moving on. Huizhong had a near encyclopedic knowledge of all the Clock Men from history and told a little story about each character as she and Crow worked their way to the middle of the hall.

Crow took note of the comings and goings of the tower guards and security forces as he listened to Huizhong spin yarns of the Clock Men of yore.

"This guy," she said, pointing at a picture of a man with wild, white eyebrows and a beard down to his stomach, "once got caught in the Clock Tower with no less than ten prostitutes. Some say the figure is closer to twenty. The only thing everyone can agree on is Shen Kuo really liked sex."

"Who doesn't like sex?" Crow asked a little too loudly.

"Crow," Huizhong started.

Before she could finish her thought, a couple with two small children strode through the Hall of Faces. Crow took the opportunity to look like yet another tourist acting badly in the big city. "Hey," he called after them, "You guys like sex, right? I mean you've got twins, so it stands to reason you like to get down, if you know what I mean."

Huizhong stared at him, mouth agape in horror and indignation. "What are you doing?" she hissed.

"Trust me. Just get ready to slap me when the time is right."

"Right?" Huizhong asked.

"You'll know," Crow said with a floppy smile.

Crow called back to the rapidly moving couple, "Hey, it's cool. Everyone likes sex."

A security guard came slowly around the corner. He acted like it was no big deal for him to be there, but Crow knew his little show irked the man to no end. Security guards either act like their presence is unobtrusive or they immediately start busting heads. Since this guy wasn't grabbing his club, Crow felt safe, but he still needed to get rid of the guy. A little diversion should be enough for the guard to go get help.

"If your wife is half as hot in bed as she is in that dress, it's no wonder you've got two kids," Crow called out to couple. "Ma'am, you've got an amazing rack!"

Huizhong slapped Crow hard upside the head and pointed her finger at him. She let loose with a long stream of Chinese curses before settling down and shaking her head slowly. "Amazing rack? What is wrong with you?"

"There's a hole with no bottom," Crow muttered as he rubbed his jaw.

He looked up at her and winked. "Fight me," he whispered. "Knock my ass down. When the hallway empties, we bolt for the door."

When she stepped back a bit, Crow took the opportunity to turn and yell at the happy couple some more. "Madam, that is an amazing ass. I wish my wife's ass was that great!"

Crow turned back to wink at Huizhong. Her fist caught him on the side of the head. One moment he was standing up, the next he was on his ass wondering what hit him. He looked up and saw Huizhong as if he was seeing her for the first time. She wasn't the pink-haired pixie that seduced him; she was a wild-haired warrior with balled fists and eyes full of fire.

Either she was the best actress in the city or he had actually pissed her off. "Sorry," he mumbled.

She stopped looking at him and peered down the hallway. Behind him, Crow could hear the click of feet running from the hallway. Huizhong reached down and grabbed his hand. Before she helped him up, she squeezed his hand hard. "S☐ pì y☐n" – damned asshole – she hissed.

With a grunt, she hefted him to his feet. He moved his jaw a few times to make sure it was still connected and said, "Yep. Sorry about that, I needed to hurry them along."

Huizhong still looked like she was ready to kill him. Crow backed up slowly and held up his hands. "Huizhong?" he asked. "Are you still there."

She advanced on him until they were almost nose-to-nose. Instead of punching him again, she planted a quick kiss on his lips and moved around him. "Good thinking," she said as she headed to the door. "You not only cleared the hall out, you let me hit you with no repercussions."

"Nice punch."

"Thank you. Mab taught me. I used to punch trees."

"You and Chan," Crow said as Huizhong pressed the edges of a recessed door. "He used to make me kick trees."

She exhaled as the door quietly opened. Crow hurried through and Huizhong secured it from inside just in time to hear voices in the hallway. "Shh," she said, holding her finger up to her lips.

Crow nodded and looked around the room. It was pretty much as he remembered; endless rows of neatly stacked and labeled boxes. The detritus of hundreds of turns of Clock Men leaving everything behind when they walk out of the Clock Tower and squint at the suns for the first time in ten turns.

Huizhong finally turned and faced him. "They're gone. Sounded mad that we'd disappeared, though. How's your jaw?"

"Hurts like *Dìyù*," Crow replied. "Hey, is all this stuff here forever?"

"No, only the important things. The cleanout crews work day and night to catalog useful papers, but the rest goes in the incinerator."

Crow squinted his eyes and cocked his head. "Where is this incinerator?"

"Downstairs. Where else would you put an incinerator?"

"People go down there all the time, right? Don't answer that. I was just thinking, if I wanted to get rid of evidence of something – something bad – I'd burn it. What do you think are the chances Chenming's stuff has been sorted?"

Huizhong nodded, understanding what he was getting at. "You think his journal might already have been burned. I wouldn't worry about it. There's so much junk down there it'll take until the end of time for it to all get burned. The master incinerator keeps tight control on what gets burned, too."

"What if someone snagged it before they locked up Chenming's lab?"

"You're thinking Robinson got in there? He was Chenming's lap lizard, a brutal little man, but he wasn't smart enough to work on his own." Huizhong said.

"Desperation makes people do desperate things. Desperate people can accomplish miracles sometimes," Crow replied.

"Why would he even try?" Huizhong asked. "Why would anyone make a grab for Chenming's diary? Sure, it would be worth a fortune, but the Clock Tower guards would hunt a thief to the end of the world."

"If I were Robinson, and I'm just assuming it's him – it may not be. If I were Robinson and thought there was something that could implicate me, I'd get rid of it posthaste. In all the confusion, he could have snuck in, snatched up the journal, and burned it within hours of Chenming's death."

Huizhong shook her head. "Protocol states on the death of

a Clock Man, the entire building is placed on immediate lockdown. Everyone inside is escorted out. You blended in with the crowd, I was an employee. The upper floor was sealed within minutes. I doubt Robinson would have had a chance to get in there."

"Think it's still sealed?"

She shrugged. "I don't know; I got out of town as quickly as I could. What happened with Chenming was unprecedented. I wouldn't be surprised if his lab was still sealed."

Crow pondered. His brow furrowed. He looked like someone who had just eaten something crunchy and tasty and realized it could have been a *cāngyǐng* fresh from the dumpster. "Okay, I say we go up first and if we can't find the journal upstairs, we go down. Sound fair?"

Huizhong nodded. "Seems like a simple enough plan."

"The best ones usually are. Where's the elevator?"

She pointed at a non-descript door in the middle of the room. "Right over there. We'll be going almost to the top, plenty of time for someone to catch us in the act."

"Think anyone will notice?" Crow asked, suddenly concerned.

"I doubt it. These elevators run all the time. Most people will be watching 101, anyway. They had the new floor built and ready for occupancy within a few hours."

"The power of magic," Crow muttered.

As they rode the elevator up a hundred stories, Huizhong watched the city transform from dark alleys and madness to a glistening gem. Crow watched with stars in his eyes. For all his faults – and there were many – he genuinely loved this city. She wished she could see it through his eyes. All she ever saw was the darkness and violence, but he saw something different.

Crow had seen the worst things Croatoa had to offer and still managed to keep upbeat about the place. The constant buzz of the city set her on edge, but it seemed to energize him.

They were fundamentally different people, she guessed. He hid his dark side, the one that pinned her to a wall and grinned while he choked the life out of her, under a blanket of alcohol and bad jokes. She hid hers, the one that seduced and helped murder him, under a shield of disdain.

Maybe they weren't that different, after all. Two people who had stared the darkness in the face and walked away from it.

"They make these elevators slow on purpose," she said to break the silence and derail her train of thought. "It's supposed to allow the Clock Men time to reflect on the job and the responsibility."

Crow snorted. "If they want to know what they're doing is important, they should get down there and talk to the people who need the power to make food and light. Go talk to the kid who keeps his light on all night so the monsters won't come."

Huizhong didn't have a response to that. For all his fluff and bluster, Crow really believed in his city. She edged closer to him. "I always liked taking the elevator; I did it every night before I went home. The city is amazing at night, an ocean of flickering lights."

He looked at her with a hint of sadness in his eyes. "It's amazing from below, too. I know it's not your forest, but the city itself is amazing. It's a living, breathing thing. Not always easy to deal with, but beautiful in its own way."

"Once you peel away the bad things."

"The bad things are what make it amazing. You can't have the good without the bad."

Again, she didn't have a response to that. Every time she thought she had Felix Crow figured out, he surprised her again. Huizhong looked out the window and tried to imagine it without the people under the pier or the junkies or the babbling street preachers praying to gods they'd never meet. But she couldn't and she didn't feel she ever would.

After a short eternity of seeing the world through

different eyes, the elevator finally dinged. Crow pulled himself away from the window with an obvious effort. "Time to see what ol' Chenming was up to," he said. "You ready?"

Huizhong nodded. This was what Ao Shun told her she was holding onto; the dark place in her soul that had to be explored before she could find some closure on it. Right across the hall from the elevator was a set of double doors with a magically charged seal. Beyond those doors were the horrors she had run from when she fled Croatoa with her tail tucked between her legs.

"I've got to say, I'm not looking forward to this," Crow said. "Let's get this done. I've got a conversation scheduled for later today and I don't want to be late."

She grinned despite the sinking sense of dread in her stomach. "How do you plan on getting through the seal?"

He looked at her with a serious set to his face. "What? I thought you had a key."

"Why would I have a key?" she asked, taken aback.

His face split into a grin. "Just kidding. This isn't like Fei's door. That thing was meant to keep out an army. This seal is meant to deter employees from getting themselves in trouble."

He fiddled around in his jacket, going through pocket after pocket before holding up a small piece of bronze and jade. "Master key. You learn some useful things being a cop, like how to disable low-end security measures with a bit of metal."

Crow moved the little gadget around the glowing edge of the door until he found what he was looking for. He gently eased the device closer to the door until the air felt like it was going to pop. Then, with a slight hiss, the glowing edge of the door flickered out of existence.

"What did you just do?" Huizhong asked.

"Re-routed the seal. When that seal was in place, you could be the strongest person on Aluna and not open that door because the magic generates an opposite reaction. The harder you pull, the stronger the seal becomes. Fortunately, these seals are set up in loops. Find the first part of the loop and you can force the loop into something else, a master key for instance. When we leave, we'll pull that out and no one will even know we were here."

He motioned at the door, "Would you care to do the honors?"

Huizhong hesitantly reached out to the door. It was cold and smooth under her fingertips. The last time she was here was a nightmare she'd relived again and again over the past months. Inside the main room on the hundredth floor was where she'd felt her will become subsumed by Chenming Zhang's. She watched herself fighting Crow, screaming in her own mind as her body tried to kill him again.

A slight push and the doors opened silently. The lab was exactly as she remembered, right down to the torso of a man Chenming left as a gruesome greeting. Last time, the man was alive and floating in gelatin; now his corpse rested in cracked and dried out gunk.

Crow sucked in his breath and let out a low whistle. "They closed the doors immediately after Chenming hit the ground, right?"

Huizhong nodded. She was unconscious when Crow managed to kill Chenming Zhang, but the chaos at the bottom of the terror was still burned into her mind. At first no one understood what had hit the street. It was just a mass of flesh and metal. As soon as someone recognized The Clock Man, the tower shut down. She and Crow managed to escape with the crowd just before the bars dropped.

"That was, what, six months ago?" Crow asked, prodding at the remains of a little dragon. All that was left of it was a pair of wings and a head attached together by a mass of wires. "This little guy was alive last time I was here."

There are things people aren't meant to play with, Huizhong thought as she looked around the macabre scene. It was terrifying when it was alive, but it just seemed sad now that everything Chenming Zhang had wired together was dead and rotting. So much waste. Wasted lives, wasted talents. And all for what? So a man could try to seize immortality? All his talents and he still hit the street at a couple hundred *zhàng* per second.

"Huizhong," Crow said quietly.

She snapped back to the world at hand. After all the terrors that had been birthed here, the result was a dead, dusty room. "Yeah, six months ago."

"Did you know it takes turns for a corpse to decompose?" Crow said absently. "Like over ten turns. When I was on the force, we tracked down a serial killer. Real piece of *lā sh*□. He used to capture young girls, dress them up, poison them, and then position their corpses like schoolgirl dolls in his basement.

"Anyway, he'd been at it for turns when we finally nabbed him. I went down into the basement and found row after row of dead girls. He'd arranged them like they were in school. The oldest had been down there for nearly twenty turns; she was a skeleton in a frilly dress. He took a new girl from the slums about every six months. Our forensics guys were fascinated. They had pristine examples of what decay looks like every six months for twenty turns."

"That's horrible," Huizhong said.

"Yep. Terrible," Crow said distantly as he examined a table. He poked and prodded at something that might have been alive in the distant past. "Bad people out there."

Huizhong stayed rooted in place, unsure if she could make herself go further into Chenming's floor of bad ideas come to loathsome life. "Why would you tell me that story?"

He looked at her and smiled sadly. For the first time, Huizhong got a glimpse of the weight on his soul and it was terrifying. "Because it made you forget about where you are right now. As bad as this place is, there's always something worse out there."

"Pessimist," Huizhong said. "There's also something better out there."

"Realist," Crow replied. "Sure, there's better stuff out there, but you're not one of those people that's going to get to experience the best life has to offer."

"How do you know that?" Huizhong asked, terrified he might be right.

"We can smell our own," Crow replied and moved further into Chenming's workshop.

Without another word, and with thoughts of dead girls all neatly arranged, she followed him. All around her were things that shouldn't be; drawings of dissected and rewired creatures, brains with plugs in them resting in jars, and all manner of failed experiments.

An entire floor of the Clock Tower consisted of about one hundred and thirty thousand square hands of space. Not huge by warehouse standards, but big enough to be intimidating and filled to the brim with shelves and experiments and notes.

It was clear no one had been up here since the event. There were no piles of papers, no boxes, no obvious signs of sorting. The room was sealed up and forgotten until the cleaning crews could get into place. Crow moved rapidly toward the northern edge of the floor, pausing occasionally to examine something or move papers around.

As they got to the Northern edge, the mass of machinery and paperwork gave way to a brightly lit, open space with a single enormous desk and a view of the entire city. It was here that Chenming Zhang worked his magic and kept the whole of Aluna powered and moving. The chair was turned, facing the darkening skies. The first stars were shining. *Dàjiě* and *Xi□ojiě* were hiding tonight, so the city would have to wait until morning to feel one of the mothers' warmth.

Crow walked past the desk and stared out through the floor to ceiling windows. "Dark night tonight," he said. "Most people think crime is worse when the sisters are both shining full on, but it was far worse when they were gone. A night like tonight is bad news for everyone out there."

Huizhong glanced out the window, but something about

the desk chair caught her eye. Why would Chenming's chair face out the window? She approached the chair cautiously and spun it around with her foot. The corpse staring back at her made her repeat "forty dead girls" like a mantra.

"I see you found Robinson," Crow said. "Good thing, too. If he was hiding in this room, we might never have found him."

The six-month-old corpse leered at her with sunken eye sockets and retracted teeth and gums. His skin hadn't liquefied yet, but it had turned tough and leathery. All around Robinson's body, decay ruled supreme. Considering the place, though, Huizhong wondered how long it would be before the man rose from his chair and tried to slaughter them.

"The renegade magic must have kept him somewhat preserved," Crow said as he stared down at Robinson's dead body. "How does it feel to be locked away and left to die, asshole?"

Huizhong sensed Crow's anger rising and tensed. The last time he got mad, he nearly killed her. To her surprise and relief, he backed down quickly and grinned. "At least he got to move around instead of being stuck between two stones. Of course, he probably died of dehydration and I hear that's not a fun way to go. I wonder why he didn't take a dive out the window."

"He didn't want that book to fall into the wrong hands," Huizhong said. She reached toward Robinson's corpse and stopped. Just a body, she told herself. Just another dead body. *Forty dead girls. Forty dead girls.*

His fingers felt like *Wěidà de xīyì* hide after it had been left out to dry and crack in the summer suns. She jumped when she tried to peel a finger back and it broke off. Part of her wanted to examine the finger, part of her wanted it as far away from her as possible. Huizhong tossed the finger over her shoulder and kept prying.

In all, Huizhong broke off six fingers trying to get to the diary nestled between Robinson's arms. By the end, she was choking back putrid bile that poured from her overactive imagination. She got the book, though, and did it without throwing up.

"Nice work," Crow said when he saw the shocked look in her eyes. "It's not everyone that gets to desecrate a corpse."

"Not helping," Huizhong replied. "And I don't think breaking off fingers counts as desecrating a corpse. Don't you have to perform a *Hēi mófǎ* ritual or have sex with a corpse before it becomes desecration?"

Crow chuckled, but didn't offer to help her out. "Whatever it takes. I usually desecrate the living. When they're dead, they're less interesting."

Huizhong flipped through Chenming Zhang's diary and did her best to ignore the sick feeling in her stomach. "There is something so wrong with you."

"Just one thing? I must be getting slow in my old age."

Each page she flipped through pushed Huizhong closer and closer to the madness of Chenming Zhang. His script, neat and tidy for the first half of the book, slowly and deliberately changed until chaos reigned supreme. His letter positioning didn't change, but the script that was so precise in the beginning changed to pointed letters and screaming text by the end.

"'The voice came again last night,'" Huizhong read out loud. "'It told me tales of immortality. I thought I was going mad, but really all I found was the ultimate sanity. Why should anyone die? Why should I die? I, who have given so much, should be able to live forever. The voice taught me how. All it wants in return is a way I have with magic.' Chenming was hearing voices. He really had lost it."

"Well, he had cut parts off his body and replaced them with mechanical pieces. I thought it was obvious that he'd lost it."

Huizhong nodded slowly. It was one thing to see the end result of his madness – the clinking, clacking thing he became. It was another thing to get into his head and see the genius he was turn into the madman he became. People like Chenming Zhang – brilliant magician, brilliant surgeon – weren't supposed to go insane like average people. There was supposed to be a big push, an otherworld shove that would take the best and turn them into the worst, not a slow, tedious descent into madness like an average person.

Crow looked around the room, picking things up and examining them closely like he was looking for clues. Huizhong focused on the diary. He was in there, she was sure of it.

She rubbed her eyes and flipped through the little book. As his mind rotted, the voices in his head became more insistent until he started venturing out of the tower. "'I killed a homeless man tonight and ate his soul. It tasted like spicy sauce on fish. There was a zing of flavor at the end that made me smile and lick my teeth. Later that night, I realized it wasn't his soul – that can't be eaten – it was his ... himness. The essence of him that tugged at the bits of the universe, tinged with sorrow and the tiniest bit of magic. We are all part of the universe. We are all magical things. We are all bits of the Heavens. We have been molded into horrible life and given faculty to understand our place. That was the greatest crime in the universe. And that is the wrong I intend to right.'"

Crow stopped and stared at her. "What was that last line?"

Huizhong flipped the page back. "'That was the greatest crime in the universe'?"

"No, no. Before that. Something about the Heavens."

She scanned the page, looking for the line she had just read. "'We are all bits of the Heavens.'"

Crow dropped the statue of a dragon holding a mug. It bounced once on the bare stone floor before shattering. "Chenming Zhang figured out how to make Heaven's Powder," he said.

"What?" Huizhong asked. "How could that be? He was a

Clock Man. And a doctor before that. How would he … why would he make something like that?"

And then it hit her full force. Her half-forgotten trip through the universe and all the jangly little bits that made it up. Each part was connected, yet separate. The essence of a person intermingled with the universe and held in place with a bit of magic.

"He made it because the voice told him to. But you know what? I don't think he was crazy. I think someone really was talking to him."

"Who?"

Crow furrowed his brow in concentration. "You said there's an incinerator down in the basement, right? Ever been down there?"

"Once. During orientation for my job at the gift shop they took us down there and explained there would be no funeral for anyone who got in the way of the Clock Tower."

"Does it have any tunnels?" Crow asked.

28 | The Madness of Madam Chow

When Crow and Huizhong left, Chan breathed a sigh of relief and sat with his back to the wall next to Kevin's room. The boy was alive and that was the most important thing. Whatever he had done or had done to him in the city, he was alive.

After the night, he was emotionally exhausted. Kevin running off into the dark city, Crow and Huizhong dancing around the idea that they both had a thing for each other, even the slaughter in the tea house, left him wanting nothing more than to pull the cover of darkness over his head and forget the world.

But Chan did not believe in quitting. He could rest when the job was done and The Beast found or when he was dead. Until then, no matter how much his bones ached or his head pulsed, the battle had to go on. Leaving, no matter how enticing an idea it might be, was out of the question.

He rapped on Kevin's door, not really expecting the boy to answer, but hoping to assuage his guilty conscience. "Kevin, are you there?"

There was no sound from the room and Chan half worried that the boy had run off again. It was unlikely, but not outside the realm of possibilities that Kevin had returned to Fei Long's apartment long enough to get something and then snuck back out the window.

Chan rapped again and Kevin finally responded. "Go away, I'm trying to sleep."

"You do not sound like you are sleeping," Chan said. "You sound wide awake. I was just hoping to make sure you are okay."

"Fine," came the terse reply.

"Crow and Huizhong think they have found The Beast," Chan said. "They are heading out now. Do you need anything?"

"I need to be left alone."

Chan crossed his legs and assumed his meditation position. There would likely be little sleep tonight or tomorrow and everything he could do to rest would help him survive the next couple of days. "Good night, then," he said and closed his eyes.

A few moments passed, just enough time for Chan to feel his heart rate slowing, before the door to Kevin's room clicked and opened slightly. It was a way Kevin had of communicating; he would explode and then the anger would leave him. After the anger was gone, he was another boy like any of the millions of boys on Aluna. The open door was an invitation, a way for Kevin to open up slightly without having to apologize.

Chan's joints creaked as he stood. No matter how many times he visited a healer, no one could tell him how to stop the creaking and popping. 'It's just a part of getting older," they'd say and then nod sagely. It was the kind of half-hearted answer that ultimately drew him back to the traditional medicine of his youth.

Kevin was sitting on his bed, stroking Dino's feathers. The dinosaur looked content, at least as content as a predatory bird-lizard can look. "We saved each other tonight," Kevin said without looking up.

Chan noticed the wild look in Kevin's eyes and knew something terrible had nearly happened, but he also knew pressuring the boy wouldn't work. He'd been forced to grow up a lot in the past six months and the stress of that either made diamonds or coal.

"Are you okay now?" Chan asked, trying to finesse information out of the boy.

"We're fine," Kevin replied. He had that flat tone he got when he didn't want to talk.

Chan nodded. "I can see that. I am happy you are safe, both of you. I have grown ... fond of both of you."

He turned and started to leave when Kevin spoke. Rather than pulling information out of him like rotten teeth, the boy was offering it up. "Someone wanted to eat us tonight," Kevin said. "Three someones, actually."

"Dragons?" Chan asked.

"People," the boy replied. "Well mostly people. They were gross, all covered in scabs in ground-in dirt. They shoved me into an alley and two of them tackled Dino. I got a few licks in on one of them, but it didn't stop him."

"You are big for your age, but you are still small for an adult. In time, you will be able to break things and people with your fists."

"I know," Kevin said. "You told me that over and over and over and I still let my ego get in the way. Eventually, I might be as good as you, but not now."

"You will exceed even me," Chan replied.

Kevin bowed his head and said, "Thank you."

When he raised his head again, there was strength in Kevin's eyes. It was the kind of strength that can only come from meeting one's demons head-on and conquering them. Most martial artists do it at some point in their lives, but it was rare for a ten-turn-old to overcome his *Lóng de chéngzhǎng*.

From the look on the boy's face, whatever he had done was causing him immense guilt. Chan waited patiently while Kevin decided what to say and what not to say.

"I killed two people tonight and Dino killed one, too."

Chan rocked on his heels. The last thing he expected to hear was Kevin had killed someone. "Was it the men with the caked-on dirt?"

"Three of them," Kevin reiterated. "Only one guy survived and that was because he ran away early on."

Chan sat on a chair and asked, "How did you kill them?"

"Dino shredded one of the guys, I killed the lead guy by bouncing him down the alley and blew up his friend's leg."

Silence fell across the room as Chan struggled to process

what Kevin had just told him. The boy didn't belong here, he knew that when he snatched him from Earth. His hubris had introduced an outside influence into an already unstable situation.

"Kevin," Chan said, "listen to me carefully."

The boy nodded, but his smile remained plastered to his face.

"While I think what you did was both miraculous and justifiable, there are those out there who would call you a *gwai lo* and seek to stop you."

"What's a *gwai lo*?

"It means a ghost man, but people use it to describe foreigners. Anyone who's not supposed to be here is a *gwai lo*. People will always call you *gwai lo*, but that doesn't mean you need to adopt the mannerisms of the *gwai lo*."

Kevin patted Dino's muzzle and thought for a long a time. Given his lack of money, not-so-great understanding of the world, and youth he was stuck. Chan sympathized with him; he was always the outsider, the one who didn't quite get people, the stranger even among his friends. Even Crow, for all his faults, still looked at Chan as something of an oddity.

"What if I don't want to be … what was it? *Gwai lo*?" Kevin asked.

Chan nodded. "Yes, *Gwai lo*."

"What if I make people look at me as something other than *gwai lo*? They don't have to respect me, but as soon as things start exploding around them, they'll learn to fear me."

"There is nothing wrong with being an outsider," a woman's voice said behind them. "I am an outsider and I wouldn't have it any other way."

Chan turned to find Mrs. Chow standing behind him. She'd snuck in through the open door Crow had created but never fixed. She looked tired, almost like she'd been in the fights with Chi You himself. Her eyes were still hard, but her shoulders were slumped and her dress was tattered.

"Mrs. Chow," Chan said, not sure what else to do, "you

honor us with your presence. I was sorry to hear about your bar; only cowards would do that."

She bowed slightly. It wasn't much of a bow, but it was a bow and that was the first time Chan had ever seen her bow. "I apologize for coming in unannounced, but I couldn't seem to find a door to knock on."

"Crow," Chan said simply.

Mrs. Chow shook her head and sighed. "That man has a thing for destroying doors."

"It is one of his many gifts," Chan agreed.

She shook her head and ran a hand through her black hair. "Let's cut the crap, Chan. Formality was never my thing. Thank you for letting me in."

"As you wish," Chan said. He motioned toward the boy on the sofa with the dinosaur snuggled up next to him. "You remember Kevin."

"Of course," she said, smiling. "How have you been?"

"I killed two people," Kevin replied. "They were trying to eat me."

Mrs. Chow took the blunt statement in stride. Most people would have assumed he was lying or shook in their shoes, but she just smiled and nodded. "I was about your age when I killed my first person. He tried to muscle in on my territory so I rammed a knife through his eye."

"I used magic," Kevin said.

Chan motioned to the couch and said, "I was trying to explain to him what being an outsider was like."

Mrs. Chow looked at Chan with a querulous expression on her face. Then she looked at Kevin and finally looked back at Chan, shaking her head in wonder. "You're explaining to him what it means to be an outsider? Did you miss the part where he's from a completely different planet?"

"I was aware of that," Chan said, bristling at her words.

"Because, if you think you understand what it's like being an outsider, I've got news for you, buddy; this boy can tell you volumes about what it means to be an outsider."

She pointed a finger at Kevin and smiled at him. "Don't you ever go trying to fit in. People who fit in get lost in the flow and stop being themselves. When I was a young girl, I learned if you want something in life you have to take it. No one is going to give you a good life; you have to seize it and never let go. And you cannot have a good life if you spend it trying to fit in."

"You are not helping," Chan said.

Mrs. Chow shot him a sidelong glance and snorted. "Everyone I've ever known has told me I would never amount to anything because I came from the streets. Yet, here I am – one of the greats."

"Great at breaking the law," Chan muttered.

Mrs. Chow clucked her tongue. "In another place, in another time, beating people up for money could be illegal. In other places, speaking to the wrong gods could be illegal. Your study, the art of hurting people, *is* illegal in some places. Laws are made by people in power to support their goals. Breaking an unjust law is civil disobedience."

"And it will still get the police called on you," Chan replied.

"I can handle the police," Mrs. Chow said with a casual wave of her hand. "What I cannot handle is someone blowing up my bar and killing my patrons."

Chan nodded in agreement. "The *Qīng Bāng* went too far. They attacked us on the street with combat magicians."

Mrs. Chow shook her head. "Chan, don't be a fool. The *Qīng Bāng* do not work with combat magicians. For all their power, they can't afford them. Very few people can afford to hire combat magicians. Also, it wasn't the Green Gang that blew up my bar. I know their symbols and the one on my wall was meant to look like theirs, but it wasn't one of theirs."

"Perhaps whoever painted it was in a hurry," Chan said.

"Initiates in the Green Gang are expected to draw that symbol perfectly every time. It's drilled into them. A mistake can cost the life of a member. Someone just wants us to think the Green Gang blew up my bar. It's probably the same people that hired the combat magicians to attack you. Someone with a lot of money, but not a lot of understanding about the local gangs."

Chan sat back and thought. If there was one person in Croatoa who knew enough to say with certainty that the *Qīng Bāng* did not blow up her bar, it was Mrs. Chow. The woman was nefarious, but she was well informed.

"If the *Qīng Bāng* did not blow up your bar, who did?"

Mrs. Chow got up and paced around the room, examining trinkets and art Fei Long had amassed during his long reign of power. Most pieces were dismissed out of hand, but she held one aloft and asked, "Can I have this?"

"The owner is dead," Chan replied. "You can have anything you want from this apartment."

She pocketed the piece she was holding up. It was a ceramic figurine of two people intertwined a strange type of sex. "Thank you."

"Do you know who blew up your bar?" Chan asked.

"Not a clue," she replied. "But if I ever get hold of them, they're going to pay and pay dearly."

"Can I help?" Kevin asked. Chan choked back a desire to yell at him. Who in their right mind would want to help Mrs. Chow do her dirty work?

The famously dour Mrs. Chow smiled a warm, sad smile at Kevin. "My dear boy, you have no idea how much I appreciate the sentiment, but this is beyond you."

Kevin clenched his fists and narrowed his eyes. Chan felt the tell-tale sparkling in the air and hoped the boy wasn't about to kill them all. "Kevin, it is not an insult."

"I have skills," Kevin pleaded. "I made Dino. I killed two men tonight with my magic. I can help you."

Mrs. Chow must have sensed the power building in the air because she took a step back from the boy. Although her enterprises were strictly non-magical, she had been around long enough to recognize the energies building up.

"Chan is right," she said. "I didn't mean you couldn't help, I meant you shouldn't help. If I bring you in to help me, it'll paint a huge target on your back. Every gang in the city will be coming for you and I can't have that on my conscience."

"Let them come," Kevin said. His eyes turned bright blue and electricity crackled in the corners of the room. "I can handle anyone."

"I'm sure you can," Mrs. Chow said quietly. "You're very powerful. But this is something I have to handle on my own. It would make me look weak to have someone as powerful as you help me and I cannot afford to look weak right now. Even if it wasn't the *Qīng Bāng* that blew up my bar, they have brought dishonor on themselves by not responding. I have a meeting tonight with someone that needs a stern talking to about that."

The power surging in the air calmed as Kevin backed down. Chan was no stranger to magic. He'd spent time among the wild women in the North and was familiar with the taste and feel of magic. All magic has a sense of place, a vague, deeply-rooted idea that even though this feels weird, it is perfectly normal. Northern magic felt different from southern magic, but it took a trained soul to understand what the differences were. Kevin's magic felt otherworldly.

"When you two are done doing whatever it is you have planned, come by the bar. It's not completely rebuilt, but what good is power if you can't abuse it to make people work round the clock to fix something?"

"What are we planning on doing?" Kevin asked.

"You are going to wait here," Chan replied. "It is far too dangerous for you and you are far too important."

Kevin frowned and clenched his fists again. The air around them seemed to come back to life. No matter what else, the boy was rapidly gaining control over his powers. Chan held up his hands and said, "This is not helping, Kevin."

"Important how?" Mrs. Chow asked.

Chan shot a look at her and realized he'd spilled something important. "What?" he asked.

"Important," Mrs. Chow said. "You said he was too important."

"I only meant it was important to get him home safely."

"But that's not what you said. You said he was too important. Important for what?"

Chan glared at her and shook his head discretely. "I misspoke."

Kevin glanced at Mrs. Chow and then at Chan. A strange look came over his face, like he was halfway between being bemused and understanding a stray fact that had eluded him. "You never misspeak, Chan. I've only known you for a bit, but I've never known you to be anything but precise."

Chan shook his head and worried that the entire plan was going to come unfurled and take half the city with it. The Furious Fae, the same group that had sent Huizhong into town, had contacted him about the boy. It was with their help that he extracted Kevin from Earth before the Beast's minions could get to him. He didn't know the full extent of their plan, but he knew Kevin's power was very important.

"It is time I was honest with you, Kevin," Chan said. "The Furious Fae wanted you brought from Earth. The Beast wanted you brought from Earth. I suspect even the Clock Man wanted you brought from Earth. Earth magic is very rare and very powerful. The *Tao* has a plan for you, but I am not privy to its machinations. All I know is I was supposed to save you and take care of you. Over the months, I have become quite fond of you."

"What about my parents?" Kevin asked.

"I have never lied to you, Kevin. They are here in Croatoa somewhere, but no one seems to know where. Hopefully Huizhong and Crow will figure out where they are."

"And then?" Mrs. Chow asked.

"Then we will kill everyone and free his parents. But Kevin needs to stay here."

The air cracked and pulsed again. It was the first time Chan had ever spent in close proximity to a sorcerer and the effect was terrifying. He was used to a physical opponent in his face. Dodging, blocking, punching, kicking; these were all easy things. Magic was everywhere and nowhere and Chan was feeling out of his league.

"If Huizhong and Crow find my parents, I'm going with you. And I'm going to kill The Beast."

29 | Beastly

"This is what Diyu smells like, I'm sure of it," Huizhong said.

She covered her mouth with her hand, but it didn't do much good. The smell – a mixture of rot, fish, and sulfur – clung to her nose and worked its way into her brain.

"I'd say breathe through your mouth, but I'm not sure I want this smell in my mouth," Crow replied. "If madness and horror smell like anything, this is it."

The elevator had stopped after far too long and dropped them in one of the dank tunnels that crisscrossed the city. Flickering torches lit the way down the stone-lined walls. A glowing liquid dripped from the ceiling and pooled on the floor.

Huizhong looked up and the felt the weight of the city bearing down on her head. She was never much for closed spaces. At least the creeping horror of claustrophobia was almost enough to make her forget the smell.

Crow seemed unperturbed. He reached into his jacket and pulled out a flask. He took a huge swig and offered the metal flask to her. Huizhong took it and felt the burn of cheap *baiju* slide down her throat. She coughed and handed the flask back.

"Good stuff, right?" Crow asked.

She kept coughing until she thought her lungs would explode. Distantly, she felt Crow's hand patting her back. When the coughing fit finally subsided, Huizhong gulped air. "I think it burned out my sense of taste. Where did you find that stuff?"

Crow chuckled. "See, now you can't taste the air. A buddy of mine makes this stuff in his back yard. It's infused with *chi*."

"*Chi*?"

"Well, that's what he says, anyway. Personally, I think he just smiles a lot while he's making it. It's potent stuff; the cure for whatever ails you."

"It cured my sense of taste and my sense of smell," Huizhong said, wishing she had something to wash the horrid stuff down.

"Well, we're halfway there, then. As soon as it kicks in, your fear of tight spaces will drift away, too."

Huizhong looked at him with her jaw agape. "How?"

He smiled that smile that made her hate to love him, that roguish grin that spoke of too much free time on his hands and a life that generally went his way whether he wanted it to or not. "You looked around and tensed up. Lots of people do that when they're scared of something. In this case, it had to be the tight space."

She shook her head and wondered how someone who could be so daft could also be so observant. Then it hit her; he understood everything. If he could pick a bomber out of a crowd or catch minute details about how she was standing, he probably knew and understood more than he ever let on.

He put his hands on her shoulders and smiled. "Don't worry. Lots of people get freaked out in tight spaces; everyone has a phobia. Mine's *zhīzhū*. But if you want to get back to free air and no walls, we need to move."

Huizhong nodded and mustered her courage. She'd been face-to-face with a dragon, infiltrated a secret society, and touched a creature from another planet; she could handle this.

Crow grabbed a torch from the wall and headed slowly down the tunnel. Huizhong grabbed another one and followed along. As long as she could see the light from Crow's torch, everything would be okay. She did her best to not think about being alone down here in the pitch black with the city ready to collapse on her or how when it fell, it wouldn't kill her. Somehow, she knew she'd stay alive, buried in rubble and struggling for each breath for days or weeks until the world above finally forgot about her and she spent the rest of eternity covered by rocks and dust.

Maybe it would be appropriate. Hadn't she helped do the same thing to Crow? Maybe it would be *yinguo* in action. Cause and effect, only the effect snuck up on her months after the cause.

"You're not thinking correctly," Crow hissed from in front of her. "I can hear the way you're walking. Quit worrying about the tunnel and start thinking about that weird bird thing the kid has or how Chan promised to show you a Northern Dragon style form. He never shows anyone that form. I asked for months and he refused to teach me; you smile at him and he goes all blubbery and promises to show it to you."

Her mind focused back to the reality of solid walls and torchlight. She followed Crow's voice, locked in on it and used it to pull her back to reality. "What do you mean, blubbery?"

"Chan's not much with the ladies," Crow said. "I don't think he gets out all that often. He's never very good around women, except Mrs. Chow and I'm convinced she's a demon or something sinister wearing a skin suit."

Huizhong chuckled. Of course, Crow would assume there was no way someone couldn't like him. "Maybe she's just not into you. That doesn't mean she's a demon."

"No," Crow said. "But it does mean she's heartless. I've known that woman for over a decade. She hated me the minute I first walked into her bar as a raw new hire on the force. I wasn't even there on official business – word among the police was she gets left alone. All I wanted was a drink."

"Tough first day?" Huizhong asked.

"Yeah, it turned out that way, but a drink at lunchtime helped dull the pain."

Huizhong chuckled and shook her head. "She hated you? You?"

Crow smiled. His eyes glittered in the torchlight. "See, you've forgotten all about being underground. Just keep that feeling and you'll be fine."

She stopped in the middle of the tunnel and realized he was right. The walls weren't closing in anymore. As soon as she realized she wasn't afraid, Huizhong immediately realized she was still underground and the panic nipped at the edges of her consciousness. She choked it down, but it was still there, hanging out like an eight-legged *zhīzhū* in a web.

"Keep talking, Crow," Huizhong said.

He kept pressing on through the tunnel and she kept following him, terrified to lose the light from his torch. "No," he said. "It's your turn. Tell me about Ao Shun."

She thought back to the big dragon stalking through her forest, that ebon beast with the heart of pure … whatever dragon hearts were made of. "He's not bad."

"Never said he was," Crow replied. He'd stopped suddenly and was waving the torch around wildly. He flicked at something on his jacket and held the torch to the ground. "*Fèi wù hu□y□n xiéshén,*" he muttered and stamped on something on the ground. "I hate *zhīzhū*. Useless evil spirits. Anyway, why'd he send you back? Why not … what's her name? Mab?"

"I don't know exactly," she replied. "He seemed to think I had unfinished business or something. I was having bad dreams. Since I'd already been here, I guess he thought I'd do better than Mab."

"He struck me as kind of a jerk."

Huizhong nodded and then mentally kicked herself for doing something no one could possibly see. "He could be, but he could also be nice. He's a dragon. They're, uh…"

"Different," Crow said. "I know."

"I was going to say wise," Huizhong said.

"But then you thought better of it?" Crow replied distantly. "Seriously, I've never heard anyone say good things about dragons."

"How many do you know?"

"People or dragons?"

"Dragons," Huizhong replied with a huff.

"Only the one," Crow replied. "But so far it seems to me one hundred percent of the dragons are jerks because every one I've met has been a jerk."

Huizhong forgot all about the tunnel or the flickering firelight casting shadows of demons on the walls. "But you've only met one. And not even in the flesh."

"There is that," Crow said. "I hear they stink."

"Ao Shun has pretty bad breath, but that's because he eats raw lizards and terror birds. Other than that, he just smells like a dragon. Kind of sulfur-y, kind of lizard-y."

Crow stopped in front of an old wooden door. The door had to be ancient, yet it looked brand new. "Someone's been using this door," he said. "The hinges are freshly oiled and did you notice how clean the tunnel was?"

"I was trying my damnedest to ignore the tunnel."

"It's awfully clean. Far cleaner than I'd expect from an unused tunnel. Did you notice it's got *zhīzhū*, but no webs?" He motioned at the door and grimaced. "Whatever we're searching for is probably down here. Pity we don't have your good buddy Ao Shun as backup."

"Why?"

Crow put his ear to the door and grimaced. "Because it sounds like there are a lot of people in there."

"What?" Huizhong asked. "Why would people hang out down here?"

"That's the million-*yuan* question, isn't it?" He nudged the door open and stood back.

Huizhong reeled from the noise when Crow opened it. Voices, both mumbled and screamed, wafted out the open door. There was a faint odor of something she couldn't quite place coming from the doorway. It was a familiar scent, but distant in the way things smell when they're not in the right place.

Crow adjusted his hat and jacket for maximum effect and threw a roguish grin over his shoulder. "Shall we see what all the ruckus is about?"

He seemed completely unafraid. Like most things in life, he let the strangeness of the situation wash over him without tainting him. Ao Shun, Huizhong reflected, would be impressed. The dragon was the ultimate *Taoist*, a creature that never let the world get to him. Crow had to be a close second.

"Should we maybe get Chan and Kevin first?" Huizhong asked. Crow may not be nervous, but she was. Walking into a place like that had bad idea written all over it.

Crow waved a hand dismissively and walked through the door. She had to admire his poise. Not many people would have the guts to walk into a strange place like they owned it.

The door opened to a large room lit by flickering torches. All around them people bustled, intent on their work. No one paid them any attention as Crow strode through the room. At one point, he even stopped and clasped a worker on the back and pointed at a barrel the man was pushing on a cart. A brief exchange took place before Crow slapped the guy on the back and gave him a thumbs-up.

Crow continued walking around, occasionally interacting with someone while Huizhong held back. She didn't catch what Crow was saying because the noise inside was a deafening maelstrom of creaks, grinds, and screams.

He finally made his way up to a central point and put his hands on his hips as he looked around. Crow looked for all the world like he was in charge of everything. Huizhong stood next to him, unsure of what else to do.

He looked over at her and frowned. "This is where the *Tiāntáng De Fěn* is coming from. All these people are making it, but they're all whacked out on it. I couldn't get a straight story out of anyone. One guy said it was ashes, another said it was magic. Have I told you how much I hate poison suckers? I hate poison suckers. They're too hard to deal with."

"What now?" Huizhong asked.

"Now, we find someone who isn't getting high on the supply," Crow said. "Shouldn't be hard to find a normal person in a sea of losers."

Without warning, all motion in the cave stopped. Everyone turned and made for the closest exit in neat columns. Huizhong started to say something, but couldn't articulate what she was thinking. The people filing out were more like machines than people. Humans laughed and joked, shoved and prodded; these people left with the picture of efficiency and sameness.

When the last person left, he shut a large door behind him. In the suddenly eerie silence, the sound of the door locking sounded like a thunder crack. The screaming gave way to quiet sobbing. In way, the sobbing was worse than the screaming. The overall din of the room made the screams seem distant and ethereal. In the quiet room, the sobbing was far worse. It sounded like someone who knows he's going to die and just wants the pain to end.

"What's going on?" Huizhong asked.

Crow shrugged. "No idea. Maybe it's lunch time in the cookery."

"I will tell you," a voice said from the shadows. "If you survive."

The voice rattled Huizhong's clothes and set her teeth on end. The smell hit her full-on in the face. When the shock passed, she remembered where she'd smelled it before. She tapped Crow's shoulder. "Watch yourself, Crow. We've got a dragon here."

"Soon you will have dragons everywhere," the voice said. "We will retake our world."

Huizhong tensed. She raised her fists as if they'd be useful against what was lurking in the shadows. Dragons were at the top of the food chain before humans showed up on Aluna. They hunted and killed whatever struck their fancy. Their long lives and patience allowed them to be perfect hunters. Dragons were incredible killing machines armed with fangs and a preternatural understanding of magic. A single human, no matter how strong, was no match for a dragon.

She looked at Crow and was surprised to see him

smirking. "We beat you before," he said. "We can do it again."

"So certain are you?" the voice asked. "Do you honestly think we'll be playing the same game again? I see no reason to fight you. All I have to do is give you what you desire and let it poison you by inches."

"Cool," Crow said. "I'd like something to drink. Something not poison, if that's not too much to ask."

"Always the joker," the voice replied. "Always finding something funny, always playing the fool. How does it feel to mask your pain with *baiju*, Crow?"

"Pretty damned good," Crow replied. "Unless it's not good *baiju*."

"What are you playing at?" Huizhong hissed. "That is a dragon. You do not crack jokes at a dragon."

"Trust me on this one," Crow said. "I may or may not know what I'm doing."

"I assure you, child. You have no idea what you're doing," the voice said.

The dragon was fast. Far faster than anything that big should be. One moment, it was circling them, hiding in the shadows and taunting its prey, the next it was right in front of them. Huizhong and Crow took an involuntary step back. Most people on Aluna, when they thought of dragons at all, thought of them as magical things. Standing nose to nose with three-hundred-hand long beast was a great reminder that dragons were predators. Its whiskers twitched, sensing things that only a dragon would understand. Gigantic eyes watched them from a head bigger than a person. When the creature smiled, it showed off a mouth full of teeth as long as Huizhong's forearm.

Ao Shun was black as night, but the dragon in front of them was bright red. Its snout was narrower and the whiskers were longer, but it was the meanness in its eyes that terrified Huizhong. Ao Shun would hunt and kill humans for food if it came down to it, though he claimed people didn't taste good. The dragon in front of them looked like it would happily hunt humans for sport and decorate its lair with their bones.

Huizhong pulled herself together and did her best to stay calm. "Red dragon. Ao Qin, I presume," Huizhong said. "I read about you in a book. You're the mythical Summer Dragon Queen."

The dragon clucked and huffed. "At your service, although not so mythical," she replied, tipping her huge snout downward.

"You know," Crow said. "I never thought I'd live to be old enough to meet two dragons."

Ao Qin coiled in on herself and watched them with glee and madness in her eyes. "We are not dead yet, little thing."

"You're a dick, too!" Crow said. "The other dragon I met was a dick. Is it normal for dragons to be total dicks?"

In the blink of an eye, Ao Qin's muzzle was back in Crow's face. "Don't tempt me, human," she said. "I would take a great deal of pleasure rending you limb from limb or giving you a barrel ride."

"The one that goes over the falls or another kind?" Crow asked.

"The kind that gets very hot."

"Crap! I was hoping for the waterfall one."

Ao Qin slowly retreated and coiled up in the middle of the room. She watched them with an intense face. Giant eyes burned into Huizhong, like she was reading her soul and not liking what she found. Her gaze slowly shifted to Crow.

Out of the corner of her eye, Huizhong saw Crow wave. She pinched her nose and shook her head slowly, wondering how the man kept himself from getting killed.

Ao Qin watched them impassively. Huizhong felt a trickle of sweat roll down her cheek. Her head was pounding. At least the room was large enough to not trigger a panic attack, but everything else was pushing her buttons.

"Why are you here?" the dragon finally asked.

"Why is anyone here?" Crow started.

Huizhong held up her hand and Crow stopped talking.

"We were looking for you."

"Shut up," Crow hissed.

Ao Qin smiled and grunted happily. "Why would you look for me? And, more to the point, what made you even think to look for me?"

"Everyone says you're responsible for Heaven's Powder," Huizhong said.

"And run the quietest gang on the planet," Crow added.

The dragon rose to her feet and stretched lazily. Huizhong could tell she didn't have a care in the world. Ao Qin didn't care why they were looking for her or how she and Felix had thought to look down here. She was giving the drug away and didn't seem perturbed by its popularity.

Ao Qin strode calmly back to Huizhong and Crow. She stuck her snout right next to them and exhaled a burst of air before taking a deep breath and holding it. "I smell the ocean," she said. "The ocean and questions and – my favorite – fear. Mr. Crow reeks of cheap *baiju* and desperation. Now, I'll ask again: why are you here?"

No one spoke. For once even Crow shut his mouth and watched warily. "You have some people here that aren't supposed to be here. I'm going to free them."

"And how do you propose to do that?" Ao Qin asked

In a heartbeat, Crow changed from the fun-loving jokester to something extremely menacing. "You sure you want to know?"

"My dear boy", Ao Qin said. "I have lived through ice ages, wars, and more strife than you can even imagine. You don't frighten me. Nothing frightens me."

Crow balled his fists. Huizhong wondered if he was going to punch the dragon, but he closed his eyes and relaxed. The old Felix Crow came tumbling out. "You may think you're hot snot on the gangster scene, but you're really just cold boogers on a toilet seat."

Ao Qin turned her head and stared like a Sorority girl trying to figure out math. "I'm sorry," he said, "but I don't know what that means."

Crow's eyes focused on Ao Qin's massive visage. He flashed his evil grin, the one Huizhong always suspected he learned when he was a cop, and winked at Ao Qin. "It means I'm not your lackey."

A pair of stone pillars on either side of the dragon exploded. Huizhong instinctively covered her face with her hands as if mere flesh could stop the stone from pummeling her fragile flesh. The force of the explosion pushed jagged rocks across the vast cavern.

Somehow, the explosion was directed directly at Ao Qin and most of the stones slammed into the dragon's scaly hide. There was enough force in the explosion to shake the dragon back and forth. One rock hit her in the side of the head and slammed Ao Qin's giant head to the side. She dropped to the floor and the lights went out in her eyes.

As the dust settled, Huizhong saw Ao Qin's motionless form on the floor. She was covered in a fine, gray dust. Bits of rocks slowly slid off her and still she didn't stir. Huizhong breathed a sigh of relief. The only dragon she'd spent any time with was a vicious bastard, but Ao Shun didn't have the manic glint in his eyes that Ao Qin had. It shouldn't have surprised her, but it seemed each dragon had a distinct personality.

Unfortunately, Ao Qin's personality was mean.

"See," Crow said, pointing his thumbs at his chest, "they're not so tough. All it takes is a few *jin* of stone."

Huizhong couldn't believe his flippancy. Her heart was still pounding in her chest and her brain was still dumping adrenaline into her blood. She felt like she'd just been put through the ringer.

A cacophony of rocks echoed in deep bass undertones around the cave. Four eyes locked onto the source and found Ao Qin calmly staring at them. Strong, stumpy legs pushed and she rose to her feet, tail flicking about and whiskers twitching. The dragon shook her whole body, trying to dislodge any stray bits of stone or dust.

"She looks pissed," Crow said. There was a waver in his voice that Huizhong had never heard. Even when he faced down the monster that Chenming Zhang had become, Crow seemed nonplussed. To hear even a hint of fear in the man's voice sent shivers down Huizhong's spine.

She forced herself to focus and remember what months spent with Ao Shun had taught her about dragons. He used to tell her stories of the Dragon Wars and the glorious ways his kind had fought against what they saw as human aggression. When he got to the part where the dragons surrendered, Ao Shun's whiskers and tail twitched violently. That was one of many times Huizhong feared for her life around the dragon. They were wise creatures – a life of thousands of turns practically guaranteed that – but they were still predators in their hearts and any predator could be dangerous when it was angry.

"Run," Huizhong said.

Crow looked over at her. She locked eyes with him and yelled, "Run!"

All around them the air crackled and popped. Hints of sulfur filled the air. If *Diyu* was real – and she had no reason to doubt it at that moment – they were stuck in the middle of it. Of all the ways she thought of herself dying, being roasted alive by an angry dragon was not one she wanted.

Huizhong grabbed Crow's hand and tugged. He hesitated for a moment, but turned on his heel and followed her. They made it less than twenty steps before a red blur passed them and they found themselves face to face with an angry Ao Qin. She stalked forward, head low and whiskers pulled back.

As they backed away, Crow mumbled, "Wǒ kào. How in the name of Guan Wu did we beat these things?"

"We had numbers," Huizhong said. "One on one, there's not a soul from this planet that's a match for a dragon."

Ao Qin darted forward. Her snout slammed into Crow, sending him flying. Huizhong turned and ran to where he fell without thinking. Asshole. Psychopath. Whatever. He was her asshole and psychopath and he owed her a conversation.

She knelt by his side as he struggled to suck in air. "Relax," she said. "You just had the wind knocked out of you."

Crow closed his eyes. His body tensed, hands clenched into fists. Huizhong stroked his forehead, thinking he might be dying. Finally, and with great effort, he took a deep, wheezing breath. He rolled to his side and coughed uncontrollably.

"So weak," Ao Qin said. "So pathetic. Your magic is puny, human. Let me show you what real power is."

Crow continued coughing and wheezing, but managed to extend his hand. He held it there, shaking violently, with his middle finger extended. *"Cao ni ma bi,"* he said through choking breaths.

"I think I'll pass," Ao Qin said.

The crackling air felt heavy. Power surged all around them. Huizhong felt her limbs first get heavy then stop working entirely. She flopped forward onto the stone floor. Her face hit the floor and bounced. Even though she couldn't move, she could feel the stone caress her face and hear the sickening crack in her skull as her nose broke.

"Take her," Ao Qin cried.

Huizhong heard footsteps pour into the cave. Rough hands grabbed her and picked her up. She wanted to scream, wanted to lash out and smash everyone that dared lay their hands on her, but her body wouldn't cooperate.

Her mind immediately returned to the terror of Chenming Zhang's fingers in her brain. Then, he had taken over her brain and made her body do things she didn't want and couldn't abide. Now, her body simply failed to respond.

Ao Qin's workers held her up so the dragon could examine her closely. Her fetid breath washed over her. Bile poured into her stomach. She watched, completely helpless, as the dragon sniffed her. Her long tongue probed her face.

"What should I do with her, Crow? I'll bet she'd be delicious. I could eat her a bit a time so she could enjoy watching me eat parts of her body."

"Let her go," Crow hissed.

"Do you know how dragons prefer to eat?" Ao Qin asked. "Of course not. You're just a puny human. What could you possibly know of the true rulers of this land?"

As Ao Qin talked, Huizhong caught a brief glimpse of a man in an impeccable suit. She tried to call out to him, but her mouth didn't work and he disappeared anyway. She wanted to sigh, to cough, to do anything to prove she was still alive and not in Diyu.

"You're digging your own grave, babe," Crow said. "Pretty soon it's going to be your body on display at the museum."

Ao Qin grunted and snorted. She managed to make the dragon laughter sound sad and worried. "The skeleton at the museum was my daughter," she said.

"Let the girl go or I'll do everything in my power to reunite you with your daughter."

"Finish this dance, Crow," she said. "Bring me the boy or she dies. I'll let you experience firsthand how dragons eat when I roast her legs while they're still on her body and eat them. The next day I'll do her arms. Then the flesh on her torso. Then everyone dies. And you will get to watch it all happen.

"Bring me the boy, Crow, or know her last days will be spent in horrifying agony."

30 | Get Ready To Rumble

"We've got bigger problems than we thought," Crow said as he walked into Fei's apartment. He barely noticed Chan and Kevin staring at each other as he headed straight for the kitchen and flung open cabinets. "Like three-hundred hands bigger. Maybe bigger than that."

The cabinets were ideal in ways Crow couldn't understand. Who neatly stacked dishes by size then color when it was easier to leave them in the drying rack until they were needed again? The first cabinets contained Fei's plates and bowls, and the second cabinet looked to be neatly labeled dry goods. Crow was about to slam the door in disgust when something caught his eye.

Nestled behind a cluster of soy sauce and vinegar bottles was a bottle that looked like it didn't belong. Crow eased the bottle out and whistled appreciatively. "YI-DI's Masterpiece. Hundred-turn-old *baiju* they say was created by the god of alcohol himself. You guys want some?"

No one responded, so Crow shrugged his shoulders and poured himself out a few fingers. The smell wafted to his nostrils; cleaning solution to some, home to him. He allowed himself a moment to think back through the evening – the sneaking, the diary, the big freaking dragon – before an image of Huizhong being carried away by an army of drugged up losers hit his brain.

The *baiju* went down more smoothly than its smell would imply. Rather than tasting like window washing fluid or something to get stains out of upholstery, it tasted of sweet, rotting fruit and warm blankets on cold nights. As the liquid burned its way down Crow's throat, he closed his eyes and tried to let go of the night.

Huizhong was out there and he needed an Earthling magic user to get her back. The kid could probably take care of himself – maybe, dragons were tough critters, but Kevin was powerful – but Huizhong was a different matter; she was reluctant to give into her violent tendencies. That was a failing on her part.

Crow downed the rest of the *baiju* and said a small thank you to YI-DI. His nerves were still jittery, but at least he didn't feel as concerned. The drink had smoothed the rubble in the road, not eliminated it. One by one, the cells in his nervous system decided to work. Crow stood up straight and proud.

And immediately fell over.

Cursing, Crow rose to his feet and looked around the room. Kevin and Chan were staring at each other warily. "Guys?" Crow asked. "Is anyone home?"

Still no response.

"I hope I didn't walk in at a bad time," Crow said, "because I've got even worse news than the damned giant, red dragon that lives under the city."

Chan made the slightest tilt of his head. Crow knew he was listening, but wasn't sure about Kevin. The boy's glare could cut through dragon scale. "Okay," Crow said. "So, worse than the giant dragon. The bad guys have Huizhong."

"That is unfortunate," Chan said.

"Unfortunate?" Crow asked. He downed his drink and went back for the bottle. YI-DI's magical alcohol would calm his nerves and let him think clearly.

"Yes," Chan said. "Unfortunate."

Crow leaned against the bar and drank hundred-turn-old *baiju* straight from the bottle. "What is going on here, guys? I just told you there's a dragon that lives under the city and her followers have Huizhong."

Kevin's eyes locked on Crow. Just for a moment, he understood the boy's sorrow. Everyone in the room had lost parents, but only Kevin had been taken to a whole new planet. Crow empathized with him. His own upbringing in the orphanage was far from pleasant. Instead of disc games in the park, Felix Crow got a cot with a lumpy mattress and cold water.

"He killed someone," Chan said, pointing at Kevin.

"And…?" Crow asked.

"He used magic to do it."

"Ugly people in an alley. They were going to kill and eat me," Kevin hissed. "Now Captain Aluna over here thinks I did something wrong."

"Oh, the *Wàngjìle*," Crow said. "Don't worry about it. The forgotten get killed all the time. I've killed a few of them myself. One time, when I was still on the force, my team was told to go in and clean out the alleys. What a waste. We caught a lot of grief over that mission. Half the city wants the *Wàngjìle* killed off, the other half wants to give them medals for eating the first half."

Crow could tell Chan was fuming; his gray eyes locked onto Crow's and held them tightly. "It was wrong."

"Wrong?" Kevin asked. "Should I have let them eat me?"

Chan whirled and started toward Kevin. The boy rose and the dinosaur leapt to his feet, hissing and twitching his tail back and forth. "Chan," Crow said. "He has a point."

"He should not have been out alone. It is not safe out there."

Crow took a deep drag off the bottle of *baiju* and wiped his mouth with the back of his hand. "It's not safe anywhere. Weren't you paying attention? There's a *hùnzhàng* dragon living under the city and it's holding Huizhong."

"A real dragon?" Kevin asked.

"The real deal. Whiskers, huge eyes, big teeth. It's a beast."

Crow thought for a moment and then chuckled to himself. "What?" Chan asked.

"It's just funny," Crow replied. "All this time we were thinking there was a human calling himself The Beast, but it's actually a dragon down there; an actual beast."

"Will she be okay?" Kevin asked.

Crow could see the worried sparkles in the kid's eyes and knew he and Huizhong had bonded somehow. He, personally, never had a mother or even a mother figure to bond with. The women who ran the orphanage weren't exactly the maternal type.

"That's tricky," Crow said with a sigh. "The dragon – her name is Ao Qin, by the way – says she only wants you."

"I'm sorry, Crow," Chan interjected. "I like Huizhong, but her life is nothing compared to Kevin's. She is normal; he is not."

"Do you trust him?" Kevin asked. "Do you think she'll let her go if she gets me?"

Crow shook his head sadly. "Not a chance, kid. More likely she'll kill her and you and sleep on your bones."

"See," Chan said. "That is one more reason Kevin should not go meet this Ao Qin."

"How many *Wàngjìle* did you kill again?" Crow asked.

Kevin replied without thinking. "Three. Well, I got two, Dino got one."

Crow nodded slowly. "Those *Wàngjìle* are tough old bastards. It must be from a healthy diet of rotting things, tourists, drugs, and alcohol."

"Crow, he does not need encouragement. Taking Kevin to Ao Qin would be disastrous."

"He killed two *Wàngjìle* with nothing more than magic and that feathered thing with the claws. Didn't you say he fought off three combat magicians? Sounds like he can handle himself."

Chan's eyes hardened. "This is not your decision."

"No," Crow replied, "and it's not yours, either. He needs to make the decision."

"He is ten," Chan replied.

"By the time I was ten, I had started to work on being on my own. Of course, I hated the orphanage, so that might have had a lot to do with it."

Chan folded his arms across his chest and grimaced. "And look where it got you. Alcoholic ex-constable with a huge chip on his shoulder."

"Said the guy who thinks he's a hero from a pulp novel. You fight for a living, Chan. It's all you know how to do."

"At least I can make it through the day without sedating myself," Chan replied in a huff.

Crow smiled. It was the evil grin he used to throw criminals before he beat confessions out of them. "That's because you're permanently sedated. When you get to the end, the only thing you'll be able to say about your life is that it happened and you punched a lot of people. I'm a waste? At least I've solved problems. What have you done other than act like you're the toughest guy on the planet?"

"Guys," Kevin said quietly. "Let's calm down."

Crow looked at the boy and winked. "Consider this a life lesson, kid. Sometimes you've got to kick your old master's ass."

Chan eased his left leg back. Crow caught the motion out of the corner of his eye and reciprocated. If his former master wanted a fight, maybe it was time to beat some sense into the man.

Crow tensed and released the muscles up and down his body. Joints popped and muscles warmed up. It had been a long time since he'd fought Chan. He lost then and lost hard. But Crow had learned a trick or two on the constabulary that should help. Besides, how would Chan's fist fare when the furniture exploded around him?

Chan was a slave to his own honor. As soon as Crow stepped into a fighting stance, Chan had to commit or face the dishonor of backing down. The master cupped both hands in front of himself and bowed his head before returning to his fighting stance. Both hands were open and extended from the body to better deflect incoming blows. Crow knew from experience that those open hands could become fists in the blink of an eye.

Crow bent his knees, lowering his body to the floor, and put his fists up in front of his body. Chan might have the speed and coordination to make a fist before his punch smashed into a target like someone's face.

Turns of practice in the fighting rings had taught Chan to be as fast as light. His hand didn't even seem to move. One instant it was close to his head, the next it was near Crow's head. A normal person would have been pulverized – nose smashed, facial bones broken, brain rattled. He practiced his punches every day and every day they got a tiny bit better until some would say he had the fastest punch in history.

Crow had turns of alcohol abuse and only practiced Wushu intermittently; mostly when he was drunk and angry and needed to take it out on a bag full of old clothes. Unfortunately for Chan, Crow had two things going for him: a naturally fast reaction time and a bit of magic that had been conferred on him that allowed him to sense energy swirling before an attack.

He barely registered the punch had happened. All Crow really knew was his head had jerked to the side. It was only a glimpse of Chan setting up another punch that confirmed Chan was trying to hit him. Or kill him. With Chan it was always difficult to tell whether he was royally pissed off or just mildly annoyed. The turns of stoic asceticism that Chan lived in had taught him emotions were the root cause of most of society's ills.

As Chan's hand retracted and he set up to throw another punch, Crow punched at Chan. The punch was deftly blocked. Crow may have been slower, but he was strong enough to knock out teeth. Both men backed off and examined each other. Chan's face had taken on the blank look he got when the fight was engaged.

One of the many things Chan taught Crow was to eliminate his emotions. "Anger is the fight killer," he used to say. "You think it makes you stronger, but it only makes you reckless."

It was one of many things they disagreed on. Crow embraced his emotions, but controlled them. "Ready to get your ass kicked, old man?" he asked.

They circled each other like predators, each looking for an obvious opening to exploit. They'd fought before - probably dozens of times - but those were sparring sessions. This fight was the real deal. Crow took advantage of the furniture in the apartment and circled until the tea table was between them. It wasn't much of a barrier, but it would slow down Chan enough to give him a tactical advantage.

Chan responded by kicking the tea table. The old table, made of dark, heavy wood, flew at Crow's face. He barely managed to get his hands up before the table slammed into his arms and pushed him back, off balance and almost ready to fall. Chan seized the advantage and charged forward. Unlike the tea table, Crow could sense Chan's movement slightly before it happened.

He was off-balance, but managed to twist enough so that he lurched to the left. Crow's mind flashed on a play he saw about a drunken *Wushu* master who staggered about while fighting, but still managed to take revenge on the people who had killed his daughter.

The *baiju* burned in his veins, deadening his fear and enhancing his willingness to take risks. Chan seemed surprised that he hadn't hit anything but air, so Crow lunged forward. His fist found Chan's ribs, but it lacked enough power to take down the master.

Chan's foot was a blur as it sailed past Crow's head. That side kick was famous, one of Chan's legendary techniques. It was said that Chan's kicks were so fast they could set the air on fire. There was no flame in its wake, but Crow knew he'd be lying on the ground and holding his face if Chan had managed to hit him.

Crow embraced his new-found drunken fighting style and half-staggered, half-ran at Chan. Chan threw a slow right punch that Crow saw coming long before it could hit him. He lurched to the right, thinking he was okay, only to find Chan kicking him mid-step.

In the amount of time it took for Crow to step to the side,

Chan hit him square in the stomach. Crow fell back into the book cases that lined the Fei's wall. A porcelain figure of a man holding a snake teetered and fell on Crow's head.

He rubbed his head and moved just in time for a flurry of strikes from Chan to break the bookcase Crow had been leaning on. An elbow in Chan's ribs made the master back off. Crow's mind recognized an opening and lashed out at Chan's knee.

Fast as he was, Chan was faster. Crow's foot almost hit the side of Chan's knee, but the master moved slightly at the last moment and Crow landed forward of where he wanted to be. The full force of his body falling slammed his ribs into Chan's waiting elbow.

Crow wasn't unskilled, but Chan had experience on his side. He'd fought everyone from rank amateurs to some of the best on the planet and he was smart enough to recognize their strengths and weaknesses. Crow's ability to see a strike before it came was damning, but there was always a solution. If he couldn't hit Crow, he'd set him up to hit himself.

Chan watched as Crow held his ribs and grimaced. He could have finished him right then and there, but it would have accomplished nothing. Mastery was not being able to beat anyone to death; it was the ability to let the opponent to come to the realization that the fight was over. Crow stood upright and smirked, but there was a grimace in that smirk that said the blow to his ribs hurt more than he wanted to admit.

A fist sailed at Chan. He deftly blocked it and pulled Crow slightly off balance, just enough to trip him up. Again, Chan was waiting. As Crow started to move away, Chan pushed forward. It didn't look like much, but the marriage of Chan's forward momentum and Crow's need to escape combined into enough force to send Crow staggering backward. He tripped over an errant foot stool and wound up on his back.

Chan didn't hesitate. He didn't want to put Crow down,

but if the man wouldn't back off he would have to be encouraged to stop the fight. Crow put his hands down to get back up just in time for Chan to kick the foot stool into Crow's arm. He fell back to the floor with an oomph.

Chan darted forward and landed with a knee on Crow's chest and his hand wrapped around his former pupil's throat. Crow kicked his legs up, trying to hit the back of Chan's head, but the old Wushu master squeezed harder.

It was a common misconception among people that the purpose of a choke was to suffocate an opponent. Chan realized it was much easier to squeeze the arteries in the neck, starving the brain of blood and oxygen until it shut down.

Every time Crow tried to move, Chan followed the movement and squeezed a bit harder. Eventually, the world started to fade from Crow's eyes. Chan, like Crow, knew exactly how long to squeeze. At exactly 45 seconds, as Crow started to lose consciousness, Chan released his grip.

Blood and oxygen flowed back into Crow's brain. Restarting the brain took time, though, and Crow rolled to his side. He held his head in his hands and squeezed. "*Pìy□n*," he gasped.

"Are you two done?" Kevin asked. He'd been hiding on the couch and doing his best to stay out of their way as the fought. It was the first time he'd seen either of them fight and he had to admit Chan's skills were incredible.

"Are we?" Chan asked.

"Fuck you," Crow gasped.

"We are done," Chan said.

"Good," Kevin replied. "Because we have to save Huizhong and the rest of the planet."

31 | Opiate

Huizhong's cage was tiny. Whatever magic Ao Qin had hit her with faded slowly leaving behind a prickling taste on her tongue and an itch deep in her skull that she couldn't scratch even if she could move her arms. She'd heard stories of the jail cells in Croatoa from the few of Robinson's friends who had survived an encounter with the police, but a thirty-by-thirty-hand cell would be luxurious compared to a cage that wouldn't let her move at all.

Ao Qin's minions had caged her and positioned the tiny prison so she could see exactly how much trouble she was in. If the main floor, with the empty-eyed minions cooking vats of foul-smelling sludge, was scary, this room was straight out of the worst nightmares of the world.

Across from her were two more cages, presumably just like hers. Those cages were populated by leering decaying corpses. She was going to die and it was going to be a horrible, withering death surrounded by madness and horror.

"Do you like your accommodations, my dear?" a voice asked.

Huizhong tried to turn her head, but the cage held it tightly. She tracked with her eyes and caught glimpses of a man in a suit as he walked just outside the periphery of her vision. "Who are you?" she asked.

"I am both a ghost and the most important person on the planet. I like to greet all our guests. No one is supposed to know I am here, but one of the perks of great wealth is the ability to go where one wants. As far as this planet knows, I am at my home increasing my wealth."

"Yet here you are," Huizhong said. "pestering me."

He stepped into her view and she got her first look at the man in the suit. He was an older man with gray hair and dark eyes. The corners of his lips were curled up in a sneer. Given the suit, the sneer fit him. He had an aura of casual severity about him, like he was used to getting what he wanted.

The man leaned close to her, close enough that she could smell the sweet scent of desert spices on him. His eyes burned into her, but she held his stare and remained steadfastly defiant. His eyebrow cocked up and he leaned back without taking his eyes off her.

"Do you know who I am, pretty lady?"

Huizhong tried to shake her head, but wound up bumping her head on the bars. "No," she replied.

"I shouldn't be surprised," he said. "I never found the limelight to be all that enticing. One can accomplish so much more in the shadows. My name is Hoqwua."

"Oh," Huizhong replied, rolling her eyes. "Him. What do you want?"

Hoqwua spun slowly in the room, gesturing to the remains in the cages and other things Huizhong couldn't see. "What does anyone with money and power really want?"

"More," Huizhong said. "That's what all this is about? More money and more power?"

"Power, mostly," he said. "I have more money than most gods, but you can never have too much power. Do you know what power is, my dear?"

Huizhong started to answer, but he held his hand up and waved off her reply. "Don't worry about it. People with no power have no concept of what power really is."

"Is it locking people up and killing them?"

He stood very close to her again, close enough that she tried to scoot away. His hand traced her face, her neck, her body, leaving a phantom trail behind it. Huizhong shivered. She desperately wanted to wipe the places he'd touched.

"Locking people up and killing them is certainly part of power. But power, real power, doesn't happen on a small scale. Right now, I have absolute power over you." His hand stroked her body again and again she shivered in repulsion.

"You might control my body, but you'll never control my

mind," she hissed.

Hoqwua grinned as he touched her. "That, my dear, is where you are wrong. Any idiot with enough muscles can make people do what he wants them to do. That's ruling through fear and it's the sign of an amateur mind. Power is people doing what you want them to not because they're afraid of you, but because they cannot do anything else. Imagine that; a whole world of people ready to do my bidding because that is all they can do."

"What about your friend the dragon?" Huizhong asked. Her whole body felt like bugs were crawling all over it.

"Ao Qin?" Hoqwua asked. "She is a means to an end. I have control over her, too. The great red dragon of the South belongs to me. A man who controls a dragon; how is that for power? Does it get you excited? I know you girls are attracted to power."

"Stop touching me," Huizhong said. "You've proven your point; I'm completely at your mercy. But you still haven't told me how you're going to control my mind. It would take a lot of *baiju* to make me want to do your bidding. Especially in the bedroom."

Hoqwua held up his hand and showed her a purple ring on his finger. Just like the one on Jolan's finger, this one seemed to sparkle and dance in the firelight. He tapped it with his thumb. "Do you know what this is?"

"A ring?"

"Oh, my dear, sweet thing. So naïve. Yes, it is a ring, but what is unusual about it?"

"I don't know. I never could afford high-end jewelry."

Hoqwua held the ring up so he could see it better. "High-end. I suppose that's one way of looking at it. There are a few dozen of these rings in existence. All of them, save two, belong to my family. The secret, you see, is in the metal. I own the only known mine in existence. Without that mine the plan would never have come to fruition."

Huizhong knew she had to keep him talking. The longer

he talked, the longer she stayed alive. Plus, there was always the chance he'd screw up somehow. "Plan? What plan?"

"Control, my dear. Control."

"I'm going to die, anyway. You may as well tell me the whole plan."

He tapped his chin and shook his head. "You think you're clever, don't you? All you have to do is get me to tell you every detail and escape, then you can go back to the world as a hero. My dear, you are incorrect; you're not going to die. You have no magic in your body, so you're useless to the grand plan. But, a pretty girl like you can always have uses to a man like me."

Huizhong tensed. "I'll fight you to the end of the universe."

Hoqwua laughed. "You'll do no such thing. I'm sure by now you've noticed our minions down here obey without question. Don't fret about them; they're happy in their subservience. Most people need someone to lead them, to take away their fears and concerns and tell them what to do. Left to their own devices, the average person will make bad decision after bad decision.

"We take that pain away from them and teach them the joy of obedience. When you're under our spell, you won't even notice it. All you'll feel is the supreme joy of serving someone who is truly better than you."

She remembered fingers in her brain, controlling her body as she silently screamed in the dark recesses of her mind. And suddenly a piece of the puzzle snapped into place. "You're using Chenming Zhang's technology to control these people, aren't you?"

He grinned and his smile sent shivers down her spine. She'd been around predators her whole life and knew what that grin meant. There would be no escape, not even into the peace of death. "Ao Qin wanted the secrets to controlling human minds and the ability to do it efficiently. Chenming Zhang graciously provided that skill in return for a shot at immortality. Together with my metal and another of Ao Qin's little tricks, this city – nay, this whole planet – will soon be back in dragon hands where it belongs. And with my metal, I will control the dragons. Now, if you'll excuse me my dear, I have pressing matters at hand. The next time we meet you will be my willing slave.

"And I intend to take full advantage of your charms. Sleep well, Huizhong. I will see you soon and you will want to be well rested; I am a man of hearty appetites."

He turned to leave, but stopped short. "Don't worry about your friends saving you. You see, we know full well Crow will reach out to Chan. They'll be dead before they make it down the elevator. Two birds with one stone. All we really want is the boy; your Crow and Chan are superfluous and, frankly, they know too much."

Huizhong thrashed and raged against the cage. The metal bruised her body and left her head spinning. Two minions with dead eyes appeared in front of her and began attaching things to her head. She fought them every step of the way, but it was no use. She couldn't move enough to keep them from pasting wires at her temples.

The wires ran across the room where a minion plugged them into a machine that hummed and clicked. Green magic raced along the console. It would only be a matter of time before the magic plunged into her brain and left her a ready and willing slave of Hoqwua.

A minion pierced her arm and she felt something flowing into her body. Her panic slowly began to fade. She'd be a slave, but honestly what had she done with her life, anyway? Palling around with dragons was not the way to fame and fortune. As if fame or fortune was something for a person like her. Those were for better people.

Huizhong tried to shake her head and clear the alien thoughts of mediocrity from her brain. She bumped her head and used the pain to pull herself back to the world. The green magic raced up the wires to her temples. She felt distantly like she should be screaming and crying, but couldn't bring herself to do that. It would be fine. Hoqwua was a nice man. Perhaps they could become friends.

Perhaps they could become more than friends.

The magic hit her temples and she felt herself slip away into the abyss. It was better this way. She might not be free, but at least she could be happy. That old Huizhong was a party pooper, anyway. And, seriously, why didn't she ever fix her hair? It was so tacky.

Deep inside her brain, the old Huizhong watched and waited. She could see out of her eyes and feel the world around her, but she couldn't move anything. In a cage in a mental cage, she thought to herself and chuckled. The packet of Heaven's Powder had long since worn off, but she still felt connected to the universe and that gave her strength to be patient and wait. It might take turns or decades, but old Huizhong was looking forward to the time she'd be able to slam a knife in Hoqwua's back and disappear.

32 | We All Fall Down

The Monastery of Hope had seen better days. Only a few days ago, the grounds were cultured grasses and neatly arranged topiaries; the tireless work of a timeless monk. Now, the ground was littered with empty packets of Heaven's Powder and broken people. Hope, once a wise and glorious thing, had fallen to the masses and been corrupted by their insatiable desires.

The Golden Monk's body was hung by his wrists from the pagoda. Crow stepped over the slumbering body of a young man who'd never seen a good day in his short life and stared at the monk. He scratched his head and pointed. "That's, what? Thirty feet up? These junkies can't figure out how to make it through the day, but they can figure out how to hoist a golden corpse up there using crap they found in the alley."

Chan grunted. "People can be clever when they want to be cruel."

"Who takes the time to hoist a corpse like that? These people need jobs," Crow said with a sigh.

Kevin and the dinosaur stuck close to each other as they looked around the ruined monastery. There was sorrow and curiosity in his eyes. Chan felt the weight of the world collapse on his shoulders. If only the Beast hadn't discovered Kevin. If only he'd been faster, he could have gotten to Earth and saved the boy's parents. If only. If only. If only.

But he hadn't been faster and now the boy that should be enjoying childhood on his own planet was leaking his innocence all over the grounds of a despoiled holy place. It was like watching his own childhood come to an end all over again.

"Where is the tunnel, Crow?" Chan asked.

Crow ignored him and kept staring at the suspended monk. There was a hint of regret in his eyes, something that didn't creep into Felix Crow very often. "Hey, kid," he called out. "Ever seen the corpse of an immortal?"

Kevin stood next to Crow and stared up at the monk's body. There was no shock in his eyes. "Why is he gold?" he asked.

Crow shrugged. "It seemed like a good idea at the time."

The boy's fingers stroked Dino's feathers idly, like he was using the dinosaur as a safety net or a way to remember he was still alive. "Who was he?"

"This, my boy, was the last monk of Hope. This was a monastery built a few hundred turns ago and sealed off toward the end of the Dragon Wars. This guy tried to broker a peace with the dragons and failed miserably. We were already winning the war, anyway. His people turned to spinning yarns to give people false hope. He fell in love with gold and became gold himself. When he found out what he'd done, he walled off the monastery and was never heard from again. I'll bet you anything, this guy was at the very root of everything that's happened. He knew my name. He knew Fei Long's name. He probably knew Chenming Zhang personally. Which means he probably knew about the dragon. He watched all this happening and didn't lift a finger to stop it."

"Should we cut him down?" Kevin asked.

Crow snorted and shook his head. "Why?"

Kevin looked up at Crow and then back at the hanging monk's corpse. "He should have a burial or something."

"He's dead, kid. Let the vermin eat him. Whatever he was is no longer there; all that's left is a corpse that doesn't even have the common decency to rot."

Crow gave the monk one last, sad look before striding up the pagoda. He adjusted his hat and looked around the remains of the monastery. His gaze stopped in some places, eyes searching for something. As he looked, he got more and more frustrated.

"What are you looking for?" Kevin asked.

"The way into the tunnels. It's got to be here somewhere,"

Crow said, motioning with his hand. "All the time that guy spent meditating you'd think he'd be able to post a sign. 'This way to the underground lair' would be all it had to say, but he was too busy trimming the bushes to write anything."

Kevin cocked his head to the side slightly and asked, "Why would it be along the walls? Didn't you just say it's underground?"

Crow held up a finger and looked like he was about to say something snarky. He opened and closed his mouth. Finally, he said, "That's a good point."

"Dragon War era monasteries were built on a centralized plan," Chan said. "They were intended to remind the monks that centeredness in all things was important. If they got too far into the spiritual side, they lost their humanity. If they fell too far into the pleasures of the flesh, they lost touch with their spiritual nature."

"Why do you know that?" Crow asked. "No offense, but it seems a bit off your beaten path of beating people up."

Chan shook his head and remembered why he was so relieved and sad when Crow left his tutelage and joined the police. For all his innate skill, Crow never did master the esoteric nature of Wushu. He wanted to learn to punch and kick, but never wanted to understand the deeper meanings of the art. By eschewing the spiritual side of Wushu, Crow missed out on the deepest aspects of martial arts; the stuff that looked like sorcery, but was nothing more than what could be accomplished with training and introspection.

"You never understood the spiritual and philosophical aspects of what I taught you," Chan said.

"All I ever wanted to do was kick some ass," Crow replied. "You were far too interested in all that spiritual feihuà."

"Flesh is just flesh," Chan said. "You are far more than skin. When you understand that, you will be ready to transition to something more."

"Okay, let's say you're right," Crow said.

"I am."

"About the monastery," Crow said.

"About that, too," Chan replied.

Crow rolled his eyes and gritted his teeth. "Then, if these monasteries were built around a center, that would be the most logical place to look, right? When I first came in, the Golden Monk was sitting in the pagoda. I'm not an architect, but that looks to be about the center of the yard."

Kevin ran up the steps to the pagoda with the dinosaur in tow. He looked around intently, even stomped his foot looking for a hidden door or something similar, but there was nothing to be found. "It's just wood," he called out.

"Okay," Crow said. "You've got a couple hundred turns to kill and want to build a tunnel. No one talks to you, no one visits you, but there's always the chance someone will break in and you want to keep your secrets. Where do you hide the tunnel entrance?"

"In the center?" Kevin asked.

Chan pointed at Kevin and said, "He is right. Monks of his time were obsessed with centeredness. This was, of course, before your people showed up with their weird ideas of a god that can become three gods. The entrance is almost assuredly at the center."

Crow looked over at Kevin stomping around the pagoda. "Anything?" he asked.

The boy shook his head, but continued stomping. Crow walked up the steps to join him in his mad quest. Chan examined the writing on the pagoda's pillars. It was an old dialect, barely even remembered anymore, but some of the words remained in use today. He ran a finger down the front of the pillar, tracing hundreds of turns of history under the tip of his finger. The Golden Monk had lovingly detailed the pillar with his thoughts about life and the world around him. "'I must keep this place alive'," Chan whispered, "'for without Hope, all is lost'."

The Golden Monk had seen the world change around

him, peeking out from his hidey hole while Croatoa grew like a cancer. The city swallowed the monastery whole, not even realizing it was there. It was subsumed to the whims of a city that felt hope was a thing for the weak. Over time, his handwriting never changed. He maintained a dispassionate tone for the whole of his writing. It had to have been a feature of being so isolated, so alone, but still feeling superior to everyone else. He had to have suspected his walls would be breached someday, but the monk never fretted about it.

His life was clinical and sterile. It was a series of mindless tasks meant to strip away his ego, but all it did was strip away his humanity until the monk was little more than a wind-up doll with strange skin. While Crow and Kevin searched, Chan continued examining the pillars that held up the pagoda. In the end, the Golden Monk was as much a mystery in death as he had been in life.

On the second pillar he checked, Chan found something that he didn't understand. "Crow," he called out. "What do you make of this: 'She lies below'?"

Crow shrugged and shook his head. "Could be burials. Some of these monks were into weird things."

"What's wrong with burial?" Kevin asked. "My grandmother was buried; it wasn't so bad."

"It doesn't happen much here," Crow said. "That's Earth stuff; we usually light a bonfire and drink all night long."

"You do that anyway," Chan said.

Crow tipped his hat to Chan. "Someone died somewhere. It would be improper to not give a proper farewell."

Dino hooted and chirped excitedly. Everyone turned to see the dinosaur with his head down and long tail twitching in the air. He was scratching at the dirt just beyond the pagoda and sniffing wildly. Kevin tentatively walked across the pagoda and dropped down next to Dino. The deinonychus looked up briefly and chirped before returning to scratching away at the ground.

"What's wrong with him?" Crow asked, peering across

the pagoda, but not moving.

Kevin touched Dino's head and felt excitement and the thrill of the hunt. But there was no way he could be hunting anything in the dirt. The dinosaur's thoughts were a jumble; he could smell something but couldn't figure out where it was coming from.

"He thinks there's something down there," Kevin said.

Chan stood next to them and looked down at the dirt. He swept his foot around and found nothing but an endless supply of sand. "There is only more dirt."

Crow dropped down and scooped away the dirt with his hands. The fine sand kept flowing back into the hole. He grunted and thrust his hand deep into the soil. Chan nodded appreciatively. Iron hand training was at the very heart of Wushu and it was good to see his former student had been keeping up with his studies.

He winced and yanked his hand back out. "There's something down there."

"More dirt," Chan said dismissively. He wished they could get on with the task at hand.

Crow shook his head and flexed his hand. "Whatever it is it's rock hard."

"Could be a rock," Kevin said.

"Ha, ha. Be a pal and help me scrape this off. I promise you there's something down there and it's not just a rock."

With Kevin, Crow, and the dinosaur all flinging sand into the air, Chan decided to move off and keep looking around at the pillars. As he walked past a bush, a screeching sound caught his ear. He spun and checked on Kevin and the dinosaur, but they were all happily digging in the dirt. The screech – it sounded like a gate opening or closing – hit him again.

This time, Chan was ready. He turned to his left and found nothing but a manicured shrub that smelled of spicy urine. He doubted the monk used the foliage for a bathroom, but monks could be odd fellows, so it wasn't completely outside the realm of possibility.

As he peered at the shrub, something glinted in the sunlight. Chan leaned closer, but he couldn't see anything that should reflect the light. He pushed his hands into the shrub and found himself staring at a pipe buried deep inside the bush.

"Crow," Chan called. "I've found something."

Crow sauntered over, covered from head to toe in dust and sand. "What?" he asked.

Chan pointed at the shrub and said, "This."

The pole in the ground was nothing special. It looked old and possibly predated most of Croatoa's short history. "Could be a bathroom pipe," Crow replied.

"Even though it smells like urine here, it appears to be on the outside of the bush, not the inside of the pipe."

Crow rubbed his chin and shrugged. "How'd you find it?"

"I heard something like a gate closing," Chan said. "Then the light from the mothers reflected off it."

Crow slapped Chan on the back and grinned. "I'll make a detective out of you yet."

Chan didn't know what that really meant, but decided to take it as a compliment. He pushed his way into the bush and tried to peer down the pipe. After a few hands, the thin pipe was nothing but blackness. "I cannot see where it goes."

"Couldn't get down there anyway," Crow said. "Still it's peculiar. Who puts a pipe in the middle of a monastery? I met a guy who said the Golden Monk still had some access to the world. The monk even knew my name. I'll bet you this pipe was how he was communicating."

"And that means there is something under this monastery," Chan said, scratching his chin thoughtfully.

Crow grinned and fanned himself with his hat. "Just like we thought."

"Um," Kevin called out. "Chan. Mr. Crow; we found something."

What they had found was an ancient, hinged doorway made from a metal none of them had seen before. The door was half-eroded from age and the constant pressure of the sand on top of it. The metal was deep purple with tiny pink sparkles in it. Chan knelt down and touched the door. The heat of the day had seeped into the strange metal.

"Look familiar?" Crow asked.

"No," Kevin said. "Why?"

"Chan? It's your chance on *Take a Gamble*. What does it look like to you?"

Chan shook his head. He'd never seen anything like the metal on the door. "I have no idea."

Crow fished around in his trench coat for a while before he finally pulled out a tiny ring and held it up to the sky. The ring was largely purple, etched through with pink and other colors. It was hypnotic to look at, in the same way that lava lamps became popular because they were so fun to look at.

"Look familiar?" Crow asked.

Chan and Kevin shook their heads slowly, eyes never leaving the ring. "Where did you get it?" Chan asked.

Crow chuckled and shook his head. "Found it on Jonal's finger. No reason to go tossing out a perfectly good ring just because it was on a dead junkie. Point is, that grate is the same metal as this ring. You know what that means? It means this grate was from Hoqwua's mystical mine. He went out and collected all the purple metal from that mine. Except this bit."

"What kind of metal is this?" Kevin asked. "I've never seen anything like it."

"Dunno, kid," Crow said, shrugging. "Whatever it is, there's only one place on the planet where it comes from and only one guy who controls it."

Chan dropped down and stroked the metal. It was roughly hewn, jagged and malformed in places. Something tugged at his mind, some tiny bit of information from a long time ago that he stumbled across in his studies. Crow and Kevin continued chattering away while he felt around the edges of the grate only to find it was securely fastened to the stone underneath it.

Dino nosed in, sniffing and chirping quietly. Something down there had grabbed the dinosaur's attention. Chan assumed it was food, but he'd seen the creature eat before and this wasn't feeding behavior. It reminded him of watching wild *lóng xīyì* hunting the *wěidà de xīyì* on the farm. The dragon lizards were smaller than Dino, but in groups they could easily take down a lone great lizard.

That was it. Dino was hunting. Something down there had piqued his interest. Animals only hunted when they were hungry or when there was a threat nearby. A threat like a dragon.

And that's when he remembered what was so important about the purple metal. "It is dragon steel," Chan said.

Crow and Kevin stopped talking and looked down. "Dragon steel?" Kevin asked.

Chan glanced at Crow and saw confusion on his face, too. "Dragon steel is a myth," Crow said. "No one alive has ever seen it."

"History says the metal was dark purple and sparkled like the night sky. It was supposed to be the weapon that would change the course of the Dragon Wars, but it was too rare to outfit an army with *daos* made from dragon steel. Magic and numbers, of course, ultimately won the day."

Crow looked at the ring in his hand with fresh eyes. He held it up the suns and whistled appreciatively. "So, old Hoqwua controls all the dragon steel on the planet. No wonder he wanted it all back; this stuff is probably priceless."

"What's so important about it?" Kevin asked.

"They say it is toxic to dragons," Chan said.

"Someone who controls all the dragon steel on the planet could control the world. If word of this got out, the dragons would likely attack just to make sure no one could use it on them," Crow said.

"Another war with the dragons would be disastrous. We

are many more than we were during the last wars and our people are concentrated in large cities. Imagine what a few dragons could do to Croatoa," Chan said. "We must stop him."

"Well, let's get going. That tunnel must lead at least to the dragon. If there's a dragon, Huizhong is there," Crow said.

Chan stood up slowly and brushed himself off. "There is one problem, though."

"What?" Crow asked.

"The grate is securely fastened to the stone. There is no way we can get it off without tools."

Crow pondered that for a moment before turning to Kevin. "Hey, kid. You blew up a stuffed toy and crippled some guys, right? Want to take a whack at some dragon steel?"

Kevin grinned. A huge, ear-to-ear grin crossed his face. "Yes!"

"Okay," Crow continued, standing next to the grate. "Let's see what you've got."

The boy stared hard at the grate. Chan could tell he was concentrating, but there was no tell-tale sense of lightning in the air. Kevin's eyebrows furrowed and his nose crinkled up. He waved his arms around like a mad man, but nothing happened.

"I think you should try it, Mr. Crow," Kevin said, gasping for breath.

Crow put his hand on Kevin's shoulder and said, "Never give up. You've got to figure out what amazes you and go after it. Once you've got it, you may need to slap the snot out of naysayers every day, but you have to hold onto it. Now, close your eyes and reach out to the grate with your mind."

Kevin's body went slack. He distantly felt Crow standing next to him. Chan watched with a hopeful air. It would figure Crow could teach the boy to channel and harness his destructive powers. "Relax, Kevin," Chan said. "This is just like learning Whirling Python; it is impossible to do it if you're tense."

Crow pointed at Chan and winked. "He's got the idea. Relax. I'd give you some *baiju* if I thought it would help, but I'm all out and it turns out there are all these rules about getting kids drunk."

Kevin laughed despite himself. Even from a distance, Chan could feel the tension going out of the boy. The faintest hint of electricity flowed through the air, nothing more than a whiff of ozone and a raised arm hair, but it was enough. Once he figured out the basics of a thing, Kevin was an incredibly fast learner. The air thickened and pulsed around them as energies were diverted and redirected.

There was loud popping noise, followed by the sound of Xuanwu rending the heavens in twain. The grate exploded in a mass of searing white light and shrieking metal.

As the energy in the air calmed down, Crow uncovered his eyes and blinked them rapidly. He looked at Kevin with a sense of awe on his face. "Amazing kid. I've blown up stuff, but nothing like what you just did."

Kevin beamed. It was the first time in a very long time that Chan saw the boy happy and pleased with himself. "Excellent work, Kevin," Chan said.

Crow looked down into the now exposed tunnel. He turned toward Kevin and Chan with a serious look on his face. "There's a monster down there that almost no one has seen in hundreds of turns. It's huge and powerful and has magic that can turn you to dust from a thousand hands away. Our ancestors fought these creatures to a standstill, but that was sometimes an entire army against one dragon. There are three of us and one dinosaur. The only way we're going to survive this is if we go smart and quiet."

Dino took that opportunity to hop into the tunnel and speed off, chirping madly. Crow looked from the tunnel to Chan and Kevin. His brow furrowed like he couldn't believe his plan was rejected by a dinosaur of all things. "Or," he continued, "we could follow Dino and hope for the best."

Kevin took off after Dino, calling out the dinosaur's name. Chan could have told him it would be impossible to the reel the dinosaur in now. The predator was loose and the only thing that was going to bring it back was running whatever he had smelled to the ground and killing it.

"*Aiya, n☐ yā t☐ng de,*" Crow muttered. He glanced at Chan and asked, "Are you coming?"

Chan nodded and Crow jumped into the tunnel. Chan took one last look around the light and hopped into the abyss. It wasn't every day someone got to chase a dinosaur and a young magician straight into the lair of a dragon.

33 | Lovely Day

Huizhong's visions came back with a bottle of cheap *baiju*, a pack of *bidis*, and a nightmarish vengeance. As the magical drugs coursed through her body, her mind desperately tried to escape back to the balancing rocks and solitude of her clearing. She saw the same vision over and over again: Crow, the man with the *d□ulì*, the powerful male, all going through a tunnel. The man in the *d□ulì* and the powerful male had names now: Chan and Kevin.

There were subtle changes in the vision. This time she wasn't with them and they weren't walking. They were chasing something that she couldn't make out. All she could capture of their quarry was a blur of color and a desperate desire to eviscerate something. The quarry's thoughts were so alien she could barely comprehend them. It had a complicated understanding of the world, far more so than anyone ever guessed and it felt terribly alone. The only thing it had left in its world was an all-consuming desire to protect its tiny pack.

Dino. It had to be Dino. The dinosaur always seemed willing to kill anything that crossed it or threatened Kevin, but she had assumed that was just its nature. In a way, she was right, but it wasn't a programmed response on the part of the animal. His actions were intentional and rationalized. He, like Kevin, was the only one of his kind on the planet. They joined together in their sorrow and became a pack.

As always, the vision descended into chaos. Fire and madness and death followed the chaos and Huizhong awoke to a vital need to obey Hoqwua and the desiccated remains of two corpses in cages just like hers across from her. She assumed Hoqwua left them there so she'd know she had a choice: obedience or the slow, creeping death of starvation.

Huizhong was nothing if not pragmatic, though. She choked back the insistent message to love and obey her captor and smiled at the corpses across from her. "Did I miss anything, guys?"

Their lips were pulled back, little more than leather worms on faces of ancient hide. Their gums had receded, leaving toothy grins that Huizhong, in her weakened state, found funny. She did her best to ignore the way the hands reached toward each other, as if they could stave off a grisly end with a simple touch. The fact that a couple had been left down here to die slowly came close to breaking her. Huizhong preferred to think of them as passing notes to each other or looking for a low five for a particularly clever joke.

Maybe one of them had said something about how Hoqwua couldn't get a girlfriend because he was a raging psychopath. "Did you hear the one about the psychopath that found a bloody corpse crawling toward him? Sure, he stabbed his wife again until she learned her place."

Ha. Ha. Ha. Ha.

"What has four legs and one arm? My kⁿngbù xīyì playing with my wife."

Ha. Ha. Ha. Ha.

Her mind was a whirlpool of emotions. She hated Hoqwua. She hated Crow. She hated Ao Shun. Yet she loved them all. The magical narcotics being pumped through her temples felt like a variant on the stuff in Heaven's Powder. The powder was subtle. It showed you the universe and your place in it. Most people felt tiny and powerless when they saw how big everything was how puny they were. With that kind of revelation, all it takes is a little nudge and they suddenly find religion.

And once they find religion, all it takes is a few people to tell them someone has a plan for them and they're not completely random to hold them in thrall.

The stuff pumping through her body had all the subtlety of fist to the face. She could feel herself cracking apart at the seams of her being. The drug was attacking her whole being like a *línghún xīpán* gnawing on her soul.

Huizhong dove deep into the chemical miasma, much like she had with the powdered version, and looked below the obvious pinpricks of bright light vibrating like dancers in a sea of void. Below that, she saw the inner workings of the universe once again. And in those inner workings, the places where the universe rewrote itself every moment, she found the strength to keep going.

They had moved her cage so she could, as Hoqwua put it, "watch her past come to an end." Huizhong now had a wonderful view of the floor of the cavern where drones were making Heaven's Powder around the clock. If Crow was right and the stuff was that addictive, even if she did get out of here, the city would fall apart in due time.

Ao Qin stirred. The big, blood-red dragon had been sleeping in the middle of the floor. She was a constant reminder that getting out of line had a cost and it was her magic that kept the powder flowing.

Over the past several hours, as the drugs constantly wore her mind down, Huizhong watched as a sorcerer was rendered into the odious powder before being mixed into the chemical stew in the vats. It was horridly fascinating and about as pleasant as watching tiny dragons being slaughtered for their scales. A group of dead-eyed addicts brought the sorcerer out and tossed his naked, chained form in front of Ao Qin. The dragon toyed with him, batting him this way and that as he cried out in terror.

The poor man thought Ao Qin was going to eat him, but that would have been over too quickly. She couldn't be certain, but Huizhong got the distinct impression that fear and pain were necessary for the rendering to work. By the time the dragon was finished with him, the sorcerer was a sobbing mess. His legs had been broken at the thighs and shins, his nose was bleeding, and his eyes were hanging out of their sockets.

Unimaginable agony, but Huizhong watched it all with a coldly calculating mind. In her weakened state, she latched onto anything that felt real and, unfortunately, the sorcerer's torture was as real as it came.

Magic crackled and popped on the floor. Even from as far away as she was, Huizhong could feel reality bending to Ao Qin's whims. While the world flexed and twisted, the dragon took her time rending the man from limb to limb. Every time he thought she would kill him and end his suffering, Ao Qin bit off a limb.

It started with his right leg, snapped neatly off first at the shin and then at the thigh. Then the left leg followed suit. The magic Ao Qin was working kept the sorcerer alive and aware of his surroundings as the dragon nipped pieces off his body. When she bit through the chains that wrapped around his body and brought an arm out in her teeth, the man gave up all hope.

Even from where she was caged, Huizhong could see the pain written on his face. Then, as Ao Qin took his remaining arm and left his torso on the rock, all the sorcerer's problems faded away. His mind shorted out and his pain-wracked body went limp.

Ao Qin stood over him and said something. The sorcerer started crying and screaming once more until the dragon took his head.

The sorcerer's body parts were combined with body parts from a monk from an order Huizhong wasn't aware of. The monk had taken the torture with much more aplomb, never moving or even batting an eye as the dragon did her honest best to torture the man and keep him alive as she pulled his body apart.

Horrible green flame from the dragon's mouth rendered the remains of both men into ash. The dead-eyed servants of this madhouse carefully scooped up the ashes and mixed them with wood ash from the fires before carefully pouring them into one of the large vats. Fluid coursed from the vats through tubes. Super-heated ovens turned the fluid to dust that minions carefully poured into tiny paper packets.

Huizhong didn't know how they did it, but Ao Qin and Hoqwua had managed to find a way to suck the energy out of ashes and turn magic and religion into a potent drug. They were using the drug as a weapon to bring down the city bit by tiny bit. Considering Jonal's reaction to Heaven's Powder withdrawal, all Ao Qin and Hoqwua would have to do was stop making the powder and the city would tear itself apart in short order.

In the chaos, Hoqwua would rise up and pretend to make the city safe again. Like obedient sheep, the people of Croatoa would welcome him as their ruler if only he would stop the madness. If the dragon and billionaire were thinking that small; Hoqwua had intimated he had global ambitions. Since all the magical power for Aluna coursed through Croatoa, controlling this city would be tantamount to controlling the planet.

A distant clanging sound awoke Huizhong from her reverie. Somewhere out there, something had exploded. Exploding things usually meant Crow, but he wasn't coming from the direction of the elevators. That meant there was still hope.

Ao Qin stirred when the explosions echoed through the cavern. At first, she seemed unconcerned, but something caught her attention. She sat upright with her nose sniffing at the air. It all smelled like sweat and desperation to Huizhong, but dragons had an amazing sense of smell.

The dragon raised her eyebrows and twitched her whiskers: dragon excitement from what Ao Shun had said. She rose quietly to her feet, far too quietly for a hundred-hand long creature. Huizhong watched out the corner of her eye as Ao Qin stalked slowly toward the main entrance to the cavern. The one she and Crow had come through less than half a turn ago.

"Where are you going?" Hoqwua called out.

Ao Qin sneered at him. She turned back and stood in front of Hoqwua with an evil glint in her eyes. "I am leaving," Ao

Qin said.

Hoqwua shook his head sadly and held a finger up in her face. "You belong to me," he said, "Or have you forgotten about the dragon steel?"

The dragon smiled a huge, toothy grin. "Your dragon steel is gone, little man. I can smell the change in the air."

"You think you can fit through a tiny grate? The main gate is still in place."

Ao Qin shook her massive head slowly back and forth. "I should kill you, but not tonight," she replied. "Tonight, there are strange magics out there."

Hoqwua clenched his fists and gritted his teeth. "We had a deal," he hissed.

"There is no time for your deals, little thing," Ao Qin replied. "King Yan is coming."

A strange skittering sound, like nails clicking on stone echoed faintly from the tunnels. Something was coming and coming fast. The dragon pushed Hoqwua aside and stood by the door. Her body was twisted and contorted. To an untrained eye, it would look like she was trying to make herself small, but Huizhong had seen Ao Shun do the same thing. Their bodies – half snake, half lizard – worked well with the same kinds of coiling that snakes do. From that coiled position, Ao Shun could erupt with enough speed and power to shatter a *Llmíng hóngmù* tree. Huizhong once saw the black dragon punch through a trunk sixty hands wide.

"Minions!" Hoqwua cried. "Defend me!"

A dozen men flowed into the cavernous room. Their armor glistened black and purple in the torchlight. Each one held a *kwan dao* – a short broadsword on the end of a staff. They stood at attention behind Ao Qin's bulk. Their empty eyes made them look slow and harmless, but Huizhong knew all too well what could happen when someone else took over a brain. She herself had fought Crow almost to a standstill, screaming inside her own mind as her body lashed out.

The men down below were likely going through the same

thing. Their bodies were hard and smooth, but their minds were boiling seas of turmoil. They were slaves stuck in bodies and forced to watch as someone else made them move.

Deep inside the tunnel, the clicking sound grew louder. Huizhong watched with detached eyes. On the floor, Ao Qin waited patiently, ready to devour whatever popped out of the tunnel. The men in the line didn't seem so sure. As soon as they settled into position they began fidgeting; the high cost of employing junkies as security.

Huizhong wished she could move, if only to watch the oncoming battle. Every moment she spent watching something else was a lifetime away from the machines pumping poison into her veins. Strange thoughts assailed her. Maybe Hoqwua would win the fight and free her. More and more, she wanted to please him and do his bidding.

Huizhong stamped down hard on that thought. The only thing she really wanted to do was slice Hoqwua like a *m□ngshé* and feast on his entrails. But that wouldn't be what he wanted her to do and that was wrong.

The clicking got louder and louder until a green and orange blur burst out of the tunnel. Dino didn't pause as he leapt from the entrance straight into the first person he found. His huge toe claws tore through the man's chest before he exploded off the dying man and straight into Ao Qin's face.

Dragons were reputed to be amazing fighters. They could sneak like no other creature on Aluna and old documents from the Dragon Wars showed them as terrifyingly fast fighters. Aside from their size and their natural weapons, their intellect and cunning made them fearsome foes.

The angry deinonychus moved so quickly, bouncing off her face and back into the fray that Ao Qin didn't have time to react. Dino also attacked in a less obvious way. Rather than going straight down the middle to get to prey, his hunting instincts kicked in and Dino attacked from the side.

As soon as Dino took out one person, Hoqwua's perfectly aligned fighting rows crept into disarray. The dinosaur moved erratically, drawing people to him and then dodging their kwan daos effortlessly. He was playing with them, enjoying himself, but always working his way toward the dragon.

Ao Qin finally saw her opening and uncoiled, launching herself forward like giant arrow. The stories from the Dragon Wars barely scratched the surface of what dragons were capable of. She was a red blur that could smash through walls. Huizhong could imagine the dragons of old laying waste to entire armies.

Dino wasn't an army, though. He was made for a time when creatures of nightmares roamed freely and only other nightmarish creatures could survive. By the time Ao Qin landed, the dinosaur had dodged her speeding bulk. Three-foot-long claws dug into the stone as the dragon tried to stop herself from skidding. Before she could stop, Dino hopped onto her and dug his own claws into her back.

She shrieked, a terrible keening wail punctuated by growls of anger. Dino held tight, burying talons deep inside her flesh. In his world it wasn't uncommon to take down creatures the size of Ao Qin, but almost never alone. To hunt and kill a dragon would require a pack.

A child's wail caught Huizhong's attention. Kevin stood at the entrance to the tunnel, fists tightly balled. Huizhong couldn't feel it from where she was, but she knew the air around the boy would be crackling. Chan showed up a moment later, with a wheezing Crow bringing up the rear.

The pack had arrived.

34 | Reign Fall

While Kevin was running after Dino, it was easy for him to convince himself he was as tough as Crow and Chan. The scene at the end of the tunnel was enough to remind him of just how small he was in the world. Scary looking men with *kwan daos* were falling all over each other trying to get at Dino. At least one man was curled on the ground, holding his chest and screaming in agony.

"This is not good," Chan said from behind him. "We have wandered into a massacre."

Heavy breathing and thudding footsteps announced Crow's arrival. The man was all but doubled over from the exertion of the run, but he still had a gleam in his eye. "Wow," he said, "that's a battle."

Kevin took a deep breath and tried to center himself. He knew he could always run, but he'd never be able to live with himself if he left Dino and Huizhong behind. Chan's breathing technique helped steady him somewhat, but he was still shaking.

Chan put a hand on his shoulder. The touch brought Kevin back into the world and calmness failed. "What are we going to do?" he asked Chan. "There must be twenty or thirty guys with *kwan daos* in there."

"Don't forget the dragon, kid," Crow chimed in. "That's the real threat. And where's Hoqwua? I want that bastard."

Chan drew his dao and gazed out on the floor. "We will fight," he said.

"You never were much on motivational speeches," Crow said. "Look, kid. Sorry, Kevin. If you want to cut and run, I get it. I'm scared half to death right now, but your friendly dinosaur is in there and Huizhong is in there. Whatever you two decide to do, I'm going in. I'd rather go out in a blaze of glory trying to do something than not. I've got too many regrets in my life as it is."

Kevin nodded and gulped. Visions of blood and sharp things filled his head. He wondered what it would feel like when someone ran him through with a kwan dao or hacked his limbs out from under him. "I'm scared," he said quietly.

Chan squeezed his shoulder. "So am I. Remember bravery isn't doing something when you aren't afraid of it; bravery is doing something even though you're terrified of it."

Crow put his hand on Kevin's other shoulder and said, "Hold out your hand."

Kevin held out his hand and Crow dropped the purple ring in his palm. "I'm going to want that back when we're done," he said.

His head was throbbing and he felt like throwing up, but Kevin closed his fingers around the ring and did his best to put on a brave face. He started to speak, but his voice wouldn't work, so he nodded instead.

Crow motioned out at the cavern. "Okay, here's the plan. Those guys are all focused on Dino right now, but they can't get to him. He won't be able to hold on long, so I say Chan and I move in through the back and take these guys out from behind. Kevin, if you stick to the shadows, you should be able to find Huizhong. I'd start with that area back there; that's where they were dragging her when I left. Keep small and keep safe.

"Chan, you ready to go out in a blaze of glory?"

Chan nodded. "You will need a weapon."

Crow walked calmly out onto the cavern floor and put his foot under a kwan dao someone had dropped. With a flick of his leg, the weapon flew into his waiting hand. He spun it around a few times until it fell neatly into his other hand. Despite his terror, Kevin was impressed; Crow really was a student of Chan's.

Chan squeezed his shoulder one last time and said, "You do not need luck, you have skill and smarts. Xuanwu will smile on you. He appreciates bravery."

Kevin watched Chan stand next to Crow. They calmly watched the scene in front of them. With a nod, they both strode into the fray. Chan's first strike severed a man's head and Crow was smiling when he slammed the blade of his kwan dao into a man's back.

Kevin shook his head, trying to focus on the task at hand. If Crow was right, this path should take him past the worst of the fighting. His hands were shaking, but he sunk low to the ground and set off. Out of the corner of his eye, Kevin kept watch on the battle in case it shifted toward him. With his other eye, he sought out places to hide if need be.

The cavern stank of sulfur and disease. If Crow was right and this place was where they made that strange powder, it made sense. Back home, he'd heard that people who made drugs ruined every place they made them in. If the teachers in his school wanted to keep kids off drugs, all they'd have to do is bring them to this place.

There were cages along the wall with skeletons and rotting corpses. The whole thing reminded him of one of the horror movies he used to watch on his tablet when his parents thought he was sleeping. In the movie, death seemed so distant and fake, like the people making the movie were desperate to scare people watching it. Kevin watched the whole thing – some movie about a guy who captured women and killed them with a knife – and slept like a baby that night.

That was fake, though. Reality was a different story. The noise was bad enough, but it was the smell that really got to him. In addition to the sulfur, there was underlying current of copper that reminded him of the time he put a penny on his tongue at school. The skeletons and dead people in the cages weren't movie props, they were the real deal.

The totality of life dropped into Kevin's young head. The death itself didn't scare him – Chan had taught him death was nothing to be feared – it was the fact that someone could make him die that scared Kevin. The idea that all those people in the cages died because someone more powerful than themselves decided it should be was soul crushing.

He stood up a little straighter and focused on the back wall. If that's where he needed to get, he wouldn't let anyone stand in his way. Crow was right, it would be better to go down fighting than slowly die in a cage.

On the other side of the cavern, the battle raged on. Kevin spared a glance and could barely make out what was happening. It was a mass of flashing silver and splashes of red. Somewhere in that mess, his friends were fighting for their lives.

Kevin turned back to his path only to find a man with tattered clothes and ebony eyes staring at him. The man didn't say a word as he raised his kwan dao.

The blade narrowly missed Kevin's head. An instinct to avoid strikes – something Chan drilled into him – allowed him to move without thinking about it. While part of his brain was still processing what to do about the man trying to kill him, another part had shifted into survival mode and was busy calling the shots.

As the silver blade sailed past his head, Kevin's mind reconnected. The survival mode integrated with the thinking mode and he ducked just before the man could cut his head off.

A *kwan dao* was a heavy weapon. During training with Chan, Kevin learned that the best way to use the weapon was either slicing or stabbing and experts learned how to move swiftly from one to the other. Stabbing was easy. Slicing with a long, heavy weapon was decidedly more difficult. Kwan daos didn't accelerate very well, so it was necessary to keep them spinning whenever possible.

The blade on the man's kwan dao disappeared behind his head. Kevin ducked under the short blade on the other side and darted into the man. The best way to slow someone down was to get very close to them and jam up their body.

While he was entering, Kevin pulled his foot back and slammed it between the man's legs. The man blocked it, but

Kevin was expecting that. One thing Chan drilled into him over and over was dealing with armed opponents required a weapon of one's own. Weapons perform two functions: they increase range and increase power. Most people see weapons as physical objects, but a weapon can be mental as well.

By pulling his foot back, Kevin purposely telegraphed his attack. Chan had a lot of experience fighting and he shared those experiences with his pupil. Weapons overcame people's natural responses in a fight. Rather than do the simplest, easiest thing in a fight, a person with a weapon will attempt to use that weapon for everything. The easiest way to block Kevin's kick would have been to twist at the hips and use his legs to absorb the kick. A slightly more complicated response, but still effective, would have been to put his foot out and block the kick that way.

But the man forgot he had feet and legs. His focus was completely on the *kwan dao* in his hands and he used it to block Kevin's foot. He struck down hard, hoping to shatter Kevin's leg, but he fell prey to the boy's trap. With the *kwan dao's* blade forward, Kevin never would have attempted to get close to the man, but the blade went up as the man blocked the kick, giving the boy an excellent opening.

Kevin twisted as the wooden edge of the kwan dao struck his leg and let the force spin him around. Halfway around, he turned the rising kick into a spinning rear kick that exploited the hole in the man's defenses left by moving the *kwan dao*. This time his foot slammed into the man's groin. Before he could react, Kevin had grabbed the man's *kwan dao* from his weak fingers and started to spin backwards.

By the time the signal that his testicles had exploded hit the man's brain, Kevin was already bringing the sword edge of the *kwan dao* into play. The man's legs gave out as the pain worked its way through his body. He hit the ground on his knees, hands cupping his crotch, just in time for Kevin's blade to bury itself in his neck.

Kevin cursed himself for not practicing *Shāmò Xuànfēng*

more often, but he honestly never saw himself needing to use Desert Whirlwind. On Earth it would have been a completely useless technique – after all, who fights with *kwan daos* on Earth anymore? On Aluna, the technique had just saved his life.

He pushed the man's body with his foot and tugged at the blade embedded in the man's neck. It came free with a wet pop. Kevin continued toward the back of the cavern without a second thought to the man with the nearly severed head.

No one else accosted him as he jogged toward his goal. From a distance, the rock face of the cavern looked smooth and tidy, but as Kevin got closer and closer, more details resolved. He snuck along the edge of the wall until he found an opening.

Kevin decided two things: There may be more openings and the longer he stayed close to the fray, the more likely he was to get drawn into it. He cast a glance across the cavern and caught a glimpse of Chan dodging and slashing. The big dragon was still writhing around, snapping at Dino who was holding onto its back with his huge claws. He wanted to help, wanted to unleash whatever power was flowing through him and end the fight once and for all, but he still couldn't completely control his magic.

For a brief moment, he saw everyone fighting as their constituent parts. Instead of bodies, he saw bits of energy and matter flowing and clashing. He started to push out his power, but a voice in his head told him it wouldn't work. He blinked and the fight returned to a mass of bodies. His own uncertainty had just shut him down.

He cursed himself and ducked into the opening. If he couldn't help Crow, Chan, and Dino, he could at least help Huizhong.

Kevin found himself in a tunnel lit by torches burning with faint green flames. He stared at the fire, wondering what would cause it to burn that color. Maybe the fires on Aluna were normally green. No, the candles in the apartment burned orange and yellow, just like fire should. There had to be some magic working here. He snatched a torch off the wall and started forward.

One step in front of another, he told himself. Whatever was waiting at the end had to be easier to deal with than the dragon and the army. He jumped every time he heard a sound, wondering what kind of horrors were lurking around him. The echoes running up and down the tunnel made it difficult to tell where sounds came from.

The tunnel was short, maybe fifty feet or so, but it felt like an eternity. At the end, it opened into a smaller cave. There was another cave with steps carved into it, leading up into darkness. Kevin checked his torch and started forward.

Again, it was another short cave that felt eternal. Thankfully, his torch lit the way reasonably well. At the top, he found a cave with three cages and a window cut into the rock. The cages were horrible things; metal molded around a person, trapping them completely and binding them in place at the same time. Two of the cages held dead people, but the other one held Huizhong.

Her eyes were closed and there were tubes pushed into her temples. Strange green and purple energy flowed through the tubes from a box on the floor. Kevin walked quietly toward the box, worried it might explode or attack him. He nudged it with his toe and it didn't respond, so he focused his thoughts on it.

Energy in the room drained out of the air and into his body. He pushed the latent power into the box and peeked around at what he found. Inside was the remaining mind of a madman and dark thoughts of a wife pushed to suicide. It was a living thing, dark and angry, and constantly battling itself for supremacy. The madman hadn't always been that way, but very few people are born truly mad. He grew to madness after he amassed enough wealth and power that no one dared reel him in when he started off the cliff. The woman was his wife, a woman that loved him deeply even as she watched him turn to *yúkuài de nǚhái* to satiate his twisted desires. He left a trail of their broken bodies behind before he turned his attentions to his own son and daughter. The daughter died from shame and the son followed in the father's footsteps, destroying everything he touched in a never-ending quest for money and power.

The box was meant to teach people the price of disobedience and slowly break down their defenses until all that remained was joyous subservience. Somehow or another, the inventor had found a way to trap magic in the slime running through the box. The slime pushed the horrible history into whatever it touched, forcing the victim to succumb to thoughts of slavery or suicide.

Kevin snarled and cut the tubes with a swipe of the kwan dao. The magic inside spewed all over the small cavern in globs of purple and green goo. It hit the walls and sprayed his face, leaving a sickly, sticky goo that stained clothes and souls.

He tugged the tubes connected to Huizhong's head until they came off with a pop. Her eyes remained closed, though, and Kevin hoped the magic goo hadn't finished its dirty work. He wiped her face and said a small prayer to Chan's god.

"Wake up, Huizhong," he whispered. "I need you to wake up."

Her eyes fluttered open, then closed again. She took a deep breath and exhaled slowly. "Hello," she said quietly. "Did I miss anything?"

Kevin's heart grew. She was still alive and seemed okay. "Not much," he said, hoping to be as cool as Crow, "just a fight with a dragon and the corpse of an immortal."

She tried to nod, but the cage held her too tightly to move. "Can you find a way to unlock this thing? I have a terrible itch."

He searched frantically around the cage, looking for anything that would open it up. All he found were locks with no keyholes. "I think there's a trick to it. Give me a minute."

Huizhong chuckled. "Don't worry, I'll just talk to my

friends while you search."

"Your friends?"

"The people in the cage across from me. I call them the Yangs, but I don't know if they're married or anything. They don't talk much, but they're great listeners."

Kevin turned his head and looked at the other cages. The occupants were emaciated corpses, dry and dusty things with sunken eyes and lips pulled back into sneers. "They talk to you?" Kevin asked.

Huizhong's voice was sing-song and giggly. "Most of the time, no. But I talk to them."

"You've only been here overnight," Kevin said. "That stuff they were pumping into your head must have been potent."

"Do you want to know a secret?" she asked.

Kevin kept searching the cage for a latch or anything he could use to get her out. Something nagged at him about the other cages, though. "Sure," he said, not really paying attention. "I can't figure out how this thing works."

"Ask them," Huizhong said. "They were here when I checked in. Maybe they saw something."

"They're dead," Kevin replied, "They didn't see anything."

"The dead see all kinds of things. Things you and I don't see because we're still chained to our bodies. Ask them; they'll know."

Kevin kept searching cage, not really paying attention to her. She was drunk or something and wasn't making much sense.

"Ask them," she said again. "They'll tell you what you need to do."

He got the feeling she wasn't going to let it go. Besides, maybe the other cages would have some indication of how to open this cage. The corpses, a man and woman, seemed to be trying to reach for each other. Whatever monster locked them in let them die slowly from lack of food and water. He peered around the edges of their cages, but still couldn't find anything.

"You need to ask them," Huizhong said again.

"Fine," Kevin replied. He looked the corpse of the woman in the eye. "Do you know how to open these things?"

All they gave him as an answer was an empty stare and teeth that seemed far too big. He looked them up and down until something caught his eye. On the woman's finger was a familiar ring. His eyes shot back up to her face. Sunken eyes peered back at him. Her face was distorted in death, but when he looked closely a part of him died.

"Mom," he whispered.

The other corpse, now that he looked past the decay, was clearly his father. The dragon had claimed to have his parents and she was right about that. She had neglected to mention they had died slowly in cages, desperately reaching for each other until the life seeped out of them.

"Oh, no," Huizhong said. "Kevin, I'm so sorry."

Kevin took a deep breath and tried to calm himself. He knew anger would cloud his mind and degrade his skills; that was something Chan harped on all the time. But the hurt built inside of him, poisoning his heart with whispered tales of revenge.

"Kevin," Huizhong pleaded. "You must control yourself. Please. I promise I'll do whatever it takes to help you."

The air grew angry, like a cloud of rage had fallen into the small cavern. Energies crackled and hissed like serpents as Kevin rode his pain. They had been here the whole time. He could have saved them if only he had known where to look. If he could have controlled his power, he could have found them and saved them and they could have gone home.

Home.

There was no home anymore. The boy he was died by inches on this horrible planet and all that was left was an empty shell with the power to shake the world to its foundations. If the people who lived here couldn't keep things together, he'd have to do it for them.

Kevin reached out with his mind and let his rage attack the cages. At first, they twisted with screeches of metal bending and tearing. Fissures soon appeared along the tubes, splitting them into swirling masses. He pushed harder and the cages flew apart, landing on the stone floor with loud clanks before skidding across the cavern.

The corpses stayed upright and Kevin almost let himself believe he'd been wrong, that his parents were still alive, but in desperate need of food and water. Pieces slowly fell off the bodies. First a finger, then a hand, then an arm, all landing softly like dried-out leather. The remainders of the bodies fell together, as if they had one last shot to be together and took it.

A hand on his shoulder startled him. Kevin turned around, eyes blurred by tears, to find Huizhong standing freely. His rage hadn't confined itself to the cages his parents were in, it had destroyed hers, too. Feeling completely lost and empty, he collapsed into her waiting arms and held on tight as if she were the last person in the world.

She held him and cooed and whispered. He couldn't make out what she was saying, but it didn't matter. The words were there and the arms were there and for the moment she was the whole world to him.

"Well, well, well," a voice said. "Isn't this touching. I guess the stories about you were true, my boy. Not many people can do this to one of my cages. They were meant to hold sorcerers and you destroyed them like they were made of noodles. Bravo."

Kevin didn't let go of Huizhong, but he turned his head to see a man in a gray suit staring at them. Whoever the man was, he had a mean glint in his eyes, like a P.E. teacher about to punish the class for not being athletic enough.

"You're a monster, Hoqwua," Huizhong said.

"Small-minded people always think those of us with vision are monsters," Hoqwua replied.

He had a strange looking weapon in his hand, like a

primitive gun. Kevin knew from talking with Chan that guns were very rare on Aluna. For whatever reason, the Alunans never developed firearms, even though their fireworks displays were spectacular. The second settlers were pulled through in their sleep, so their weapons didn't come along with them.

Hoqwua pointed the device at Huizhong and Kevin. He smirked when he noticed Kevin looking at it. "I suppose you wonder what this is, don't you boy?"

Kevin no longer cared about living or dying. His soul felt empty and he wondered if Chan was right when he said people who die are set free from their soul traps. Maybe, somewhere far from here, his parents were living. He rolled his eyes at Hoqwua. "Gosh, Yogi," he asked, "is it a gun?"

Hoqwua's brow furrowed, like he understood most of the words, but was lost on the meaning of the sentence. Of course, Kevin thought, he probably wouldn't know about Yogi and he may or may not even call the weapon a gun. No matter. He focused on the weapon and reached out to the atoms that made it up. One little flick and …

"Don't," Hoqwua snapped. "Put your puny powers away, child, or I'll kill both of you."

Kevin felt he didn't have much to live for, but he couldn't assume the same of Huizhong. Maybe she had a life somewhere safe and sane. Her life wasn't his to take. He backed off the weapon and pushed himself away from Huizhong. Maybe he could take the shot and she could get away. The weapon in Hoqwua's hand looked like it could fire one shot before it needed to be reloaded.

"What do you want, Hoqwua," Huizhong asked. "More torture? Your last bit didn't work. I still don't belong to you and neither does he."

Hoqwua's face darkened and the true man stared out from behind the friendly mask. He was ugly. From skin to soul, Hoqwua was an ugly person hiding behind a veneer of civility. "Well, if you won't come freely, that's fine by me. I'll just break you the old-fashioned way. You don't need both legs or both arms. In fact, they just get in the way. As for the boy, I'm not interested in children, but Ao Qin wants his magic."

"Does that gun even work?" Kevin asked. "It's looks it'll explode if you try to fire it."

"Gun?" Hoqwua asked. "That must be one of your primitive Earth words. This is a divine fire rod. It packs and concentrates the power wasted on fireworks into something smaller and easier to carry around."

"It's a gun," Kevin said. "And not a very good one at that."

Hoqwua raised the weapon and pointed it directly at Kevin. "It's good enough to kill you."

"I thought your master down there wanted him alive," Huizhong said.

"My master?" Hoqwua asked. "Oh, you mean Ao Qin. She works for me."

"She works for you?" Huizhong asked. "How is it that a dragon works for the likes of you?"

Hoqwua twisted in place and fired the weapon out through a window overlooking the battle below. His finger twitched and the device belched fire. The roof of the cavern erupted in a mass of flames and hot rocks. The explosion brought the fight on the floor to a standstill. "That's how," he said.

"You just blew your one shot," Kevin said. "Now you have to reload."

Hoqwua shook his head and pulled a duplicate weapon from behind his back. "The beautiful thing about being rich is I can afford duplicates. Not that I paid the creator of this device for his work. When he was done, I had him brought here. Now, let's go."

Kevin spared a look onto the floor of the cavern and felt his heart sink even further. Hoqwua's shot had disrupted the fight. Dino had panicked and hopped off Ao Qin's back. The dragon had him cornered, but the dinosaur's hopping and dodging kept him safe. The battle had shifted; Crow and Chan were fighting a losing battle.

"You see, boy," Hoqwua said. "you cannot win this fight. The world will be mine. Now, move or I'll shoot her in the spine and let you watch as I take her."

The weapon jabbed Kevin's ribs, spurring him forward. Huizhong shoved Hoqwua's hand away and got a backhand for her troubles. She dropped to one knee and cursed. "You're a weak little man, Hoqwua."

"And you're out of time, *chāng fù*," he replied. "Now move."

By the time they reached the cavern floor, the fight was over. Kevin had to admit to himself they never really had much of a chance anyway. Like so many things, it seemed like a good idea at the time, but there was no way it could have worked. Crow and Chan were formidable fighters, but against thirty people and a dragon, they were fighting an uphill battle.

Crow was still snarling and jabbing his kwan dao at anyone who got too close. While he and Chan were focused on the people in front, a few of Hoqwua's men snuck around behind and tackled them.

Hoqwua jabbed Kevin in the back again and shoved him forward. Kevin dropped his head and marched. He shoved his hands in his pockets and found something. A small bit of smooth metal was lurking. He felt along the edges of the ring and wondered exactly how to play it. Supposedly the metal would kill a dragon, but how? Did he just have to let Ao Qin touch it? How do you get a dragon to put on a ring?

As Kevin and Huizhong were marched across the floor, Kevin caught Crow looking at him. There was a gleam in his eye, like he had been planning the trick with the ring all along. Maybe the fight was just a ruse to get Ao Qin off guard.

Ao Qin stopped snapping at Dino and turned her great head. The dinosaur took the opportunity and bolted. His strong legs propelled him across the cavern and into one of the many caves. Kevin wanted to yell out for him to stop, but he understood Dino's terror. Up close, the dragon was massive. Her body rippled with muscle and barely restrained power.

The dragon sat on her haunches and glared. Smoke twirled lazily from her nostrils. Hoqwua forced Kevin and Huizhong to their knees not far from where Chan and Crow were pinned. "This is the child," Ao Qin said. Her voice was deep bass and felt like thunder rolling across the sky.

"My name is Kevin," Kevin replied.

"Kevvvviinnn," the dragon said, "such a strange name for a creature of such power."

"Power?" Kevin asked.

"Leave him alone!" Huizhong shouted. "He doesn't deserve any of this!"

Ao Qin growled rapidly; dragon laughter. "No one deserves anything that happens to them. The *Tao* does not work that way. There are good things and there are bad things, and more often than not, the people who experience those good or bad things have done nothing to deserve their lot in life."

"What do you want with him?" she asked.

The dragon snorted. "He is old enough that he doesn't need a mother. Let him ask his own questions."

Kevin took a step back, nearly tripping over the severed head of a man. The dragon was so close he could smell her. She reeked of too much fish and the musty underworld. "Why did you let my parents die?"

Ao Qin dropped her body so her face was even with Kevin's. He looked into her amber eyes, glowing faintly, and saw nothing even remotely human. "They did not matter to me," she said, "that's why. You, however, are very important to my plans."

She pushed her muzzle close enough to reach out and touch. Her whiskers twitched, sensing something only dragons understood. Enormous nostrils expanded as she breathed in his scent. Her giant eyes rolled back in her head. "Delicious. Your planet's magic is so different from our own. It works the same way, but the flavor is intoxicating. I must visit Earth sometime, maybe incinerate some of your royalty."

"What are your plans in the meantime?" Crow asked. "Hang out down here and act scary?"

Hoqwua strode between Kevin and Ao Qin and put his hands on Kevin's shoulders. "My plan, actually," he said. "This planet needs a leader. Ao Qin worked with me because she saw the vision."

Ao Qin growled quietly and her eyes narrowed. Kevin was no expert on dragons, but he knew dogs and people did similar things when they were angry. "What vision?" Kevin asked.

"A shining new world where people understand who to look to for leadership. It will start with this city. Once Croatoa is on board, the rest of the planet will quickly fall into place. I had the money and the vision, my scaly friend had the magic and the experience. Soon, dragon and human will understand their place in the new world order."

Kevin shrugged away from Hoqwua's grip and stepped back. The man's eyes were wild. Not only was he drunk on his own power, there was something else that felt wrong about him. "What is our place in your world?"

Hoqwua adjusted his suit and smiled. "Your friends will die; they're unnecessary and know too much. The girl will come with me. You, my boy, will become the basis for the next great push. Your magic will change this world in ways it hasn't seen since the first wave of settlers came through. Their Earthly magic was lost over the millennia, diluted and washed away, but yours is fresh and it will create more converts.

"Chenming Zhang stumbled across a way to control people's minds, but it only works in this building. Good enough. We kidnapped some people and made them slaves. Ao Qin knew how to use the ashes of sorcerers to create religious experiences. The small-minded fools love their religion, even if they won't admit to it, so it only made sense to turn their religions against them. The best weapons are the ones you don't see coming.

"Now that we have you, though, we'll be able to do so much more."

"Okay," Crow said, "so, you're *n□o cán*. No one in their right mind would want a whole planet."

Ao Qin rose until her head was well above Hoqwua's. "His magic is mine," she rumbled.

Hoqwua sighed. "We've been through this. We need his magic to make the next generation of Heaven's Powder. You got the parents."

"The parents had no magic," Ao Qin snapped. "They were of as little use as you have been."

She nudged him with her nose. From a dragon's point of view, it was a light tap, but it was enough to make Hoqwua stagger back into Kevin. Instinct took over and Kevin caught him before he could fall. Rather than thanking him, Hoqwua righted himself and shoved Kevin. "Never touch me again, boy."

Hoqwua turned back to Ao Qin and hissed, "And you, never shove me again. You were nothing when I found you. Just another wasted dragon. I made you."

"You trapped me," the dragon growled. "Erected your gates while I slept and forced me into helping you. But I knew I could play along because it was convenient for me to let you do all the work so that I might reap all the benefits."

Hoqwua's gun was in his hand, but he hadn't pointed it at the dragon yet. Ao Qin's eyes were glowing brightly. Kevin took a step back while the tension in the room escalated. His parents had fought before and it was scary enough then. Hoqwua was obviously unhinged and the dragon was the biggest, most dangerous thing he'd ever seen.

All around them, the remaining minions lost interest in the captives and watched the fight with growing concern. As they started backing away, a cold pit opened in Kevin's stomach. It was bad enough to be killed by a dragon, but getting killed because of someone else's argument was almost too much to bear.

"I think we wandered into an ongoing argument," Huizhong said. She put an arm around his shoulder and gently pulled Kevin back.

"And here I thought these people had their *lā shī* together," Crow whispered. "Aside from a few neat tricks, these guys are crazy."

"They may be crazy, but they are still dangerous," Chan said. "We should leave before things get any worse. We can contact the police, let them ply their trade down here."

As the argument intensified, the air in the room grew colder. Ao Qin was sucking the power out of the room to fuel her magic. Hoqwua was actively pointing his gun at the dragon. They'd had this same argument over and over, but this time, with the prize in sight, neither was willing to back down.

Hoqwua and Ao Qin's voices raised until they were shouting at each other. The dragon roared and Kevin heard the hiss and bang of Hoqwua's gun. The explosive head flew into her mouth and exploded. Ao Qin looked like she couldn't believe a human had harmed her.

"Your magic is useless! Technology is the future." Hoqwua yelled. "Now be a good girl and incinerate the boy so we make more Heaven's Powder."

Ao Qin shook her enormous head slowly. Amber eyes opened and glared at Hoqwua. "Let me show you what dragons do."

Her legs shook as she rose to her feet, but she made it. For a creature that just had an explosion that could shatter rock go off in her mouth, she looked downright amazing. Color drained from Hoqwua's skin as he realized what he had just done. Ego has a way of making claims that skill can't back up. For all his strutting and preening, Hoqwua's one and only skill was amassing things. He was an excellent finder and hoarder of money, he could do amazing things with wealth, but a fighter he was not.

Ao Qin, on the other hand, was old enough to have fought in the Dragon Wars. She had fought entire armies at a time and felt the cut of magical steel. A freak electrical storm damaged her navigation and she lost sense of where she was. In the end, she wound up in the caverns under what would one day become The Clock Tower.

So, she slept until Hoqwua showed up with an offer: Join me or never leave these caves again.

He had put up dragon steel gates in the tunnels and even Ao Qin wasn't fool enough to try leave through the Clock Tower lobby. She waited and bided her time until she became a fixture. And fixtures get the best intel in the world because no one notices them anymore.

Hoqwua stepped back slowly, desperate to get the world back in order. "You don't want to do this," he cried, desperate to sound forceful in the face of the giant he had imprisoned. "If you kill me, you'll never escape."

Ao Qin's growling laugh echoed around the still room. She tilted her head to the side and winked at Kevin. "I have all the power I need. I just won't be putting it in your pathetic drugs."

Her ribs expanded as she filled her lungs with the dank air in the cavern. Amber eyes darkened until they were blood red. The temperature in the room dropped suddenly as Ao Qin sucked the energy out of it. "Run!" Crow yelled.

Dragon fire was a mixture of their native ability to use magic and a strange evolutionary tick that allowed them to expel flammable gasses. When the two things combined, the flames incinerated everything they touched. Normal fires take time to burn, dragon fire worked by burning and destroying matter at a very basic level. In the case of burning magical things, the resultant energy release was phenomenal.

Kevin turned on his heel and started sprinting. He didn't

know where to go. The cavern was largely empty and there wasn't much to hide behind. Out of the corner of his eye, he saw Chan and Huizhong running for all they were worth toward the entrance to the tunnels. Behind him, he could smell the sickly scent of dragon gas forming. The air was already heavy with magic, all Ao Qin had to do was pull in and direct it and the world would erupt in fire.

He was halfway across the cavern with no place to hide when he felt the magic click into place. A roar, like the fires of Diyu had been released, filled the cavern. *This is it*, he thought, *I'm going to die.*

His legs kept pumping, though. He ran with everything he had, but safety was still too far away. Already the heat from the growing fireball was licking at his back. It would only be moments before it encompassed him. He wondered if it would hurt or if it would be over quickly.

Something slammed into him from behind and the world went dark. The roar of the fire was deafening, but it wasn't as hot as it should have been. Maybe he died quickly and was already a ghost. Ghosts can't be burned, can they?

If he was a ghost, though, why did it feel like someone was lying on top of him? Ghosts can pass through walls, so why couldn't he move?

He'd only been dead a few moments and was already sick of it. Death was dark, heavy, and smelled faintly of alcohol. It was also digging into his shoulder and felt prickly on his face.

"Hold still, kid," Crow whispered. "I'm moving."

"Are you dead, too?" Kevin asked.

The dead Crow moved and light flooded back into the world. Kevin stared up at the ceiling and wondered what happened. Next to him, Crow was sitting on the stone floor and patting out a small flame on his boots.

"Remind me to thank Chan for the jacket. I figured surviving the explosion at Madam Chow's was luck, but I might be wrong." He looked up and down the sleeves of his long coat and grinned. "I'm never washing this again."

Kevin looked at Crow and wondered what he was talking about. The world felt muddy and his thoughts were sluggish. He could see Crow clearly, but there was still a chance he was an illusion. Kevin poked Crow on the arm and was both pleased and startled to realize he could touch the man. Ghosts can't be touched, so that left only one option.

"We're still alive," he mumbled. "How?"

Crow flicked the collar of his jacket and grinned. "Your buddy Chan gave me this. It was supposed to provide protection, but I've never had the opportunity to test it out."

The idea of a magic jacket made Kevin chuckle. No wonder Crow always wore it, even when it was hot outside. "Is the dragon still there?" he asked.

Crow swiveled his head and nodded. "She busy eating what's left of Hoqwua. I don't think he's dead, though. That blast of flame must not have been full power. Wait, she's headed our way."

35 | Take It All

Ao Qin's body, like all Southern dragons, was low to the ground. She moved like a snake in an undulating, weaving pattern that looked like it shouldn't have been as fast as it was. The sight of a huge, rapid-moving mass of scales and teeth heading straight at him was enough to make Crow wonder where his life had gone wrong. He yanked Kevin to his feet and handed the boy a *kwan dao*. "If we're going down," he said, "we're going down fighting."

The great red dragon of the South weighed nearly ten thousand *jīn*. She moved like a raging torrent of water flowing through a ravine, easily avoiding anything that got in her way. Crow nudged Kevin and they split up. If they were together, Ao Qin could have just eaten them both at the same time, but by breaking up, they would force her to choose a target.

Before she could get to them, a whirling silver object sliced through the air and embedded itself in Ao Qin's neck. She skidded to a halt and twisted to find out who had dared interrupt the hunt. Chan stalked across the floor. His *dūulì* covered his eyes, but his clenched fists and purposeful stride betrayed his anger.

Ao Qin snapped at him as she tried to pull the sword free from her neck. On a human, the effect of a sword through the throat would have been a serious issue, but dragons were made of sterner stuff. To her, a sword in the throat was a nuisance instead of a threat.

Huizhong followed up behind him, *kwan dao* in one hand and her dragon stone blade in the other. She took a few steps and threw the *kwan dao*. It hit Ao Qin straight in the neck, embedding itself under her jaw where flesh was soft. Despite two blades in her neck, the damage Dino had done to her back, and the explosion in her mouth, Ao Qin fought on.

No one had fought a dragon in centuries. They were reclusive creatures and, even during the height the Dragon Wars, there weren't that many of them. Armies had to search for months to find a dragon to slay as the war wound down and many young men and women who wanted to tell the tale of how they fought the greatest of beasts were let down.

The ones who did fight a dragon and lived to tell about it, had a very different viewpoint. They had the right to tell the tale of slaying the dragon, but very few ever talked about it and no one ever bragged about it. Like most things in life, the having was not so great as the wanting.

A few tales managed to leak out of the Dragon Wars and those were so unpleasant most people assumed it was propaganda. Unfortunately, they were not. Fighting a dragon meant not only fighting the largest predator on the planet, a creature that lived for hunting and was armed with teeth and claws that could rend metal, but also a predator that could breathe fire and was extremely adept at magic.

Fighting dragons meant coming face to face with the worst *M☐qīn* Aluna could conjure up in her evolutionary broth. Entire armies fell to single dragons, lost in a tidal wave of claws, teeth, magic, and green flames.

Crow stabbed at the other side of Ao Qin's neck with *kwan dao*, but she was too fast for him. In dodging Crow's attack, she opened herself up to Huizhong's knife. Dragon Stone wasn't particularly dangerous to dragons – they made it, after all – but when Huizhong's black blade sliced just below Ao Qin's eye, the red dragon howled in pain and anger.

The distraction gave Chan enough time to retrieve his *dao*. Purplish blood erupted when he pulled the blade free. Teeth that could pierce metal snapped at him, but Chan evaded her mouth. He swung the sword in a lazy arc, drawing her attention toward him. As she swung her snout at him, Crow jammed his blade into the other side of her throat.

Ao Qin thrashed and snapped her teeth at the attackers on either side of her body. As anyone who had fought in the dragon wars could attest, being at either end of a dragon was the worst place to be. Next to their stomach was the safest place; from there the teeth and claws couldn't reach. But being near the head or tail meant being in the danger zone.

As she thrashed around, first Crow, then Chan felt the impact of Ao Qin's head. Her head was the size of an adult human, but weighed more and was attached to muscles and ligaments that were meant to hold that massive head up.

Crow landed in heap, gasping for breath. He'd had the wind knocked out of him in a fight, but this time it happened twice in rapid succession. First Ao Qin's head forced the air of out his lungs, then the hard fall did it again. His lungs were burning for air, but he couldn't seem to suck any in. At least one rib was broken, probably a few more cracked. Much as he hated to, he knew he'd have to visit a healer in the morning. If he lived that long.

Gasping and croaking, Crow struggled to his knees. Finally, whatever was blocking his breath subsided and he gulped down air. Through blurry eyes, he saw Chan struggle to his feet long enough to get slammed across the room when Ao Qin's tale whipped into him. Huizhong went down next, after Ao Qin's head slammed her across the cavern.

Chan struggled to his feet and limped across the cavern, sword in hand. Ao Qin, now that she no longer had to deal with multiple attacks coming at her, focused her efforts on him. The room went cold. Strange energies played across the floor and ceiling of the cave.

"Run!" Crow yelled. "She's going to light a fire!"

Chan limped faster. His legs didn't want to move and each breath was searing agony. The *dao* in his hand felt heavier than the broadswords Master Smith trained with, but he kept going. He could feel the world changing around him, cold air and crackling energy threatened to suck the life out of him. He knew he had to move faster and he hoped the old legends were true.

He was almost within striking distance when Ao Qin's

ribs expanded. Only a few more feet and then one last task before he could die with honor. She reared back, preparing to spray the world with gas.

"*Tā māde ni□o*, Chan, move!" Crow screamed.

During the last bit of the Dragon Wars, an archer loosed an arrow just as a Northern Winged Dragon was about the spritz the world. When the dragon opened its mouth to spray the gas, the arrow found its way into the dragon's mouth. The gas spray suddenly stopped. The dragon still slaughtered almost everyone, but a few people managed to escape the grisly fate of their brethren.

There was a sac at the back of a dragon's throat that sprayed the gas. The sac was only exposed just as the dragon sprayed gasses. Magic ignited the fuel and the resulting fireball was enormous. But until the dragon decided to use it; the sac was hidden deeply within her skull.

Timing was everything. Chan could smell the first hints of gas coming from Ao Qin's mouth. It smelled like lamp oil and old fish with a hint of the worst *baiju* on the planet. But it didn't have to smell good to be flammable.

Ao Qin opened her mouth and Chan flung the *dao* once more. The gas erupted from Ao Qin's mouth just as Chan's dao severed her fire sac. Without the sac to aspirate it, the fluid inside the sac dropped into the back of Ao Qin's mouth. She gagged and coughed, spitting out the *dao* and a mass of yellowish liquid. Her mouth opened again and she screamed to the heavens in agony.

Her body convulsed, twisting around maniacally. A long tail slammed into Chan's chest. He heard the ribs break and hit the stone the floor with a thud that rattled his brain around in his skull. Desperate fingers clawed at the floor, trying to pull himself up and rejoin the fray. His body convulsed and he fell back to the floor coughing. Each cough brought up a thick, semi-liquid mass with it. Breathing felt like he was rubbing his bones together and with each necessary breath he wanted to scream.

Kevin watched the events unfold with horror in his eyes. The smells of the battle assaulted him. Run a person through with a sword and it's only a matter of time before the stench from a perforated bowl leeched into the air. The faint fish scent of the Ao Qin's fire gas. The sickening coppery scent of blood. Urine and feces and the musky odor of dragon and fear.

Ao Qin's snout caught Crow in the head. It happened so fast even his gift didn't see it coming. One moment he was standing, the next everything went black. He barely registered hitting the ground. Kevin saw Crow go down and lie there like a rag doll as the man's beloved hat rolled across the stone floor.

When he saw the hat roll away and Crow didn't try to retrieve it, Kevin feared the worst. It wasn't supposed to happen this way. The heroes were supposed to enter and, after a tricky, but ultimately safe, fight, they were supposed to walk away unscathed. Maybe someone would get a scratch or a black eye, but they weren't supposed to be coughing up blood or dead. This wasn't how the world was supposed to work.

He clenched his fists and glared at the dragon. She was still thrashing her head about, flinging blood and flammable saliva everywhere. Her eyes were wild with pain.

Everyone was down except Huizhong and the boy. A massive claw, easily capable of rending Kevin in two, swiped toward him. Huizhong tackled Kevin moments before the claw could kill him. They rolled on the ground together before coming to halt.

"Are you alright?" she asked.

Kevin tried to move and found he was mostly still mobile. He nodded and gave Huizhong a thumbs-up sign. "You?" he asked.

She nodded and rolled off Kevin. "We've got to get out of here."

"No kidding," Kevin replied. "Back through the tunnels?"

Huizhong cocked her head, but seemed to understand which tunnels he was talking about.

"They're neat," Kevin said. "you'll love them."

"Come on," she said, taking him by the hand.

Ao Qin stopped thrashing and let out a long, low growl that shook the cavern. It was the kind of deep bass that moved clothes and rattled souls. Everything stopped and even the air felt tentative. Kevin tugged Huizhong's hand and turned around. The dragon's eyes were full of rage and madness and pain and more than a hint of worry. She'd been alive for a millennium and other than a stray storm, nothing had scratched her; now these little things had done unspeakable damage.

The dragon was a blur as she darted forward. She batted Huizhong aside with a casual claw. Kevin gasped as a maroon stain spread across Huizhong's shredded blouse. He turned back to Ao Qin just in time to be shoved to the floor by her snout.

Kevin hit the ground hard and tried to backpedal away. Ao Qin followed him, growling the whole way. From the ground, she looked every inch the massive hunter she was. Whiskers twitched angrily as Ao Qin bared her fangs. Blood and *lóng hu□ zhī* coated her teeth, staining them red and sickly yellow.

Her eyes narrowed and Kevin prayed to every deity he'd ever heard of that she didn't eat him. The bared teeth broke into a dragon-y grin. Ao Qin's tongue darted across her teeth. "Your people are gone, little Earthling," she hissed.

He desperately wanted to say something witty, to be more like Crow, but all Kevin could do was shiver and mumble prayers to deaf and blind deities.

"Gods," Ao Qin hissed. "You people and your gods. Tell me, boy, have you ever seen one?"

Kevin thought about that for a moment, remembering the odd tales he'd heard over the turns and the theories that god was in everything. No matter how hard he thought about it, though, he couldn't remember an instance where he felt the presence of a god. The bulk of Ao Qin standing over him was closer to any god he'd ever been, and she wasn't even a goddess. He shook his head, wondering what the dragon was getting at.

"Dragons figured out long, long ago that whatever fingerprints a god would leave behind have been wiped clean. Now, we float on the *Tao* and do what we will because there will be no judgement. There will be no afterlife. After I suck the life from your bones, your world will switch off."

Kevin kicked her in the snout. It was one of the kicking from the ground techniques Chan loved to talk about. Neither of them ever suspected Kevin would use it to kick a dragon in the teeth. Ao Qin chuckled and casually swatted Kevin's prone form across the floor.

"You are so small and weak," she hissed. "How did your people ever defeat mine?"

Kevin was curled in a ball. He pretended none of this was happening and he was at home watching T.V. and Tina was still alive. For a brief, shining moment, it was true. He was there. He was home.

Then Ao Qin growled and the vision vanished. Kevin groaned. He wanted to cry, but refused to show the dragon she'd won. Chan always said quitting was never an option. As the dragon peered over him, Kevin wondered if she was right. Would he simply cease to be? No, it couldn't be. Death was just a change. But it was a change that took people away from each other. People like his parents, rotting away in cages not far from here, or his friends, slowly bleeding out on the cavern floor.

Delicious anger rose in his heart. Chan always said anger was the enemy, but it felt so right to get mad. Kevin kicked Ao Qin's snout again and again. Who was she to have taken his life away from him? Who did she think she was?

"I hate you!" he screamed as he kicked her.

Ao Qin's rapid-fire grunts mocked him. "I'm okay with

that," she replied. "Your hatred means nothing to me. All that matters to me is the latent power in your bones."

He kicked her one last time and glared. "It's not in my bones, dumbass. It's in my whole body."

"Which is exactly why I'm going to eat you rather than boil away your useless flesh. Then I will have truly taken everything from you."

Kevin reached in his pocket, trying to find the ring Crow had given him. She was close enough now that he could touch her, so now was the ideal time to spring a little surprise for. As he dug around and found nothing, a horrible thought occurred to him.

He looked around frantically, but the ring was nowhere to be found. Crow was going to be pissed.

"Did you know, boy, that there is a monk that still lives in a monastery not far from here? I have spoken with him, but he has been silent lately. He taught me the spells to suck the life out of the world around me. He thought he was offering me eternal life, but I'm already functionally immortal. That monk didn't understand the true power he was giving me. The strange man upstairs wanted to live forever, so I traded secrets for his secret of controlling people. Hoqwua provided the means, I provided the magic. He thought he was in charge, which suited my purposes. With your power added to mine, nothing will stop me. I already have half the city addicted to Heaven's Powder. I'll build an army of slaves and take back the world for my people. Then we'll feast on Long Pork and gnaw on your bones."

Kevin shook his head. It was such a convoluted plan, there could be no way it would work. Yet, here he was and everything Ao Qin wanted was happening.

"Now, boy," Ao Qin said, "enough chitchat."

Kevin strove to remember the feeling he had when he blew up the floating dragon or killed those guys in the alley. He closed his eyes and reached out with his magic. He sensed her, the total alienness of a dragon.

Again, she chuckled. "Your magic is weak, boy."

She pushed back and slammed his magic down. For all his power, Kevin was still a novice. Ao Qin had centuries to practice her own skills. He felt the magic push into him and, with it, his last weapon was lost.

"Now, you might feel a tearing sensation as I bite your limbs off," Ao Qin said. "That's perfectly normal."

A tingling started at the base of Kevin's spine and worked its way up. The tingling turned into a tugging sensation, like someone was ripping away a part of himself he didn't even know existed. He struggled to hold onto whatever that part was, but he didn't even know how to hold onto something that didn't exist.

The tingling turned to burning sensation that worked across all the nerves in his body. He opened his mouth to scream, but the pain was so intense it was all he could focus on. At only ten-turns-old, Kevin learned why some people preferred death to life.

The sensation stopped suddenly, leaving Kevin panting on the floor. Distantly, he heard something shrieking in pain and the familiar chirping and growling of an old friend. Kevin forced his eyelids open and watched Dino kicking around something amber and soggy.

Kevin understood the game well enough to know when his pain disappeared, Ao Qin was busy with other tasks. As powerful as she was, even the mighty Red Dragon of the South had trouble keeping her magic working as she had an eyeball torn out of the socket.

She flung Dino off with a shake of her head and turned back to Kevin. One glowing red eye glared at him. For all the pain, for all the suffering, he was going to be the sacrifice that would make things right. When his power was hers and the boy was nothing more than a wasted shell, she would blow out of her prison and take the city by storm. Maybe a visit to Hoqwua's ancestral home would be in order, too.

Ao Qin opened her mouth and licked the terrified boy's

face. His fear and power were delicious and soon they would all be hers. Power unlike anything Aluna had ever seen. After wreaking a little vengeance, her kind would once again rule this planet.

And she would rule the dragons. That kind of power was worth losing an eye and flames for.

Kevin saw Dino hit the ground hard. Deinonychus was never made to handle rough landings and he left a trail of feathers behind him as he skidded across the rough floor. Yet another friend ruined by this planet. No, scratch that. It was all the dragon. She killed his parents. It was because of her that he was brought here. Now Tina was dead, Crow, Chan, and Huizhong were all hurt, possibly mortally. And Dino wasn't moving.

Kevin let his anger flow and channeled it into the strange magic in his body. He grabbed onto her fangs and held on tight. "You want my power?" he snarled, "Here, have it all."

Ao Qin's body stiffened as power flowed through her teeth and into her skeleton. Powerful muscles spasmed, tearing sinew and breaking bones. Slowly, painfully, her giant body collapsed under its own weight into a whimpering pile on the floor. She tried to block his magic, but Kevin's rage shoved her pain aside and pushed further. Nerves lit up as magic poured through them.

The pain and magic overloaded her system. With a quiet whimper, the dragon that had seen a thousand turns and plotted to overthrow the world, died an ignominious death broken and beaten on the cold stone floor. The rock in the cavern would remember this moment and whisper tales of it to anyone who cared to listen far into the future.

36 | Falling Down, Standing Up

Chan and Crow, bruised and battered, sat at a table in a darkened corner of Mrs. Chow's bar. Chan wouldn't admit it, but every movement hurt. He had stopped coughing up blood, but for how long he didn't know. On the other hand, he'd fought a dragon and lived to tell about it, even if it was his progeny's magic that had delivered the final, decisive blow.

Crow sat perfectly still. His mind was still reeling at the sheer madness of Hoqwua's plan. The man had to have been insane because no one in their right mind would attempt to cage a dragon and then partner with it. He wondered how long she'd been down there. Long enough to have lost part of her mind, at least.

A waiter came by and set a pair of glasses and a ceramic bottle with the image of Yama's face on it. Crow expected Chan to ask for water instead of *baiju*, but the man remained steadfastly motionless. With a grunt and groan, Crow poured out two glasses of Yama's famous *Dìyù Hu*□. The colorless liquid sparked in the low light. Chan still hadn't moved and Crow contemplated taking the drinks for himself.

In the end, he sighed and slid a glass across the table at Chan. "Drink up, buddy," he said. "If slaying a dragon doesn't earn you a drink, nothing will."

"You two slayed a dragon?" Mrs. Chow asked.

Crow jumped. Admittedly, his mind was elsewhere, but Mrs. Chow's ability to sneak around was almost preternatural. He motioned to a chair and mumbled, "Yeah. Big one."

"I don't think there are small dragons, Crow," she said. "They're supposed to be big."

"Technically, we didn't kill it," Chan said. "That was Kevin."

"Oh, now you're alive," Crow said. "He's right, though,

we fought hard, but in the end, it was Kevin's magic that took the beast down. If it hadn't been for him, we'd be dragon chow."

"The beast? As in The Beast?" Mrs. Chow asked.

Crow tapped his nose and said, "The very same. A big, red Southern dragon with a huge chip on her shoulder and a massive superiority complex."

Mrs. Chow snatched Crow's glass from his hand and downed the contents before he could react. She let the *baiju's* soft fire warm her insides as she pondered the news. "Interesting."

"What is so interesting about that?" Chan asked.

She smiled her most frustrating smile, the one that promised there was a wealth of knowledge that she wasn't going to share. "Is the *Tiāntáng De Fěn* still out there?"

"I'm sure it is," Crow said, "but there's no way to make any more. This city's going to have a massive withdrawal soon."

"That is not going to be a good situation," Chan said.

"Between that and the ongoing war between the police and the Green Gang, things are going to get a might bit ugly around here," Crow added. He leaned back in his chair and downed a shot of *baiju*. "I think I might need to get out of town for a while."

"We cannot leave," Chan said.

"What do you mean?" Crow asked. "Of course we can leave."

"We were partially responsible for what happened. It is our duty to make things right."

Crow held up his hands. "What? We didn't start this. We didn't even want this. You were looking for the kid's parents. Huizhong was looking for whatever it was she was looking for. Me probably."

"You really aren't all that hot that a woman like Huizhong would come looking for you," Mrs. Chow said.

Crow put on his best shocked face. "How dare you,

madam?"

Mrs. Chow snorted and took another drink from his glass. When Yama's fires of *Diyu* subsided, she smiled warmly and said, "Don't take it personally, Crow. But if she really wanted you, she'd be here right now. Take it from a woman."

"You're a woman?" Crow asked.

Mrs. Chow glared at him until she saw the sly smile creeping across his face. "I'm sure you don't have much experience with women, Crow, so I'll forgive you that insult. For now."

Crow laughed. He took his glass back from Mrs. Chow and refilled it before sliding it back in front of her. "You earned that drink. Anyway, I still don't get how we were even remotely responsible for what happened and what's about to happen."

Chan sniffed his drink and sipped it. He wrinkled his nose, but downed the *baiju* with a grimace on his face. "I was looking for Kevin's parents. Huizhong was looking for herself and a sense of peace. Kevin wanted his parents. What did you want?"

"To help people," Crow said as innocently as he could.

"You have never helped a soul in your life, Crow," Mrs. Chow said.

"Because every time I try to help someone, dragons intervene."

Chan poured himself a second glass of *baiju* and sipped it. Crow suspected this was the first time Chan ever tasted alcohol, which meant the rest of the evening could be fun. Nothing's more fun that trying to move a drunken martial arts master who doesn't want to move. "I don't believe you. Aside from your little dragons, I don't think you care much about helping anyone or anything."

"I've changed," Crow replied. "New leaf."

"I don't think you've changed. I'm not sure you even can change," Chan said.

"Not true, not true," Crow said. "Earlier today I never

would have even thought about changing. That's a change."

"It only counts when you follow through with it," Chan said. "Thinking about something and doing something are two very different things."

Crow drank his *baiju* and wiped his lips with a napkin. "See, I even wiped my lips. But what about you, pal? Here you are drinking and using contractions."

"I have not been using contractions," Chan growled. "They are an abomination of the language."

"'Technically, we didn't kill it' and 'I don't think you've changed. I'm not sure you even can change'," Crow said, counting off each time on his fingers. "You've changed, man. I'm not even certain I know who you are anymore."

Chan's gray eyes swirled as he pondered the facts. Deep in his mind, gears were turning and replaying what he had said. When he confirmed Crow was correct, Chan nodded. "Perhaps I am becoming more relaxed."

"You still haven't answered what you wanted, Crow," Mrs. Chow said.

"Neither has Huizhong," Crow replied.

"She is not here, though. She took Kevin and went back North," Chan said. There was sadness in his voice. Over the past months, he had grown quite fond of the boy. Although, considering the state Croatoa was about to find itself in, leaving was the safest option.

"Smart kid," Crow replied. "Smart woman. Get away from this madhouse."

"Spill it, Crow," Mrs. Chow said, "or there won't be any more *baiju*. What did you hope to gain?"

Crow started to answer with his usual dismissive flippancy, but thought better of it. "Back when I went into the Clock Tower and Chenming and his gang of miscreants killed me, I delved into my dark side. I wanted to find The Beast and kill him. Her. Whatever. At the time, I thought it was a him."

"Why?" Chan asked.

"Truthfully, there wasn't a good reason. I didn't have

much going on at the time and had spent my free time wandering around the city. I saw all the Heaven's Powder hopheads and it seemed like there were more of them every day, so I thumped one until he said something about the Beast. Then I found that book Huizhong stole and it was open to the section on the Monastery of Hope. One thing lead to another and here we are."

Chan stared at him in disbelief. "You did all this because you were bored?"

"Not everything has meaning, pal. Sometimes the *Tao* just leads you where you need to go," Crow replied with a wave of his hand. "Sometimes it's interesting, sometimes it's a pawn shop."

Mrs. Chow laughed out loud. "You are an interesting man, Mr. Crow. You set out to, what, take over the city? And wound up saving it instead."

"Well, I had help," Crow said, "but that's the general gist."

A man materialized next to their table and bowed deeply. "My sincerest apology, Madam Chow, but I have a message for you."

"Fuck off," Crow said, "We're celebrating."

The man looked like any random person on the street, but there was a hint of steel in his eyes that set Crow on edge. There was a certain look police officers were trained to keep an eye out for when on patrol, a kind of hardness the gangs developed. Where one gang member showed up, there were usually more nearby.

The man forced back his edgy eyes and did his best to look humble and harmless. Crow could make out the outline of a long dagger, a short stick, and a few other things hidden away under the man's tunic. His knuckles were enlarged, a sure sign of iron hand training or, at the very least, a lot of punching.

"I am sorry to interrupt," he said, "but this is of paramount importance."

He handed Mrs. Chow a rolled-up message and Crow caught a glimpse of a tattoo on his forearm. He stood patiently by while she cracked the seal and read it. Her eyebrows rose then her eyes narrowed and a scowl crossed her face. She rolled up the paper and handed it back to the man. "Tell them I own this place legally and it's nothing more than a nightclub, not a 'den of iniquitous behaviors'. Tell Jacob at the bar to get you an envelope to take to them. If they have problems, they can come directly to me."

The man bowed deeply and retreated. Mrs. Chow sighed and turned back to Crow and Chan. "Well, that's one less problem. The police are back to their usual demands for payment instead of killing my people."

"That guy was Green Gang," Crow said. "Why was he coming to you?"

Mrs. Chow smiled and rose. She rose and adjusted her dress before fixing them with one last smile. "The drink is on the house, gentlemen. Welcome to the new Mrs. Chow's."

She retreated into the club. Crow looked at Chan and shook his head. "You knew that, didn't you? You knew she runs the underworld. No wonder she wanted The Beast gone; she didn't want the competition."

Chan nodded. "Sometimes it is good to have the ear of people in high places."

"Think she could spare a table? I owe a guy a table and these look pretty nice."

Chan cocked an eyebrow, but didn't say anything. He was used to Crow's idiosyncrasies. There was a time when Crow spent the better part of a week seeking out a velvet painting of a dragon spinning records in a bar. Chan never did find out why it was imperative that Crow get that painting, but he finally managed to scrounge it up in an old apothecary in the religious district.

"One thing still bothers me," Crow said as he stared into his glass. "Well, actually two things. You said someone shot an explosive arrow through Lo Pan, right?"

Chan nodded, wondering what Crow was getting at.

"Okay, someone also blew up Mrs. Chow's bar and tried to pin it on the Green Gang. At first I blew it off, but I'm wondering who did that. All of Hoqwua's people were brain-dead zombies; they couldn't have pulled that off and they couldn't have shot the arrow. The police don't blow up bars or people, they just beat the snot out of people they don't like. And there's no way the Green Gang would blow up Mrs. Chow's place, let alone try to pin it on themselves."

Chan's head felt fuzzy. He never drank, so the alcohol was hitting him harder than he expected. "What are you trying to say?"

"I think there was someone else involved, someone not police or Green Gang or Hoqwua or Ao Qin."

Chan's head flopped forward on the table as the room spun around him. "Too much," he mumbled. "We should figure it out later."

Crow sighed and downed another glass of *baiju*. "Well, buddy, we've got a little time before the city self-destructs; what do you feel like doing?"

"Let's finish this bottle and see what happens."

*****

Huizhong sat in her clearing and sighed contentedly. Kevin sat in front of her. His body was still, but she could sense the edginess coming off him in waves. "Just breathe," she told him.

Kevin took a deep breath and let it out slowly. The rumbling magic flowing out him settled down, but didn't quite stop. He was fortunate to have trained with Chan. The Master of Fists may not have been the easiest person to understand, but he certainly understood discipline and had taught his student that lesson well. Kevin was young, but he was already far more disciplined than most adults.

"Feel the world around you," Ao Shun's voice rumbled. "Feel its ebb and flow. That is the voice of the *Tao*. If you follow it, things will be easier for you. If you fight it, the *Tao* will roll over you like a *dàlàng* and you will either learn to follow the *Tao* or drown in your own misery. It doesn't require you to follow a strict path, it just encourages you to flow with yourself."

"What am I looking for?" Kevin asked.

"You don't need to look for anything," Huizhong said. "Just follow the flow and see where it leads you."

"What if it leads me to kill a dragon?" Kevin replied.

"Then you kill a dragon," Ao Shun said.

"What if it's a baby dragon?" Kevin asked.

"Then definitely kill it," Ao Shun said. "Baby dragons are spiteful, ugly things. It is only after we mature that we grow into marvelous specimens like myself."

The crunching of boots on gravel interrupted the evening's lesson. Kevin's eyes slowly opened and he blinked several times just to get his eyes to work correctly again. "How did I do?" he asked.

Huizhong patted his leg and said, "You did great. Chan would be very proud."

Kevin's head drooped. "I miss him. I don't miss the constant training, but I miss Chan."

"The city is about to explode," Ao Sun said. "You are safer up here and Chan and Huizhong's boyfriend are needed in Croatoa."

"He is not my boyfriend!" Huizhong snapped.

"Then why did he give you a gift before you left? Is that not normal in human relationships?" Ao Shun asked, cocking his head to the side.

When Huizhong had unpacked her baggage, she found an odd thing. Nestled in with her neatly folded clothes, was a small object wrapped in gauze. When she unwrapped it, she found a statue of Ho Hsien-Ku. It was the same Immortal Maiden that she and Crow saw when they walked through Fei Long's lobby. Somehow or another, he had managed to steal it, wrap it up, and secret it away in her luggage.

It was just like Crow himself; an odd gesture that teetered between being romantic and being creepy. She was examining it when Ao Shun nudged open her window and stared at the statue with emotionless dragon eyes.

"Giving me a statue Ho Hsien-Ku does not mean we are dating," Huizhong said.

Ao Shun settled to the ground with a satisfied groan. He must have been hitting the weeds down by the river again; whatever was in them settled the big dragon down immediately. He laid his whiskers back along his face. "Crow is an important piece of the puzzle, no matter who he is."

"He is a weapon," a woman's voice said. "Nothing more."

The dragon snorted and rolled his eyes. "You are just jealous that the *Tao* didn't choose one of your warriors."

"They would have been better choices," the woman said.

"Your warriors are impressive, there is no doubt about it. But they are rigid and predictable. They would have been found out and eliminated before they could carry out the mission. Chan trained them well, but he, too, is too rigid. Felix Crow is chaos personified. That is why he succeeded. Look at what he has accomplished without even trying; Hoqwua is dead, Ao Qin is dead, we now know of her plot and Hoqwua's dragon steel mine."

"I still think bringing Crow in was madness. At least the boy will be safe."

Kevin looked up to find a woman with black hair and a bow slung over her shoulder. She grinned down at him with a twinkle in her eye. "Hello," she said. "You must be Kevin. My name is Mab and we have a great deal to talk about."

"Is now really the right time, Mab?" Huizhong asked. "We just got here."

Mab fixed Huizhong with a stern look, then softened. "Of course. You both must be exhausted. Sleep. We will talk in the morning. Your dinosaur is around here somewhere."

"Dino can take care of himself," Kevin said. "He's a survivor. What happened to your leg?"

Mab looked down at her wrapped ankle and smiled. "I wasn't paying attention and twisted my ankle. Don't fret about it; I'll be fine."

"You're a survivor, too," Kevin said.

"As are you, child," Ao Shun said. "Power such as yours will draw every sorcerer on the planet looking for you. I can't promise you the world, but we will all do our best to make sure you're prepared for it."

Kevin's head spun. This morning, he awoke to an apartment filled with statues of naked women and now he was going to sleep after killing a dragon and speaking with another one. Even worse, he was being told people wanted his power and would probably kill for it. One thing he knew for certain was his power was his and his alone. He'd learn everything he could and use it to keep what was his, no matter the cost.

This may not have been home, but at least it was interesting.

Notes

I admit I stole the name of Aluna from my son. It was a place he used to tell stories of when he was a wee lad. His stories revolved around a high-tech place where war and action were the norm. I took the name – something he still insists I owe him money for – and changed what the planet was like. Oh, ah.

This was my first true fantasy novel. I did a bit of research and found there were no hard and fast rules about fantasy, but it was generally accepted that there needed to be magic and dragons. Coincidentally, Chinese *Wuxia* novels have similar rules.

I've never been overly into fantasy, there's some really good stuff and some not-so-good stuff out there, but most of the fantasy novels I've ever read focus on the really big stuff. Armies go to war, evil kings take over kingdoms, stuff like that. Every time I read one, I always kind of wondered about the little people in those worlds. Not everyone is born to be a hero, some stumble into it. Those are the stories I like. Hence, Croatoa. It's a city full of crime and vermin, even though it's powered by magic.

All the Chinese in this book came from Google Translate, so I can't attest to its accuracy. I do, however, have a logical out: Old Chinese sorcerers dropped into Aluna a couple thousand years ago, so the language would have drifted over time. That means I'm off the hook about perfect translations and so is Google.

Some elements of the story were pulled straight from Chinese history. The Green Gang was a real gang in turn of the century Hong Kong. They were the progenitors of the modern Triads. Hoqwua was a real person, too. He was a trader back in the day and was reportedly extremely wealthy.

History is mum about whether or not he buddied up to dragons.

Speaking of dragons, Ao Shun and Ao Qin are two of the historical Dragon Kings (the North and South, respectively). The East and West Dragon Lords are Ao Guang and Ao Run. Traditionally, all the Dragon Kings are male, but Aluna is a wild and not-so-wooly place.

Many of the place names are references to famous Chinese martial artists from history. Looking them up is your homework. Good luck.

At any rate, I hope you enjoyed this book. The story isn't over yet, so look for a sequel at some point in the future.

Thank You

No novel makes its way into the world without some help from people other than the author. These people provide support, feedback, criticisms, and generally work to make the book a better experience for the reader. I'd like to thank S.K. Holmesley, Sylva Fae, and RobRoy McCandless for your help and guidance.

I'd also like to thank my wife for all her support and guidance, as well as putting up with this little endeavor and my son for coming up a planet of Aluna, even if his was quite different from my own version of the planet.

Alunan History

c-0, current day

c-.5, Crow kills the Chenming Zhang at the behest of Alyssa Zhang. Alyssa disappears.

c-2, Huizhong arrives in Croatoa

c-3, Ao Qin starts talking to Chenming Zhang

c-5, Crow leaves the police force

c-20, Hoqwua discovers and traps the sleeping Ao Qin

c-30, Hoqwua discovers he has access to Dragon Steel

c-300, The last dragon is sighted. It's Ao Qin. She slinks into the caves under Croatoa after she's wounded in an electrical storm. Ao Shun leaves the south for the north.

c-500, Croatoa is founded

c-550, The last monk of Hope walls off the monastery

c-550 – c-750, the second dragon wars

c-750 – c-1000, relative peace

c-1000-c-1200, the first dragon wars

c-2000, the first Chinese wizards arrive

Translations

Moons – Big Sister: Xiǎojiě
        Little Sister: Dàjiě
Suns – Big Mother: Dà māmā
        Little Mother: Xiǎo mǔqīn
Hope – Xīwàng
Shit - lā shǐ
Crime Alley - Fànzuì Hútòng
Heaven's Powder - Tiāntáng De Fěn
Green Gang - Qīng Bāng
Dǒulì – conical hat
Changsha – jacket
Xīyì – lizards
Niǎo lèi – birds
Páxíng dòngwù - reptiles
Qún – flock
Hǎizǎo – seaweed
Xiangqi – Chinese chess
Zhìyù zhě – healer
Wěidà de xīyì – great lizard. Used as horses on Aluna
Gong-Detian - goddess of luck
Zhōngyī - traditional Chinese medicine
Sun Simiao - famous traditional Chinese medicine doctor
Dāpèi gǒu – lap dog
yáng zǐ è – Chinese alligator
xiē – scorpion
jiǔhòu tǔ zhēnyán – after wine, spit out the truth
Xīyì – lizard
mábù – linen
yǒngyǒu – owns
wǒ kào – Well fuck me, holy shit, etc.
Dìyù – hell
Cāngyǐng – fly
Jièyān – quitter
Yāpiàn – opium
Kāfēi – coffee

Yīshēng – doctor
Báichī – moron, idiot
Dàshǎgè – big dummy
Móguǐ – Devil
Chéngfá zhě – Punisher
Shén Jiē – God Street
Zhīzhū - spider
fèi wù – useless
huǒyǎn xiéshén – evil spirit.
Ao Qin – Red Dragon of the south
Jiānhùrén – Guardians
Chídùn - slow witted
Hēi mófǎ – Black Magic
tā māde niǎo – God dammit
Shí rénzú – cannibals
Lóng de chéngzhǎng – Dragon's growth
Wàngjìle - forgotten
Hùnzhàng – damned
Fèihuà – nonsense
Fàngqì Xīwàng – abandon hope
Lóng xīyì – dragon lizard
Kǒngbù xīyì – terror lizard
yúkuài de nǚhái – pleasure girls
Dìyù huǒ – Hell Fire
jùxíng jī – Giant chicken

About the Author

Eric Lahti is responsible for the Henchmen series of paranormal adventures featuring gods and Valkyries and the Saxton stories featuring a man and his talking gun. *Greetings From Sunny Aluna* is his fourth novel. He currently resides in Albuquerque, New Mexico where he works as a programmer during the day and a writer at night. Eric is currently working on a new book about ghosts, ghost hunters, and all the powers of Hell.

Lahti's Works:
Henchmen
Arise
Transmute
The Complete Saxton
The Clock Man and Other Stories

www.ingramcontent.com/pod-product-compliance
Lightning Source LLC
Chambersburg PA
CBHW020652110726
47901CB00001B/153